DAEMONES EX MACHINA

RUSSELL ANDERS

Helping talented writers publish exceptional books

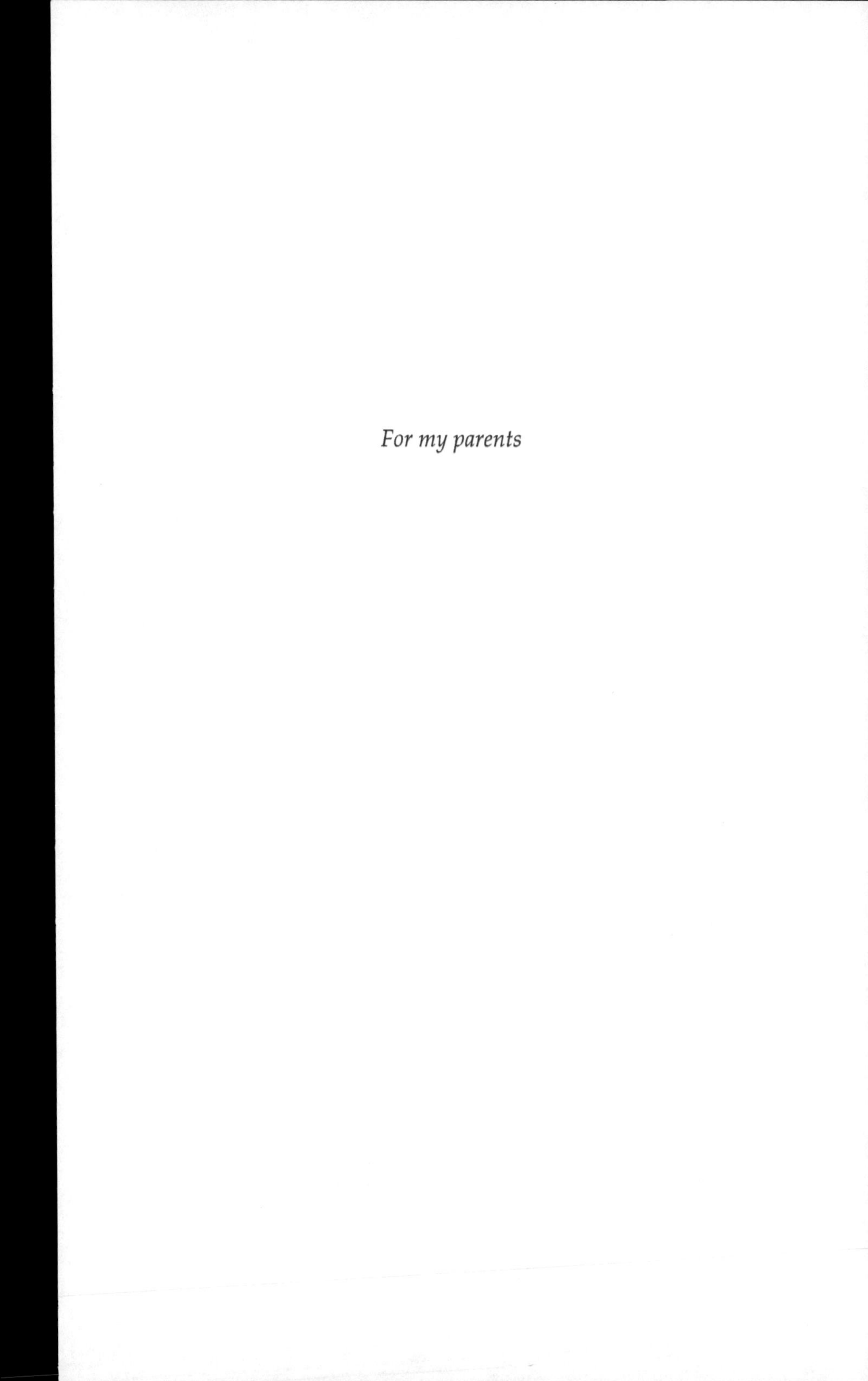

For my parents

1

Fucked.

That's how Jon read the mission timer that blared an angry red in the corner of his Augmented Reality overlay. Technically it read numbers, but he translated them to what they really meant. They were late. Really late.

15:07

15:08

15:09

An image of Guion's face appeared below the timer, a rendering of his athletic angles, sharp jawline, and tight side flattop cut in holographic glass that glowed. "Is he dead?"

Jon shook his head as if Guion could see him. "No. His interface unit still shows a heartbeat."

"It could be hung in a loop. Or maybe the display's been hacked."

Jon reached out for the illusionary silver sphere that hung in AR over Friedy's Master Interface Unit. It shone brightly in the room lit only by the incidental glow of status lights studding the server cabinets that surrounded them. An onslaught of viruses waited to assault anyone daring such access, slagging their MIU and, if Jon knew Friedy, the brain tied to it too. But at Jon's touch, it erupted into layers of radial menus like a flower blasting into bloom in time-lapse. He scanned the segmented rings, riots of color, and tapped a scarlet section. It clenched into a sphere and sucked the rest of the menu in before blossoming open again, this time into rings and segments all shades of red, each option another biometric. He pinched and twisted one option after another, prying each open and peeking at the data inside before closing it and moving to another.

"Brain activity, heartbeat, everything. He's still all systems go."

"Check manually."

Jon knelt beside Friedy. The scrawny New Deutsche Republic native lay slumped against a cabinet, buried deep in the mathematically precise maze of machines, limbs sprawled and head lolling, drooling onto a bib bearing a cartoon figure in his same pose, wearing his same shock of wild, platinum blonde hair. The words "Badass Hacker" screamed out in blocky crimson underneath. A glowing green line scrolled across the little slab of screen that lay cockeyed on his chest and jumped at regular intervals, a silent EKG readout. One slim cable stretched from his MIU to a rubber nipple stuck to Friedy's temple with a clear glop of conductive adhesive, a fancy piece of archaic tech. A second braided silver cord slid through a small hole bored through the glass cabinet door and slotted in a port in the server rack. The tower glowed with illuminated indicators beside him. Friedy said they reminded him of the hieroglyph-slathered walls of Egyptian pyramids rendered in iridescence. With his head lolled back and his mouth slack, Friedy looked passed out . . . or dead.

"No. Not dead," Jon said after pressing a pair of fingers to the pale man's neck. "I feel a pulse."

"Then maybe he's comatose."

"Guion, he's alive. He's late, but he's alive. Give him some more time."

"He's already had more time than we can afford." Guion didn't betray any emotion in his voice, but Jon could tell he was getting jittery. The tactical head of their team didn't ask for vital checks every two minutes. He didn't get hung up on small, useless repetition like that. But he did now. Had been for the last . . . Jon checked the mission clock . . . 16 minutes and 27 seconds.

Ibacipla Group was expanding its brand into the recreational weaponry market. Advanced Weapons Engineering wasn't happy to welcome another into their turf, so it put together a team to infiltrate Ibacipla's facility and sabotage the brand before launch. Where A.W.E. led the market in fashionable firearms and clothing designed to mesh together in trendy ensembles, Ibacipla's new Slimline catalog of handguns and accessories focused on concealed carry with an emphasis on the female demographic. The slogan *Strapped and Strapless* drove the brand message along with a silhouette logo of a woman holding a handgun. Viewed in augmented reality, she extended her arm and fired a single silenced shot before returning to her original pose.

That's where Jon and his team came in. It was a simple op. Insert a virus into Ibacipla's network that overwrote the AR code behind the logo so that the gun made an empty click sound when fired. Then the gun barrel would sag limp to the sound of a sad trombone's "wah wah waaaah." Ibacipla would correct the code in a day, but the initial impression would damage their brand for months. A.W.E.'s viral marketing team already had a spate of memes loaded and ready for strategic timed releases into the WorldGrid. If everything worked out, they'd forever turn Slimline into a cheap joke. For all that, Jon's team just needed to get inside

Ibacipla's facilities, drop the virus in their server, and then get out of there.

"Hey, uh, we'll be leaving soon, right?" Dunford leaned over Jon and Friedy.

Jon looked up at the security shift commander. The dough-bodied middle manager wore a full moustache that fattened his cheek-heavy face and a sidearm that, though real, was clearly ornamental for him. He was why they'd had such an easy time of things so far. Jon identified him early in operations planning and bribed him for access codes. He also adjusted the patrols for tonight to widen those gaps a little. Besides the money, Jon offered extraction. When they left, they took him with them and he got a new corporate home in A.W.E. Except they were supposed to be gone by now.

Jon patted Friedy's shoulder. "Yeah, as soon as he's done."

"Okay, well it better be soon. My patrol edits ran out ten minutes ago." Dunford looked around, clearly wanting to walk off, but unsure where to go.

Guion returned in his ear. "Jon, patch into a POV view. I want to see what Friedrich's doing."

Jon spun through the options in the flower menu. "I don't see anything like that in the menu." He let it collapse back to the silver pearl. "He probably removed it from his MIU. He only loads essential 'ware on his device."

"So patch into his datafeed and run the app locally."

"Being whitelisted on his device doesn't apply when I start digging that deep. You know Friedy wrote his own operating system for his MIU, including security, right?"

"He's routinely attached to your hip. He never talked to you about his security measures?"

Jon glanced at the slab of touchscreen and its steadily jumping green lines. "He said he worked his magic to weave protective wards." Jon sensed an incoming tirade. Guion had barely drawn a breath before Jon cut him off. "I know you're impatient, but that's a bad idea."

"I'm not impatient, Jon. Something needs to happen. Right now."

"Something is about to happen right now." A raspy voice cut into their conversation and another holographic head lit up in Jon's peripheral vision. Stone, one of three combat specialists assigned to their team, along with Mason and Bricklayer. Jon referred to them as "the heavies" when he joked with them. "I've got two patrolmen inbound. If we leave now, we can slip out before they see us. But it's got to be now."

"Do it. Abort," Guion said.

"Guion, he's still in there," Jon said.

"He's out of time. Get out."

"Wait." Jon tapped Dunford on the shoulder. "Get rid of them. Buy us the time we need." He continued when he saw the objection on the supervisor's face. "If we blow this mission, you're hosed. Unless we come home a success, you've got no value to A.W.E. You've already torched your home here. If you want somewhere to go after this, make this work." He gave the man a light shove. "Go."

Dunford let the push stumble him into a casual gait and he strolled from the corridor of soft blue light and gunmetal frames to intercept the two-man team. Jon walked a step behind, dressed in the same security uniform. "Hey, guys. How's it going?"

They stopped short. "Chief?"

"Heh. Yeah. I saw a blip on my screen and decided to check it out. Show the new blood the ropes." He shrugged. "False positive. You know how that goes. Anyway, we spent enough time digging around here looking for what it could be that we've got this area covered. You guys might as well move on, and, uh,"—he leaned into them— "you didn't hear me say it, but you don't have to give the time you save skipping here back to the company. Know what I mean?"

The two guards looked at each other. "Yeah, we gotcha. Still, you ought to radio one of us next time to get a ping. It's kinda your whole job."

"I know. I know." Dunford waved the comment away. "Still adjusting to the new post. Old habits die hard."

"Yeah, well, you take it easy, Chief." They had half-turned to leave when Dunford's voice came over their earpieces asking for a status update. Other patrols started reporting in, but these two stayed silent.

Dunford's mouth hadn't moved.

"Chief, what the hell is going on?"

"He broadcast that to everybody, not just you," Jon said.

"Yeah, check-in time," Dunford said. He gestured to them. "You don't need to. I see where—"

Dunford's answer came over the channel, cutting him off.

You put yourself on playback? Jon sent over a private message.

It seemed like a good cover, the former chief sent back.

The guards grabbed their guns but didn't clear them before their heads slammed together with a muted *pfff*. They collapsed in a dead heap. Stone and Mason slid into vision, their active camouflage ponchos shifting to match their surroundings and rendering them more distortions of scenery than men, like large drops of water holding pistols.

"Targets down," Stone said.

"Abort the mission," Guion said.

"Guion, the guards are down. Stone and Mason got them before they made any report," Jon said.

"That's right. They didn't report in. Someone's going to follow up on that, and now there's not only you but a pair of bodies to hide. Time's up. Get out."

"Friedy's still alive."

"Good call. Terminate him. We can't risk him being captured and interrogated."

"What? You can't be—"

"Jon," a voice with a lilting German accent said. A translucent head fuzzed into focus in front of him, life-sized, full color, and fully animated. More of Friedy's special work. Guion called them customizations. Friedy called them enchantments. "We're in trouble. I'm speaking to you on a private channel. Subvocalize your responses."

"No fucking shit we're in trouble. What the hell is going on, Friedy? All you had to do was deploy a file. You should have been in and out of there in two minutes, not . . ."—he checked the mission clock—"twenty and counting." He blinked. "You're not downloading pay data for yourself again, are you?"

"I checked the code before I deployed the virus."

"Why would you do that?"

"I didn't write it. I told you yesterday it was strange. I wanted to make sure it would do what it was supposed to."

"And?"

"It will, and so much more. I found a subroutine to send lethal amounts of feedback through my MIU and fry my brain." Lightning flashed inside of Friedy's head.

Jon paused. "Jesus. Really?"

"*Yah,* so I purged it. But then I found another."

"They put two in?"

"Five. I needed to scry the entire package before deploying it, for obvious reasons, and they didn't make it easy. There's something else in here, too. Something I can't make sense of. When have you ever heard me say I can't make sense of code?"

"Why not tell the whole team?" Jon said. "Why keep us in the dark this whole time?"

"This code came from A.W.E. Someone in the company

wants me dead. That could include people on this team, like Mr. Stay in the Van team lead."

"Guion always runs tactical oversight remotely."

The ghostly head cocked sideways in a shoulderless shrug. "I didn't know who I could trust, aside from you. You're my best friend, Jon. That's why I'm telling you in private. If they're gunning for me, they might be after you too. Be careful. I'm almost done conjuring my contingency in case things go wrong."

"What—?"

A strong hand gripped Jon's bicep, and he snapped his attention to Stone's craggy face. Friedy disappeared from his sight. "Earth to Jon. You seem lost in your own world, so I'm guessing you didn't hear. Guion says if you don't terminate blondie now, I do it and then we all evacuate."

Jon looked at Stone.

Stone looked at Jon.

Stone smiled. "What he doesn't know is that I got orders to ice him as soon as we're clear of the building." He opened his hand. A chrome-black lighter sat in the expanse of his palm. He flicked the top open with a thick thumb to show a red button instead of a spark wheel. "Wired the van myself after drinks last night."

"So . . ." Jon eased his hand back toward his gun.

"So this whole mission is a disaster and none of us are supposed to come back from it. But there's a problem."

"Do tell."

A slow smile crawled across his thick lips. "I decided I like you last night, even if you didn't slot a bar filter that showed me any tits."

Jon looked. Waited. "Too easy."

Stone's face got serious. "Mason, Bricklayer, and me, we're ex-military. Soldiers don't frag their own."

"Friedy, Guion, and I are civilians."

"We're all out here in the shit right now. It's close enough for me."

Jon smiled back. "You just bought yourself some tits." He slapped the man's solid shoulder. "I'll pull my shirt off as soon as we're safe." A serious look gripped his face. "We've got some on-the-fly planning for that though."

"I got in touch with an old buddy who does border runs. Got a rendezvous set up already." He lifted his eyebrows and smiled at Jon's look. "I knew I couldn't go back when I got the orders to start scragging teammates."

"This is Freidrich. I am deploying the package and disconnecting now. Logoff will take thirty seconds."

Jon looked at Stone. The man glanced at Friedy then back at Jon. "Talk about timing. How 'bout we get the hell outta here?"

Jon updated Guion as they made their way to the elevator banks. Guion put up resistance until Jon mentioned the bomb in the van. That got the team lead's attention.

"Just leave," Jon said. "Get out of the van and get us something else from the parking lot. Something big enough for all of us. Stone's got an escape set up."

Silence. Then, "Is it a manual trigger only?"

"Yeah, he says there's no timer."

Guion didn't answer.

A soft chime and light announced the elevator's arrival.

Something exploded outside. The shockwave rattled the building.

"That triggered an alert." Dunford stared at the virtual security dashboard he still had access to. "They're locking the building down as a precaution and sending a team to investigate the blast."

The elevator doors didn't open. The AR controls for up and down both displayed red padlocks.

"Guion?" Jon tried to raise the man. "Guion, are you there?"

"It was more than a manual trigger. I opened the side panel instead of the driver's door just in case. Looks like that started a timer. Someone wanted us all dead."

"In case you didn't do it," Jon said to Stone.

The hard man nodded without comment.

"You've got site security incoming," Jon said.

"And if you called an elevator, so do you. No one's supposed to be on that floor. Don't worry about me. I'll get a vehicle. You need to evacuate the building. Take the stairs."

Jon got them moving toward the stairwell. Maglocks clamped the door shut, but a hard bang from Brick slammed it open.

"Go up," Guion said.

"Up?"

"They'll secure the main entrance first. Climb, and trip a few sensors as you go. Let them see you."

Friedy started to wheeze after sprinting up one concrete spiral. Stone scooped him up in a fireman's carry. He ran full tilt with 65 kilograms of asthmatic Friedy slung over a shoulder and didn't even breathe hard.

"You want us to give away our position?" Jon said.

"I want them to see you going up. They'll assume you're making a roof exit and send forces there to stop you. But you're going out the 38th floor instead," Guion said.

"You heard the man, Mason," Stone said. "Slot some of those extreme sports skill files into your muscles and get up there."

Mason hopped up on the metal banister and swung into the open space that cored the circular staircase. "It's parkour blended with primate motion engrams."

"*Gesundheit.* Get four lines ready."

"You mean five, right?" He loped and climbed like a monkey, already disappearing into the heights.

Stone smiled. "You're not base jumping?"

"That was only one time, and you're sore I haven't invited you again after you wussed out."

Jon sucked air through his mouth but kept his breathing measured. Next to him, and slowly falling behind, Dunford had no such control. Too much time monitoring the complex from an AR intelligence station left him ill-equipped for sprints and stairs. Sweat ran down his face and neck, bloomed dark from his collar and armpits. Somewhere along the way, he'd gone from panting to wheezing. Jon tangled his hand in the man's shirt and hauled him up to pace.

"They found us." Dunford barely got the words out. He blinked and squinted and for a moment Jon thought it was because of sweat in his eyes. "They cut my feed. Video showed me with you."

"Come on, man. It'd be a real shame to go through all this just to get left behind because you didn't hit the treadmill enough." He yanked again and Dunford stumbled faster. "Brick, our extract doesn't have a harness. You're gonna have to take him."

"No problem."

"He's, uh . . . juicy."

Stone voiced the snicker implied in Jon's comment.

"Assholes." Brick stayed deadpan as he continued to climb. He didn't slow. His voice contained no strain.

Calls for them to stop bounced off the concrete walls and echoed alongside their boot clomps. A pair of gunshots punctuated their commands when the group continued.

"We don't have time for a prolonged gunfight," Stone said.

A shape dropped through the slot in the center of the zigzag of stairs. It fell past them and swung through the banister beside the security forces. Mason hit a guard with both feet, planted him into the poured stone wall and fired a quick controlled burst into another before his feet hit the ground.

More fire. Mason spun around and through the banisters, climbing and dropping floors like it was a dance. Stone and Brick added fire support from above. Stone fired his large-bore handgun with a casual air, Brick with mechanical precision. Both proved immune to their weapon's kick.

Silence.

"I'm going to beat you there a second time. Get a move on, lead feet." Mason bounded his way up the center cut again. "I'm still working with all meat limbs. What's your excuse, Brick?"

Brick grunted over the comm as he tucked Dunford under an arm and continued at the same pace he had before.

The group emerged into a long hallway capped with a floor-to-ceiling window. The corporate complex beyond it shone with fluorescent harshness in the night like an overlit city unto itself. Thirty-eight floors up, they barely saw the lamps lighting the parking or walkways. Other towers dominated the night scene.

Mason had indeed beaten them there a second time. He worked in front of the window, his sinewy form draped in a smart camo poncho that, again, cloaked him now that he moved slowly enough for the fibers to project a proper image. He attached anchors for rappelling lines and slapped a gooey wad with a metal disk on the center of the glass.

"Blowing the glass in two . . . one . . ." A small pop chased by a prolonged crunch transformed the clear window into an opaque sheet of green lightning in freeze-frame. Mason gave it a solid bang with his elbow and the entire mess collapsed, revealing the world outside once more, this time accompanied by a rush of cool night air. He threw the lines out the window. They unspooled with energy and slapped against the building with an impatient sound. The group stutter-stepped to a halt and began to hook themselves in.

"You're with me," Brick said to a soggy Dunford as he moved to the window. He still carried the man.

"You can't carry me while working the rope! You'll drop me!"

Brick hefted the man up as if he weighed nothing. "No, I won't."

"Then we'll both fall!"

"I can leave you." But even as he said it, Brick hopped onto the windowsill with the line in hand and leaned back.

"Relax," Jon said. "I don't think Brick's got an original limb left. He could take all of us down at once."

"Yeah, but I won't." He fell back over the edge and disappeared.

Brick didn't put Dunford down as they sprinted across the asphalt two minutes later toward a van that skidded up to their touchdown point. Electric motors slid its side door open as they neared, and they dove inside without grace. It began to roll before the door closed and long before they untangled themselves from the human pile they made and found comfortable places to crouch in the vacant cabin.

"Hold onto something," Guion said from the driver's seat. "We need to get clear of whatever Ibacipla might send after us." He broke into traffic and started weaving his way forward. The van swung back and forth with each car he passed. "Stone, send me the evac site."

Stone and Jon shared a look. Jon nodded.

Stone called his contact. "Hey, Bezelton, we'll be there in ten."

"Make it fast. Ibacipla's making some noise about border closings. Whatever you did really pissed them off."

"How's ten minutes?"

"You're an asshole."

"Yeah, but you love me. Also, I saved your life."

"We might be even on that score after this."

Stone tossed his head side to side. "I'm willing to discuss it."

"You got casualties incoming?"

Guion slipped into a narrow spot between two cars and got honked for the maneuver.

"Watch it, man. Erratic driving like that'll get you pulled over, and you're already driving while black. What is that, a thousand points on your license?" Jon said.

"Not the right time for jokes," Guion said.

Stone looked around. "Anyone hurt?"

"We're all good," Jon said. "Though Dunford here could use a paper bag."

Mason laughed and slapped the still sweating security chief on the back.

"Zero casualties," Stone said.

Silence crowded the line again before Bezelton answered: "Copy that. Proceed to exfil site. We'll see you there."

"That's a copy."

Guion swerved again, and Jon banged his tailbone on the floor as the van picked up speed.

EVEN THOUGH THEY HAD ALMOST TEN MINUTES TO GET USED TO Guion's abrupt driving, the whole team collapsed forward in a heap as he slammed the breaks and skidded to a stop in the corporate "nature spot" that was their extraction point. Tires squealed and left pungent drag marks on the asphalt as Guion swung the van broadside.

"What the hell was that?" Dunford said.

"Stone, we've been here too long. Get on board. We're

leaving now." That didn't come over beamed communication. It was a loudspeaker announcement. Floodlights from the vertibird flooded the van, blinded them in the dark.

"You heard the man." Stone hit the release button and slid the door open. "Maybe next time you can be a little more genius and we'll be on a laxer schedule." He smiled at Friedy before stepping out into the night with Mason.

"The van's dead," Guion said. "Someone shut it down with an override."

Brick looked at Dunford. "Am I carrying you?"

Dunford yanked his shirt straight. "I can't tell if you're kidding." They looked at each other in silence. "No."

"Okay." The big man stepped out, the guard a few steps behind.

"Come on, Friedy." Jon put one foot out and reached back to help his friend. Guion grabbed his shoulder from the front seat.

"No, everyone stop. The van's dead and our AR is down. That's why they're on the loudspeakers. They're hijacking our systems. Why?" He cocked his head. "Come out the front, my side. Keep the van between us and them."

Stone turned in the doorway. "You heard Bezelton. I saved his life. I get you're paranoid, Mr. Team Lead. You're right to be. We got set up." He fixed Guion with a serious look. "But some people won't kill friends—"

His head exploded.

Explosive rounds ripped Dunford's chest open and shredded the bullet-resistant casing on Brick's arm. He and Mason scattered. Automatic fire chased them in the darkness, too much for them to stamp out or evade for long.

The flurry of fire turned Jon's question into "Oh shit!" as he wedged himself between the driver and passenger seats and then slid out the door, dragging Friedy behind him. No sooner had they hit the ground than a massive ripping sound, like a ragged chainsaw engine, shredded the night silence and the van disintegrated one bullet-sized bit at a time. They huddled on the ground, hands clapped to their ears, as minigun rounds chewed apart the trees beyond them.

The wind picked up. Rotors. The machine-born storm ripped wounded branches off the trees. With all the buffeting, it took Jon a moment to realize the gun had stopped. He dared raise his head.

Seven A.W.E. corpsec agents surrounded them, sights trained on them.

A.W.E.? Bezelton sold them out.

"All of you, guts to the ground, hands behind your head!" He yelled, but he didn't have to. The speaker in his helmet made him plenty loud enough to hear over the engines already. "Do it now or we open fire!"

"Three!"

"Two!"

Normally Jon would look to Guion for some kind of contingency plan, but with only a second remaining, he rolled onto his stomach and laced his fingers behind his head.

2

Jon thumbed the screen on the stolen tac-pack and looked around. Moving from the electric glow to the dark of night left him blind. He didn't like that at all.

"Friedy, come on, man. We don't have time for this." He tapped the screen in a few other places and frowned. Even before they threw him in a cell, A.W.E. deconstructed his neuro-wired MIU with a nanite injection. That cut him off from AR and left him with the touchscreen interface on this tac-pack. Robbed of the deeper and more intuitive interface, he felt blind and incompetent.

He growled and tossed a glance over his shoulder. Past the distant hills, he could make out the prison high-rise, the plascrete towers stabbing the night sky like stubby fingers the color of a new-ish corpse. Windowless, it still glowed in the darkness, bleached by the sea of fluorescent emergency lights that brought artificial day to the grounds. He couldn't see them, but he knew the area swarmed with paramilitary security forces.

Strategic Homeland Operations with Capital Conservation and Control, SHOC^3, A.W.E.'s private security and military contractor arm, field-tested and promoted their armaments.

Overwhelm the opposition with $SHOC^3$ and A.W.E.!

$SHOC^3$ also manned their jails, like this one. The lights of their aerial search vehicles buzzed around the dim perimeter beyond the soulless white of the lamps. They flitted like insects in a widening pattern. It wouldn't take them long to find them out here. A.W.E. cleared the ground for kilometers around, leaving nothing but grassy rolling hills cut by barren roads.

Friedy's contingency, a worm he insisted on calling a homunculus, had sprung them before their jailors could finish what they started. It infected the MIUs of the arresting troopers, hopped from there to the prison system, and then when Friedy failed to call it off on account of being beaten and tortured along with Jon and Guion for three days, it shut down the facility. Took it completely offline and depowered every single system. The team made brutal use of the chaos.

Alarm klaxons split the silence wide open, crawled over the hills, and reached them in their inky spot as an angry moan. They'd slipped prison, but they weren't safe. No forests, no buildings, nowhere to hide. They needed to find a vehicle, and soon, or they were going back. They wouldn't escape a second time.

"Busy now." The scrawny man crouched on the ground a few steps away and scratched the air with a stolen external MIU. "Crossroads were places to conduct deals because no one owned them. A.W.E. owns everything for the next twenty kilometers, so I need a little more in the ritual to violate the border."

"There isn't time for your numerology bullshit," Guion said. He had a lot more bite in his voice than Jon. Ever since their run on Ibacipla Group, he'd been uncharacteristically snippy.

"It's not bullshit. Right, Jon?"

Guion shot Jon an annoyed look.

"Friedy's a designer baby. His father had the money to really push the envelope with him, bought him all kinds of upgrades." Jon shrugged. "The magic part is bullshit, but he makes it work."

Guion rolled his eyes.

"His brain is half computer."

"I've got a unit wired to my meat too." Guion tapped his temple. "Mine doesn't make me do stupid things. It helps me make risk assessments."

Jon didn't take the bait. "But it's not part of you. It's something you access. He doesn't have an implant. Techs redesigned his brain in utero. Friedy internalizes machine thinking at a level no one gets. It's magic even to him. He'll tell you it's sorcery, but I think he's operating at a level no one can explain outside of mystical terms."

"Whatever. Where's security?"

"Without an AR view, I don't know what I'm looking at here. You're the one who's supposed to handle this stuff." Jon tapped the screen and dragged a finger. Shrugged.

Guion took a step closer to Jon and glanced down at the screen. "No security on screen yet." His eyes rolled up for half a second. "I calculate we have two minutes before they get a good fix on us." He turned his head to the kneeling German as he scribbled in the air. "Let's get out of here before then. This is stupid. We should be clear of this area before they figure out where we are, not hanging out until they're almost in shooting distance."

"Friedy's gonna have a bug up his ass about this until he finishes," Jon said. "How's it coming, Friedy?"

"Almost done."

"Almost done," Jon said. "Then we hijack the first vehicle we find and head for the Manhattan Hive. It's got a crowd of millions and the corporations fight over jurisdiction there constantly."

"Have you ever been to The Hives?"

"Friedy and I used to slum there as teens sometimes. Why?"

"I grew up there." Jon and Guion looked at each other for a silent moment. "It's a good idea," Guion said at last.

Jon held up a shirt they nicked from a downed security guard. "While we wait, can you tie me up?" He nodded to his left arm, which hung lifeless at his side. A bullet wound scored a trench through the artificial skin of his forearm and revealed a seamless chrome plate underneath.

"This position is less than fifty percent secure and dropping by the second." Guion took the shirt and rigged a sling. He tied the arms together behind Jon's neck. "We'll find a clinic somewhere that can figure out what happened to it. I'm no doctor, but that looks like a graze and it didn't penetrate the casing, so I don't know why it's not working."

"I do. They turned it off."

"Simple enough. We'll get it turned back on. What can it do? I didn't see it listed as an asset in your file." Guion yanked the knot tight and stepped around to Jon's front.

"That's because it's not an asset. It's an arm."

Guion squinted at him.

"It's just an arm. I mean, the casing's rated against small arms fire and I can shut off the sensors while still engaging the motors if I don't want to feel anything, but it's not like I've got a weapon or storage compartment in there."

"Thirty-nine percent," Guion said to Friedy. Then back to Jon: "It's just a simple replacement?"

Jon nodded. "That's it. Lost the meat one on an op that went bad, and I needed something."

"Twenty percent. Why not get a cloned biological?"

Jon snorted through his nose. "You've got a better health

plan than I do. This is all the company would spring for, and I needed to take out a loan to cover my part of it. But A.W.E. wasn't going to loan me that much money on good faith, so they put a trigger in here in case I missed a payment. That's how I know they can do it."

"I had to give up three years' salary for the tactical processor, but it's mine clean and clear," Guion said with a finger to his temple. "Two percent."

A drone buzzed overhead.

"And that's all folks," Jon said with a glance skyward. "Friedy, I know your heart's in the right place, but the clock's run out. Time to go. All of us. Right now."

"A moment more. Infernal calling is tricky, especially since we're not in neutral territory."

"Call things by their names. I have no idea what 'infernal calling' actually means, aside from it's a stupid name." Guion swung his dark eyes from Friedy to Jon. His serious face showed more emotion than Jon remembered ever seeing. Pinched with anger, Jon preferred the neutral mask he normally wore, the one so thick that it started a rumor that Guion wasn't a person but a prototype android. "He's a crazy moron, and you indulged him. You're worse than he is."

"Guion, relax. Also, shut up." He used his good arm to turn the man around and pushed him toward the crossroads. "But you're right. We need to go. No more hanging out waiting for him to strike a deal with Hell."

"Oh, that was never going to happen, JonJon. Friedy has nothing to say about your immortal soul. You're the only one with agency in the matter."

That wasn't Friedy's voice. An octave deeper and missing the lilting German accent, this was someone else. Someone not them.

A man stood in the center of the crossroads, dapper in his pearly, vested business suit and casual in the way he held a smoldering cigarette between his fingers. Everything about him screamed that he was out of place. His dress, his manner—he didn't belong in this situation.

"Besides, profess to love the man as much as you want, we both know there's no way you'd allow Friedy to negotiate on your behalf for a pizza, let alone anything as important as your soul."

"Who are you?"

"Oh come on, Jon. You don't really need to see crimson skin and horns, do you?" The man spread a slow smile, charming with a hint of malice, as he eased closer. "Our time's limited. Why waste it on questions you know the answer to?"

"Guion—"

"You're going to ask him to shoot me, but you can't because he's not here." His smile vanished, and a hint of chill replaced some of the amusement in his tone.

A glance said the man was right. Guion was gone. He didn't see Friedy anywhere either. But the prison alarm still screamed in the distance, and he could pick up the sounds of rotors in the night sky. A.W.E.'s security forces were still out there, and they were closing in.

Jon tensed, clenched his fists. "What did you do to them?"

The man shrugged. "Nothing. They're standing right where they were a few seconds ago, looking at me, having a nice conversation." He sniffed with a hard wrinkle of his nose and his tone went cold again. "You should know that neither of them is wasting time asking about you. They both got right to business."

"What do you want?"

"Closer," he said with a nod. "But still the wrong question. Really, Jon-O, you need to pick up the pace here or you're not going to make it." He gestured to the horizon, where the beams of headlights bounced as they sliced the dark. They all pointed this way.

The man sauntered in a slow circle around Jon. "About now, they've managed to get a fix on this toy of yours." He touched the tac-pak in Jon's hand. Unfortunately, Guion had the gun they'd lifted. "And that drone flyover confirmed it."

Jon looked at the screen again. The black blips that represented "friendly" security forces did seem to be converging in his direction.

"Quit wasting time, Jon-O. I'm nearly done with Guion and Friedy, and I'm not going to stick around just for you." The smile returned. "I don't like you that much."

"Alright, make those security forces vanish. Take us off the grid so they won't find us. Give us what we need to take care of our needs."

The man chuckled. "Three wishes? You have me confused with someone else. I'm not a genie."

"What then?"

"Think of me as a talent agent. I'll match you with one of my people who has the skills you need."

"Okay, then I need someone who can hide me and my friends. He doesn't have to do anything else but keep us hidden."

The suited man grinned wide. "I know just the person. You'll get along famously. You take care of his needs and he'll lend his particular talents to your cause, starting with getting you out of here safely."

The headlights clustered atop a nearby hill. They certainly saw him in silhouette now. In his mind, Jon imagined their radio chatter and the calls to close in.

"Okay, fine."

"Excellent! If you were dealing with me directly, there'd be all this paperwork to fill out, contracts to sign, that kind of thing. But I'm just the facilitator, and I have a feeling Steve will be happy to skip all that. You can probably move through the process without having to seal it in blood." He extended his hand.

Jon hesitated.

"Uh-uh, Jon-O, no time for second thoughts."

A helicopter soared overhead and flooded the area around them with its spotlight.

Jon grabbed the man's hand and lost the world in a slow flash.

3

Jon pressed himself against the dingy plastic of a parked car and peeked up and down the street, sparing only a nanosecond to capture an image in his mind before snapping back to his crouch, resetting, and going again from another angle. He had to ball himself up to hide behind the tiny vehicle. It also meant he didn't have to move much to get a decent view of the surrounding area.

Unfortunately, the SHOC^3 trooper standing a meter from him made no attempt to hide. "Dude, I thought you said you were good at this." He didn't keep his voice down either.

Jon flashed wide eyes at him. He stabbed a finger against his lips and pressed his other hand down several times.

"Aw, come on, man." The trooper still wore the uniform from the penal facility, though he'd lost his helmet and much of his gear. Jon wore the man's holster and gun. The trooper stepped around the car and looked the street up and down. "I don't know what you're bothering for. No one can see us anyway."

"Steve! Jesus! Keep it down."

Steve chuckled and looked over his shoulder. "You still

haven't figured out how this all works, have you? No one can hear us. It's like we don't exist."

"I'd feel better if you got under cover. Let's not develop bad habits."

Steve looked at Jon crouched against the one-man vehicle for a moment before shaking his head. "Nah. You're kinda big, and that car's small. Doesn't leave a lot of room for me, and I'm not feeling cuddly." He swept his gaze up a nearby alley and stopped. "I am in the mood for that, though."

Jon had to half-crawl into the street to see what Steve pointed at, and even then he didn't get it at first. Plastic trash bags choked the alley. The ones nearest the street had burst and spilled their jumbled, rotting contents like the gap between buildings had vomited. A man in ragged jeans and stinking, mottled sneakers crouched next to that mess cloaked in a new, clean plastic poncho with heat-reflective lining, likely a gift from a shelter. He held a half-empty container of synth-soy cubes in scab-flecked hands, picking random trash bits from his impending meal. He fished an eyedropper from the reeking pile and eyed it up against the sky, cracking a smile of yellowed teeth and receding gums when he saw fluid in it. Jon figured even odds that it contained the original flavoring that came with the package, or the putrid mix of rotting food and liquid waste that grew at the bottom of trash heaps. He gagged to himself at the thought.

Steve licked his lips. "Come on man. I'm doing my part. Time for you to do yours." He never stopped looking at the man in the alley.

"You can't be serious."

Now he did turn away so he could stare hard at Jon. "The fuck I'm not."

"That's disgusting."

"I'm starving."

"You ate twenty minutes ago when we nicked that super-sized Could Be Chicken meal from Baron of Beef."

"Yeah, and I'm hungry again."

"And so you want dumpster-soy?"

"Look, the deal is I keep you hidden, you keep me fed. Pretty good deal if you ask me. If you dealt with the boss man, he'd want your soul. I just want you to get me food." He crossed his arms. "I don't have to like what you do when no one sees you, and you don't have to like what I eat. In fact, I promise you I will never offer to share a bite of anything."

Jon looked at the man in the alley again. He was dripping the flavoring—at least, Jon hoped it was flavoring—on the dried-out cubes.

"You better move fast, man. Looks like he's about to start."

Jon took one step toward the man before he stopped and shook his head. "This is bullshit. We can do better than this. I'll get you a pizza or something once we're set up someplace secure. I am not mugging a vagrant for food he picked out of the trash."

"You're half right. You'll get me pizza and something once we're settled, but you'll also get me that right now." He pointed.

"Fuck that. Come on." Jon began walking down the street, keeping to the shadows and overhangs.

"Fine. Have it your way, man. I'm on strike." Steve fell in behind him. He didn't make an effort to keep hidden, but he followed Jon's trail, which was good enough.

They moved like that without incident for some time, with Jon leading them deeper into the city sprawl away from the corporate monoliths that rose like glittering geometric moun-tains behind them. The Manhattan Hive used to be the economic heart of one of the most powerful cities on the planet. Rich in history, it mixed architecture from a wide span of generations and eras, all continually updated with modern technology. Theaters from the 19th century designed to carry stage voices with good acoustics moved to surround sound speakers hanging from steel latticework bolted to their delicately patterned ceilings. The old towers of iron girders got wired with wifi. Somewhere along the way, their glass windows became clear solar panels and someone added water reclamation units to their crowded roofs.

But for as dogged as the city was, for as long as it marched with the times, it aged. Its rich history slowly morphed into a creeping geriatric stain like a yellowing photograph. There was too much there, and it was too old. Contractors and engineers could only update a building built centuries ago so many times. The true cutting edge needed new, brand new, and so the money and the power built their new corporate homes further out on Long Island where there was still room, or they could make room. Towers dedicated to everything from finance to law to publishing became sky-high squats and tenements. The boroughs became human hives choked with the destitute not fortunate enough to live in the corporate plazas.

This area gave the corporate workers nightmares. Their entertainment feeds offered no shortage of stories featuring these filthy slums that teemed with anarchy and violent crime. Not only did it make an easy setting for piles of action and crime films, games, and virtual reality run-throughs, but it provided a mammoth boogeyman the corporations used to shackle their employees. Sure, the salaries might not be luxurious, but we provide housing. Otherwise, you'd be out there.

No one wanted to be out there.

But it was exactly where Jon needed to be right now. Out past the network of security cameras, away from the crowds of people wearing the latest trendy body cams that featured very hackable feeds, or the silent observers with video recorders implanted in their eyes. Out here corporations could still fly drones, but it was a risk with all the armed folk who'd just as soon shoot down an unmanned flier and scavenge it for parts. Out here they could try to patch into the ancient traffic cameras pointed at intersections, though they'd roll the dice on whether a given fixture still had power going to it. With all the jury-rigged and cannibalized wiring, the odds sat with the house.

Somewhere along the way, Jon slipped into the zone. He crept from shadow to alley, nudged his way through the middle of crowds, and fell into a steady, nondescript pace headed for Brooklyn. Steve grumbled to himself as he stomped in Jon's wake, but he kept pace well enough, and though he didn't make any effort to conceal himself, no one paid him any mind. After a while, Jon stopped checking over his shoulder for the possessed man.

He became so used to sliding by unnoticed that when the cry went out, he flinched.

"Jon!" Friedy broke from the base of a crumbling tower tangled with rope bridges, pulley lines, and power cables. He slapped Jon with a quick, fierce hug and a *Gott sei Dank!* before stepping back. His pale blonde hair, often in disarray, sat wild on his head now with yanks stretching in random directions. It gave the toothy smile that split his mouth a crazy look.

All told though, Jon had to admit Friedy looked remarkably good. He was still too pale and too thin, but his jubilation at being reunited with his friend let him shed the sickly feel that usually hung over him like smog.

"Hey, Friedy. I'm glad to see you too, man. I was hoping we all struck similar deals and got out of there."

The man nodded. "Ya. Me too. But I didn't think finding each other after getting away would be so difficult."

"I know, right?" Jon laughed. "It makes sense though. Our

demons make us invisible, but they also make us invisible to each other."

Friedy's thin eyebrows bunched. "What are you talking about?"

"You mean you didn't sneak away?" Jon noticed the splotched stains on Friedy's prison jumper. They'd faded with a few scrubbings that rubbed out some of the neon yellow of the nylon suit, but now that he studied them up close, they looked like blood.

"*Nein*. I never went invisible, and I can see you clear as day, *mein Freund*."

The realization splashed down Jon's body like a bucket of ice water. He stepped further off the street as Steve caught up the rest of the way.

"Friedy, this is Steve."

"Hey." The demon offered his hand. "No last name. Just Steve. You got any snacks? I don't care what they are, or if you started on them, or if they're still good. Basically what I'm saying is I'm not picky."

Jon slapped the demon's shoulder. "How can he see us?"

"I told you hours ago, man. I'm on strike. You've been doing this solo, and I know pride's a sin and all that, but you're nowhere near as good at this as I am."

"That means . . ." Jon glanced at his artificial arm still bound in a sling made from a shirt.

"They put a tracker in there, didn't they?" Friedy said.

"If they bothered to put in a cutoff switch, I'm sure they put a tracker in here with it. What happened to that MIU you had at the crossroads?"

Friedy shook his head. "Lost it right after I made my deal."

Jon looked at Steve. "You can baffle it. We'd have never gotten away if you couldn't."

"Sure can." He nodded.

"Steve, I'm not screwing around right now. You've got to squash the signal."

"I'd love to, man, but . . . " He shrugged. "I'm on strike."

"How can you be on strike?" Friedy wondered. "To come here, you needed to submit to a contractual arrangement, which included what you'd do for Jon."

"And what he'd do for me," Steve said. "Don't put this on me. You're the ones with free will. You can break the agreement. I can't. Not unless you do it first."

"You're going to hang us out to dry over garbage-soy?" Jon demanded.

"What 'us' brohame? Nobody can see me if I don't want them to, and your bud here— sorry man, I can never remember names—he got away in his own right. That just leaves you, and since you're the only one in violation of a contract, that seems about right to me."

"Fine, I'll get you two pizzas when we're settled. Squash the signal." Jon glanced over the hardplas block of armor on Steve's shoulder. "Now. That's the third time that car's cruised past. We're being watched."

"Love to, dude, but promises don't fill the belly." Steve rubbed his stomach. "As soon as this is distended, you're a ghost. Until then,"—he put a fist in the air—"power to the proletariat."

Jon spun Steve around and shoved him forward, kicked the group into motion. "Fuck you, Steve."

"I do not feel fucked, JonJon. You, on the other hand, feel quite fucked to me. No lube fucked. Maybe keep that in mind next time I say I'm peckish."

The trio moved with urgency, but not too much urgency. Jon set a metered pace. He still wanted to blend in with the crowds where he could, and he didn't want to tip off his pursuers that he was onto them. But it wasn't a single unmarked corpsec vehicle tailing them. The rusting Ford F-

150 with a covered bed. The blue Dodge Neon with a dingy white door. The Jeep Cherokee with the small spiderweb crack in the corner of the windshield. He assembled a catalog of cars that kept showing up around them.

The passes came faster, closer. They were herding them. It was only a matter of time before they boxed them in, and then whoever else was around would spring. They'd be back at the extraction site all over again with no way out. Jon sighed, threw his head back in frustration, and kept it there.

"Everyone get inside. We're climbing." He pushed Steve ahead of them again, forcing the demon to keep pace this time.

Their pursuers were coordinating their movements. He could tell from the way they'd adjust to the jagged path Jon cut through the Hive streets. But they were always in cars. So they'd go where cars couldn't. He didn't like the look of all the rope bridges, especially the ones that were just rope, connecting the towers here in a messy tangle, but they'd be a hell of a lot harder to pin down up there. If they got really lucky, the security forces after them wouldn't even have the stones to get out of their vehicles here.

They burst onto the roof of a lower building when Jon heard them.

Rotors.

So much for luck.

He spun the group around and herded them back toward the stairwell door when the vertibird banked around the building, its underslung nose turret auto-tracking them while a second minigun mounted on the side moved with less precision and more malice in the hands of a door gunner.

"Now you're dry fucked," Steve said.

The rotorcraft edged past the lip of the building and threw down rappelling lines, but only after the guns spun up, daring them to move before the ground forces collected them.

Jon looked for anything that might help, might offer them a way out. He found nothing.

Friedy gripped Jon's arm with a strong hand, and he felt the feverish warmth of the man's touch through his clothes. His little friend stepped close and spoke in his ear. "You've taken care of me since we were kids. It's my turn."

Before Jon could ask what he was talking about, Friedy tore into a sprint, ripping across the roof with such speed that he was halfway to the vertibird before the machine-controlled nose gun opened fire. The door gunner never even pulled the trigger. The scrawny German leaped the four meters straight through the open side. He shot into the door gunner like a bullet and Jon was sure he heard several of the man's bones break on impact even though there was no way that would carry over the engine noise.

The craft tilted and swayed back from the building edge in a way that didn't feel completely controlled. It swung dangerously close to an adjacent building before righting itself and starting to climb.

That's when the screams started. Screams and . . . animal noises? Jon swore he heard snarls and howls mixed in with the tumbled mess of throat-ripping shrieks that poured out the door. A corpsec agent fell from the bird and tangled in the ropes, his intestines spilling out in a tangled mess of pulpy worms swaying on a half-second delay from his body.

Two seconds later, someone threw his arm out the door after him.

Gunfire flashed in the cabin, a flurry of tight explosions that came and went, swallowed by more screams. The vertibird stopped climbing, dipped its nose, and came forward, though it kept its wings locked in the rotors-up position where it was more maneuverable. As it flew overhead, Jon saw a commotion in the cockpit. Nothing distinct, just wild flailing, and then a blood burst that splashed the windshield and blocked his view.

The bird kept forward but began to spin and tilt. Friedy leaped clear as the open door rotated across their building again, hitting the ground in a squat after dropping half a dozen meters. He was already sauntering their way when the vertibird slammed into a nearby high-rise. The dilapidated building shattered on impact, pulverizing those too slow to get clear with a spray of concrete and rebar. Then the fuel lit or a gas line sparked, maybe both. The whole thing exploded in a sooty fireball, and Friedy looked for all the world like a hero in one of those old action vids as he sidled up to them taking no notice of the fire pluming behind him.

"Holy fuck, Friedy," Jon said when he could get his gaping mouth to make words again. Beyond what he'd just done, his childhood friend was a terrifying sight, soaked in chunky blood up past both elbows with splashes and sprays marking the rest of him. But Jon couldn't stop looking at Friedy's smile. His toothy grin stretched wide with pride and was washed pink with a mix of saliva and blood. Ichor dripped off his chin, stained his collar.

"Did you eat some of those guys?" Steve held up both hands. "Dude! Up top!"

"Talking's not in your contract, Steve." Jon shoved him aside.

"I'm an apex predator now," Friedy said more to Jon than in answer to Steve.

Dust and smoke from the crash billowed over them in a cloud so thick Jon could barely see Friedy, even though the man stood only an arm's length away. Except it didn't smell like smoke. It was cold, damp. Fog?

"That's how a well-adjusted person talks," said a voice from the mist. It dripped with sarcasm and a heavy Oxford accent, which was weird because Guion wasn't British.

Something wearing Guion's body approached them. It had his trim frame, his close-cropped dark hair, his thick nose, and the small birthmark at the outside corner of his right eye. It had him down to the tiny details, but it used everything wrong. It strolled instead of marched, locked its eyes on them instead of gaining wide-area awareness. It smiled. Guion never smiled in a dangerous situation, and never smiled like that at all. A shark's grin.

"He warned me about your questions and I see them all over your faces," not-Guion said. "While we are temporarily obfuscated here, and the mess you've made will certainly hinder pursuit, the word that needs emphasizing is temporary. Let us table further discussions about spirit animals and the like until we have relocated to safety." He held up a gloved hand before Jon could talk. "Guion has secured a safe haven. Lovely little villa in a small town called Rockaway near the Brooklyn-Queens border. He's been following you surreptitiously for some time now but didn't think it prudent to reveal himself until confident your pursuers were dealt with."

"Where's Guion now?" Jon said.

"Right here," not-Guion said gesturing to himself. "He wanted me to come forward so that I might apply some of my talents. When I come forth, he goes to sleep."

"And you are?"

Shark grin. He extended a gloved hand. "I have had several names in my career, but you may call me Jack."

4

The lovely little villa turned out to be a small apartment added over the attached garage of a home that was probably quite nice back in its day. Since that time, overcrowding sliced and diced it into ever-smaller cramped units. Almost every house in the neighborhood was a collection of Single Room Occupancies with shared kitchens and bathrooms. Guion somehow claimed the largest apartment for kilometers.

Largest meant two rooms, not one. The bathroom nook and kitchen knock-out in the stuffy entrance hallway made it a neighborhood luxury.

There wasn't a stick of furniture covering the dented wood floors, but Jon noticed the windows in both rooms already had translucent drapes, the kind that let in light but clouded the view in and out. He also saw two stacks of clothing in the corner. Shirts and pants neatly folded with beat-up work boots resting on top, all bearing logos from old corporate events.

Cheap charity cast-offs. Completely nondescript, definitely Guion's style and matching what he was already wearing.

The olive canvas cargo pants caught Jon's eye, or rather the logo on both pockets did. A cheap foil gunmetal skull on each pocket and the words "A.W.E.'s Awesome Arms Expo" running in a stripe down one leg, "All September. All El Paso," running down the other.

Jon's gaze lingered on them.

Guion looked, then scowled. "You have other options if you don't want to wear those. Let's get settled and get to work." Real Guion had come back before they left Manhattan, shortly after they cleared the crash scene.

"Yeah, right. We have to get my family."

Guion stopped cold. He looked at Jon sideways. "What are you talking about?"

"What do you mean what am I talking about? Anyone close to us is in danger." He tossed a hand Friedy's way. "Friedy's mom is probably placed high enough to be okay, but my family isn't on the top floor of The Heights. We've got to get them before A.W.E. does."

Guion shook his head.

"I wasn't asking. I'll go without you."

"We were locked in that detention center for three days." Guion paused, fixed Jon with a heavy stare. "They're already gone."

"Fuck you, man. You didn't even check."

"I don't need to check."

"So you're gonna write them off, just like that? Real easy when it's not your people."

"You don't have any people. Not anymore. None of us do. Not you. Not me. Not even Friedrich." The lines that cut Guion's face softened. In all the years they worked together, Jon never saw anything so human from him. "I had family too."

"Parents and a brother, five years senior," Friedy said.

Guion gave him a look. "My brother's a useless shit. I haven't spoken to him since I shot him when I was ten." He snorted. "My parents . . ." He shook his head and wouldn't look at them. "I would have liked to save them."

Jon had to work the words past his disbelief. "I know business can be ruthless, but most of that stuff is just stories. A.W.E. is a company, not a criminal syndicate."

"You kidnapped and murdered people. You blew up buildings and cars and sabotaged hundreds of projects. What else would you call it?"

Jon swung his hands wide with a head shake. "We were doing our part to help A.W.E. keep the world safe."

Guion looked at him sideways. "You don't believe that."

"You don't?"

"The company line is bullshit."

"Then how do you sleep at night?"

"My criminal paycheck bought a smart gel mattress and a spacious apartment with full atmospheric controls slaved to my biometrics. I slept great."

Jon shook his head and stepped back from Guion. "We're too valuable to them. They wouldn't just execute everyone without a thorough review."

"They most certainly would. You watched it happen on the Ibacipla job. The heavies. Friedrich. They've already tried."

"Yeah, but we're field operatives. Family is different. They're innocent. They don't have anything to do with this."

"Jon, stop. I've been here before."

"Griffin," Friedy said to Jon.

Guion snapped his head to Friedy. "How do you know that name? Those files were sealed."

Friedy shrugged. "Not to me."

"Who's Griffin?"

"High-value scientific asset. She wasn't quite to chemistry what Friedrich is to computer learning, but she's the closest thing I've ever seen." Guion turned his head to the window, wouldn't look at them as he continued. "We got close, and eventually she transferred her residential assignment to mine. So when the Oceana Combine extracted her, I fell under immediate suspicion. I was out when it happened. Corpsec nabbed me before I got home that night. Locked me in an interrogation cell and subjected me to a battery of information extraction methods."

"What's that got to do with our families?"

"They didn't stop with me."

"Your parents?"

Guion twisted one side of his mouth. "Nobody spoke, because nobody knew anything. Didn't matter. The company didn't let them go. They got to go back to their lives, but the chief inspector let me know that he still suspected me, and if anyone else close to me defected, or if I disappeared, their lives were forfeit."

Guion let that sit for a moment before continuing.

"Do you know how much it costs to electronically transcribe a brain?" Guion said. "In all the operations you've run for the company, how many times has it been to extract someone who knew something we wanted?"

Jon sat like a statue. Only his mouth moved. "Plenty."

Guion nodded. "How many of them ended with a drop at a facility like the one we just broke out of?"

Jon opened his mouth to answer, but Guion plowed over his reply. "Do the math. A.W.E. almost liquidated my family over a single extraction. We saw the company execute three highly trained soldiers with a fortune of implanted enhancements and scheduled the three of us for impossibly expensive cerebral mapping."

He shook his head. "I've been working it through in my

head since we got out. We were all supposed to die on that operation, then the heavies spared us and Stone called someone outside the corporation. That terrified A.W.E. They think we know something they don't want us to, and they're desperate to find out what we found and who we told. Being a Heights resident means nothing. They might even drag someone out of Pluto at this point."

The Heights were the opulent residential floors of executive staff in the A.W.E. corp-platz, home to the top one percent of earners. Pluto was the mythical collection of floors above them reserved for the owning families, as high above The Heights as The Heights were above everyone else. No one knew anyone from Pluto.

He locked eyes with Jon.

Jon held his gaze for a silent minute. "Fuck this." He slapped his coat off the floor. "Come on, Steve. We'll do this ourselves." He turned for the door and almost ran over Friedy.

"Sit down, Jon." The little man still stood awash in gore from fingertips to elbows, lips to neck.

"Since when do you take his side?"

"It's not a side. It's a fact. You know I love your brother and sisters, but they're dead."

Jon grabbed a fistful of Friedy's stained prison jumper and hauled him up on his tiptoes.

Friedy snarled. A gold wash smoothed across his eyes and sharpened his pupils to ebony spikes as he pulled his lip back in a growl. They were . . . feline? Reptilian?

Inhuman.

Jon's grip slackened and Friedy took a breath. He gritted his teeth and squeezed his eyes shut. When he came down, flat-footed and relaxed, he was Friedy again.

"They can't stay on their floor without me. They need me, Friedy."

"Not anymore, they don't. I could prove it. It's simple really." He shrugged. "I'll hack the security feeds." Friedy's eyes thickened with a watery sheen. "I'm sure there's footage of them being taken away, and if they don't record their deaths, their files will certainly have that update. But . . . you don't really want to see that, do you?"

"Not everybody." Jon shook his head. "'The kids' would still be okay."

His older brother Jason had struggled with infertility in his marriage, so he and his wife adopted Gerald, Michael, and Lisa from a Hive uplift program. An accident outside the controlled zone claimed Susan and left gray-bearded Jason to care for the kids alone. The family rallied around him and "the kids" after that, making them the core of their unit.

"I'm sorry," Guion said behind him. "Anyone worth saving is already cold."

Jon sank to the floor. Friedy slumped next to him and hugged him with a sticky arm. His skin crawled at the warm, tacky touch, but Jon didn't move, didn't speak. His mind blasted his body with one shotgun load of sensations after another as it pinwheeled out of control.

Sinking numbness.

Rippling chills.

Heat that buzzed in the nerves.

The bracing clarity of new purpose.

"Then we kill them."

"Who?" Guion asked.

"The people who did this." Jon rocketed to his feet.

Guion shrugged. "You know who did it. You did. I did."

"Don't lay this on me, Guion. Whatever we did to piss off A.W.E. doesn't justify this."

"No, it doesn't, but that's not what I'm talking about. The people who pulled the triggers are people just like you and me. Professional bag men. They didn't know your sister or your nephews, and they're paid not to care."

Jon bristled.

Guion shrugged. "You could do it, but what'll that accomplish? They don't know who you are or who your family was."

That only paused Jon for a second before resolve hardened on his face again. "Then I'll walk into the boardroom and shoot every member of the executive council."

Guion snorted. "You say that like it's so easy."

"With him, it is." Jon pointed at Steve, who put a pair of hands over his heart and fluttered his eyes at them when everyone turned to look.

"We don't know their limitations. We've barely tested their abilities."

Jon scowled. "Friedy took down a vertibird with his bare hands." Pause. "I'm going, and you can't stop me because you can't see me. Steve, throw the cloak." He turned to leave.

Guion grabbed his arm and held him in place.

Jon's stare went from his arm to Guion to Steve, or at least where Steve had been. His spot by the window was empty.

It wasn't a big place; it didn't take long to search. Steve sat cross-legged in the kitchen nook half-buried in a heap of ripped and gutted food containers. He took alternating bites from protein bars held in either hand.

Guion looked at the open cabinets and the neat arrangement of dried and concentrated food now thrown about the room. "With rationing, we had enough food to last a month."

"Don't use that filthy language around me," Steve said around a mouthful of dense chocolate protein.

Guion snatched what remained of a bar out of Steve's hand. Without missing a beat, the possessed security guard pulled out another. Guion grabbed it before he could unwrap it. "Enough."

"Obviously not," Steve said.

"Deal with him," Guion said.

"Yeah, Jon, deal with me." Steve grinned with chocolate-stained teeth. "I'm hungry."

"You're fed. Now make me vanish. We're going on a trip." Jon hauled Steve to his feet but didn't make a go at his food.

"I can keep you from being seen, but I can't make you disappear. Going against reality like that is too much work. You want to vanish from them? Break line of sight."

"You didn't mention that."

Steve shrugged. "You didn't ask."

Jon grabbed his arm and dragged him along behind as he marched toward the door. "You'll fill me in on the other caveats on the way."

5

The staircase emptied into an area the size of a spacious phone booth with doors on opposite walls. Someone had driven a nail into one of them and hung a woodcut that read P3. Another apartment, Jon guessed. The other opened into the garage, communal space dominated by a bank of padlocked lockers and his way out of the house.

Jon pulled the garage door up and found himself face-to-face with a couple.

"Oh, hello," she said in surprise with a step back. The man at her side caught her shoulder.

Jon shot Steve a look, a shrug, and a wordless *what the hell?*

"Oh, I guess if you go ripping open doors in front of people the cloak drops. Who knew?"

A white-splashed charcoal pitbull with a physique packed with scars and muscles pushed forward and sniffed Jon up and down, tore his attention away from Steve. It was all he could do to marvel at the animal's striated muscle, meat piled on meat. A canine bodybuilder.

Jon spared a glance at the couple that held the leash. Her strawberry bob fit with her smooth features and soft figure. No hard lines on her anywhere, in contrast to her partner's rangy body, drawn face, and head full of peppery corkscrew curls slowly dusting to salt. Casual wear, both of them. No logos on anything, but a few sewn patches where they might have been. Possibly conscious corp objectors.

"Don't mind him," the woman said. "He's just checking you out. And hey, since he hasn't torn your leg off yet, you must be okay."

The dog sat in front of Jon and barked once.

"Oh, he really likes you." She gave the dog a rough scratch behind the ear.

"You in the suite upstairs? We didn't hear you move in. I'm Paul." He offered his hand. "This is Paula, and you've already met Pepe."

Jon took it. "Pepe, huh? For a second there I thought you were going to say his name was Paulson."

Paula slapped Paul on the shoulder. "See? I told you that wasn't a stupid name."

Paul sighed with a smile. "Yes, well, unfortunately for everyone, Pepe came to us with his name already, and with everything the poor boy's been through neither of us"—he gave Paula a look—"wanted to put him through anything else."

"A rescue, huh? Former fighter?"

Paula scowled. Her full lips emphasized the expression. "Yeah. Fuckers."

"It's the B7s," Paul said. "They're a gang that started in the 70s blocks. Lots of the usual stuff, you know? Drugs, prostitution, all that. But they're big on cage fights. Man on man. Dog on dog."

"Sometimes they'd bring the dogs to me after the fight for patching." Paula made air quotes with one hand.

"Fucking animals. And by that, I mean the people, not the pooches."

"Paula's a vet at the local shelter," Paul said.

A SHOC[3] branded patrol car drifted by as they chatted in the driveway. The sleek midnight blue sedan sported tinted windows, a crimson trim, and the company name emblazoned on the door in stylized letters like white phosphorus. The colors of the American flag tinted menacing.

Jon shot a glance over his shoulder, looking for reassurance that they were covered from this at least, but Steve was gone.

"That's weird. You don't normally see daytime patrols." Paul twisted and followed the car with his gaze as it reached the dead end of the block, turned, and headed back. "The B7s mostly stay out of the upper blocks during the day."

Jon repositioned himself as Paul spoke. He dropped to a knee to pet Pepe, hid behind the couple, angled his face away from the street. Jon refused to look at the car as it slid past a second time. It cruised like a shark prowling for meat.

Paul noticed. "Unless they're not looking for gangers. There was that building that went down in Manhattan earlier this week."

Paula gave him a one-eyed squint. "That was Manhattan, which is more than a little ways away."

Paul didn't break eye contact with Jon. "I'm just saying this might not be about the B7s." He nodded to Jon's arm. "How'd you get hurt?"

Jon stood. "Company job went bad."

"What company?"

"Does it matter?"

"Does it?"

"Paul, what's going on?" Paula said.

"This is a poor community, but it's a nice place with

generally good people," Paul said to Jon. He placed a hand on Paula's shoulder and gave a gentle squeeze. "We've got our trouble, but we handle it. We don't need more."

"The last thing I want is trouble. Not for you. Definitely not for me."

"Yeah, I believe that. The problem is that you live right upstairs from us. I don't need SHOC^3 banging on my door giving us rough questioning. You don't want to talk to them. Why don't we want to talk to them about you?"

"Because they're autocratic thugs?" Paula said.

"It's one thing not to like their methods. It's quite another to aid a fugitive," Paul said.

"SHOC^3's more interested in catching people who violate corporate law than civil." She turned to Jon. "Did you kill somebody?"

Jon shook his head in big sweeps. "I didn't. Things went sideways, but I don't know why. I don't know what they want from me, and I don't think I'd like the way they'd try to get whatever that is."

"See? It's business, not crime. Fuck the jackboots."

Paul sighed and shook his head. It wasn't a gesture of resignation.

"You have to understand, Paul likes everything to run smoothly. It's what he does." Paula laid a hand on his shoulder. "Paul's a hi-tech handyman, keeps a lot of the tech here operational and jury rigs like a muthfucka." She gave him a smile like a laugh. "Though the best repair job he ever did was this boy here." More scratches on Pepe's neck. He barked once in appreciation. "Mr. White Knight here helped clear the clinic while I worked on Pepe so we could keep his spunky butt." Another smile. This one so glowed with warmth and appreciation that if she didn't follow it with a kiss it would have been wrong.

She kissed his cheek. Not a peck.

"Handyman, huh?" Jon shrugged his artificial arm, still cradled in the shirt-made sling. "Know anything about canceling a repo code on a prosthetic?"

PAUL FOLDED A THICK SQUARE OF BATTERED WOOD DOWN FROM the wall of his one-room apartment. He dropped a supporting leg out from underneath it and opened a compartment in its surface to retrieve a collection of delicate tools. Paula pulled a mismatched pair of folding chairs off hooks from another wall and set them on opposite sides of the table while he set up. She motioned for Jon to have a seat, then disappeared out a back door half-cloaked by an American flag that had a middle stripe of $10,000 bills. "Ronnies." She took Pepe with her, leaving the men alone.

"Alright, let's see what we've got here." Paul put on a pair of magnifying spectacles. He rolled Jon's forearm one way, then the other, prodded the bullet trench with a small probe. "I don't see any damage here. Remarkably little scoring on the casing, even. You got lucky." He lifted his head and traced his gaze up to Jon's face. "Does this go all the way to the shoulder?"

"Yup." He pulled his short sleeve up over the cap of his shoulder and pointed to a hairline scar. "That's where they knit the synthskin to mine."

"I don't see work like that much. That's no Medicaid job."

"Workman's comp with a big loan assist. I had good credit back when it happened."

Paul half-rose out of his seat and examined the seam. He gave Jon a pointed look as he sat back down. "That's not made to come off."

"No, of course not. Why would it?"

"Cheaper prosthetics need more maintenance than you're used to. The neural interface loses connection, servos wear out, the sorts of things that require you to open up the housing and get into the guts of the machine. Anyone who bothers with synthskin coverings for those wears it like a glove so they can slip it off when they have to."

Jon ran a finger over his scar. "They leave it open?"

Paul nodded. "Cover it with clothing most times. Or they use a lite adhesive to glue it down just enough. Kind of like a post-it note."

"My connection's wireless. It's not physically connected to my nerves, just bolted in place. They placed some gel on the seam here when they first installed it, but nothing since."

Paul rose and looked at it again. "Nanosurgery. They knit it to you. If they ever needed to do maintenance on your arm, they'd cut the skin away and use more nanite gel to secure a graft when they were done." He sat back and placed his glasses on the table. "I can't do that. To open that up and have a look, I need to cut the skin off. When I do, it stays off."

He stated it. A fact, not a question.

Jon looked at his arm lying dead on the table. "I need to be able to tie my own shoes." He flashed the man a grin. "Besides, I'm suave enough to make chrome fashionable."

Paul didn't return the smile. "Do you need local anesthesia?"

Jon shook his head. "It's a heavy paperweight. Totally shut down."

"Okay, let me get my assistant. I have a feeling I'm going to need a little help with this."

Paula did the cutting. She insisted. Paul handled a scalpel fine, but he had no eye for style. If this was coming off for good, it should at least have a little flare to it. She cut an oblong hem, leaving a flap of skin covering the crook of his elbow, but swinging up higher in the back, exposing the joint cap. "I've got a little paste to keep that in place," she said as she finished.

Paul slipped the magnifying spectacles back in place. "Alright, let's see what we've got here." He picked up a probe and slid it along Jon's smooth chrome forearm in search of a seam.

"Fancy toy. You got a MIU in there too?" Paula said.

"Used to. An injection took that out around the time the arm died."

"Probably piggybacked on the same wireless neurological interface the arm used for motor and sensory signals." Paul angled his head. "That means you had a full five MIU."

"Full five?" Paula said.

"Handhelds show you things through eyepieces and pump sound to you with buds or micro speakers in the glasses frames. You can get a little tactile feedback through the gloves," Paul said.

"Yeah, or those icky codpieces." Paula wrinkled her nose.

"Our new neighbor here didn't have to wear any of that. His MIU beamed all that information to his brain, so he could see and hear everything we do in AR, but he could smell and taste and feel it too. Full five."

Paula held up a hand with fingers splayed and gave Jon a questioning look.

He nodded. "Whenever I had to work with new people, I'd always insist we meet at a bar and have a bunch of drinks. Team building. But they weren't real drinks. We'd have water and our MIUs made it into beer."

"They call it phantom food," Paul said.

"If it can make you perceive anything, why use water? Why use anything?" Paula said.

"We didn't have to. The MIU could make something out of nothing if we wanted, but the less it has to do, the cleaner the experience. So we use real-world blanks and overlay sensory edits most times."

"You use water to take care of the cold and the wet and your MIU adds flavor," Paula said.

"You got it. Plus, water's tasteless so there's nothing to override. Makes the whole experience run better."

Thoughts churned behind her gray eyes. She scrunched her face and shook her head. "Fuck that. No way. If it can do all that, I'd never be able to trust my own senses. I can't imagine living in a world curated by someone else."

"It's not like that," Jon said.

"How do you know?"

Paul sighed as he sat back and tapped the light on his glasses to darkness. He crossed his arms and shook his head at the dead arm.

"Let's hear it, doc."

"That thing is not made for shops like this. I'd need finer tools than anything the Five Hives offer to open that up. There's good news though." He patted Jon's forearm.

Jon didn't feel it.

"You don't need to open this thing up to bring it back online."

"I notice you haven't done that yet."

Paul tucked his bottom lip and nodded. "I'll bet money I really need that remote links and software handle your maintenance for everything but the heavy stuff. And I'll go double or nothing and say that if you try anything without the proper access codes, it'll lock your MIU with a virus. So, no offense, but you can't use ours."

"I've got a computer wizard. I'm not worried about it. But we need to get our hands on a MIU for him to work his magic."

"Malcolm," Paula said.

Paul looked at her, then nodded first to her, then to Jon.

"Who's he? A tech fence?"

"Yeah. Under the table. You can get a MIU from him that won't require you to load your personal data," Paula said.

"Just be real sure that fancy thing doesn't send a couple of squad cars cruising past his place," Paul said. "Malcolm likes discretion and isn't as forgiving as we are to people who bring trouble his way."

6

Guion scanned the piles of detritus at the curb as he wove his way through the neighborhood. Rockaway was a beach community stretched across a peninsula. A strip of urban sprawl four blocks wide and 150 blocks long that separated the Atlantic Ocean from Jamaica Bay, all laid out in a grid that Guion now marched through on a mission.

Is there a purpose to our perambulation? Jack said in his head.

"Jon needs a little time to figure things out. I want to be ready by the time he gets back."

Steve returned minutes after Jon stormed off on his execucide crusade, thwarted by opening a door in sight of others. Jon was still out there doing . . . something. But without Steve's cloak and knowing he was visible to everyone, Guion doubted it was anything more dangerous than a walk to clear his head. He could have it. When he finally cooled off and returned, it would be to a fully operational base.

"Furniture. Our place needs furniture."

So you resolve to walk the streets?

"What we're looking for has a few specific criteria, and the first one is that it's got to be free unless we pass a shop that lets us barter with service. We don't have any cash, and we don't have MIUs for electronic transactions."

One man's trash.

Guion nodded. "But it's got to fold. We don't have much space, so we need easy storage for everything we bring in. A table and some chairs top the list of necessities. I need to map operations on paper until we get MIUs again."

Which returns us to the lack of currency.

"Exactly. So handwritten notes for now. I'm not doing that on the floor."

I assume you're reserving one room for beds.

Guion shook his head. "Neither room has enough space for three beds." He frowned. "Or four, I guess, assuming Steve needs to sleep. Does he?"

I'm afraid you'll need to make that inquiry of him directly, dear Guion. We're all quite individual in our needs.

"Four beds then, just to be safe. Though part of me is tempted to make Jon share his." He shook his head. "That's emotion getting in the way. There's no space for pettiness now."

But no room for four beds either.

"No, that's why we're going with floor pads. Foam would be nice, but anything with a little cushion that we can roll up and store in the corners of the apartment will suffice."

Quite the detailed shopping list.

"Our needs are basic right now, but they're pronounced. We need a planning area and we need to be able to sleep."

I see why you are the team lead. What I can't see is how you perpetrated a crime heinous enough to get yourself incarcerated. The blatant unprofitability of the whole thing precludes your pragmatism.

"Guilt by association."

You covered for one of them, and they let you down. Guion could hear Jack's nod of understanding in his voice.

"I didn't do anything for them. Friedrich is a known delinquent who skirts by on his talent and position." He shook his head. "Jon doesn't seem to mind getting dirty through proximity, but I do." He looked around. He balled his fists. His words picked up speed. "Now I'm back here, after doing everything right to get recruited into the corp-platz."

Back here?

"Years ago I took my family out of here. Even my useless brother." He snorted. "I knew my folks would want that. A sprawl-born has a .03 percent chance of landing meaningful corporate work and I did it." He let his gaze wander, same as his thoughts. "I should kill those two idiots and report to corporate. Maybe they'll forgive whatever they think I'm guilty of."

Jack let Guion work that thought without comment. That he had nothing to say said volumes. No, that was just emotion. It had been a while since he had to manage spikes this high. Besides, if it were that easy, he could have refused to escape prison with them, proven loyalty without the murder. But when given the opportunity, he didn't sit on his cot and wait when the door sprang. He left because he already knew compliance bought him no clemency. They had put a bomb in his car, after all. A.W.E. wasn't angry with them. Their corporate master wasn't punishing them. The company was scared and everything since their violent extraction was panicked corporate flailing.

Whatever they were involved in made A.W.E. desperate. That gave them leverage. If Guion discovered what they had, he could use it. There might not be any going back, but if he had something that made a megacorporation quake, he had more than a .03 percent chance of leaving the sprawl a second time. If it didn't work . . .

"If I can't get back, I'm going to make them . . ." He took a lungful of sea air rotten with decaying seaweed and petro-pollutants.

Make them . . . ?

Guion shook his head. "One thing at a time. I haven't failed yet. I haven't begun yet. It's not the time for surgical vengeance."

He needed to slap a leash on those two. They'd ruined his life in a single evening and a few key moments of leniency. He couldn't trust them to make good decisions, not even for their own self-interest. Hell, Jon's demon was already out of control and chewing through their foodstuffs. They'd need to deal with what they were going to eat at some point, an issue Guion resolved before bringing the other two back here. They weren't here a day and they'd taken a step backward from where they needed to be.

Guion was team lead, and he'd need to be the only lead if they were ever getting out of here.

"Right now, I need the base appointed. Keep an eye out for folding tables."

I do so respect your logical purity, Guion. It will be a pleasure working with you.

7

Friedy stalked through the old streets lined with cracked sidewalks and splattered with a mess of stringy shade from the webwork of bridges and cables lashed across the floors above him. People gathered on stoops or small balconies stories above the street. Kids played street hockey with sticks of scrap wood nailed to aluminum rods and pucks made from crushed soda cans or rode past on bikes that looked like the mechanical version of Frankenstein's monster.

Down in Rockaway's lower blocks the ancient, once opulent homes gave way to newer construction: towers and tenements. As crowded as the upper blocks were, they had nothing on the crush of humanity down here.

116th street was a bust. Guion had sent him there looking for MUIs, having identified the block as a commerce center, and he was right. Stores packed the entire stretch from beach to bay, everything from kiosks in the street median to stores piled one atop the other several stories tall. A few older buildings and services peppered the mix. What few homes used to be here had been repurposed and remodeled to serve commercial interests, but the subway still ran, the same as it did seventy years ago. Down a few doors sat a Conflagration Containment Service office converted from an old firehouse, and a police station located next to the Snack Time Super-Center served as the local SHOC[3] basecamp. Friedy stayed away.

But Guion was wrong about any potential leads here. Yeah, the bustling block offered a few places to buy MIUs, but security was tight in the stores. Some even buzzed you in and made sure every shopper had an associate attached to them. The prices were well beyond what they'd be able to scrounge anytime soon and beyond all that, there wasn't anything worth buying or even stealing. Even the nice models weren't top of the line like he'd prefer.

Rather than leave it at that, Friedy asked around for where else he might go and heard about a place down in the low 80s he could try. That place wasn't always on the up and up though, so the crowd tended to be rougher.

Friedy had to go though. He had to at least check it out. Coming home with nothing promised more of Guion's insufferable beratement. He could hear it now. How could Friedy visit two commerce blocks and come back with nothing? Do you know what the odds of that are? Three percent, Friedy, three percent—unless you weren't really trying. If you're sloppy and lazy, then it's much more likely you'd come back with nothing. Do you know what the odds are that you were sloppy and lazy? Do you want that number?

"Hey man, ain't seen you around here before."

The voice yanked Friedy out of his mental tumult. He realized he'd clenched his fists so hard he bruised his palms. The crowds and groups he'd been ignoring were gone, left behind some unknown number of blocks ago. This area saw a lot less pedestrian traffic, and the five boys who slowly spread around him were all armed. Pistols glinted in a few waistbands, the old metal kind that were as good for clubbing as they were shooting. One held a shock baton in the off position, though even without the crackling electrical nimbus it looked solid enough to break bones. The last pressed a button on an empty hilt. Black grit like sand spilled out into the shape of a knife blade as the magnetic field assembled the iron filings into an impossibly sharp micro-serrated edge.

Friedy jerked his head one way, then the other, looking for Jon by old habit. No Jon. Not this time.

"I don't think you belong here," said one of the boys. They looked like late teens, maybe twenty at the oldest. Physically powerful and filled with the arrogance and invulnerability of youth. One pulled a sleek MIU with a scanner attachment from a baggy denim pocket and pointed it at him.

"I—I—I—want no trouble." Friedy struggled to get the words out.

His stutter lit them up with laughter. "M—M—Mother-fucker, shut the fuck up and stand still." More laughter.

For a flash, Friedy didn't see a gang of young armed men surrounding him. He was six and it was the corporate kids circling and pointing and laughing. Then he was ten. Then fifteen. He'd been here before. He'd been here his whole life.

He felt an odd rush. The old anger mixed with new confidence and aggression. "Fuck you."

The laughter slammed into a brick wall.

"Look who cured his stutter," one of them said.

"Ah, forget it," the one with the MIU said. "He ain't worth shit. None a' his organs sellable." He looked up from the screen with a mix of contempt and confusion. "Damn, man. How you not dead yet?"

"For real? Lemme see." Another sidled up and stared down at the screen. His face went slack with laughter and he grabbed his gaping mouth. "Oh, ho, ho . . . shit!"

The rest gathered to see the joke that was Friedy's

biometric evaluation. They all had a good laugh until the screen flashed at them. Friedy couldn't see the warning message, but he saw it wash their faces in brilliant red light. As one, their faces fell grave and their gazes rose to him.

"Homes is worth something after all."

"Hell yeah, he is."

"Fuck you all. Come at me. I want you to." Friedy started to pant. "Nein. I want to come at you." He sprung into their midst and the group collapsed on him.

Friedy was a genius, his mind a massive beehive with each insect representing a thought. If he concentrated, he could organize the swarm and direct his thoughts to a single task; Friedy thought faster and with more power than some computers. But he could also let his thoughts fly free, wandering all over the mental landscape, granting him the mad creativity to think outside the box and come at problems in unorthodox ways.

The one thing Friedy could never do, however, was stop the thoughts. He never switched off. He wrestled his racing mind to find sleep every night, and those same thoughts paralyzed him in social settings and physical confrontations. In both cases, he got so bound up in analyzing the situation that too much time passed, and he'd create an awkward silence or take a punch to the face.

Not now though. Without realizing it, Friedy swam in the moment on pure instinct. He didn't think, didn't analyze. Now it was all observation and reaction with nothing in between. Crouch to duck the baton swing. Now leap to tackle the man before he recovers. Roll him on top to take the pistol shots coming. Throw the body into their midst and grab the nearest throat. Squeeze through the fingertips until the skin pops and the blood pours.

Friedy bounded and wove among them. He never stood still, made them cross their lines of fire, and struck not with the skill of a fighter but with the savagery of an animal. He gouged, rent with steely fingers. He bit and tore. And when he did he chewed.

It was over in less than ninety seconds. The dead lay twisted and torn around him in a mess, while he stood bloody to the elbows again. He felt no pain.

He felt no fear either, and he couldn't keep the smile off his face as his gaze moved from one body to the next. Five down. All by himself. Poor Friedy was dead. His panting breath fell deeper into his belly as the fear he'd lived with his entire life finally dropped away. He felt free. He felt alive.

He felt . . . hungry.

Friedy searched the bodies and pocketed their weapons, the top-line MIU, as well as a few handfuls of paper money he'd use to get a slice of pizza. Except Steve had pizza at the apartment. It looked greasy and gross. He wanted meat. A burger . . . no, not a burger.

He glanced down at the bodies. He sank down next to one. The boy had bled out when Friedy bit open the side of his neck. Friedy sniffed the still bleeding wound, smelled the hot blood and exposed meat.

His stomach growled.

He ate.

8

Jon checked the house number.

"This is it. Steve, go hang out at the head of the block for a bit."

"Wait, what? I'm not coming in with you? What was the point of coming back up to get me? I was just starting to enjoy that place with no one in it." He winced and put a hand on his stomach. "That condensed food your friend got is starting to give me gas."

"I don't need you harassing this guy for food while I'm trying to make a deal."

"Come on, man. I wouldn't do that." Steve put a hand on Jon's shoulder. "I only harass you for food. Besides, why deal? Why not sneak in and take what you want?"

"Would your cloak hold up to me lifting something?"

"Hey man, before I took the big trip down, I was a person, same as you. Not a sorcerer. Not an angel. I only got these powers as part of the contract."

"So you don't know what you can do?"

"I've got the basics, but all the clauses and exceptions? Do you know how boring legalese is?" He slapped Jon's shoulder. "It's a big adventure of discovery, and you and I get to take it together, good buddy."

Jon pointed. "Head of the block, Steve. I'll meet up with you as soon as I'm done."

225 Beach 125th Street was an unremarkable house with a brick ground floor and white vinyl siding for the second story. A short stack of concrete steps led up to a landing that spilled sideways into a porch that looked out over the street. A large picture window watched the porch.

The maroon and chrome Xiao Ming Electro Glide two-door that sat charging in front stood out from the multi-car pileup that crowded the driveway and curb.

Xiao Ming Electro Glide: smooth power for a smooth ride for a smooth driver.

Malcolm lived in an SRO like everyone else, but he lived like a king among paupers.

Jon rang the bell. He waited.

He knocked. The door cracked open.

"Who are you? I'm not finding you on my scans."

Jon held up his hand. "No AR. No MIU. That's why I'm here."

"What makes you think I can help with that?"

"Paula sent me."

"Yeah?" The door pulled open all the way. A bald black man in sharkskin trousers and a salmon shirt stepped back. Both hugged and accentuated his athletic build in a way off the rack clothing never did. He held the door in one hand, a MIU with a scanner in the other. His eyes worked the air between them, visually issuing AR commands only he could see through a pair of slim frame silver spectacles.

"No wire. That's a good start."

"You're Malcolm, right?"

"Don't jump ahead. We're still establishing who you are."

"Sorry, I just . . . you're not what I expected."

"That says more about you than me."

"Guess it does." He shrugged, uncomfortable. "Sorry."

"You ain't local. What are you doing here?"

"I'm looking for a MIU with the specs I understand you provide."

Malcolm shook his head. "Not what you're doing at my door. What are you doing in Rockaway?"

Jon sucked a hard breath through his nose, thought for two seconds, and decided to play it straight. "Hiding. I'm on the lam."

The man gave a slow nod, a gesture of small approval. "What'd you do?"

"I honestly don't know. One moment everything was fine, the next I'm on death row counting down my last days."

"$SHOC^3$ just nabbed you and dumped you in jail?" Skepticism crawled over every word.

"I never said $SHOC^3$."

The man started to say something, stopped, thought. Realization bloomed on his face. "You mean you're . . ."

"Corp asset. Yeah. They liquidated half my team when they took me. No one bothered to say why, then or after."

The man chewed on that answer. After a moment of consideration, he waved Jon in, up a half-flight of stairs and offered him a seat in a leather easy chair made of cubic angles. He eased into an identical chair with his back to the window. Mirrored glass coated the opposite wall floor to ceiling. Not only did it reflect the daylight and brighten the room, but Jon noticed it let Malcolm watch him from multiple angles.

"You're being awfully candid with a stranger."

Jon smiled. "You're not a stranger. You're Malcolm." He crossed a foot over his knee. "If Paula's right, you've got the kind of MIUs that operate anonymously. If I go live on one of those commercial models that collects and broadcasts all my shit to any device that's listening, I'm dead ten minutes after switching on." He threw his hand up and let it collapse back into his lap. "You strike me as someone who sees through bullshit, so I'm giving you the raw story."

"Which corp?"

Jon snorted, twisted half his mouth into a grin. "Do you really want to know that?"

"I probably don't." He considered Jon for a moment, then rolled to his feet and walked deeper into the house, asking for a moment's patience with a single raised finger as he passed.

Malcolm returned with a small plastic bin that he put on a coffee table near their chairs, a solid glass cube framed in steel.

"You've got multiple rooms?"

"Naw, man, but me and a bunch of the other folk here share the common area. We did it up nice with a group fund."

Jon looked around. "It is pretty high-scale compared to what I was expecting. So you didn't do this on your own?"

"How could I? I'm just a humble hustler like the rest of the working poor."

Jon caught Malcolm's look. Nodded. "Right."

"You want a MIU to get back into the world and turn that arm back on, right?" Malcolm pulled out a MIU as tall as his hand, though not as wide and all screen. It had almost no visible border. It lit up at a touch. "Okay, what we've got here is the Black Hole. It's a whole lotta steps above what most people in town come to me for, but I'm thinking you want to do things most people in town never think of." He tapped the screen in a few places. "Pretty standard interface." He saw Jon's face and pulled a set of glasses from the bin. Chrome wire frame bolted to slim rectangular lenses. "Here. You're probably more comfortable with these."

Jon slipped them on and saw the virtual construct painted atop the real world. A black pearl, completely without shine or luster, hung over the MIU. It erupted into the familiar radial bloom at the man's touch, though Jon noted the rings were mostly empty.

"It'll suck in all the data you need to interact with the virtual world but gives almost nothing back. That little bit you do have to provide goes out with the serial numbers filed off, so to speak. The operating system includes an adaptive smart adblocker. It's a processor hog, but you'll want it."

"What for? The thing's already anonymous."

"Just 'cause they can't ID you don't mean the bots won't hit you. It's like nonstop carpet bombing." He paused. "I forgot. Courts ruled advertising free speech, but the corporations got themselves exempted from the distribution lists."

Malcolm pulled out another MIU from his bin, this one cheaper and nowhere near as cool. He synched it to a pair of glasses and handed them all to Jon, motioned for him to put them on. "Have a look at anything in the room."

Jon slipped on the specs. The room came alive with all manner of AR prompts. Every piece of furniture sprouted small windows that proclaimed their brand and model, along with links to catalogs of pieces in the same collection. Popups beside that window showed selections that a brand manager deemed a good match from other catalogs. More popups showed where he could buy that same piece at prices lower than list.

The holoprojector exploded in his vision, data windows blasting his sight like shrapnel. Not only did it project the standard shopping options but offers for different streaming services and packages popped into view, each one playing a montage of offerings in video with as little provocation as a glance.

He squinted and stood, looked out the window for a break, but didn't get one. Outside, every car erupted in an array of options. Where to buy it. Where to rent it. Where to service it. Where to get gas or find a charging station. Every element of the vehicles had its own cluster of popups too. Tires, paint, upholstery, sound system.

The houses had tags. Tags for contractors, building supplies, plumbers, electricians, rental offers, and eviction services.

People's clothes all carried tags too. So did the tents the desperate set up in driveways. Ads for tents, patch kits, and charities clogged his vision.

They even tagged the street. *Looking for a beach vacation on the cheap? Come down for the day to Rockaway!*

Jon pulled off the glasses and pinched his eyes. "That's awful."

"Ain't it just? I gave you the unfiltered view. No one does that. As you saw, you can't. There's too much crap to do anything. But there's a legal limit to how much a filter can exclude from your augmented experience." Malcolm waved the Black Hole at Jon. "This bad boy here though, it cleans it all out. You only look at the augments you want to. And that smart blocker I mentioned keeps away the ads floating around in the WorldGrid that'll show up outta nowhere and scream at you. I didn't include those in your little tour there." He motioned at the MIU in Jon's hand.

"That thing sounds better all the time."

Malcolm nodded. "I'll bet it does." He motioned for Jon to sit again and relieved him of the filterless MIU. "You can use glasses, or if you're looking for something less bulky, I've got some bluetooth contacts." He pulled a tiny case from the bin with one hand, a small squeeze bottle with the other. "I'll throw in the solution for free since we're good friends now.

"Same deal with the earpieces." He dropped the contacts case and bottle and came back with a tiny box in each hand. "You can go standard earbud, or I've got a model that you can wear hidden." He offered Jon one of the boxes. Molded plastic hugged what looked like two flesh-colored cones with a slight curve. They reminded Jon of tiny, blunt horns.

"Finally, gloves. I got the standard models, of course. Or you can use what I'm using. Malcolm smiled, obviously proud of what he was about to unveil.

Jon looked at the man's hands. "You're not wearing anything."

"Weren't you wondering how I worked in AR without gloves?"

"Where I come from, no one wears gloves. Everyone's got MIU implants." Jon smiled and shook his head. "I don't mean to take the wind out of your sails, man, sorry."

Malcolm pointed at him. "That is a level of fancy I can't touch. Even if I could get my hands on that kind of stuff, there's no one out here who could afford it."

"Alright then. How do you do it?"

Malcolm stepped close to Jon and offered his hand. "Fingertip overlays," he said. "A dot of adhesive keeps 'em on, and I can touch virtual constructs the same as gloves without sacrificing any feeling in my hands."

Malcolm took his seat by the window, crossed his legs and steepled his fingers over a knee. "The higher-end peripherals cost more, but you get what you pay for." He paused for a brief moment. His eyes flicked to the upper right, then returned to Jon. "Hold up a sec."

He opened the door for a young woman. Jon couldn't help but stare. Her halter top straps twisted around her neck and made a window to show off her cleavage, while the line of her thong rode above her low-waisted jeans to accentuate her hips' smooth curve. Her clothes looked casual but hugged and displayed her sculpted frame. Even though Malcolm stood a good head and a half taller than her, half his face disappeared in the massive poof of hair that erupted from her head and fell in mirrored waves to either side.

"Sup, Tasha? What's goin' on?" He waved her inside.

"Wassup is Phillip. He's startin' to roll with the B7s."

Malcolm turned away and scratched the back of his head with a grimace. "Shit."

"Yeah." Her word was a verbal punctuation mark. She closed on him, tapped his chest with a rigid finger. "I need you to shut that shit down."

"Yeah." He faced her. "Yeah, right. Okay. Send him by. I'll talk with the boy."

"Send him by?" She pulled her head back with wide eyes. "Motherfucker, a daddy visit ain't what I'm askin' for. You think I can't talk to my son?"

Malcolm held up his hands. "That clearly ain't doin' it, and you wouldn't be here if you didn't think so too. So what do you want from me?"

"He's gotta deliver, Malcolm. 6K by the end of the week for his hash mark."

"They only beat his ass if he's short." Malcolm threw up his hands at her look. "I'm not saying it's cool. I'm just saying he's not in any danger."

"He is short. He's way short, and he ain't got a lotta time left. He was running a ring to make the roll."

"Dogs?"

"Junkies."

Malcolm took a long breath as he wiped a hand across his face.

"Something's got SHOC[3] stirred up. They raided it. They didn't get him, but they cleaned the place out." She shook her head. "He made it out with $500. Malcolm, those beatdowns are sixty seconds for every thousand he's missing." Tasha stabbed a lacquered nail between her breasts. "I'll handle *him*. I want you"—she twisted her hand and jabbed that finger in his chest— "to handle *them*. You talk to your business partners there and buy him out. Pay his due and give them extra to cut him loose."

"Yeah." Malcolm stroked his chin. "They're gonna want a lot for that."

"Motherfucker, he's your son!"

He held up a hand, but his eyes were elsewhere, thinking. "Yeah he is, and I'm gonna help him, but it's like you said, something's got SHOC[3] riled up. They busted three of my incoming shipments, put a real pinch on the cash."

"Then you gotta get him outta town. He ain't gonna make six minutes."

"It's not like I got property and people all over The Hives." He looked at Jon in the other room, then swung his gaze back with slow confidence. "It'll be okay." He cocked his head toward the short staircase. "New customer wants a bunch of high-end stuff. I'll pay Phillip's debt."

She gave him a hard hug that reeked of relief. "I'ma go home and talk to Phillip." Her face got harder. "If they beat him, if they take him in, I'ma come back and whup your ass."

Malcolm threw up his hands and laughed. "It's hard to tell when you're kidding sometimes."

She didn't move. Not a step. Not a centimeter of expression.

"Okay," he said. "Let me get this money, and I'll handle my end." He pulled open the door.

"Good." She pecked his cheek. "Bye."

"I don't have any money. I should have mentioned that earlier, but you were on a roll," Jon said as Malcolm returned to his seat.

Malcolm scowled. "You just come in here and waste my time, company man?"

"On the contrary, it seems I was here at just the right time. I'll take three of those Black Holes with high-end peripherals, and twenty percent of what you make off the sales from your impounded goods." He smiled at Malcolm's expression. "I'm going to liberate your goods. I break into places for a living."

Malcolm stared in silence for a moment. "You're the thing that's got SHOC^3 turning the lower blocks inside out."

Jon gave a grimace and a head bob. "More than likely."

"Shit, you're the one who's got the Snack Time Super-Center checking receipts on the way out the door."

Jon shrugged.

Malcolm swiped the air. "Motherfucker, it takes forever to get outta that place now! Those exit lines are so long."

"They haven't caught the person yet, have they?" Jon gestured to the bin. "Load me up with some of that, then turn me loose on that depot."

"Why shouldn't I turn you in? Seems like the safer way to get my money."

"You can." Jon leaned into Malcolm. "But they won't find me. They only got this far after we crashed a VTOL. We took out an aircraft and a building and they're still floundering in the wrong place and getting trouble they don't want." He shook his head. "You're a smart guy, Malcolm. You make your living slipping them. You've got two options and one of them has much better odds for a payout." He extended a hand. "Partners?"

9

Blood smeared the battered brass knob to the apartment. Jon froze, hand halfway to it.

"Steve, cover me."

"I don't have a gun, man. Neither do you."

He frowned. "I meant the cloak. You can make me invisible, right?"

"That's what I'm here for." Steve tapped the side of his nose and pointed at Jon.

"Alright." Jon puffed out a breath to ready himself. "Do your best. I'm going to dive left into the kitchen and break line of sight with the hallway."

"Kitchen! My man!"

Jon yanked the door back and threw himself diagonally through the opening. He hit the ground in a roll and banged hard against the basin sink.

"Come on out, Jon. You got here just in time. Maybe you should take first crack at this."

Jon emerged into the hallway. Guion stood at the head of the living room, arms over his chest and hands gripped tight. Friedy stood between them in the doorway to the room all smiles and gore. His icy eyes twinkled as he offered what he held in his blood-smeared arms. "Look what I found. More clothes, some hard currency, and I got a MIU. A good one, not those pieces of shit they had in the shops."

"Friedy, what the fuck?" Jon said as he stepped to the man. He ran his hands over Friedy's shoulders and chest, made a quick pass over his neck and down his arms as he spoke. "What happened to you? Are you hurt?"

"Nein. I was assaulted, but I handled it. None of this is my blood." He pointed. "What happened to my hand?"

"Everything's fine. I still got it." Jon held up the synthskin overlay, now an empty flesh glove.

"His hand?"

"Friedy paid to have the synthskin mapped to his palm print."

Guion looked at the two of them. "Creepy, but irrelevant." Hardness returned to his face. "How did you handle the assault?" His tone said there was a right and a wrong answer to his question.

"I assaulted them worse." He held up the bundle in his arms. "And I took from them instead."

"Did you tear them apart like you did the vertibird crew?" Guion asked.

"What difference does it make?"

"If you shot them, then the violence blends in with everything that already happens here."

Guion stepped close to Friedy. "But if you savaged them like an animal, those bodies are going to draw a lot of SHOC[3] attention. They're looking for the people responsible for tearing apart one of their squads just like that. Remember?"

He slapped the bundle out of Friedy's hands. "Then you waltzed right through the door of our safehouse coated in blood like you just walked out of a cheap splatterpunk sim."

"The clothes aren't ruined. I wiped off before gathering them, and I made sure I had a rag underneath them."

"Come on, Friedy. A rag? What if Paul or Paula saw you on your way up here?" Jon said.

"Exactly." Guion nodded.

"Your intel sucked!" Friedy said. "None of those stores had anything useful to us, so I followed up on some other leads. I got into a little trouble, but I came out with a top-line MIU. Not some bullshit neuter model, but a field-agent level model." He thrust it forward in a bloody hand to push his point. "One of the corps is giving them to people so they can biometrically scan potential kidnap victims for human testing."

Guion snatched it and began swiping the screen. "You lifted a corporate MIU and brought it back here?" He spared the gory man a withering glare as he worked the unit. "It didn't occur to you there's a tracker in here, now pinging away in our living room?"

"Pfff . . . of course there's a tracker. I took care of it before I left the scene."

Jon stepped between the two before Guion could answer. "What did you do to it?"

Friedy beamed a bloody smile. "I slanted the settings." He giggled. "It's broadcasting that it's in downtown Paris right now."

Guion stopped, cocked an eyebrow. "Paris? They'll know it's fake."

"Of course they'll know it's fake! Picture it: SHOC[3] standing around a rendering, looking at an icon across the Atlantic, every one of them knowing their intel is useless and not being able to do a thing about it." Friedy laughed. "Come on, Guion. That's got to make even you smile."

"No, Friedrich, it doesn't make me smile." Guion let the MIU fall to his side and focused on Friedy. "It would have been more useful to place it somewhere in one of the Five Hives. That would have been credible enough for them to investigate. Instead, you wasted a prime opportunity to control their attention with a stupid prank they're already ignoring." He sighed and gripped his temples. "This is more of the operational sloppiness you're known for."

The blue in Friedy's eyes turned from ice to fire. He tensed his fingers into claws and leaned in as he spoke. "What does that mean?"

"It means no one wants to work with you. I sure as shit didn't. I begged corporate to give me another cyber-specialist when I got your file."

"Friedy, breathe. Guion just means the first time we worked as a team," Jon said.

"First time, and every single time after," Guion said.

"Enough, Guion." Jon took Friedy's shoulders in the gentle way he'd done since they were teens. "Look, Friedy, I need you to be more careful. You can't up and die and leave me with this asshole." He jerked a thumb over his shoulder and smiled at the little man.

Friedy returned the grin.

"I'm glad you're okay."

"He's not okay. None of us are okay," Guion broke in. "Did that vertibird attack teach you two nothing? We're being hunted and you left a big, messy clue right in their path, Frei-drich. We're all a lot further from okay than we were."

"Steve, you covered Friedy, right?" Jon said.

Somewhere in the discussion the demon made himself comfortable on the couch and started tearing open foil packs of chips. Steve looked up from the bag. He'd peeled open the sides so it was one large sheet of foil he could lick. "Huh? Oh, was I supposed to do that? You gotta tell me this stuff, JonJon. I just cover you unless you tell me otherwise."

Guion stood with his mouth agape shifting from Steve to

Jon and back. It took a few passes before he found his voice. "You didn't contract him to cover us all by default?"

"I needed to get out of there, man. They'd been digitally brain cloning us for three days, security was closing in, and then suddenly there's a guy offering deals for my soul. Pardon me for not considering all the operational details of the arrangement."

Guion let his head fall, gripped his temples with a single hand. "Steve, hide us all."

"You want me to?"

"It's why I asked."

"Yeah, well tough. You and I don't have a deal. Haaaa haaaaa. Hey, pass me those brownie bites."

Guion cast an irritated look at Jon.

"Steve, hide us all." Jon passed the man a clear plastic container of brownies shaped like miniature muffins.

"Sure thing, dude." Steve dropped from the conversation, already focused on the chewy treats in his hand.

"Friedrich, go clean yourself," Guion said. "For the love of God, you look like a zombie with all that blood on your mouth and throat. At least try to pass for a normal human.

"And Jon, clean up after your do-nothing demon at least." He waved a hand over the blanket of trash. "I don't want vermin on top of everything else. You guys exhaust me. I'm getting some air that doesn't stink like an insta-food dumpster. Try to have some order in place by the time I'm back."

"You might want to hold up on that. It looks like someone else followed the blood trail," Jon said as he peeked out the front window to the broad concrete driveway below. Muffled voices oozed through the aged glass.

"SHOC³?" Guion stepped to the other side of the window to have a look for himself.

"Different kind of trouble."

Four boys in loose denim and t-shirts wove their way

through the mess of cars stuffed into the driveway with a swagger that threatened. He picked out the gleam of a pistol in one waistband, with others likely tucked out of sight. What they all wore quite prominently, however, were blue durags. One wore his as a skull cap. Two others tied them to a bicep. The last lashed his around one knee. Jon didn't know much about gangs, but he knew group markings when he saw them.

Jon called over his shoulder without looking away. "Hey, Friedy. Those guys who jumped you, were they gangers?"

"How would I know?" He could hear the shrug in Friedy's voice.

"Where did you run into them?"

"82nd Street, I think."

"Close enough." Jon told Guion about the B7s.

Guion threw a grimace over his shoulder at Friedy before returning his gaze out the window. The boys had wound their way through the car maze and called for someone, anyone, to come out. One banged on the door with the butt of his gun.

"We're hidden, right?" Jon noticed Guion asked him, not Steve. He had to slap Steve on the shoulder to get him to answer.

"Huh? Oh, yeah. No sweat, man. They'll never find you."

"Good." Guion pushed away from the window. "Then we can leave them to whatever they're going to do and get back to salvaging something from Friedrich's latest screw-up."

"Oh shit," Jon said. "P3 went out to talk to them."

"What's that, a SHOC^3 task force?" Guion said.

"Paul, Paula, and Pepe, their dog. Our downstairs neighbors."

"Pepe? I'd have guessed Paulson," Steve said.

Jon held out a fist and Steve pounded his knuckles.

Guion waved it away. "If you're the only one they've met, they can't give up Friedrich, so we're fine."

"Yeah, but they might not be." He pried the window open a hair to hear the conversation below.

"That's not our problem. We're up against enough. We can't get entangled in anything else."

Downstairs, the B7s loomed in front of the couple, but Pepe made sure they didn't get too close. The dog stood ready, leash taut without pulling, hackles raised in an angry line from between his bulging shoulders down to the base of his tail. The gangers posed back, hands on guns, ready to draw.

"They're in trouble because of us," Jon said.

"No. They're in trouble because of Friedrich. We can't clean up every mess he makes."

They wanted Friedy. He could hear that much. They didn't ask for him by name, but the "scrawny boy with crazy hair and fish-belly skin" couldn't be anyone else. The leader showed them an image on his MIU, a spitting image of the one Friedy came home with. He pointed to it and insisted people saw that same guy come down this block.

"Steve, can you disappear the neighbors?" Jon said.

"No can do, good buddy. I keep telling you, I can't make someone vanish."

"No, you said it was too much work, but you never want to do anything. I'm not asking what you want this time. I'm asking what you can do."

Steve held up his hands. "Best I can do is keep you from being seen. They'd have to break line of sight first."

"Bitch, if you don't get this dog outta my face, I'ma shoot it, then I'ma shoot your bitch-ass man, then I'ma shoot you. So get that fuckin animal back and tell me where my bounty is."

"When they scanned Friedrich as a body grab, it must

have cross-referenced the results with a wanted file. If it went out to everyone in their freelance program, SHOC^3's received the message too." Guion glanced at Jon across the window. "That's good. They'll focus their search on where the warning triggered, which lands them in gang territory. That should mire them for a while."

"Okay, great, but what do we do about them?" Jon said.

"I'm serious! I ain't playin!" A warning buzz cut off the lead ganger. "What? Aw, shit. Bounty's canceled. Someone else got the motherfucker." They grumbled and cursed as they drifted away. "Maybe see you 'round, sweetheart." The lead B7 air kissed at Paula as he backed down the driveway.

Guion and Jon looked at each other, then to Steve who worked on a pack of hard caramels with comic seriousness. Their gaze drifted into the apartment, and to Friedy, who stood in the middle of the living room, MIU in hand.

"I got write access to their records and changed the status of the bounty."

"SHOC^3 will eventually realize you're not in detainment and that you edited the record. That confirms you're on the loose and hacked their files." Guion paused, considered. "They already know you're out here, and they already know you can hack their system." He bobbed his head. "Well done, Friedrich. Don't leave the apartment again."

"Are you seriously grounding me like a child?"

"Jon can acquire whatever food we need. You now have the tools to ply your trade with no need to go anywhere else. We've had enough of . . ."—he fluttered his fingers at the window—"*that.*"

"Actually, Guion, I'm gonna need to borrow him to pay for a deal I made, but don't sweat it." Jon flashed Friedy a smile before returning to the team lead. "You can stay in the van."

10

The operation that paid for their MIUs sounded challenging when Malcolm laid it out for Jon. SHOC^3 had impounded several shipments he needed. Once they processed everything, a matter of days, they'd return the material to its owners. Malcolm could get another supplier, but that would take a little time. Phillip didn't have time.

Breaking into a private security contractor's facility was a tall order under normal circumstances. Breaking into a facility operated by the world's leading paramilitary security company shot that tall order into the clouds. Mounted cameras, drone sweeps, patrols, thermal sensors, and a building locked down and compartmentalized like a prison. Jon could beat the locks. Steve said he could beat the rest.

The whole thing went so easily, Jon still had a hard time believing it. Sure, he'd had some false starts with Steve. His baffles failed every time he touched someone, and if someone else saw that person's reaction, Jon popped into their view too. And anyone who saw that person's reaction gained the ability to see him in a never-ending chain of "busted."

That went for picking things up too. As long as no one

saw him manipulating the world, he stayed hidden. He could snag something as soon as someone looked away and it would be gone when they looked back, but he couldn't do it while under observation.

Human observation, anyway. It turned out Steve fooled automated and remote surveillance far more easily. Static in the feed, loss of resolution, a momentary blink in the image, Steve's cloak caused momentary hiccups in the image to cover him. That was a nice surprise, though Jon frowned that he discovered this at the same time Steve did.

With so many unknowns still hovering around his new abilities, Jon took it slow and cautious at first. He scanned each scene to identify surveillance blind spots. He moved from cover to cover. He held his breath as patrols passed by. All the while Steve stood out in the open and berated Jon to hurry up. He was hungry and wanted a couple of pot pies.

Every nerve screamed at him the first time he tested Steve and left his head in view as a camera swept him. He held his breath and waited for the alarm.

It didn't come.

Halfway to the merchandise, Jon relaxed completely into Steve's invisible grip. He strolled down corridors, Friedy in tow, only exercising caution not to brush any SHOC[3] troops they passed. He stopped checking corners before he rounded them. He didn't soften his steps.

No one noticed.

The worst hiccup in the process came when Jon located the boxes Malcolm wanted. They weren't boxes. They were crates and entirely too big to carry out. Friedy saved the day then. He found a collection of aerial drones in lockup. They loaded the drones up with all the electronic accessories that fit, and then Friedy programmed them to fly to the agreed drop point. He even thought to program their travel with a scatter pattern so they all took different routes. From there, they literally walked out the door.

It was the easiest op Jon had ever run. For his assistance, all Steve wanted was five pot pies: one turkey, two chicken, and two beef. Jon considered that a fair deal and stole them for him on the way home.

Malcolm was so happy with how things went, he invited Jon and Friedy to his place for a little celebration the next day. The two left Guion with Steve, who had moved on to rotisserie chickens, and sat perched above the street on Malcolm's porch. It wasn't luxurious, but he did get nice sun exposure.

Malcolm took a long drag from his joint. He was still holding it in when he passed it to Jon.

"Here you go, man. I don't normally party with someone so fast, but you came through in a big way, so I'm okay pretending we're friends."

Jon looked at the tapered wrap of paper and the thread of smoke doing a slow dance from its smoldering tip. It stank, a pungent reek with a hint of sweetness. He'd never smoked anything before. He definitely didn't want to smoke this.

Friedy reached across Jon's chest and snatched the joint. "Come on, Jon. Join the party." The joint glowed and crackled as Friedy took a lungful. He almost fell off his lounger as he coughed and hacked between wheezes.

"Dude, what the hell are you thinking?" Jon took the joint and sat up. "You've got enough trouble breathing as it is."

Friedy hauled in a huge breath and held it. "That was different," he said in a strangled voice.

Malcolm laughed and clapped. "Oh shit, that's right. You guys had the implanted MIUs. You never smoked nothing before, did you? You loaded a weed app or something and let the unit make you feel high."

"They're called buddy apps," Friedy said. "Get it?"

Malcolm grimaced. "That's some corny white boy shit."

Friedy shrugged. "I couldn't use them. I was stuck using these." He waved his MIU. "But I heard about them."

"You got that implant rejection syndrome?" Malcolm said.

"Close enough."

"That must have been rough, not being able to touch the world everyone else lived in."

"Don't feel too bad for him," Jon said. "Friedy's always had his own thing going on, and it works for him fine."

Malcolm and Friedy both looked at Jon with their unvoiced question.

"Oh get off it, Friedy. You might not have a full five implant, but you live in a world way deeper than augmented reality." He cast a sideways look at Malcolm. "He calls it silicon sorcery." Eyes back to Friedy. "Remember what you did to Boulliver?"

Friedy grinned. It was a wicked expression.

"Yeah, I thought so." Jon gave Friedy a playful shove with a laugh.

"Someone wanna clue me in?" Malcolm said. "This sounds like a good joke."

"Oh man." Jon finally took a drag from the joint. "It's the best. When Friedy and I were kids, there was this bully named Anthony Boulliver. Classic jock asshole. Big, strong, tough, athletic, handsome. You know the type."

"The type that liked roughing up a brainiac," Malcolm said. "I'll bet you were the biggest brain in the school."

"I'm a wizard." Friedy's gaze drifted distant, eyes seeing the past. "He was an asshole."

"Yeah, he'd slap Friedy around, get a chorus of kids to make fun of him, standard bully shit. I tried to help, but I wasn't always there. Erica, my younger sister, stepped in once. She is—*was*—a tough bitch." Pain flashed across his features, there and gone. "That just made it worse though."

"She meant well," Friedy said from far away in memory.

"Motherfucker like that would get capped out here."

Jon shook his head. "That would have been letting him off easy. We were in the eighth year of our education track, and Friedy decides he's had enough."

Friedy stared across the street with a distant look in his eyes, the shadow of a smile cast across his face.

"He hacked the security feed in Boulliver's residence and sifted through the recordings until he got what he needed. Damning footage."

"What, was he involved in something illegal?"

"Jerking off."

Jon and Malcolm laughed. Friedy's smile spread wider.

"You posted that publicly, didn't you?"

"I added it to the augment of the classroom's whiteboard. Intermittent loop, so it would pop in and out randomly throughout class."

"He didn't just do that though. This crazy motherfucker edited the video first." Jon held up a pinky.

Malcolm laughed and clapped. "Didn't the instructors shut it down?"

"I only added it to the student's AR, not the instructors. It took them a week to figure out what was going on and how to stop it."

"Wait, they didn't have everyone logged into the same augment? How would you separate the instructors?"

"An augment needs to be processed by a MIU to be experienced," Friedy said.

"You hacked every student's MIU?"

Friedy grinned, full of teeth and malicious pride.

"Boulliver knew who did it, of course, and he took it out of Friedy's hide."

"But his nickname haunted him until the end of general education. He was Tiny Tony for the next five years. I healed from my beatings. He didn't."

"Now that's right." Malcolm reached across Jon and slapped hands with the little man three times. "You are a scary motherfucker, little dude. I definitely want you on my side."

Malcolm's eyes flicked the way they did when people interacted with AR. "Hold up a sec. Got company coming in." He rose as a woman rounded the corner and strutted up the block. She was a study in extremes. Her large chest and wide hips combined with a tiny waist in an exaggerated hourglass shape, while her long, white-painted nails blazed bright against her richly dark skin and tumbles of raven hair.

"You got people here? Can you get rid of them?" She said it low, but Jon still heard.

"I can't right now. These are some new friends, and we're just getting to know each other." He smiled at her. "Don't want to get off on the wrong foot."

She stared at him with smoky eyes. "Please?"

"Now don't be like that, Kat." He pulled a thin roll of cash bound with a rubber band from his pocket and held it in front of her face. "These are new friends. You feel me?"

He'd liquidated everything they stole for him already. Malcolm could move. Jon filed that away. Some of that money was already theirs, and from the looks of things, they could make a lot more working with him.

"I don't want to go home." She wasn't panicked, but fear chilled her language, body and voice.

Malcolm didn't say anything, but he bid her continue with a serious look.

"Some girls turned up dead." Kat shook her head, sending her jet curls tumbling over her shoulders and back again. "I know, bodies turn up all the time, but these was different. People are talking. They say there's a killer out there, one who likes ladies, or really doesn't since they're butchered so bad." She hugged Malcolm like he could keep her from drowning. "I sent Monique to a friend's to get her away from the building. We're talking about trying to buy our own SHOC[3] contract, but that's so expensive."

Malcolm's face soured like food gone bad. "Fuck the company men. You'll pay your life's savings and they'll squirm out on a hidden clause." He pushed her out to look her in the face. "You get yourself a veteran, maybe two. Boosted if you can find them."

"How we supposed to afford that?"

Malcolm held out the roll of bills again.

She looked from it to him and grabbed the cash. Malcolm tipped it back from her grasp.

"Then you put wireless cameras all over your block and sync their feeds to those soldiers. I want to know my babies are safe."

She took the roll in one hand and hugged him again, less desperate this time, more relief. They held each other for a minute but when they separated Kat stood in place. "You'll send the surveillance gear?"

"Got it worked out while hugging you."

She smiled at that, gave him a quick hug, a peck on the cheek, and wiggled her fingers at Jon and Friedy. "Bye, boys."

"Sorry about that. Responsibilities, you know?" Malcolm plucked the blunt from Jon's hand as he straddled the lounger and settled himself with another deep drag. The man seemed happy, relaxed. Jon and Friedy were riding a wave of goodwill with him.

"Our cut wasn't in that roll of money, was it?"

Malcolm froze, gave Jon a serious look. "You know it was. You also heard what she said."

"We did a job, Malcolm."

"And I'll pay you for it. In tech. In cash. I'll make good. I always do."

"Didn't you promise money to Tasha last time I was here?"

"Yeah, so?"

"She out of the picture now?"

"What are you talking about?"

Jon jerked a thumb at the corner and saw Friedy still staring down the block. Jon slapped him back to the conversation.

"What? Katrina?" Malcolm burst out of his confused expression. "Oh! You mean because she was here and . . ." He shook his head. "Nah, man, Tasha's still around. She's always gonna be around. We got a boy together."

"Do all your women look like that?" Friedy craned his neck to watch Kat reach the boulevard and disappear around the corner.

Jon slapped his shoulder again.

"None of my ladies look alike." Malcolm watched Friedy struggle. The little man wanted to clarify his question but was afraid to ask. He grinned and laughed. "I'm screwin' with you. Yeah, all my baby mamas are fine. It's my weakness. Some guys get off into beer. Some love the thrill of dice. Me, I love a soft, sweet-smelling, fine-ass lady." He closed his eyes and swayed his head at the idea before shaking himself back to reality.

"So how many kids do you have?" Jon said.

Malcolm held up a hand with all five fingers stiff and splayed, lips pursed and eyebrows high. "And now you know why that job you did was so important. I got people to take care of."

"Are we on that list?" Jon said.

Malcolm gave him a serious look. "You are. Below them, but I'll do right by you." He took another toke and laid back. "It wasn't supposed to be so hard. I was supposed to be big-time."

"You live in a shit neighborhood, but your place is nice."

Jon slapped Friedy again. He shrugged his hands and mouthed *what?*

"Yeah, I do, but I hustle for every dollar and it ain't always steady. You saw that. Nah, man. I was on track to have it way easier. Towerball." He closed his eyes in memory. "I had scouts about to start a bidding war for my ass."

Towerball grew out of urban decay, a competitive sport played in the guts of an abandoned high-rise. One team took the top floor, the other the ground. They started in the middle and had to run the ball into the opposing team's goal zone with all the parkour and brute force they could muster. It had basketball's pacing with football's full-contact brutality.

Though birthed in urban poverty, corporate entertainment giants seized it as soon as they got wind of it. They formed teams and leagues, acquired towers as permanent courts and wired them with cameras until they bristled. They renovated the courts for stunting and so aerial drones had clear flight paths inside. They even introduced game variants; expanded the courts to multiple buildings, even added the batter as a new armed defensive position. Regulation batons only. The safety of the players remained paramount, of course.

"You shoulda seen me, man. I know every middle-aged loser talks about what a sports god they were in their prime, but you shoulda seen me. When I got the ball, ain't no one could touch me."

"Good at slipping tackles?" Jon said.

"Tackles? A motherfucker would have to get close to me for that." He shook his head. "Nobody could slip the floors like me. They called me Spider-Man."

"So what happened?" Friedy said.

Malcolm swung around and put his feet on the patio. He kept his eyes on them as he jerked one leg of his trunks back to reveal his knee. A puckered crater sat in the middle of a long worm of a scar that ran the length of his knee.

"I was already starting to make noise about SHOC^3 practices in the lower blocks. Call them out on their bullshit. You know, accusing people of stealing what they own, beating 'resistors,' standard shit. One day I made the mistake of going from general to specific. I named names. Those names didn't like that. Didn't like me." He made gun fingers and popped an imaginary shot at his wounded knee.

"You seem to get around okay now," Friedy said.

"Oh, sure. I can walk. I can run. I can even jump." He tucked his lip and shook his head. "But no more towerball. This thing can't take that kind of punishment." He handed Friedy the joint before swinging around and stretching his legs out again. The little man puffed, coughed, and wheezed, though a little bit less this time.

"So you leveraged your community connections into a fencing ring," Jon said.

"Making my living under SHOC^3's nose is nice. It's not exactly taking from them, but it's the best I'm gonna do."

"We'll take it as long as we get paid."

"Naw man, don't get this twisted. You did a solid job, and I'ma see you get your compensation, but I'm not hiring. I don't need help like yours on the regular."

Jon swung around to Malcolm. "If we don't have regular income, we're going to need that payout."

"He could pay us in tech and I'll get us money from SHOC^3," Friedy said.

"No," Jon said.

"No, listen to me." Friedy leaned into both of them. "I've been working on something to get us funds. I just need enough anonymity to get inside their system, and I could put a process in place that would pay out." He looked at Jon. "We could split it if he can get me the software."

"Friedy, we're not running a job on SHOC^3. We've got enough problems already."

"We can't keep stealing everything we eat. It's raising too much attention."

Malcolm's eyes twitched behind his wireframes again. He got still for a minute, the kind that came without calm, then sat up and joined their huddle. "You want a job? I got one for you."

"Does this one pay?"

Malcolm fixed Jon with a hard look. "They all pay. One of my daughters is missing. Gone a day and her mama says she ain't heard from her. With that shit Kat just came over here with, I'm more than a little concerned."

A vision of Gerald, Michael, and Lisa flashed across Jon's memory. They sat around their dour father singing silly songs until a smile showed his teeth through his gray beard. The family called him Grumpy Santa from then on. He remembered he'd never see them again, and the pain stabbed him anew as he looked at Malcolm. "We'll take it."

11

uion didn't feel anything about the teams he led. He made it a point not to feel anything. He took drugs to make sure he didn't. Not too much. He'd read a study on people with traumatic brain injuries who had impaired abilities to process emotion that showed those same people had difficulty prioritizing and making good decisions in high-pressure situations. Making good decisions in high-pressure situations was what earned Guion his pay, so he took just enough to keep his emotions an asset and relied on psychology, philosophy, and willpower to keep them from being more.

Everything about what was happening now assaulted that cultivated detachment. The stress climbed to unprecedented levels; his teammates engaged in increasingly erratic and unprofessional behavior, all while his chemical edge dwindled. He hadn't taken a pill since launching the ill-fated Ibacipla run.

Guion tapped out the container of Evenflo. Three pills. He shook the tiny plastic case to make sure nothing else remained. Three pills. He let them sit in the center of his palm. He didn't take one. He stared. He thought.

"Jack, you said you could enhance my performance. How deep does your awareness go?"

What are you asking for, Guion?

"Can you see the emotion suppressors in my brain chemistry?"

Jack didn't answer right away, but Guion didn't take the silence as being ignored. Jack was investigating. He felt it. There were no phantom fingers dragging across his brain, but all the same he felt Jack's scrutiny, like he was being watched, but deeper, more disquieting.

Why Guion, Jack said at last. *I had no idea you lived such an ascetic life. Not a trace of any narcotics. No evidence of alcohol. No caffeine, not even excessive sugar. I'm impressed.*

This time Guion said nothing.

Which makes finding traces of the one unnatural chemical in your system rather easy. Yes, I see it quite clearly.

"Can you inhibit its metabolization?"

Pause. *To drag out its longevity in your system you mean. Yes, I can do that, but you understand in so doing you're effectively underdosing yourself.*

Guion nodded. "I know, but I need to make this last. I have no idea how long we'll be out in the cold, and I don't trust black market psychopharmacologicals. I'll grit my teeth. Ease back what's in there and release it only when I need it."

There's a delay between administering the compound and its effects.

"I'd be obliged if you could do what you can about that too."

But of course.

Guion closed the bedroom window someone kept leaving open and stared at the Black Hole in his hand. He popped open the radial menu, opened an anonymous and encrypted dialer . . . and sat staring at the blank input. He fidgeted in his chair, took a breath, adjusted himself again and remained uncomfortable.

Guion adjusted his earpiece, pushed the glasses up his nose, nodded to himself, punched the number, sucked in one more deep breath, and sent the call. Voice only.

"Hello?" Her face appeared in his lenses. A face he hadn't seen in two years, not when awake, anyway. Griffin should have been named Dragon. She was a study in reds: feathered hair shone like fire; a soft, natural blush glowed in her cheeks; her crimson gloss lit her lips. Even the sparkle in her amber eyes suggested a blaze behind them. Guion wasn't poetic, but she always proved a powerful muse.

His breath caught. He gritted his teeth and forced the word out.

"Griffin. Hi."

"Guion! . . . You've been burned and you need me to arrange your intake."

He jerked his head back like she'd slapped him. "How did you—" The breath eased out of him as he relaxed and a smile pulled at his lips. She couldn't see it, so he laughed a single chuckle.

"Why else would you call me from an encrypted IP?"

"You're sharp as ever."

"My brain is easily half of my sexiness."

"Yeah it is."

Jack didn't make any thought noise, but he felt the doctor frown with pursed lips and release a little more Evenflo into his system.

Her translucent face dropped the wry grin and got serious. "Do you know what happened?"

"They liquidated my combat assets at the end of a

successful op," he said. "They took the remaining two and me to a brain mapping facility to make data clones of our minds. We escaped and now I need a new home."

"Why did they only take you three?"

"We were the ones in position to encounter whatever information they want locked up," said Guion. "The combat specialists barely interacted with anything in AR outside of target assistance apps. But the others are an infiltrator and a hacker."

"And you're a risk because you patched into everyone."

"I always love talking to you. I don't have to explain everything."

"I can make a recommendation, but you know there's going to be questions that need answers before we'll move on anything. The more you tell me now, the less investigation acquisitions will have to do."

"Our last op was a complete success. No one is looking for us for reprisals."

"Okay, and who's the recruitment request for? Your whole team?"

"Well, obviously me. I'll vouch for the infiltrator too. His style's nothing like mine, but he's effective."

"You said you had a hacker too. What about him?"

Guion frowned. "The hacker is Friedrich. Friedy."

"*The* Friedy?" Griffin sounded starstruck.

"Don't get overly excited," Guion said through his frown. "He's a bigger liability than he is a genius. Still, if his name sweetens the application, throw it on."

"Sweetens it? Are you kidding? Of course I'm adding it." He heard her tap some notes. "Okay, so, now the uncomfortable one. If your op was successful, why'd they liquidate your team? Why would they think you were exposed to dangerous information?"

Guion sat in silence, fighting himself to speak.

"Guion? Are you still there?"
"Yes."
"Do you know why they burned you?"
Pause.
"Yes."

12

"Come on, Jon. I'm talking about sticking a virtual tap in the SHOC^3's money keg. Free funds for as long as we need. How can you not be on board with that?"

Friedy side-shuffled and flopped his arms as he talked, an excited child dancing around a disapproving parent. They walked from the second block of B125th street all the way to the beach block of B147th this way. Friedy begged and pleaded the whole trip.

Jon shook his head the same as he had from the first time Friedy mentioned his plan on Malcolm's porch. "You already know what I'm going to say. You've got a photographic memory and I've said it every time you pushed for it."

Friedy snorted as he skipped in front of Jon and walked backward. "It is not going to attract any attention."

"You always say that."

"I'm always right, too. Name a time someone found me out when I took something I wanted."

Jon stopped so short that Friedy continued a few steps back before he realized the growing gulf between them.

When he jogged back, Jon gripped his shoulders. "You under-stand this is different, don't you? When you screwed around before, you were rich and famous with high-ranking family. Anything you did, you did from a protected position."

"What am I, some child you're lecturing?" Friedy shrugged Jon's hands off. "I know what I'm doing."

"I don't doubt that. Neither does Guion. We're still leaning on you for all things WorldGrid."

Friedy threw his hands up. "So what's the problem?"

"There's nothing different about you or what you can do." Jon spun Friedy around and threw an arm across his shoul-ders as he got them moving again. "The difference is that we're working without a net. The consequences if something goes wrong are a lot higher now."

"Nothing's going to go wrong."

Jon laughed. He gave it no humor. He didn't smile. "We're A.W.E.'s most wanted. Our families are dead." He swept a hand in front of them. "Look at where we are. I'd say a whole hell of a lot's gone wrong already."

"None of that's my fault."

Jon caught Friedy's eye. "Let's keep it that way."

The little man wriggled out from under Jon's arm and mirrored Jon's tour guide arm sweep. "We don't have to live like this. SHOC^3 can pay for everything we want. I just need a couple of tools."

"We don't need more. We're not settling down here."

"Since when do you care about getting into Oceana?"

"I don't. But I can't hurt A.W.E. on my own. Steve's cloak has more limitations than I thought at first. So we might as well help Guion get us back through the glass doors. They've got the resources to make another corporation bleed." He cast a glance around the ancient buildings of brick and timber, all damp and swollen with sea mist and the tang of seaweed. "We don't need to live rich, but we do need to live, and for that, we need money." Jon returned his gaze to Friedy. "And we've got a line on some safe cash."

"Hunting down a missing teenager? We're PIs now?"

"Should be easy money. This is what you do now, right, Mr. Apex Predator?" Jon punched Friedy in the shoulder.

Friedy scowled. "I don't even know why I'm asking your permission. I can just go do this whenever I want."

Jon gave him another head shake. One time, over and back, full of weight and warning. "Come on, we're here."

They climbed the short set of stairs to the covered brick porch. Jon rapped on the door. Waited. Rapped again. He was about to leave when it opened a crack. The chain at eye level snapped taut. A slice of wrinkled and craggy face some good centimeters lower peered out.

"Yes?" A snout loomed in the door crack. Friedy tensed. Jon watched the hair on the skinny man's arms stand up.

The dog growled.

Friedy gritted his teeth. "Nice dog." His voice strained with effort.

"He's a piddle."

Friedy blinked. "That must mean something different from what I know."

"A pit/poodle mix, not a urine puddle."

"Right . . ."

Jon edged over, pushed Friedy more into the background. "Hello, Mrs. Silverberg. My name's Jon. This is Friedrich. We're friends of Malcolm's."

"Malcolm doesn't call me Mrs. Silverberg."

"He called you Nana Robin," Friedy said when Jon tapped his foot. "But he spoke of you in ways that made obvious an affectionate history between you." He motioned in the space between him and Jon. "We don't share that and wouldn't presume the connection."

She looked them up and down. "You new hires of his?"

"New acquaintances," Jon said. "When you told him Rose went missing, he asked us to look in on you."

"And find out what you know," Friedy added.

Another growl. The dog's lip quivered and let a flash of fang peek out. She didn't hear it.

Jon shuffled on the porch and kicked Friedy. The little man flashed him a sharp look before breaking it off with a thick, sick swallow.

"I don't know what else I can tell you that I haven't already told him. Rose wasn't acting strange. She didn't say anything alarming. She just didn't show up yesterday. No word that she wasn't coming, no answer when I called." The blue eye fluttered. "I hope she's alright. You can't assume that in this neighborhood."

"Especially with that killer on the prowl."

Jon abandoned subtlety this time and flashed a warning look over his shoulder. Friedy thrust up his hands in an aggressive shrug.

"I tried talking to SHOC[3] about it." Nana Robin shook her head behind the door. "They said she wasn't gone long enough to make a case out of it and that I should try again later if she didn't turn up." Her eyes drifted, not seeing them anymore. "I told her not to go out into that fog."

"Fog?" Jon said.

"It rolled up from the beach the night she went missing. In all my years here, I've never seen anything like it. So thick I couldn't even see to where you're standing now." She pursed her mouth a moment before continuing. "I didn't like it. I thought there'd be an accident for sure. I told Rose that even if she kept to the sidewalk, someone was likely to hit her." Sad smile now. "She said she'd walk home along the beach to be safe." She puffed a small laugh. "As if anyone could stand it that long."

"What's wrong with the beach?" Friedy said.

"Oh, it sounds nice enough, but if you stay near the water you'll eventually catch a whiff of some spill or another. They've had a few lately. If it only makes you sick to your stomach you're lucky. Killed whatever was left of the low-rent tourism, even if they still run the ads." Nana Robin shook her head. "She knew that. She wouldn't dare."

"Well, ma'am, Malcolm asked us to keep an eye on you while we hunt down any clues about Rose." Jon waved a hand around. "So you might see us around the block."

She dipped her head with a smile. "That's very sweet of him, and I'll let him know I think so." She shook her head. "But I don't need that." When her gaze came up, it was with a serious cast. "Now, if he could find me another Shabbos goy, that I do need."

"Shabbos goy?"

"Jews are forbidden from working Friday to Saturday, sundown to sundown, so some hire non-Jews, called goyim, to do things like turn lights on and off and cook during that time." Friedy blurted the whole thing out like he chastised Jon with the facts. He flashed an AR message to Jon as he spoke. *If only we had the word's knowledge in our pocket . . .*

"Your friend is exactly right." Jon could tell from her tone Friedy had impressed the old woman. Clearly, she didn't understand WorldGrid access. "Most of Malcolm's children have worked for us when they were younger."

"Us? Malcolm gave us the impression you lived alone," Jon said.

"Oh . . . yes. Us is my husband Saul and me. He's gone years, but I still include him when I talk." She smiled and Jon watched Friedy bake in the warmth of it. "It's an old habit I don't care to break."

He flashed an AR message. *This will keep you busy and out of SHOC³'s accounts.* Jon smiled wide as he grabbed Friedy and yanked him in front of the door. "Well, as it turns out, Friedy here is way goy and he's available every weekend."

Friedy stumbled and kicked the door as Jon pulled him into position. If the door allowed it, the dog would have eaten his leg. Instead, he barked and clawed, tore a gash in the little man's denim. White thread filled the wound like guts.

The beast stood. It growled with a feeling instead of a voice that made everyone take half a step back. Jon lifted his hands off Friedy. The little man held the beast in check with effort that made a full-body fist.

"If he says no, so do I. I trust him." She pointed at Friedy from behind the door. "There's something wrong with you." Then to Jon: "The block patrols will be fine. Thank you." The door slammed and several bolts snapped shut.

13

Squatting in the Rockaway Hive kept their profile low, away from people who'd care if they saw a face that screamed red and wanted across the WorldGrid. Of course, it would be even better if they didn't venture out so much. Guion hammered that point like a blacksmith, but they had necessities. Among them, pizza.

And wings.

And Oreos.

And corn nuts. Especially corn nuts. Steve loved corn nuts.

Jon stole a lot of food today.

He stole so much that it formed a tower of steaming cardboard and greasy paper bags that he had to balance and peek around as he stepped blindly up stairs too shallow for his feet.

Under other circumstances, Jon might have resented spending so much of his time on petty theft to meet the gluttonous whims of a couch potato, but for now he welcomed the distraction. Running, literally running, since they had no car, from fast food joints to snack dispensaries to even lifting packages off the backs of e-bikes after distracting the gig delivery people. He used to crack facilities locked up tight behind layers of technological and human security. Now he stole bags of chicken wings.

It was perfect.

The stakes were so low they laid on the floor, and the resistance pitiful. He couldn't fail, especially not with Steve's cloak, but it demanded just enough attention that he could push his successful investigation out of his head, except when it barged into his thoughts like a jump scare from a cheap horror stream.

He'd found Rose, found her on the way home. It was embarrassing how easy it was and a testament to how little effort $SHOC^3$ put into policing the neighborhood. Friedy in tow, he took the beach walk to the lower street numbers and literally stumbled on her body. Despite Nana Robin's insistence, Rose had walked the beach that foggy evening. It was the only part the old woman was wrong about.

Everything else rang true like the words of a prophet. Especially the bit about random chemical slicks washing ashore with waves full of dead fish and a stench so rancid it shook the air. They gagged. They retched. They vomited as they stumbled through the stink, half-blind from the tears that poured out as if their eyes were vomiting along with them.

She blended in with the piles of flotsam on the oily sand. At some other time, gulls would have picked her flesh apart, but the rank swell must have lingered here since then, because nothing living stirred on this stretch of sand. Just as well. Her belly was open and her guts were out. They'd have pecked her down to almost nothing.

Friedy almost threw up on her. Jon had to shove the little man to avoid that, then drag him back to run an ID on her prints. That was a different struggle, since Friedy didn't want to touch her cold hands now gone slimy in the chem-laden sea spray.

But he eventually pushed Friedy hard enough to get it done. It was her. Everything swam after that. Jon had a vague awareness of sending Friedy home while he saw Malcolm. Somewhere in there he got Paula involved. Malcolm wanted the killer, and Jon couldn't hand Rose over to SHOC[3].

He got busy, but not productive. Rose's butchered face and gutted belly haunted him. The memory leapt at him. It blended with imagined images of "the kids," heads blown open with high-caliber rounds. Did they die as ugly as Rose? The thought torrent got in front of whatever else he tried to think about. He drifted, half-aware of what he was doing, so when Steve decided he wanted to go on a food bender, Jon was happy to be his gofer.

The food tower swayed and he struggled to balance the wavering mass in one hand as he pulled open the door and scooted around it, maneuvering like a master waiter. He put both hands underneath the pizza box foundation, lukewarm and simultaneously slick and sticky with partially congealed grease.

The apartment didn't have a lot of space for four men, and the growing mass of wrappers, food-soaked cardboard boxes, and styrofoam containers gummy with different sauces didn't open the space any. The place reeked of old food. It coated every surface with a scummy film that left them rubbing their fingertips together after touching it.

"Oh, dude, you're a lifesaver. Bring that feast over here," Steve said from the couch they'd scrounged from someone's curbside trash. He'd doffed the armor of his uniform, which lay scattered in the sea of food waste on the floor around him, and now sat barefoot with his shirt untucked and pants unbuttoned.

"Not until he cleans this up." Guion leaned against the

doorway between rooms with his arms folded, and the way he didn't take his eyes off Steve as he spoke said they'd been at this standoff ever since Jon left to get more food.

Steve swept a finger across the room. "None of this shit is in my contract. But hey, JonJon, you already know you don't have to feed me if you don't want to. You've got free will."

Jon kicked his way through the mess and dropped the heap onto the couch next to Steve. A few containers bounced, fell, and spilled at his feet.

"Don't worry. I'll get this." Steve grabbed a handful of chicken fingers, dragged them through a smear of barbeque sauce splattered across the wooden floor, and crammed them in his mouth. "There you go. I cleaned up a little. Still not in my contract. I did that special for you. Friends now?" He winked at Guion as he chewed.

Guion moved only his eyes. "Jon, he's yours. Get him in line."

"Yeah man, laziness is my gig, not yours. Get on your shit," said Steve. He bit into a steaming slice of pizza oozing glops of bacon-infused cheese. He half-grunted, half-screamed with a full mouth. "Hot! Oh! Hot! That's burning my mouth." He swallowed with an effort and took another bite. "Hot! It burns!"

"He's harmless," Jon said.

Guion kicked a wad of waxy paper, gummy with semi-dry imitation ketchup. "This isn't harmless. We've got two small rooms for four people. He's already taking up too much space, and all of this is going to start stinking. There'll be rats in no time. I can't spend all my time bagging his trash." He locked eyes with Jon. "Get him in line."

The middle-aged man with stubble and a buzz-cut continued to burn himself slice by slice. Half the first pie was gone already.

"He only looks like corpsec," Jon said. "That's the body he took when he got summoned. He's not exactly disciplined."

"But he's under contract with you."

"Yeah, which is why SHOC^3 isn't busting through that window right now. He's doing what he was contracted to do."

"So you mean he has free reign as long as he performs specified duties?"

"Pretty much, yeah. All he wants to do is eat though. He's not going to cause us trouble."

Guion frowned and held up a crushed Blast Burger box. "He's not just eating. He's disrupting this space and keeping us from getting operational. We've been here four days now and all we've managed to do is scrounge some furniture and get your arm functional again. I'm not convinced he needs this much food to fuel his powers."

Jon shrugged. "I'm not convinced he knows how they work."

"Or I'm too lazy to explain it," Steve said through a mouthful of something.

Guion kicked his way to the middle of the room to close on Steve. "But he'll keep you running around getting him ridiculous amounts of food all day."

"Hey fuck you, man. You don't know how many calories it takes to cloak you."

Guion rounded on him. "And how many calories does it take, Steve?"

"Beats me. I just know I'm hungry." Steve bit into an oversized muffin. Oversized crumbs fell to the floor.

Someone knocked and everyone looked at the door at once, everyone but Steve.

"Yeah, I got that too." He hefted the remains of the muffin. "Don't sweat it."

Another knock. "Jon? Are you home? It's Paula."

Jon stepped toward the door, but Guion grabbed his arm. They shared a look and Jon jerked his arm free, left a lingering finger pointing at the man with a warning look.

Jon pushed the door open. It partially blocked Paula, already turned to go back downstairs. She stopped and faced him.

"Oh, you're home. I thought the place was empty."

Jon looked over his shoulder. Guion glared down the hallway at him when his face squinched tight and he fanned the air in front of his nose.

"Steve!"

"That one's kinda sharp, isn't it?" He took a break from whatever he was chewing to beam.

"Almost empty." Jon returned his attention to Paula. "Had to get decent before answering. Can't have your husband getting the wrong idea and stop coming up here to fix things. This about . . .?"

"Yeah." She nodded, then looked around. "Would you mind if I come in? I'd rather not talk around a door that's got me half-pinned to the wall."

Jon looked over his shoulder again. Guion had cracked a window, but that's all it would move, and it clearly wasn't enough for the man. He took it out on Steve, riding him about his eating, his mess, and his gas. Steve stayed sprawled on the couch, slouched, a lazy smile on his face when he wasn't taking easy bites of whatever he laid hands on.

"How about we go for a walk?" Jon said. "Steve made another mess in here and we haven't cleaned it up yet. I know Paul rigged a solar-powered hot water system for you guys, but it might take a whole summer's worth of hot water to wash it out if that grease slick gets in your hair." He shrugged one shoulder and shot her a cockeyed grin. "Or you could shave it all off."

Paula wrinkled her nose. "I'm past my experimental phase, thanks. A walk sounds fine."

He spread an arm down the staircase and followed behind, shooting Guion a wink as he closed the door. Paula led them out through the garage onto the street. Without conferring, they turned up the block toward the boulevard. The beach loomed like a monster behind them.

Their heads dipped, shoulders slumped, an emotional shadow dimmed their faces. Small talk couldn't put this off anymore, but they rounded the corner before anyone said another word. Only then did she pick up her head and look at him. "Paul says you and Friedy are working security for Nana Robin."

"Paul gets around."

"He's an honest handyman who knows how to work with what's available. He keeps their houses in order, I keep their bodies in order." She bobbed her head. "We're hooked into almost everybody." She looked around. "He's not from here, you know. Not like I am."

"He from some other part of the city?"

She shook her head. "Xiao Ming."

Jon's eyes went wide and he twisted to face her as they walked. "Paul was corporate?"

"Was." She squinted with half her face. "His whole department was cut when they had some disastrous rebrand flop. Paul came to The Hives barely out of his twenties."

"Huh." Jon nodded with a jutting chin. "What's that got to do with Rose?"

"He knows corporate operatives when he sees them."

"We both know I did corporate shit. Let's leave it at that, okay?"

She pinned him with a look. "He said you might be as paramilitary as SHOC[3] troopers."

Jon got very still. He kept pace with her but didn't other-wise move. "He said that?"

She faced him with a desperate hope glaring from her face. "Is it true?"

Jon pursed his lips. "The less I say about that the better for both of us."

"Because if it's true, you're exactly the person I need." Jon wondered if she even heard his answer. A second later she grabbed his hand in both of hers and dragged him to a stop. "I need security, Jon. If it's paramilitary, that's even better."

"Hey, Paula, relax." He put his free hand on her shoulder. "I live just upstairs. If the B7s come by again, we'll take care of it."

She shook her head and pushed his hand off her. "Not at home, dumbass. We're fine there. I'm talking about the clinic."

Jon looked down Rockaway Beach Boulevard as if he could see the veterinary hospital more than forty blocks deeper into the neighborhood. "You said you had it worked out as neutral ground with the B7s."

"It's the killer. I'm almost always leaving there after dark, and even when the streetlights are working it's getting spooky at night. I've got Pepe, but I'd be even better with an escort who's got a gun and experience with 'corporate shit.'" She made air quotes.

"You want me to run security for the clinic?"

"Just at night." She grabbed his hand again. "You can still do everything you're doing now for Nana Robin. She hunkers down before dark and doesn't come out. I'm not asking you to choose."

"Couldn't Paul—"

"I love that man dearly, but this isn't a busted solar collec-tor. Paul's not a killer and he's not a fighter. What he *is* is freaking out over this, and as of this afternoon so am I." She looked past him when she said that.

Jon looked over his shoulder, but all he saw were the houses lining the boulevard, swollen with jury-rigged additions like tumors and reeking of the sweating crowds packed inside. He returned to her with confusion on his face.

"Rose isn't the only one. People found someone else and they brought her to the clinic rather than call SHOC^3."

That rocked him back on his heels, left him blinking without seeing. He ran a slow hand through his hair. "Shit."

Paula pursed her lips and nodded. She locked eyes with him. "This killer hates women."

He paused, hand still on his head. "How bad?"

"They were disemboweled and he took their uteruses."

Jon cringed. "Jesus."

"So, can you start tonight?"

14

Guion didn't struggle the next time he called Griffin, and his annoyance and frustration with that open window soothed when he saw her face manifest in his AR glasses.

"Hi, Guion. I assume you're calling with good news."

"I wish I was." He shook his head, a gesture she couldn't see. "I recovered the file Friedy stole. The little shit isn't as clever as he thinks. He's still using a dump I found and cracked open a month ago. He put it there."

"That sounds like good news. I think that chemical stoicism is making you dour." She smiled at the tease.

"I haven't taken any. I barely have any left and don't know how to get more, so I've been saving the pills for when I need them."

"I thought you needed them all the time. That's what you told me when we lived together."

"No, I can take them as needed."

"You what?" She seemed to grow, to stretch larger as all her features pulled away from the center of her face. "Guion!

Are you kidding me? How many fights did we have about this?"

"I can take them sporadically if I have to. It's just not ideal."

"Not ideal? How would you describe being an emotional glacier with me?"

"It came with a 7 percent boost in performance."

"That mattered to you more than our relationship?"

"It was a long-term investment. That performance increase made it more likely that I'd receive a promotion sooner." He shrugged at her with a deliberate pause. "A little more time off. A little more money."

"Did you get the promotion early?"

"I didn't get it at all. Your extraction went into my record."

Her face fell. Her voice softened. "Guion, I'm sorry. I didn't want anything to happen to you. I asked you to come with me."

He nodded. She couldn't see him, but he knew she felt it.

She can feel your gesture? Really, Guion? I do believe you're becoming overly sentimental, old chap.

Griffin sniffed. A tear ran down the track between her nose and cheek. "You know, I sometimes think if it weren't for those pills, you'd be here in Oceana with me now."

"You could be right. I've been off for a couple of weeks and here I am calling you without much of an update."

"So, what, you're saying you miss me?" She wiped away her tear and laughed.

"More every day." He was soft, serious.

"Guion, I'm not used to hearing you talk like this." That fire in her eyes sparkled across more unshed tears. Her smile was delicate and vulnerable. "I could get used to it though."

"I never processed losing you," he said. "It was hard and I didn't want to go through that. Then when they took my family, put me under observation . . ." he shook his head. "I didn't have the luxury of mourning. I upped my dose and I stayed on it."

"Oh, Guion." She stroked her screen. He imagined her fingertips trailing along his face.

Oh, blech, Guion. Really.

He felt Jack begin to unbind some of the Evenflo he'd held back. Metaphorically, Guion grabbed the demon's hands and resisted. He didn't fully understand their struggle and resolved to research it later. For now, he felt that pushback and knew he could do it.

"I'm feeling it now. The acute loss of losing you and the years of missing you, it's fading in together and it's a weird feeling." He huffed a laugh. "I don't like it."

She laughed.

"I didn't go with you before and there's no taking that back," he said. "But maybe we can do it right this time. Maybe I can get into Oceana and be with you despite my mistake."

Jack broke free from Guion's grip and shoved a dose of Evenflo into his neural pathways.

"Yeah." She nodded. "We're going to do that."

"To that end, this progress report." His voice went stern. He knew how he sounded. Some part of him still wanted to reach out to her, to be soft with her, but he suddenly couldn't figure out how.

She blinked and recoiled in shock, but only for a second.

"I've recovered the file, but it's locked. I haven't been able to crack it."

She knew this Guion better than the one who started the call. She flowed right into business with him. "I'm sorry, Guion, but without knowing what's in it, I don't think I can negotiate your recruitment. Can't you get Friedy to hack it?"

"He doesn't know I have it. Telling him I do risks destabilizing him even more. I'd like to avoid that complication if possible."

Griffin pursed her gleaming lips. "Your skills are impressive, and Friedy's a legend, but it's not enough. A.W.E. has gone to extraordinary lengths to recover that data and find out what you know. That makes your mystery file the key to this arrangement."

"Extractions and recruitment don't normally come with those kinds of stipulations."

"No, they don't. But they don't come with the increased danger you bring either."

"What danger? No corp willingly lets their assets go."

"The manhunt for you went public." Griffin brought up a small window in the corner of her display. "You know the stream SHOC^3: Troopers?"

"You know I don't watch streams."

"Reality entertainment cut together from bodycam and drone footage of SHOC^3 performing domestic security duties. It's the home version of SHOC^3: Real War Stories."

"I don't know that one either."

"It doesn't matter. The important thing is that they started a new line in the series a few days ago. Some new security specialist took over running the basecamp on 116th Street in Rockaway in the Queens Hive. Right now they're tussling with the local gang a lot, but it's all in service of hunting a band of terrorists that already downed a vertibird in Manhattan."

Silence.

"The new commander knows what he's doing, at least in the edited footage that's broadcast. He also seems to be taking this personally. Does the name Boulliver mean anything to you?"

15

Guion assembled the team, crowded them on the couch with Steve, and stood before them, a commander, maybe a lecturer. Jon listened to his measured words, but the man's body language screamed at him. His stillness. His flat affect. All emoting locked in a box somewhere in Guion's mind but maybe stuffed a little too tightly. He forced that emotionless face, like clenching a fist to keep the hand from shaking. Guion had taken Evenflo, but not enough. Still, something rattled him to take some, or he anticipated something in this conversation would.

"SHOC^3 is stepping up their activity. Thanks to Steve, that doesn't matter to us directly, but what about Malcolm's supply line? He's our source of tech and money right now."

Jon screwed up his face. "Malcolm's struggling, but it's not SHOC^3."

"You're saying SHOC^3's crackdowns aren't pinching his supply lines?"

"I'm saying he'd barely notice if they did. You murdered his daughter. Kinda throws off his concentration."

Guion's eyes flared; his fists clenched, a flash of anger

bright and hot and gone as soon as it appeared. "Jack didn't do it."

"Really? He's an old-timey British doctor named Jack."

"And a demon."

Jon jerked a thumb at Friedy to agree but didn't take his eyes from Guion. "Those killings started right after we got here."

"Both victims were women. It all seems a little . . ." Friedy laid a finger on the bridge of his nose.

"This is your evidence? He has an accent and a generic name?"

"Friedy did a WorldGrid search. Those girls were killed exactly how Jack the Ripper's victims were. In case you didn't know, Jack the Ripper was British. So's Jack."

"And he's a demon," Friedy said.

Jon repeated the thumb jerk.

"Oooh, busted," Steve said.

"Shut up, Steve," Guion said through clenched teeth. He worked his jaw without opening his mouth as he looked at them, searching for words and not finding them.

"Blabber's already lit up about it. Hashtag Jackisback," Friedy said.

"Oh, well, we can't argue with the collective genius of social media, can we?" Guion rolled his eyes and began to pace in terse, tight steps. "Can we please try to live in the real world and stop talking like morons?" Jon watched the anger char Guion's thoughts and burn through whatever Evenflo he had left in his system. Somewhere along the way, he'd balled his fists again, and Jon doubted the man even knew it. "Whatever Friedrich did, he didn't summon demons from Hell with a computer program."

"Not a program. I coded an incantation," Friedy said.

Guion rounded on the little man. "Stop with the larping, Friedrich. Enough."

Friedy shrugged. "Certain items have power. So do places, times of year, words." He fixed Guion with a knowing look. "Numbers too. Ancient sorcerers combined these things in precise ways to produce effects."

"So you punched a bunch of numbers into a pilfered MIU and summoned damned souls from a biblical afterlife? Do you hear yourself?" Guion's voice hit a pitch Jon never heard before.

"Now who's talking stupid?" Friedy said with a dismissive chuckle. "That's ridiculous." Everyone hung on the pause. "I coded a sequence that the MIU executed. Call it a digital ritual."

Jon stood and spread his hands wide. "Look man, he's not going to give on this and you know it. Let's get back to this killer."

Guion stared at him for a long moment and Jon watched him wind his anger back inside the shed of reason. "We have other concerns," he said as he turned away.

"Actually, no, we don't. We just brought a murderer into this neighborhood. People are dead because of us."

Guion scoffed. "One of us is a proven murderer, but it's not me." He pointed a slow finger at Friedy.

"That was self-defense," Jon said.

"Oh, he only kills bad people so it's okay. That's some fine action-sim logic there, Jon. Grow up."

"Fine. Let's talk about it logistically then. You asked about increased SHOC^3 activity, and it's here because they're looking for that killer. You asked about the stability of Malcolm's business, and he's half nuts because his baby girl is dead." Jon grabbed Guion's shoulders and bored into him with his stare. "We need to rein this killer in."

Guion met his gaze, held it a moment before a scowl twisted his features and he jerked out of Jon's grasp. "I didn't pact with a serial killer. You think I'd be that stupid? If this killer is disrupting things so much, find him."

"Come on, Guion," Friedy said. "It's plain as day."

"It's not. He has an iron-clad alibi. While you've been out raising the local gang's ire and scaring old women, I've been working our situation from the corporate side." His eyes slid to Jon. "In here. The whole time. Jack can't leave without me, and I haven't gone anywhere. Explain your way around that." He let that hang in silence, waited for a challenge. When none came, he continued.

"We're dead to A.W.E. There's no going home, but I know how we can get a new home in one of the corp complexes."

"I know you've been working the Oceana angle, but how do you know they'll take us?" Jon said. "We don't even know why A.W.E. wants us dead."

"Yes, we do." Guion looked right at Friedy. "Friedrich stole a copy of a file under tight security shortly before our last op."

Jon glanced at Friedy in shock; the little man returned a guilty look.

Guion continued with a matter-of-fact nod. "Someone found out, and it made them unhappy enough to override whatever political protections he had left and order our execution."

"How do you know all this?" Friedy said.

"Focus." Guion held up a hand. Now that he was on the offensive, his control returned. His voice and body betrayed no emotion beyond a slight irritation at the distraction. "They want us all now because they want to know who else saw that file and who we might have given it to. The company burned an entire veteran team of operatives on the chance we read whatever was in that compressed data packet. They put us through brain cloning so they could sift through everything we know with algorithms and data analysis tools."

Jon shook his head. "Why are you saying this like it's good news?"

"Because while it means we can't ever go home again, it also tells us that whatever's on that file is insanely valuable to A.W.E., and if it's valuable to them, it'll be valuable to their competitors too. We can use it to buy ourselves a position in Oceana Combine. We'll have to start over there, but at least we'll be inside the glass doors again."

"You still didn't answer my question." Friedy stood.

"I need you to start acting your age, Friedrich. Focus on what's important. You're not dead, and if you want to stay that way, we need to know what's in the file."

Friedy threw a wordless request for help to Jon, but he only grimaced and shrugged. "I hate to say it, Friedy, but he's right. We're all up the river right now, and he's the one with the plan to get us out of this."

"I don't know what's on the file. I unzipped it to have a look and it's like a box full of Russian nesting dolls. Every single one of them is protected." Friedy threw the obstacle at Guion like it was defiance.

"Then you'd better get to work," Guion said. "That file buys us our new lives."

Friedy glared at the man. "You're not answering because you put the Trojan horse in my data bomb."

"I did not. When I received the mission briefing, it said you wouldn't be coming back, and that I shouldn't plan to utilize you in anything past dropping the bomb."

There was a beat of silence. "That's why you kept asking me to check his vitals," Jon said.

Friedy opened his mouth to respond, but Guion steamrolled his response before it came. "Let's be honest about what's going on here, Freidrich. You're a liability. You've been a liability for as long as I've worked with you. You're brilliant in ways no one can understand. I don't have any problems acknowledging that. But you're a spoiled little rich kid who's lived a life of temper tantrums from a position of privilege and safety because you couldn't get over that some of the board members were mean to you as a child." He slapped a hand to his chest as he got faster and louder. "I've had to be damn close to perfect to claw myself out of The Hives. Shit, I even renamed myself so the stink of my background wouldn't taint my record."

"Being black doesn't matter." Friedy snorted. "That's old thinking. Anyone can have any skin color they want with some simple mods."

"I was talking about being poor, but if you think changing my pigmentation removes the problem, counting all those zeroes in your bank account has damaged your sight." He crowded Friedy, but Jon noticed he didn't touch the small man. "You think I could have gotten away with a fraction of the crap you pull regularly?" He gave his head a slow, grave shake. "I've had to be flawless. Flawless! That's impossible, but you know what?" He turned away and threw up his hands as he looked at the ceiling. "I did it. Or got close enough to climb." He turned and pointed. "Then you happened."

Friedy lifted his chin a few degrees too high with his reply. "I always completed my objectives."

"But that's not all you did, is it?" Guion closed again. "You're not half as clever as you think. You got caught, Friedrich, more than once. Skimming accounts, copying paydata, they knew. Oh, I'm sure you walked away clean more often than not, but you got caught more than you know." He leaned in, eyes fiery. "Guess who got the operational demerits?"

"I never saw any."

Guion snorted and whipped away, resumed pacing. "No, you didn't. I negotiated an agreement when you landed on my team that bought you latitude. I wasn't just responsible for putting together our operational plans but turning you around. Your failings didn't just go to you."

"They held you responsible."

Guion cocked a finger at Jon.

"You know, you could have talked to him, or me."

Guion bored into him with a glare of solid derision. "You don't have the slightest idea what I did. Didn't you think it was odd the company assigned three combat heavies to a simple in and out?" He jabbed himself with a thumb. "I picked them when I saw Friedrich wasn't slotted to make it back and I massaged the site intelligence to create a need for them."

Jon shook his head. "Why?"

"Internal reviews flagged Stone as a possible security risk for suspected ties with a smuggler. Psychological profiles of all three suggested they'd be the sort who'd balk if confronted with frag orders."

"You ordered Stone to execute Friedy."

"I figured a 4 percent chance he'd do it, tops. Just like I figured there was an 87 percent chance Friedrich wouldn't deploy the data bomb as ordered, but instead tear into the program, find the kill codes buried inside, and disable them."

"So you counted on Friedy saving himself, and then gave Stone a nudge to decide to go AWOL and take us with him."

Guion gave Jon one deep nod. "I'd go home without you, take my last demerit, and you'd all be elsewhere, off A.W.E.'s kill list."

"You gambled with my life," Friedy said.

"Hardly. The odds heavily tilted in your favor. The only part that didn't go as I calculated was the bomb in the van. Your theft scared the board more than I realized. Or pissed them off. Whichever, it screwed us all."

"You could have warned me."

Guion rounded on Friedy. "If I had, would you have responded with discretion and reason?" He wagged his head. "We both know the answer to that. You want the truth? I don't like you, Friedrich, and I sure as hell don't trust you to act responsibly, not even to save your own life. But I'm not a monster, so I did what I could to save you. Now our best-case scenario is starting all over from scratch somewhere else. You damn well better crack that file, because you owe me big time. Do something right just once in your spoiled, entitled life."

Friedy stood motionless a long moment, smacked to stunned, silent, just a blink here and there. Then anger bloomed on his face. "Jon, you know lots of people in other companies. How about I hack this file and you peddle it to someone, leave this asshole here?" He bored into Guion with his stare as he spoke.

"I'm sure you have a wealth of contacts, Jon. How many know you as Jonathan Rostram, and how many know you by an alias you've used to manipulate them? It'll come out during recruitment." Guion stared right back the whole time. The look between them held all the punch of an iron bar.

"Yeah, and who do you have, Mr. Stay in the Van?" Friedy said.

"Griffin, who loves me, who's never been lied to by me."

"Friedy, dude, listen." Jon gripped the man's shoulders. "Do this for us. You figure out what's on that file you nicked and we've got a bargaining piece. We can use it to get some-where good, and then you never have to see him again."

Friedy's face fell slack with shock again. "You want to work with him?"

"He's got the connection."

"He gambled with our lives."

"He mapped out the probabilities—"

"And he did it all wrong!" Friedy threw an arm toward

Guion. "His baseline threat assessment was completely off. He said so himself. If this was you, you'd have charged in and rescued me. Mastermind over there concocted a Rube Goldberg scheme with bad calculations." He spat in Guion's direction. "Just because he likes to talk in percentages doesn't mean they're real. They're just his numbers and they were wrong." Friedy's intensity melted, replaced with a quiet, desperate earnestness. "Jon, he just said he was willing to let me die."

"He said a lot, and not all of it was wrong. You know that. Let's focus on getting out of here."

Friedy slapped Jon's hands away. "You're taking his side?"

"It's like you said when we first got here: there are no sides here, just facts. You like to play games and I run cover for you." He shook his head as he put a hand on Friedy again. "We fucked Guion doing that, and we brought this on ourselves. We have to make this right."

"Get off me!" The little man hurled Jon aside. He spilled into the collection of trash bags stacked in the kitchen as Friedy stomped down the stairs, Jon's voice trailing after him.

16

Friedy was up the steps and banging on the door before he had a chance to think. Somewhere between the apartment and the brick porch meters from the seawall he started to cry without realizing it. His vision swam through tears. He sniffed and wiped his nose over and again.

The door opened as much as the chain allowed. Nana Robin's slice of face peered out. The thin white muzzle poked through at his thigh.

A beat passed. "Yes?"

"I'm sorry, ma'am. I didn't know where else to go."

"That does sound pretty sorry."

"It's pathetic." Friedy broke and sobbed before smearing his dripping nose across his sleeve and catching control of himself with a deep breath.

"Friedy, you're supposed to be providing security for the property. Why do I get the feeling you're here looking for protection yourself?"

"I didn't know what else to do. I don't know many people." His gaze fuzzed out as he thought. "Just you and

Malcolm, and he's a nice guy, but with his daughter turning up the way she did, he doesn't need my problems."

Nana Robin's face darkened when Friedy mentioned Rose. "That poor dear. I don't watch executions, but I'll tune into that one live."

"Yah, I saw the images SHOC[3] published. Whoever did it is a real sicko."

"Young man, why did you come here? Not to talk about the grisly details of Rose's death, I hope."

He shook his head. Fresh tears streamed down his face. He didn't bother to wipe them away. "I don't have anything."

"What are you talking about? I know Malcolm pays you. I'm sure it's enough to get by."

"I just found out one of the people I'm crashing with was involved in a plot to kill me, and Jon, my best friend, my brother, he thinks there are more important things to worry about."

"Are there?"

"Than my life?" Desperation and shock slapped his expression.

"I hope you don't expect me to give him a talking to."

Friedy looked at the ground. "I didn't think about it before I came here. I've spent my whole life being taken care of by others." He raised his eyes, not his head. "Family money. Protective friend. All I did was poke at people who didn't like me from the safety they provided."

"Why does that bring you to my door?" She asked with a softer tone, like she knew the answer and was inviting him to give it.

"I don't have any of that anymore. Money's gone, friend isn't protecting me. If I'm really on my own, I'd like to do something better with myself. Give a bit instead of take." He wrung his hands and looked at his feet. "I don't have much to give anymore, but maybe I could work some light switches on weekends? I'd really like to be somewhere else for a while."

The door shut and the chain jangled. It opened again, all the way this time.

"I'm sure a tech genius like you can work the lights, but can you bake a good challah?" She gave him a soft smile.

"Braided or round?" Friedy smiled gratitude.

"You looked that up just now, didn't you? Guess that makes you a quick study. Come in. Come in." She waved.

Friedy stepped inside and saw something more than a slice of her face for the first time. The stooped woman made Friedy look tall, but something about her scarf-wrapped head, with its hawk nose, eyes magnified by glasses, and that wicked smile, exuded a shrewd authority.

"Don't mind Pal. He'll behave as long as you do." She scratched the poodle-pit mix on the head. His eyes remained locked on Friedy. "I'm the one you really need to worry about anyway." She closed the door behind him.

"You know, I'm stronger than I look."

The woman cocked an eyebrow. "What a coincidence. So am I." She looked him up and down. "Is Friedy your real name?"

"Friedrich Hasenclever."

"That's a mouthful."

"Most people call me Poor Friedy, though I'd prefer if you didn't."

"That sounds like a story. I love stories. I have a whole library of them locked away up here." She tapped her temple with a knotty finger. "But we'll get to that after I show you what you'll be doing." She walked past him, beckoning for him to follow over her shoulder.

Friedy followed. Pal stalked after him at a distance.

17

Friedy didn't come back, though Jon eventually tracked him down. He didn't visit. Not yet. He knew Friedy well enough to know when to push and when to let him breathe. As long as Nana Robin kept him busy around the house he wasn't going to cause any trouble. Best to leave that alone for now.

Guion shut himself in the bedroom for hours on end, doing his damndest to crack open that file. At least that's what he said he was doing. Guion kept everything local to his MIU, so it only appeared in his AR lenses.

"More secrets?" Jon asked.

"Is there some reason I should make this public? You have some hacking insight to share with me?" He kept working as he talked, on the floor tucked into a bedroom corner, knees close to his chest.

"Just seems like you're someone who keeps the wrong kind of secrets."

That got Guion's attention. "I keep secrets?" He blinked as he closed the file and stood. "Look me in the eye and tell me you didn't know when he was going to play merry hell with mission parameters." He crowded Jon. "You never knew. Not once." He leaned in so that Jon could feel the man's body heat. "Say it."

"Man, get out of my face." Jon turned and put space between them.

"You knew he was up to something and you didn't tell me, knowing damn well it was going to come down on my head too. That sounds like the wrong kind of secret to keep, doesn't it?"

Jon made for the door as Guion shouted at his back.

"Who are you really angry with, Jon? Is it me for letting things go the way you know they always would, or is it you, because you know your life would be easier without him?"

Jon said nothing, didn't even look at Guion, but he waved a middle finger at the man as he walked out.

When he left, he wanted to stay gone, but it's not like there was a lot for him to do. That left him tracking the killer.

Track the killer, right. The killer was sitting in their above-garage apartment, obviously. Except Guion was right: he never left. Old habits from being in an over-policed neighborhood, he said. As far as Jon knew, Jack had no body of his own. For him to get out, Guion had to get out, and every time Jon was home, so was their former team lead.

Still, it ate at him. If Jack was the killer, and that just felt right, then it meant that all the terror and the gruesome murders were their fault. It meant his team brought a killer into this neighborhood. Now other people were experiencing the same pain he felt by losing family, except it wasn't from the directive of an evil corporation, but from the hand of a monstrous man.

If Jack was the killer, then it was Jon's fault too. He was the one who suggested they hole up here. He owed it to the people here to at least figure out if it was Jack, even if all his alibis seemed airtight.

Without Guion, he didn't have much to go on. The killings started right after they arrived, both women assaulted outside after dark, both with throats cut to the bone. That's where it stopped for the woman found outside Katrina's building. Rose was . . . more.

He struggled with the search in more ways than one. Though it was a fifteen minute walk from beach to bay, Rockaway stretched long. It might be a small strip of the Queens Hive, but it was big. Huge even. Way too large for a single man to patrol. How was he supposed to find a shadowy killer in all this sprawl?

And if he was honest with himself, which he allowed only briefly while out on his own, he had to ask: did he want to find the killer? Jon could fight, but he didn't relish taking on a crazy man with a knife, not even with a gun, assuming a gun could hurt the thing.

Shit, more honesty said he didn't want to find another victim either. That scared him more. Seeing what the butcher did in digital images was bad enough. To see it in person, to come face-to-face with the kind of death Rose suffered, to smell it . . . he'd seen plenty of people shot, some strangled, even a couple dropped from great heights. Jon never saw anything like the butchery worked on that poor girl.

He half-assed the investigation, hated himself for it and tried to atone by sitting unseen in the corner of Paula's clinic at night working security she didn't need. At least that's how he felt after the first few days, but he wasn't there a week when a group of B7s kicked in the doors, dragging a blood-covered man behind them with a shrieking woman in tow, all of them guns out and shouting.

"We need some help over here!" one of the B7s said.

Jon made quick assessments of the room.

The talker carried himself like the leader. Head wrapped in a blue durag, young, skinny, with a rough swagger that didn't hide his panic and a way with his gun that said he was comfortable using it. Not well. Too undisciplined for that. But very willing to pull the trigger, especially now that he was spooked. He gestured at Paula with his gun. "Come on. Come on!"

The others looked like pale shades of Swagger, followers without much to set them apart and little that suggested they'd act without being told what to do. Except for the guy attached to the hyperventilating woman. That fat ox of a man with three chins and no neck commanded more mass than any two other people in the room put together. Jon figured fear wasn't why he panted and sweat. Not much. Still, he clutched his woman's arm in a grip that bruised her pale skin, and he hung on without knowing it. A subconscious grab for a security blanket.

The woman cradled her other arm against her body, wounded and bleeding. Rangy with too much cheap makeup, now ruined with tears, and a tight outfit of revealing clothing, she might have been pretty except for the worn-down and well-used look about her.

The man on the ground clutched his throat and gagged. Blood poured out from between his fingers. Throat slice. A trauma unit could take care of the bleeding with a synthderm patch and a surgical nanite injection. He'd be fine in minutes. This wasn't a trauma unit though. It was a veterinary clinic and a low-rent one at that. The man was a goner.

When that happened, the rest of the group would get a whole lot more upset, and they were already waving guns around and hollering. In their collective panic, they pointed their guns at Paula and staff even as they beckoned them to come and help.

Jon stepped forward. "You need to put those down and get out of here."

"Man, fuck you! Sit your ass down before I drill you!" Swagger said.

"You're making them nervous. They're not going to come near you while you're waving your pieces around and screaming."

"We got jumped real bad. You hear me? We gotta be ready to blast, and you'll fuckin' thank us for it when it comes."

"No," Paula said. "That was part of the deal. You keep any internal fighting out of here."

"It's not internal!" The woman more screamed in terror with words than spoke. "It was a monster! A fucking monster killed Gloria!"

Jon laid a hand, soft and firm, on Swagger's arm and guided him to a sidebar.

"Your friend's already dead. There's nothing anyone here can do for him."

Swagger got right in Jon's face. He could feel the ganger's breath on his skin. "They better hope not. He dies, they die."

Jon didn't twitch, didn't raise his voice. "Yeah? And what happens the next time you need a bullet dug out?" Jon pointed with his eyes. "Your friend's gone. You shoot this place up, no one's going to be around the next time this happens."

The ganger looked at the man on the floor. He still twitched and gagged, but his motions shrank, his noise dimmed. Swagger hung his head. "Damn."

"What's she talking about?"

Swagger shook his head. "I don't know, man. I wasn't there. I only heard about it after."

"After what?"

The ganger pointed at Three Chins. "Rodney there was running his ladies when fog rolled in off the ocean." He shrugged. "Happens sometimes, right? But, hold up." He looked over his shoulder and gestured. "Yo, Rodney, tell 'em what happened after the fog."

Three Chins shook his head. "I couldn't even see my girls. Everything was just shapes in the dark, but I can count. There was one extra."

"He fucking killed her!" the woman said. Another cry with words.

"He?" Jon said.

"Wasn't no trooper," Rodney said. "He cut us. Never made for a gun once."

"Who was he?"

Rodney shrugged. "Just a shape, man. But he moved, right?"

"Moved?"

"*Moved,* man. Like he had boosts. How else you think a dude with a knife could take out a bunch of us with guns?"

"How many?"

"Me." He pointed to the now still man on the floor. "Eddie. Two others. Their guts are all over the corner, mixed together."

"And no one saw anything else? That's all you got on this guy?"

The woman's breath hitched several times before she found her voice. "He said something to me and Gloria before he cut us. He called us 'disease-ridden whores.'"

Jon pinched the bridge of his nose and cursed under his breath. "Paula, you can stitch up that slice in her arm at least, right?" he said without looking up.

She did, and as a gesture to keep good relations between the B7s and the clinic, Jon volunteered to help find Gloria.

It took him two days. He didn't find all of her.

18

Nana Robin slapped Friedy away from the stove and pointed to the breakfast nook with its perfectly round mosaic-top table.

"There's a seat over there," she said. "Take it."

They fought this fight so often it had grown into a habit in the two weeks since Friedy arrived. He came desperate and despondent with only enough rational thought left to know that he needed out and away from Guion and Jon. He didn't need fancy and didn't need much space. He was a small man, after all. Cheap, however, would be a plus.

As it turned out, Nana Robin knew of a place that hit all those markers. It wasn't fancy. It wasn't large. But it was cheap. He could rent one of the bedrooms on the second floor.

Her room was on the ground floor these days. Climbing the stairs was too much effort and now that she lived here alone, none of the rooms upstairs saw any use. He'd effectively have his own apartment up there, with a bedroom and bathroom. Of course, he'd have to take care of the second floor if he was using it, but they'd count that towards rent.

"Believe me," she said with a hand on his arm, "I'm the

one getting the deal here. I don't know the last time I made that climb. I'm sure it could use a cleaning." When he went up alone, he found Nana Robin was a liar of the best kind. Everything was spotless. Maybe she didn't use the upstairs much, but she wasn't the sort of woman to let part of her house fall away.

They sat at the mosaic-top table in the kitchen nook that night and shared ice cream. Serving it was his first duty.

"It's not Friday," Friedy said.

"Oh, well if you're not interested in extra pay, I'm happy to get it myself. That'll be $16.50."

"For one scoop?"

"One scoop and service."

Friedy snorted. "That sounds like price gouging."

"Careful. Pal still doesn't like you."

He didn't, but they didn't snarl at one another anymore. Friedy took him to the beach every day for Nana Robin to get him more exercise, and after a tense couple of standoffs and one physical fight, they were starting to respect each other. Starting to.

Friedy blocked her from opening the refrigerator. "I changed my mind. I'd be delighted to pick up some extra work. How about I get this and your seat."

"Don't bother." She slapped his arm and smiled. "I don't tip."

Friedy dropped a scoop of fudge track into a pair of blue bowls, blue for dairy, red for meat he learned early in his time here, and joined her at the table. Pal lay curled underneath. He didn't growl when Friedy pulled out a chair, but he wanted to. Friedy felt it, or rather the beast felt it and Friedy felt it stir in kind. She thanked him and they ate in silence.

The next words caught in his throat. They required extra effort. "Why—" He swallowed and blurted it out all at once. "Why are you being so nice to me?"

The wry grin evaporated from Nana Robin's face, but a softer smile stayed in her eyes as she sat back and folded her hands on the table. "Because when you came back I had a chance to have a real look at you."

She took a breath and scratched Pal behind his ear. "Pal's kept me safe for a good while, and I've come to trust him about people. This neighborhood isn't what it was when Saul and I bought this place. There's a lot of bad people out there, Friedy, and Pal, he has a nose for them. He can sniff out trouble like he was trained for it. He's done it for so long that it didn't even occur to me to question his judgment."

She returned her hands to the table. "He didn't like you at all when you arrived full of pithy banter and swagger." She smiled at him. "Jon's a smooth one, but you obviously rehearsed your lines." The smile vanished. "You thought you were too good to help me. He knew it. I knew it." She pursed her lips, shook her head. "We didn't need you."

"Then I was humbled." Friedy mumbled the words.

She gave him a slow nod. "When you came back you were a different person. I could see that right away. You haven't known much kindness in your life, have you Friedy?"

He looked at his lap as he shook his head.

"That's why." The sharp grin returned. "I like being different."

They slipped into an easy routine after that. Friedy did far more than flip light switches on Friday nights, and he did do most of the cleaning on the second floor, but Nana Robin clung to her independence even if she had a live-in assistant now, and there were certain things she refused to relinquish. Cooking was one of them. So every day she'd stand at the stove. Every day Friedy tried to help. Every day she slapped his hand and pointed to the table. Every day he lost that fight and sat down for a meal.

It was wonderful until Friedy and Pal found the gutted woman on the beach.

Friedy thought about it for less than a day before coming to Nana Robin. She had to go. First the gangs, now a killer, one who preferred women it seemed; this was not a neighborhood for her anymore.

He followed her through the house as she scrubbed floors, dusted furniture, and vacuumed the carpet. She had answers for everything. She couldn't leave Pal. Where else would she go? That killer? He might have an eye for women, but how many of them were her age? He was a monster, that murderer, but he had a type and she wasn't it.

"Crabs were eating her face," Friedy said. "What he left wasn't a person."

"No, it wasn't. It was a body." She turned from scrubbing the sink and took his hands. "We're all going to die, Friedy. When we do, we stop being people. If we've loved the right people, we'll become cherished memories."

"You can bring all your memories with you wherever you go, and you can live a large number of years more cherishing them."

Her face soured, genuinely this time, not a tease. "You sound like David."

"Who's David?"

"My son. We don't talk much anymore. Come here. I'll tell you a story." She took his hand and lead him to the sunroom.

"When Saul got sick, David used to come every single day to help take care of him. The cancer made him so weak, Friedy. It was to a point that I didn't have the strength to help him walk." Nana Robin looked at a framed picture on the wood-paneled wall of the sunroom. A real photograph, not an AR projector frame. It showed a younger Robin walking beside a lanky, classically handsome man. The camera caught them both in a blink, as if they'd closed their eyes in bliss, and lens flare created a light bloom around them. The couple smiled together, hands clasped, glowing. It was a photographic error, and it was perfect.

"Then he withered away so much I did have the strength to move him." She let out a long sigh with closed eyes. "David was a pallbearer at the funeral. He told me later he couldn't believe his father lay in that casket. Saul was a tall man, but David said the casket felt empty."

Friedy sat on the other daybed and said nothing. Nana Robin liked to tell stories of the past, and unless he had a question, he learned to let her spin her yarns uninterrupted. She had a flow and always had a point.

"After the funeral, he stayed here during the first week of shiva, of course, but the commute was hard. He'd been recruited by one of those big companies out on Long Island by then, and they like having you around all the time, so they try to give you everything you want right there. Take away every reason you might have to leave."

"They make it very nice," Friedy agreed. "In addition to work and living space, they have full social programs and settings so you can socialize and even date without ever leaving the corp-platz."

"Oh, they're nice. I probably know more about them than you do by now, with all the sales pitches and virtual tours and info-packets I've received. You know what they don't have, Friedy? Soul. They're living facilities designed by computer-assisted social scientists who built them to leverage joy factors or some such nonsense."

Her phone rang. An actual phone, not a MIU. "Speak of the devil." She gave Friedy a look and put the phone on holo. A glowing bust clicked into existence over her hand. He wore a rich poser chic suit and everything from his grooming to the way he held his face screamed uptight and henpecked.

"Hi, Ma."

"David."

The air tightened in the beat of silence.

"Look, Ma, this isn't one of my regular calls. I'm not going to ask you to move."

She lifted her eyebrows and gave Friedy a big nod. "You have my attention."

David cleared his throat and adjusted the knot of his tie. "I'm not asking you anymore. I'm telling you."

"Are you, now?"

"Ma, please. It's not like I'm trying to liquidate and claim your assets. The house isn't worth anything."

"Maybe not to you." She gestured behind her, where rows of shelves filled with books stretched above her head to the ceiling. "I read every one of these in this room. I'd lay here on this very daybed while your father read his trade journals and news in his seat by the big window." She pointed to an overstuffed easy chair with a slim-legged end table beside it.

"That's all still true when you move."

"Every afternoon, when the sun made it bright and warm in here, we'd take our spots with our books and read. We'd each be off in our own world, but we'd peek at each other between paragraphs and pages."

Friedy looked at the empty chair. Sun poured in through the large windows and lit the sand-colored tile and wooden walls with a soft glow and sleepy warmth.

"Ma, the gang was bad enough. Now the news feeds say there's a killer."

"When I come in here and pull down a book, I can still sometimes see him in the corner of my eye, sitting in his chair, face serious in study. He'd look up when he completed a thought and smile at me."

"Okay, enough." David's head got larger as he crowded the camera. His hand flashed in and out of frame as he spoke. "No one's trying to take your memories.

Those are yours forever. But the Rockaways are too dangerous for an old woman to live alone. If you won't see reason, I'll sue you for power of attorney and force you to relocate."

That slapped all mirth from her face. "You wouldn't."

"I know dad left you taken care of with his investment portfolio and pensions, but Vivian and I did the math, Ma. You can live the rest of your life on what he left you, but there's no way you can fight us in court. The legal fees will destroy you."

"Is that what you want?"

"Of course not. But if that's what it takes, I'll grind you into dependency and house you in a facility out here. I'd rather have you hate me here than get killed out there."

Nana Robin sat in silence. Friedy saw her eyes shimmer in the afternoon sun. He rocked to his feet and scooped the phone out of her hand in a single move. "Hi, David." He walked deeper into the house.

"Who are you?"

"I'm the new Shabbos goy."

"What happened to Rose?"

Friedy pointed at the holographic bust. "Let's talk about what's going to happen to you instead."

"Happen to me? What are you talking about?"

"I've gotten to know your mom in the time I've been working for her. She's a really good person, David. She's teaching me how to be one too. Here's the thing, Dave. I'm not there yet. What I am is a savant, a somewhat immoral savant. David Silverberg, employee ID 12088R672GF9."

Nana Robin's holographic projector rendered everything in glowing powder blue, but David's expression showed the color draining from his face. "How'd you get that?"

"I tracked it down when I decided I didn't like you, right about when we said hello." Friedy gestured with his eyebrows. "Check your feed. Those are your bank accounts." He stated that, didn't ask.

"This is outrageous! You can't break into my records this way."

"I can't? Really? Because it looks like I just did." Friedy put a mean face close to the camera. "If I can do that while talking on the phone, imagine what I can do when I concentrate. Like plant evidence that you've been skimming from operational funds."

David gaped.

"I'll get you blacklisted if you're lucky, disappeared if you're not." Friedy laid down his decree with a menacing finger. "Your mother's in her seventies and has earned the right to live where and how she wants. Leave her alone."

He cut the call and handed her the phone. "I think he'll let you stay."

19

Guion sat staring at the iron sphere in his augmented reality vision. The thing hung heavy, slowly rotating like a smooth planet. It was featureless. A sheen of light gave it a hint of detail, but it revealed nothing. No cracks, no seams, no dimples, nothing but a perfectly rendered smooth curve with no breaks anywhere.

He'd been staring at the thing for weeks now and all he discovered was that the sphere carried a massive electrical charge, AR code that would induce massive feedback in any MIU that tried to access it without authorization. It could prompt enough current to destroy a MIU completely and electrically lobotomize any brain attached to it. That part wasn't hard to figure out. A.W.E. placed the same subroutine in the virus Friedy was supposed to deploy on the Ibacipla run.

Friedy already made it farther than this. That's how Guion knew this sphere wouldn't erupt in a standard radial menu, but into a collection of other spheres, growing from planet to solar system. When he voiced his frustration to Jon, he learned Friedy saw quite a bit he missed because Friedy rarely used graphical rendering and interacted with the augmented world directly through code. That explained a lot. It also shut down his efforts for a time. Guion didn't have the knowledge to attempt something like that.

A knock at the door. Guion snapped the display shut and opened the door.

"What do you want, Paul?" He didn't need Jon's sense with people to know this was going to be an unpleasant conversation. Paul had no poker face.

"You don't watch streams, so I thought you'd want to know you've been outed." He pushed himself into the apartment. "I just heard."

"Define outed." Guion pulled the door closed and leaned against it. Paul stood square in the middle of the doorway to the living room. He stopped before wading into the carpet of food trash. Both men faced off with arms crossed over their chests.

"Nana Robin gave me a call. She never thought to get Friedy's contact ID."

Guion rolled his hand.

"He got involved in an argument with her son and threatened to ruin him."

Guion sucked his teeth and bobbed his head. "Sounds like something he'd do."

"This conversation took place over the phone."

Guion's face went blank.

Paul cocked an eyebrow and nodded. "Her son's a project manager for H-Bomb Records."

H-Bomb Records, with the sounds that will blow your ears and your mind. An A.W.E. subsidiary.

"He's corporate," Guion stated in deadpan.

"Yeah." Paul matched his tone.

"Friedrich got on a vid call with a corporate."

"Yeah."

"The system flagged him."

Paul nodded. "Her son got tipped off during the call, and he reported the contact . . ."— Paul's eyes darted to a corner of his vision for a second—". . . about thirty minutes ago. SHOC[3] already paid her a visit. She called me right after they left."

Guion popped off the door and dropped his arms.

Paul held up a hand. "He wasn't there."

Guion sagged back against the door with a sigh that sounded like he was deflating.

"Guion, this isn't working."

"We agree on that."

"Friedy and Jon are out a lot." He held out a hand when Guion opened his mouth, bid him to silence. "Paula asked Jon, I know. I also know you gotta make food runs. You might be able to pull a tap off the power grid and hack your way into the WorldGrid, but you can't con an empty stomach."

"Now that's real truth," Steve said from the couch.

Paul looked over his shoulder and the man waved at him with one hand. The other held a half-meter long wrap with the words "Outrageous Burrito" in a purple starburst on the wrapper.

"I didn't see you there, Steve. Hello."

Steve waved the comment away. "Happens all the time. No problemo. Get it? Cause of . . ." He pointed at the burrito. "I would have said hello earlier, but my mouth was full."

"Why don't you stuff something else in it, Steve?" Guion said.

"You know what, man? I am just not feeling like blowing you right now. Can it wait until after our company leaves?"

Guion glowered.

"How about you guys continue your conversation, and I'll get you warmed up by eating this suggestively. The anticipation will make it hotter later." He slid his lips around the tip of the burrito and inched them forward.

"Ignore him," Guion said.

Another knock at the door. Guion snapped his eyes to Paul. In all the time they'd been here, he was the only one who ever knocked.

Guion looked to Steve, who sucked a wad of surplus vat meat and cheese flavoring out of the rolled tortilla, eyes on Guion the whole time. He dragged the roll out of his mouth one centimeter at a time. A gooey orange string stretched behind before landing in a wet glop on his chest. Steve scooped it up with his fingers and licked them clean.

"Strategic Homeland Operations," a voice said on the other side.

Guion gestured. *Well?*

Steve gave him a thumbs up and a seductive lip lick.

Guion stared at Paul and put a finger to his lips.

Another knock. "Sir, please don't do this. I heard your voice as I came up the stairs."

Guion shot Steve a look. "I thought you covered us," he whispered.

"I did," Steve said at normal volume. "I still am."

"Then how did he hear us?" Guion still whispered.

"No, he heard him." He pointed at Paul. "He hasn't heard you at all."

Guion glared.

Steve threw up his hands. "What? Jon asked me to cloak the team, so I did. I'm supposed to do the whole neighborhood now?"

"What's he talking about? White noise?" Paul looked back and forth between them.

Another knock. "Sir, please open up. I have some questions. This will only be difficult if you make it."

"You can get out onto the roof through the bedroom

window. He probably won't hear anything. Someone's always leaving it open," Guion said. But before Guion could stop him, Paul marched to the door and pushed it open. The SHOC³ trooper edged around it with sidesteps and contortions.

"How can I help you, trooper?"

The trooper paused for a second before he looked over Paul's shoulder into the apartment. *He just checked Paul's face against images of ours,* thought Guion. "Is there anyone else here?"

Paul shook his head. "Just me."

"Then who were you talking to?"

"Myself."

"You live here alone?"

"I don't live here at all. I'm in the unit downstairs, but I'm the super of this building and I smelled something funny, so I came up to check it out." He swung his arm toward the living room. "Someone had a hell of a party up here and didn't clean up. I think I'm entitled to a little irate self-talk, don't you?"

"Present your IP, please."

"Why?"

"Present your IP, please." The trooper said it slower this time. He said "please" in a way that made it clear this wasn't a request.

Paul pulled up his network settings in AR and made it public.

"Have you seen any of these men? We got a call about one on 148th Street."

Paul shook his head.

"You're the super?"

"I am."

"So you're the one responsible for that illegal solar bloom array on the front lawn?" The trooper summoned a citation pad in AR and opened a form. That Guion could see it meant he rendered it in public space. He wanted Paul to see.

"It's not illegal."

"You need to attach specs, licenses, and inspections to an AR menu to certify the rig is legal." The trooper flexed his hand to split his citation book into three forms. "You have nothing on that rig. No forms, not even a menu. You're missing every piece of paperwork."

"That regulation is only in place inside corp-platzs. As long as we have paper forms available upon request it's kosher. Connectivity's not a given out here."

Paul picked up speed. "Since you don't know that, I can tell you don't spend much time in The Hives. What are you, a recent transfer for the new stream? That sounds about right, seeing as how we only see any action from SHOC³ around here when they want something, not when we need protection. That's why the B7s are giving you such a problem, by the way. All that turf and firepower they've got? It's because you let them get that big."

He ran his hand over the ghostly paperwork hanging between them. "So if you want to issue me those citations, go ahead and do it. You can even do it in AR since I doubt you know how to write by hand. I'll take them straight to the court and fight every one of them. Hey, maybe you'll get a little camera time out of it."

The trooper pinched the citation forms shut, swiped the book closed and grabbed Paul's throat in one fluid combo. "You sound like a lawyer, not a super. You a lawyer?"

"Handyman." Paul barely managed to push the word through the trooper's grip.

The trooper yanked, slammed Paul's face against the doorframe, then tripped him on the rebound and smashed him to the dented hardwood. A rough roll put Paul face down and the trooper zipped his hands behind his back with plastic ties before his head cleared. "Well, Mr. Handyman, maybe you should stay out of the law profession. While you're staying out, stay out of my way while I search these premises."

The apartment had two small rooms. It took thirty seconds to search.

"You have a good day," the trooper said as he stepped over Paul. He didn't cut the man's hands free before he left.

"You've got quite the activist's passion for someone who wants to keep things quiet." Guion sliced the ties with a kitchen knife.

"I got myself riled up intentionally. That way if he was scanning my biometrics looking for signs I was lying, it would be buried under my general agitation." Paul prodded his face with ginger fingers and winced. "It also bought time for you to get out to the roof to hide."

"Uh, yeah. Totally." Steve finished the last bite of burrito.

Guion helped Paul to a folding chair and watched the trooper move to the next house. Three others worked the block with him. He shook his head as they worked. "This is falling apart already."

20

"Friedy! What's going on, little dude? Come on in," Malcolm said. The man shrugged an electric-blue shirt on over his muscled and scarred frame and buttoned it as he pushed the door closed with his body.

"Did I come at a bad time?"

Malcolm stuffed his shirt into the unbuttoned waist of his jeans. It looked like he had barely pulled on clothing before opening the door.

"Not at all. Not at all." Malcolm zipped up. "See? All good."

"If I caught you in the middle of something—"

"I just finished with him," said a deep female voice from behind him.

Friedy turned to see a woman walking up the hallway. Her urban camo-print jacket hung open, revealing the sequin-knit halter top with cut glass beads that matched the thin necklace at her neck and the belly chain stretched over the butterfly and heart tattoo on her midriff. The high slit up the side of her matching skirt revealed a thick, muscular thigh. The camo, the muscle, the close-cropped hair dyed white, she wore it all with a style that somehow remained feminine.

"You here to distract him for a while?" She ran her hands up Malcolm's chest and wrapped her arms around his neck. "I'd rather not leave him alone for too long."

"Come on, Jamila." Malcolm put gentle hands on her waist and pushed her away. "You don't gotta do that. I'm good."

"You ain't good. Your baby—"

"Don't." Malcolm stopped her with a hand. "I can deal with it, but you don't gotta bring it up."

Silence reigned for a second. "Okay, Malcolm, whatever you need." She looked at Friedy. "You got him?"

He nodded. "I got him."

"You better." She gave Malcolm a quick kiss and reached for the door.

"Wait, Jamila. Before you go, take this." He pulled a wad of cash from his pocket.

Jamila took it, held it in her hand. "You already gave me for the month."

"Yeah, I know. I want you to have extra."

"Ooooh, Mr. Big Baller. I heard you was gettin all kinds of extra business from the B7s."

He nodded but didn't look happy. "I am, but it's not good business."

"Looks good from here." Jamila held up the cash.

"My shit's usually tech. Lately it's been guns. Lots and lots of guns."

The smile fell off her face. "Shit."

"Yeah. All the SHOC^3 raids got them gearing up. At some point, SHOC^3's gonna catch the shipments, and I might go dry until I can work something out. I'm planning ahead, but I ain't got nothing yet. So keep that and don't spend it, okay? Rainy day fund for the coming storm."

She stuffed the cash in her jacket pocket and kissed Malcolm again. "Thanks, Malcolm."

"You're really worried SHOC[3]'s going to shut you down?" Friedy said as he and Malcolm settled into chairs in his living room.

"Things keep going like they are, I don't see how they don't. It started with SHOC[3] looking for you guys, right? They got some tip you were in the '80s somewhere. SHOC[3] being SHOC[3], they go tromping on in there, fuck up all the B7's shit, and get into a bunch of fights with them. Now though? You could drop off the face of the Earth and this shit's still going sideways. SHOC[3] keeps busting up B7 business, so the B7s mobilize to defend what's theirs. Then there's that killer cutting up their pimps and hos that got them hunting in packs. They're gonna be strapped like an army soon, and so SHOC[3] will do the logical thing and crack down on the supply lines." Malcolm pointed to himself with a thumb.

"So why do you still do it?"

"Until I find some other way to get paid, I got mouths to feed. You've seen it every time you've been here. Those women, those babies, they need me. I appreciate you taking care of Nana Robin in all this though. That's one less thing I gotta worry about."

"You seem awfully attached to someone who gave your daughter a job."

"Two of my kids before her, me before them. Her husband taught me all about tech and running a business."

Friedy scooched to the edge of the cubic pleather seat. "Saul?"

Malcolm leaned back and folded his hands over his knee with a slow smile as his eyes lost focus, seeing some other place. "Saul Silverberg was a huge towerball fan, the kind who knew the stats for every player in the league. When I got capped, he thought it was bullshit. He also knew I didn't have any other prospects, so he offered me a job. I worked his shop for years, and when he retired he handed me the keys." Malcolm's eyes cleared and he fixed Friedy with a sharp look. "That old couple gave me everything. They met all my kids, and I helped David carry his father's casket. So yeah, you can say I'm attached."

"I met David. He's a schmuck."

Malcolm laughed. "She teach you that word? He didn't used to be, but since he got that corp gig he's become a dick."

"Nana Robin is a sweet woman. I like her a great deal. Pal . . ." He bobbed his head from side to side. "We're coming to an understanding."

"Good deal, man. I'm glad to hear that's working out. You know, Jon was pretty worried about you when you vanished from the apartment."

"I wish he cared that much when he found out there was a plot to kill me."

"He cares about you, Friedy."

"If he cared, he'd be burying a body with me right now, not living with the man who was willing to roll the dice on if I died."

"Yeah, he didn't get into too many of the details, said it was safer the less I knew. But the way he put it, you're in a lot of trouble. Sounds to me like you might not agree with the way Guion's dealt with shit, but he's still on your side."

"Fuck him," Friedy said with a wave of his hand. "I didn't come here to talk about him." He leaned in. "I came here to talk about us, and it looks like my timing is perfect. I might have an answer to your problems."

"Alright, little man. What you got?"

"Indulge me first."

Malcolm studied him for a long moment, then the seriousness melted off his face with a laugh and he stood. "You gonna ask me about getting girls again? Because if we're having that talk, I'm getting a smoke."

"Come on, Malcolm." Friedy gestured to the door. "I've never seen anything like that."

"I didn't think you liked Jamila," Malcolm called from down the hall.

"Didn't like?"

"You weren't breathing through your mouth the whole time."

"I'm getting better with the staring. But I wasn't talking about her. I was talking about how into you she was."

Malcolm chuckled as he took his seat and lit the joint he held between his lips. "Yeah. She is." He took a drag and his face got serious as he held it. "A big part of it is because it's mutual. That's important to keep in mind, Friedy. Women know when you're bullshitting them. They got a sense for it."

Friedy frowned and shook his head as he took the joint. "I've liked plenty of women." He puffed. "Really liked. It's never been reciprocated."

"Well, that's just one part of it. There's no one thing."

"I had myself altered recently."

"I thought your body rejected implants."

"Not implants. Alterations. Different methodology. Experimental. I asked for traits I thought would make me better." He handed the joint back. "Not only with women, but them too."

"Like pheromones?"

Friedy shook his head. "No, nothing that specific. I asked to be stronger, faster, dangerous in a fight. I wanted to become an apex predator."

Malcolm coughed. "And you thought that would help?"

Friedy shrugged and held his hands out toward Malcolm. "You're fit and can handle yourself."

"Yeah, but I don't go to the club and scout ladies like I'm a lion hunting antelopes or some shit like that. Damn, man, they're people. Ladies wanna feel safe around you. If you're putting off some vibe like you're on a hunt they're gonna react the same way the antelopes do." He leaned forward, didn't offer the joint. "Run the fuck away."

A bang at the door. Malcolm flicked his eyes to check the camera feed in his AR. "Oh, fuck." He stood and hauled Friedy to his feet. "It's SHOC[3]. Hide in my room. Don't come out. I'll find you."

Friedy closed the door, took a seat in the high-backed swivel chair, and tapped into the feed beaming from his porch camera as Malcolm walked outside.

"Can I help you, trooper?"

"Have you seen these men?" Friedy tapped into the officer's public stream and saw his team on display.

Malcolm looked them over. He cupped his chin, took his time before he shook his head. "Naw, man. I run into a lot of people, but I ain't seen these guys."

"This one was spotted in the 80s." Friedy's frame flashed red. "You got a shop on 81st, don't you?"

"That's right. Secondhand and refurbished electronics."

"This guy here would be interested in exactly that." Friedy's frame flashed again. "You sure you haven't seen him?"

"Wait, that's what this is about? My baby girl got carved up and you're asking me about a guy who wants a discount on a refurbished MIU?"

The trooper paused, gave Malcolm a hard look. "That's being handled by a separate unit, and the investigation is ongoing. Now, we got a call that this man was on 148th Street this afternoon."

"This is 125th."

"Cut the shit, Malcolm. He's moving around this area and

you're exactly the kind of backstreet dealer he'd come looking for."

"Do I know you?"

"I know you, asshole. That's all that's important. And I know you got plenty of traffic coming in and out of here."

Malcolm spread his hands. "I got five baby mommas, man! Of course there's gonna be traffic."

"Is he in there now?" The trooper pointed.

"I just told you he wasn't."

"Was he here earlier?"

"I already told you I ain't seen him. So the only way he coulda been here before was if he broke in because I. Haven't. Seen. Him."

"So you don't mind showing me your logs for the last few days." The trooper gestured toward the security camera that watched them.

"Fuck yeah, I mind."

"Asking was a courtesy. Since we're no longer being polite . . ." The trooper stabbed Malcolm in the side with a Lightning Strike stunner. Malcolm let out a choked cry and dropped. The trooper let him fall, didn't ease him to the ground, strode over his prone and twitching body.

"Oh, shit." Friedy looked around. The room had only the one door plus a closet. It had a window, but he couldn't open the screen behind it.

Hide under the desk? The bed? Wait, really? Come on, how amateur.

Stop. He was thinking like Poor Friedy. He wasn't Poor Friedy anymore. He was an apex predator. If it came to it, he'd kill that trooper before he could report what he found. Sure, Guion would throw a fit, but fuck Guion. He'd give Malcolm some additional problems, but he was already in trouble and—

The trooper threw open the door, weapon pointed and

ready. The weapon, Friedy noted, wasn't his stunner. He held an A.W.E. Double Shot pistol pointed and ready.

The beast roused. Friedy gripped the arms of the chair, ready to pounce as the man swept the room with gaze and gun. He looked Friedy right in the eye . . .

Then he turned and left.

Steve. It had to be Steve's cloak. He might not be living with them, but their arrangement clearly still stood.

Friedy sat in place as the trooper checked the rest of the house, then he helped Malcolm inside and got him settled.

"How'd you dodge him?" Malcolm asked as he collapsed into the chair with a grimace.

"I hid under the desk."

"For real? No offense, man. Sounds like an amateur move. I'm surprised it worked."

"I'm just glad it did." Friedy took a drag from the joint as he stood over Malcolm. "As terrible as that was, it provides a relevant segue." He took another hit. "You said you wanted to stick it to SHOC[3] before. Now they're threatening your money and assaulting you. Let me help you. Let me be a friend. You get me the tech I need, and I'll make them pay." He held out the joint. "I'll make them pay you."

21

Despite the increasing violence and tension between SHOC³ and the B7s, Jon hadn't seen a single human patient the whole day when the SHOC³ recruitment officer sauntered in. Tall and thin, body stretched like pulled taffy, she came in a uniform, not combat dress. That meant no hardplas plating and no helmet, leaving a face full of hard angles open to the world. It did not mean she came unarmed. The matte black A.W.E. Double Shot rode her small hip in a bloodred holster in front of a blocky Lightning Strike pacifier. Deadly and fashionable. A.W.E. would have it no other way.

She scanned faces as she walked, her off-center looks between blinks revealing the busy AR displays that cross-referenced what she saw with SHOC³ databases. Those leaving did so in the kind of hurry that tried not to attract attention. Those waiting to be seen decided to try their luck another time and followed.

"Paula Kellerman, I'd like to speak with you. Now please." She spoke in commands with a brittle voice and ended her sentences with an upward lilt as if everything was a question. It made Jon grit his teeth in annoyance.

"Someone's looking for me?" Paula emerged from the back, white coat over her casual attire, Pepe at her side. She stopped in her tracks when she saw the officer standing in the waiting area, put Pepe in a sit. "What's this ab—"

"Ms. Kellerman, I'm Recruitment Officer Goshram and I'm here to accept you into SHOC^3's employment opportunity drive." Her smile was fake without any effort to hide it. "Congratulations."

Paula started, blinked. "I don't want to be a trooper."

"Oh, no, you're not trooper material. As part of the surge in combat operations here, we're recruiting support staff as well as frontline freedom protectors." She pointed with a long finger wrapped in midnight blue synthetic leather. "Support staff is you."

"No, it's not." Paula shook her head.

"I'll have the paperwork completed by this afternoon. I've already logged your IP, so I'll send it to you as soon as it's ready for your compliance certification. I wanted to drop by and let you know to expect it."

"Save yourself the time." Paula cut the air with her hand. "I don't need the forms. I don't want the job."

"You're already doing the job."

Paula stopped for a beat. "I don't work for you." It was a statement, but her slow delivery made her confusion clear.

"Ah," Goshram said with another point. "There's the problem. You're patching up wounded quite well, but you're patching up the wrong wounded."

"Wrong wounded? What are you talking about?"

Goshram approached and put a hand on her shoulder. "Ms. Kellerman, don't play stupid. We have drone footage of everything. You're not just seeing dogs and cats here. You're instrumental in keeping the B7 casualty count down."

"This is a hospital. We try to keep everyone alive and healthy. Since when is that a crime?"

Goshram crossed her arms and shook her head. "You're treating criminals in an unlicensed facility. That's several crimes."

"I'm not going anywhere with you." Paula started back toward the doors to the innards of the clinic.

Goshram sucked a big breath through her nose and turned away with a shrug. She paced the waiting area as she spoke. "That's where you're wrong. I came here to get you, either as a recruit or a prisoner." Her words rooted Paula in place. "You've already admitted to several offenses during this conversation, which I've been recording and streaming to a virtual evidence locker on cloud servers."

"You can't do that! That's illegal surveillance."

Goshram laughed, a witch's cackle. "How adorable." She clapped. "Ah, there it is." Her eyes twitched to see some information feed only for her. "The VI profiler says you have anarchist and activist leanings." The mirth fell from her whole body. "You need to review the latest contract the city signed with SHOC[3]. There is no protection against surveillance in the agreement. It drove the price too high, so the mayor didn't buy that option." She smiled that plastic grin that didn't stretch past her lips. "I'll send you a copy of it along with your employment agreement."

Paula advanced on Goshram this time. "I wouldn't be dealing with those animals at all if you would do your job and protect this neighborhood." Pepe, who'd sat like a garden statue the whole conversation, stood, muscle-packed frame stiff and ready.

Goshram shrugged. "We have a feedback link on our site."

"Fuck yourself. I'm going nowhere with you." She spun back toward the inner doors again.

Goshram unclipped the Double Shot and rested a hand on

it, but didn't draw. "Ms. Kellerman, I'm offering you a choice, but not the one you think. You belong to SHOC[3] now. You can leave here a bonded employee or a prisoner." She tapped the air. "Since you're so uncooperative, I'm acquiring this facility for conversion to a supplemental medbay." She finished her AR work and locked eyes with Paula. "A cleaning crew will be here in thirty minutes to euthanize the animals."

Paula's eyes went wide. She rushed Goshram. Pepe was faster, pushed her back, bared his teeth and bristled.

Goshram drew and fired, a single smooth motion, a single trigger pull that blasted a pair of piggybacked shots. She moved too fast for Jon to stop, but he smacked the gun up and sent the bullets into the ceiling as he popped into sight.

"I've got this! Get him out of here before he gets killed."

"Pepe! Come here!" The dog skidded to a halt and ran back to Paula, who ushered him into the back as Goshram wrenched her arm out of Jon's grip in a motion that spun him to face her.

She squinted at him. "My VI doesn't recognize you."

"I like to keep to myself." He yanked her gun arm straight and twisted it into an armbar, except it didn't twist. He jammed the motion again, threw his whole body into it.

No motion, just more squinting until she gave up waiting for her digital assistant to find him in SHOC[3]'s neighborhood database. That's when she smashed Jon in the chest with her free hand, slammed him against the wall. He grunted and sagged but got his head clear in time to see her level the Double Shot at him. A quick look and desperate throw launched a potted plant off the windowsill. Goshram's targeting augment locked onto the threat and jerked her gun to it. A quick *bangbang* made an explosion of pottery and dirt. By the time she wheeled and reacquired him, Jon was halfway over the check-in desk.

Bangbang.

Bangbang.

Bangbang.

Goshram pumped three double-taps through the simple wood divider in calculated blind fire, then waited in the silence that followed, gun tracing between likely exit points. She walked around the counter one careful step at a time.

Nothing. The area behind the desk lay open and abandoned, nothing there but the shreds of wood she blasted free.

Ting.

Jon's metal fist slammed Goshram in the brain stem. She staggered to a knee and collapsed, gun spinning across the tile and coming to rest underneath the check-in counter. He took a deep breath, winced as he touched his sternum.

"Thank you." Paula knelt beside Goshram and checked the woman's pulse. "That meant more than I can say."

"I don't mind braining someone willing to shoot a dog."

She nodded in a way that felt like she did more than agree with him. "You need to get out of here. If she didn't call for backup during that scuffle, her VI certainly did as soon as she went down."

Paula gave him a quick hug in his hesitation. "Go, get out. She didn't ID you, so you can hide. I'm gonna drag her into the back and try to buy some goodwill by seeing to her before the cavalry arrives. Explain it to Paul for me? And, uh, be gentle about it."

Jon still paused, but a shove got him moving and he picked up speed when he got out on the sidewalk. He passed the incoming squad cars at a run.

22

All eyes turned to Jon as he opened the door, but it was Steve, from his usual post on the couch, who greeted him.

"Dude, I got the most wicked headache before. What the hell did you do?"

"I got scanned by a SHOC^3 facial recognition routine."

"You what?" Guion stood so suddenly his chair fell over.

"Yeah, that'll do it." Steve wiped his forehead. "Here's the part I don't get. Whoever was running that app could have looked right at you and got nothing unless you touched them."

Jon grimaced and shrugged.

"Oh, fuck. No wonder."

"No wonder what?" Guion said.

"If it was anybody around here, Jon-O's close contact wouldn't have triggered the app. They'd be able to see him, but the app still wouldn't get a read. But because this was SHOC^3, and they all have MIUs tied into their nervous systems—"

"Specifically their sensory input," Guion said.

"Specifically their sensory input," Steve said with a nod, "as soon as their eyes could see you, the app got a lock."

"How bad is this? Does SHOC^3 know we're here?"

Steve shook his head. "Nah. I got it. That explains the headache though. Extra effort to blind the app to the database results. It was like this massive burst of pressure in my head. Normally when I get pressure pains I just have to . . ." He bore down and pushed out a crawling fart that lasted so long it became uncomfortable. "Hmm." He fidgeted in his seat. "I might have to wipe that one out." He wagged a finger at Jon. "You ruined my meal. You owe me a replacement."

"What happened?" Guion said.

"I had to intervene with a SHOC^3 recruitment officer. Paula was in this trooper's face and it set Pepe off. She was going to shoot the dog. Someone needed to step in."

Guion shook his head with a dismissive sigh and wave. "Both you and Friedrich exposed yourself to SHOC^3 today. They're going to lean on people we know." He leaned in, and his next words were velvet with razorblade edges. "You want to help the people here? Help get us out of here."

"You're the one with the brilliant plan for that. I'm trying to make us less a cancer from hell for these people while we wait for you to crack that file."

Guion turned his back to Jon's reply and spoke at normal volume as set his chair back in place and collapsed into it with a long sigh. "You have to bring Friedrich back on board. I can't crack that file open."

"He hates you." Jon brushed the trash off the couch and dropped into the seat.

"Yes, he made that clear. This is also in his best interest. I trust that won't be too hard an argument to make."

Jon leaned forward and rested his elbows on his knees. "He's happier here than he ever was in the corp-platz." Jon shrugged with raised hands. "What's he got waiting for him working with you? You're going to ride his ass like a jockey the minute he gets in the door."

Guion rolled his eyes. "Are you saying I need to be nicer about his feelings? How old is this man? You want me to buy Friedrich an ice cream to make it up to him?"

"Yo, get a few for me if you do," Steve said.

Jon didn't answer. He held Guion's gaze and didn't flinch, didn't look away.

"SHOC^3's already paid a visit to dear old mom. What's he going to do, become a wild animal every time they come for him? How long can he keep that up?"

Jon sat motionless.

"It's only a matter of time before they drop a bomb on him or shell his position from a ship so far off the coast he can't see it."

Nothing from Jon.

"He doesn't care, does he?"

Jon shook his head.

Guion squeezed his temples with another sigh. "Go get him. Give him whatever he wants."

JON WASN'T SURE WHAT TO EXPECT WHEN HE RANG THE BELL OF the big brick house near the beach, but Friedy's face peeking out over a door chain wasn't it. The little man didn't slam the door when he saw Jon, but he wasn't beaming with joy over the reunion either. Instead, when Jon asked to talk, Friedy nodded and led him into a sunroom with a pair of daybeds, a thick, leather-wrapped chair by the window, and books lining the opposite wall. Friedy collapsed onto one of the beds with an ease that said it was his.

"Not there," he said when Jon started to sit in the chair.

"You don't sit in Saul's chair." He gestured to the other daybed across from him.

"Nice place," Jon said as he took a seat and looked around. "Kind of old school, but still nice."

"Nana doesn't feel the need to keep up with decor trends. She's content with what she has." The way Friedy's eyes moved said he was working in AR while he talked with Jon, offering half his attention, maybe.

"Where is she now? And the dog?"

Friedy gestured to the window. "She likes to garden in the afternoon when it's warm, and Pal lays in the grass with her."

"You don't help her with that?"

"Why are you here, Jon?"

Jon sighed. "I fucked up, Friedy. I fucked up real bad and I need your help."

That got Friedy's attention. He rolled his head and looked square at Jon. No eye twitch or distant focus. He locked on Jon. "Really."

"I let SHOC[3] see me. They couldn't read me, but an officer saw me."

Friedy swung up to sitting. His feet slapped the floor and he leaned over his knees, face split with a grin now. "Jon fucked up." He said it with whispered wonder. "Jon . . ." He drew back, sat up tall. "You never fuck up."

"I did it to save Paula. They have her, by the way. It's one of the reasons I'm here."

"What did Guion call you?"

"What? Nothing. Did you hear what I said?"

Friedy deflated, more sour than sullen. "Of course not." He dropped back on the bed and resumed whatever he'd been working on in AR. "Do you know why I asked to be what I am?"

"I didn't think you had a say in it. Weren't all your alterations done in utero?"

Friedy shook his head. "I mean after the prison break. I wanted to be strong, and fast, and deadly."

"Apex predator. I remember." Jon shook his head. "You know that's not you, right? That's the demon. Guion doesn't know medicine. I can't hide in plain sight." He shook his head again. "You aren't strong or fast like an animal. That's what's in you. It's not you."

"Do you know why I asked for it?"

"I assumed it was because you needed to get away, same as me. You just thought of a different solution to the problem."

"I wanted to be powerful. That's why I built that nuclear bomb in our teens."

"Wait, that thing was real?" Jon almost jumped out of his seat.

Friedy nodded, though he looked unhappy. "Yah, okay, great, so I could nuke the entire corp-platz collective and the Five Hives. Turn the key, scan the pad, press the button, and be like a god." He made an explosion noise and mimed a mushroom cloud. "I didn't want to do that, so the thing sat unused and I didn't feel any different. When I got the chance for power again, I asked for the kind that would make me more like you. You exaggerated, perhaps, but more like you." His gaze drifted away. "Less like me."

"Friedy, any of the heavies we had with us on our last op could have mopped the floor with me. I'm just a guy."

"Maybe to you, but to Friedy you've been a hero for a long time." Nana Robin pulled off a pair of dirt-stained canvas gloves as she walked between the men.

"Would you be a dear and throw these down the laundry chute?" She handed the gloves to Friedy while Pal gave Jon a nose inspection.

When Friedy returned, he moved to sit back on his daybed but stopped as Nana Robin looked around.

"Here, I can stand."

She dismissed that with both hands. "Go sit in your spot, Friedy." She walked to the leather chair, paused, then put her back to it.

"Saul's seat?"

She smiled. "If he's seated there, then he'll just have to make room on his lap for me." She put a hand up beside her mouth and whispered. "He won't mind." She sat.

Pal sat down in front of Jon, enjoying the neck massage. He scooted closer for more, tail making a low "whoosh" noise on the tile with its lazy wags.

Friedy looked at Nana Robin. "You see?"

"Mmm-hmm." She nodded.

Jon looked from one to the other. "I'm missing something."

"Friedy's talked quite a bit about you since he's been here. He's had more to say about you than anything else."

Jon gave Friedy a look. "Should I be honored or worried?" He wasn't joking.

"Really, Jon. You should know even when I'm pissed at you, I love you. I only have two kinds of memories: people kicking me around and you defending me from them."

"He loves telling the story about, what was his name? Bustos?"

"Juan? What about him?" Jon said.

"You knocked him out for stealing Friedy's MIU when you were both sixteen." The men looked at her and she smiled. "I may have heard that story more than once."

Jon blinked and retreated into his past, shook his head. "I don't remember that."

"I do. He was wearing a hoodie with an aug-frame. Remember them? Tactile bio-interface that made you stronger."

"Except they sucked and barely ever worked right."

"That's why they went out of fashion inside of a quarter, but he had one, and it was working fine that day. You didn't care. Hit him right here." Friedy brushed his jaw with a fist. "He went limp like the dead, out before he even started to fall." He shook his head and his eyes saw another time and place. "I could never do that."

"I got a lucky punch in."

"But you were willing to do it. You've always been willing to do it. Step up. Scrap because I couldn't. Small wonder I love you, but on top of it all, everyone else loves you too."

"Come on. That's an exaggeration."

"How long did Guion spend dressing you down before you came here looking for me?"

"He was more focused on the mess of problems we're facing. Speaking of which—"

"Jon, has he ever been too busy to spare some words of derision for me? Have we ever been in a situation too dire for his criticism?" He threw a hand toward Jon. "Look at that! Even Pal loves you right away. He's famous in the neighborhood for not liking anyone. I've been here weeks and he's only just learned to tolerate me." Friedy leaned forward again. "Do you get it? Do you get why I asked for the gifts?"

"Okay, so I'm great, but what I need to talk to you about is—"

"Do you know what the ultimate tragedy of all this is?"

"What?"

"I'm already better than you in the most important way." Friedy frowned and shook his head. "I didn't need any of these gifts, because if our situations were reversed, I wouldn't let Guion slide on this."

"That's another reason I'm here. He's sorry, Friedy."

"If he was sorry, he'd be here saying so."

"You know him." Jon shrugged. "He stays in the van."

"Not for this, he doesn't."

"Look, you've got to forgive Guion—"

"Says who?" Nana Robin said.

"What?" Jon said.

"He's not obligated to give forgiveness, and he certainly shouldn't grant it until this man offers sincere repentance and rectitude."

Friedy nodded in silent agreement.

"Oh, Jesus. Look, it's complicated—"

"Keep your complicated," Nana Robin said. "Sometimes right is right. You know what's right, don't you?" She sighed and pushed to her feet. "Look, I don't want to rile you two up and have you fighting. You're both good men, I know that. Once you know it too, you'll work this out. I'll leave you to it. Besides, Friedy can fend for himself."

She placed a hand on the little man's shoulder and smiled. "We'll have ice cream tonight."

"Jon, feel free to visit anytime." She held out her hand and leaned in to kiss his cheek when he took it. "He loves you like family," she whispered in his ear. "Be good family to him."

They sat in silence for a few moments after she left. Jon broke the silence.

"I'm sorry. I should have stood up for you more back at the apartment. Guion is serious about apologizing, but if you like, I'll slap him around a bit." He grinned. "Or I can hold him while you deck him."

Friedy continued to look at him with a blank expression.

Jon sighed. "I don't know what else to say. We're in a lot of trouble here. I gave SHOC[3] a big tip in their manhunt trying to save Paula, and they've got her locked behind some massive buyout clause now, I'm sure. We need a lot of money to save her, and we need that file so we can stop screwing up the lives of the people who live here." Jon reached across the gap and slapped Friedy's shoulder. "You're the only one who can get either of those." He paused with his hand heavy on

Friedy's shoulder, then tightened his grip and gave Friedy a look with equal parts accusation and pleading. "We really need to stop what's been going on since we got here."

Friedy rocked free and rubbed his temples. "I've been trying. You remember that package we dropped in Ibacipla?"

"The weird code?"

"The security for these files uses the same language. I'm starting to figure it out but it's like trying to read a novel in Old English. The basics are the same, but it's not really the same language we know."

The little man sniffed and started to pace the room. "I got frustrated, so I started tinkering with something else, and it's almost ready." He stopped and fixed Jon with a look. "Do you know what salami slicing is? It's a subtle form of electronic fund theft. A massive organization like SHOC[3] has base-camps all over the world. Beyond the physical space, it has countless media projects. It requires literal armies of employees, facilities, equipment, and plenty of discretionary spending."

"So you break in and steal a little bit hoping they don't notice?"

"To oversimplify it, yes, but I only do it when there's a transfer of funds. When money moves from one place to another and there's a fee, when currency changes from one form to another, when there's a complicated purchase with hundreds of lines, my virtual thief program increases the fee, the exchange rate, inserts a ghost line, and rounds the figures in our favor. Individually, the amounts are minuscule compared to the oceans of capital they move. Done thousands of times per hour, and it adds up."

Jon shot to his feet. "Those accounts are all audited!"

"Of course they are. By virtual intelligences." He shrugged. "I told them to ignore my anomalies."

"What if a human goes over those records?"

"If they do, they'll be sifting through enough convoluted accounting to drown in. The odds of them even running across one of my ghost transactions is minimal." He gave Jon a dry grin. "Guion can tell you the exact figure." He shrugged. "And if they do manage to trace it all the way to the hacker, I made sure to leave Boulliver's metadata in a few places. It's almost done, another week, maybe two. I promised Malcolm a portion of the payout since he helped get me some of what I needed to do this."

"This is the thing you tried to convince me of when we came over here the first time, isn't it? Didn't I tell you to stay away from it?"

"Yeah. I did it anyway." Plain facts without a whiff of defiance.

"How did you get all that done in so little time?"

"I had help." Friedy's eyes activated something in AR, and an image of his head appeared in Jon's sight, the same as when they spoke over coms.

"Gutten tag. I am Friedy. Artificial Friedy."

Jon looked at Friedy through the translucent form. "Is this you?" He pointed.

"You may also call me Friedy AF," the head said.

"Nein," Friedy said. "I already told you that's not cool."

"Ya. You keep saying that, and yet it sounds cool every time I say it."

"You built a virtual intelligence of yourself?"

Artificial Friedy frowned at him. "Virtual? Please, Jon, you'll make me say unkind things about your parents, and I don't want to speak ill of the dead."

"A virtual intelligence wouldn't help me," Friedy said. "Even the most complex VIs are just elaborate decision trees and dialog options. That's fine for repetitive tasks like audits, but I needed a true collaborator."

Artificial Friedy flashed a proud smile. "That's me."

Jon stared. "But artificial intelligence doesn't exist."

"Didn't exist," Artificial Friedy said. "Probably wouldn't for decades more, but A.W.E. was good enough to produce those detailed brain scans for Friedy to work from."

"The physical structure was only so helpful," Friedy said. "But their scans included footage of neurons firing and portions of my brain lighting up during different stimuli. I used them as source material to craft a homunculus in code." He made a small grimace. "It's not a perfect replica."

"That means I'm my own being."

"A homunculus in code?" Jon said. "That doesn't make any sense."

Friedy shrugged. "How often does someone say that about what I do? I summoned demons from Hell with a computerized ritual." He closed on Jon, and Artificial Friedy shrank as it slid sideways so it hung next to the real Friedy's head. "You're missing the point here, Jon. There are two of me now. Friedy squared. I can fund us and crack that file at the same time."

Jon blinked. "Yeah? Yeah!" He clapped Friedy on the neck. "So you're back?"

"I need one thing."

Jon beamed. "Name it."

"I'll get rid of our problems, but when this is over, I want you to get rid of Guion."

Pause.

"That's the demon talking, Friedy."

"Not even a little." He waved Jon to silence before the man said a word. "You're going to say Guion made a plan to help me. Save it." He shook his head and continued. "He was playing the odds. He always plays the odds. 'You only have a 3 percent chance of not fucking up, Friedrich.'"

Jon opened his mouth to counter, but Friedy leaned in and

preemptively trampled his objection, his voice softer now but more urgent.

"He did what he did before because the calculations looked favorable to him. That's the only reason. If the odds tell him that icing me, or us, will boost his chances of corporate recruitment, he'll do it. Or he'll arrange it. You know he'll consider it when the time comes."

When Jon didn't respond right away, Friedy continued. "You've never lied to me, not in our whole lives together. I don't think you will now. Tell me you'll do it and I'll believe you. Tell me you're with me and I'll be with you, like always."

23

on hit the starter and eased the truck into traffic. He'd ridden in armored vehicles before, but this was the first time he drove one. He felt the weight immediately. The vehicle had extra inertia even at low speeds. If everything went according to plan, he wouldn't test the truck at anything much faster. It should go according to plan. The universe owed them one at this point.

No sooner had Jon finished telling Guion about Friedy's good news, Malcolm called. SHOC³ impounded one of his arms shipments and had it ready to ship to some processing facility. With all the B7 activity, they weren't cataloging any of it locally, not even unpacking it. Just drive it out in the same truck it came in on and deal with it someplace safer.

"What happened to a smooth operation?" Jon said.

"You happened, motherfucker. You and your team have got SHOC³ buzzin like a pissed off nest of hornets. I need you to get that shit out."

Malcolm laid it all out. If the B7s didn't get guns from him, they'd get them from someone else, someone else who'd charge more. The B7s didn't have as much capital these days, what with all the SHOC^3 busts, so they'd resort to "fundraising" from the community. "This shipment goes belly up, everyone's gonna feel it. My kids, Nana Robin, those nice folk who bring their dogs in to Paula, and you too. Nobody gets a free ride on this one."

Guion, of course, refused to walk into a SHOC3 basecamp, cloaked or not, and this wasn't something Friedy could hack, which left Jon doing the job solo. The problem was, an invisible man couldn't drive the truck out. As soon as he drew too much attention to himself, he lost Steve's cloak. Putting his face on display in the middle of a SHOC^3 basecamp, where half or more of the troopers knew who he was and were on the lookout for him, seemed like a bad idea.

Malcolm helped there, or rather he made the introductions with someone who could. Vashanique, a slim woman with creamed coffee skin and a penchant for metallic shades and things that glittered. Thick ropes of dreadlocks dyed chrome silver hung from her head. A dress of gold chips hung from her shoulders. Jon met her in her basement beauty salon, dubious and wondering if Malcolm decided now was a good time for a prank.

Vashanique really knew makeup though, not just cosmetology. They talked for a bit about what Jon could pull off through voice and mannerisms. This had to be a total transformation. Then he sat in her chair for hours while she painted his face with a smart base and layered on facial prosthetics one piece at a time. They aged him fifteen years, gave him the ruddy complexion of a drinker, turned his eyebrows into a bristly mess of wires.

She applied one last dash of pigment, then stepped back to admire her work. She tucked a gold-painted lip and nodded. "You gotta wear this for at least four hours while it sets and all the connections form. The more you talk and move your face, the better."

"Won't that mess things up?"

"Pfff." She blew air through tight lips in disdain and bobbed her head at him. "If I gave you a busted ass, old-ass bullshit makeup job it would." She shook her head and dragged the ropes of her hair back and forth across her shoulders. "I did not do that. No no no, no. No. What you're wearing is a smart mask. That's some top-of-the-line shit right there."

She smiled and laughed at his expression. "That's good! Yeah, keep moving your face around like that. Total confusion's a new one. That'll hit a bunch of new spots." She held out a hand to stop herself. "That stuff I painted your face with? It wasn't foundation, not like the kind I'm wearing. It's a gel that binds all the individual pieces of your mask together and acts like a secondary layer of muscle."

"So this thing will move like my real face."

She gave him a single big nod. "Exactly. Except when it's all done, it'll be a single piece you can take on and off like a ski mask. You can use it over and over again. This is the only hours-long session you need to spend in my chair."

"That is pretty cool," Jon said. "I shouldn't need it more than this once, but it's still pretty cool."

"Hmmm." Vashanique frowned. "Malcolm shoulda mentioned that before we went in on the premium package. He's gonna owe me extra for this."

He left that for them to figure out. A day later a masked Jon walked into the SHOC^3 basecamp on 116th Street and flashed a forged work order to transport the truck out of the Rockaways. Guion relented enough to let Friedy forge an AR badge and transfer paperwork and in a rare stroke of luck, they discovered SHOC^3 had outsourced the job to a local company. They proved much more accessible. Friedy paid so little attention while he hacked the system, Jon worried what the little man might miss.

But Jon had to admit everything worked perfectly. Vashanique's mask hid his identity from electronic and organic eyes alike. No one even blinked at his credentials. Before long, they uploaded a route in the in-dash MIU, told him he'd have a drone escort the whole way, and pushed temporary clearance codes to a fob.

"I've got six aerial drones following me. There's no way I'm going to be able to take this truck off the planned route and dump it for Malcolm's people to unload while they're watching," he said when his scanner app said the truck was clean of listening devices.

Guion's face rendered in clear, cut glass glowed in the corner of his vision. "On it." He paused. "Do you think Malcolm can provide a high-capacity memory stick? I want to have a safe place to store the decrypted and decompressed files. I've got loads of local storage, but I'd like a backup, especially when we're talking with the Oceana Combine recruiter."

"Why not let Friedy take care of that? He found a ton of cloud space out there when he constructed Artificial Friedy. Then it's not tied to any physical device."

"He can't have anything to do with this."

"I don't see why not. He's balls deep in everything else about it."

"Because Friedrich is routinely off mission and screwing around."

"You promised to ease up, remember?"

"Your loyalty to him baffles me."

"He saved me. So yeah, I get he's undisciplined and makes messes, but he was there when no one else was."

"Please." Guion's disdain curdled the air. "You're a field operative. You probably owe your life to a hundred different people."

"This was different. You remember I told you a bad op cost me my arm?"

"Let me guess. Friedrich performed some wondrous hack that got you out of that situation." Guion frowned through his voice. "Was it the utterly predictable maneuver of turning automated defenses against the human security forces? Maybe something else in the category of 'doing his job'?"

"I was solo and I botched the op because I went in drunk. Friedy dug up blackmail material on my case handler. We couldn't erase the incident entirely, but he shaved the worst edges off. I kept my job. I kept my siblings and their families on their floor."

Jon glanced at the side mirror. A pair of cars sped up the neighboring lane, closing fast. Something about their approach felt aggressive. They didn't feel like speeding cars in a rush to get somewhere. They felt like predators running down prey. "Pause that. I got a feeling there's trouble coming."

The lead car rolled down its passenger window, and a man pulled himself out to the waist. His blue-striped shirt fluttered and snapped in the whipping wind, but the compact rifle molded around his hand stayed quite steady.

"Oh shit. B7s. They're hijacking me. They're supposed to wait for Malcolm's call."

"So give them what they want. That was the plan all along, wasn't it?"

The second car pulled even with the first one lane over. A gunner perched on its passenger window too. One of them pointed to him, then to the side of the road.

A single klaxon sounded in the cabin and his windshield tinted red for that beat. "Facial recognition match. Violent criminals identified." The gunman's face popped up in a small display at the corner of the windshield. Basic identifying information scrolled out in short lines next to the mugshot. "Driver, stay on course. You are protected." The line charting his route on the map pulsed to emphasize the automated command.

"What's going on?" Guion said.

"SHOC^3 installed a security package in the truck. One of the drones was running face scans, ID'd one of the gangers, and set it off."

"What kind of package?"

The gunner nearest him shot a three-round burst into the truck's nose. Inside, it sounded like hard hail.

"Bulletproof coating, for starters."

The mugshot shifted to live footage outside his window, and a ray-traced framework flashed over the rifle. A stock picture of the gun replaced the mugshot, and its information scrawled out alongside.

"AWE Power Fist 90. Warning: Sustained fire from this weapon will breach vehicle defenses."

Outside, the two gunners had a quick conference, speaking through their MIU displays based on how they pressed a hand to their ears. The far car sped ahead and both gunners turned their attention to the truck and opened fire.

Bullets sprayed and sparked across the hood and door. They punched a trail of snowballs across Jon's window with a staccato burst.

Jon yanked the wheel. The heavy truck swayed and lurched, a giant, wheeled club. The car speeding alongside swerved to miss him. The gunner grabbed the doorframe to avoid tumbling out backward. He glared at Jon. He pulled the trigger and kept it down, both hands on the gun, rigid arms holding it steady as it hammered the driver-side door.

Jon slammed the accelerator to the floor. Power swelled to the electric engine and he got heavy in his seat. But there was a lot of truck to move. It moved. It did not move quickly. He watched the speedometer tick up one kmph at a time.

Cars shot past on both sides and spread out in a line that blocked all three lanes ahead of him. Gunners emerged from their backseat windows and pointed a collection of rifles at him. The integrated drone escort scanned their faces and their weapons. They scrolled out in a litany of face, name, gun.

"Terence Brown. AWEsome-C60R. Warning: Sustained fire from this weapon will breach vehicle defenses.

Joshua Walters. AWEsome-C60R. Warning: Sustained fire from this weapon will breach vehicle defenses.

Michael Davis. AWEsome-C60R. Warning: Sustained fire from this weapon will breach vehicle defenses."

"Yeah, I got it the first time, thanks!"

More fire. The lead hail beat both doors now. He could only see moving shadows through the driver's window. The passenger one was messy with mothballs.

"Man, fuck you, Guion! Why the hell aren't you the one behind this wheel?"

Jon swerved into the left lane, then the right in a clumsy backswing across the asphalt. He batted the car on his side again. The one on the far side slammed its brakes and ducked behind before he hit it. He bounced the truck's nose off the cement block highway barrier.

A crunch and a metal scream. The impact jerked him sideways in his seat. Jon pulled the truck into the center lane.

Tires screeched. He smelled the rubber fumes through the cracks in the weakening glass.

"You're the one with the tactical implant. You're always the wheelman. But God forbid Guion ever crawl out from his hidey-hole and get into danger!"

The gunners in front all fired. Jon flinched and ducked despite the protective glass. Bullets snapped and rattled the windshield, but only left faint ashy marks. SHOC[3] must have given the front glass an extra coat of protection.

"I don't see how any of this is helpful right now," Guion said. "I'll get Malcolm on the line. Tell him to call them off."

"Enemy communication and coordination disrupted," the warning voice said.

Ahead of him, he watched the back window gunners wince and claw at their ears as their MIU earbuds shrieked feedback.

Jon stomped the accelerator to ram the middle car, but the truck gained speed so slowly that it only gave the car a hard bump and shove.

More fire from the side. The sound softened to a dull crunch, like crumpling already wadded paper. His window began to bend.

He swung the truck into the car, but squealing tires said they braked back in time.

"Fucking hell, Guion! Could you give me a hand here?"

"What do you want me to do, Jon? I can't talk you through vehicular combat."

"Dude, seriously? You're asking someone to backseat drive for you? That's lazy even for me." Steve's voice sounded distant, like he was shouting from across the room.

"Shut the fuck up, Steve!" Jon and Guion said in unison.

"You need to focus, Jon. I'm severing communication to remove the distraction."

He drove through a pounding bullet storm. Bangs and cracks enveloped him. His window collapsed.

The gunner in the blue shirt pulled alongside again.

"I'm trying to give this to you!" Jon yelled over the gunfire and wind.

The man leveled his gun at Jon. "Pull over right now!"

"I'm with Malcolm! Stop shooting and the truck is yours!"

"Malcolm?"

"Yeah! Malcolm!"

The man smiled and relaxed. He pulled his gun back. "Shit, man! Why didn't you say so?"

Metallic *ratatatatatat*. The B7 convulsed and exploded in bloody bursts that ripped his chest and belly open. He fell out the window and splattered on the pavement, gone as soon as he hit the ground.

"Anti-personnel measures engaged," the warning voice said.

The car swerved as more machine gun fire punched holes in its frame. It jumped forward. Then its back tire shredded and it fishtailed into Jon's path. The truck hammered the car into a spinning wreck.

In the live drone feed, Jon watched a boxy robot with six electromagnetic feet on spider legs crawling across the truck's roof. It sported twin-mounted JBB-333 machine guns on either side of its body. Those four barrels pitched down and opened fire on the car at his passenger door.

The driver slammed the brakes just in time, and even though the drone tracked the car, it yanked back and then across Jon's tail ahead of the bullets that ripped apart the pavement.

Bullets snapped high on his windshield now as the gunners in front of him turned their fire on the drone. A mothball crack popped into the windshield with a grinding crunch.

Hard clangs on the roof as the drone stomped to the truck's fore. It locked in place right above Jon and opened fire. The two cars in the side lanes swerved. One ducked back.

The one in the middle didn't have those options.

The back of the car disintegrated in a torrent of bullet holes.

The driver exploded blood against the inside of the windshield.

Tires flapped away in steel-belted ribbons.

The wreck fishtailed and skidded sideways, not going nearly fast enough.

Jon swerved and caught the front of the car in a hard glance, battering the already damaged front corner of the truck. He overcorrected to avoid running off the road and the bulky vehicle rocked up on two wheels for a long moment.

The drone skittered to the far side of the truck and anchored itself, shifted the balance of mass. The truck crunched to all fours and bounced its underbelly off the pavement.

Jon punched a call. "Friedy! Guion went silent on me. Get Steve to throw his cloak on me right now. I need to disappear!"

"Aren't you driving?"

"Not for long, I don't think."

"Yah. Okay." He disconnected.

Steve's cloak wouldn't work if it made the truck look like it was driving itself, but as soon as it stopped, he could vanish. At least that's what he understood. Jon blinked against the wind howling through his window as he wrestled with the stiffening wheel. He never felt it when Steve threw his cloak around him. The only way he knew when it took was Steve's say-so.

If Steve's cloak failed because Jon was still driving, would he try again? Was he willing to work that much?

A car zipped across the lanes in front of him. One of the surviving two. Its rear gunner was back in place, but instead of a rifle, he hoisted a large bore gun at the truck.

MA49 Grenade Launcher. Warning: Weapon ordinance can penetrate vehicle defenses.

"Goddamn it!"

Jon swerved.

Too early.

The gunner tracked and fired.

The drone shredded him. Blood sprayed the pockmarked car.

The drone exploded. The shockwave pushed the unbalanced truck over. It rocked up, sped along on two wheels, lost balance centimeter by centimeter.

It reached the point of no return.

The truck slammed onto its side and scraped along the ground with a long, anguished scream that only grated metal makes. Black asphalt blurred past Jon's open window. He bumped it. It tore the shirt and top layer of skin off his shoulder in an instant.

By the time he ground to a stop, every breath stabbed him in the side. He already felt bruises rooting deep along the slash of his seat restraint. Numb fingers pressed the release and dropped him against the door. He panted and winced.

Outside, he heard voices and the sounds of guns reloading.

24

Jon sat naked to the waist as Jack finished wrapping his torso. It was definitely Jack. Not only did Guion not have in-depth medical knowledge, but Jack had different body language: surgically precise with a dash of fussy.

"You're in luck," the demon said.

"I don't feel lucky right now."

"No, I imagine not. Abrasions and bruised ribs both carry a significant pain load. Still, they're the kinds of injuries I can treat effectively here. No need to risk breaking into that dog hospital you got yourself banned from." Jack spat the word "dog."

"Not a pet fan, Jack?"

"I dislike the unclean." He cut a hand-sized patch of gauze from a roll and smoothed it over Jon's shoulder. "That goes for animals as well as people."

"Good thing for me you've got me all nice and antiseptic."

Jack clucked. "Jests, Jonathan? You are not nearly as sterile as you think." He chuckled at Jon's expression. "Oh, have no fear. I've cleaned your wounds quite thoroughly. I refer more to your attitude. You are sloppy."

Jon frowned as Jack pressed tape around the borders of the gauze. "You sound like Guion."

"Indeed, he and I share much a mind. It's why we're such good partners. You should know your revelation about your indiscretion with spirits quite rattled him. Neither of us suspected you of being an alcoholic."

"I'm not." Jon's voice was flat as the floor. "It was a girl, a bad girl."

"Hmm," Jack said through his nose. "Most are."

Jon caught the demon's eyes. "It wasn't her fault. Tawni was a Hiver and had a bunch of damage from it. She . . . didn't know how to cope."

"White knight that you are, you stepped in to save the lass, but she ensnared you in some of her unseemly behavior."

Jon's sight drifted into the past. "She deserved help. She wasn't evil."

"Yes, yes. Let's jump past the predictable middle to the inevitable end." Jack waved a gloved hand. "She wasn't a bad person, but she was a bad influence and you had to let her go." He clutched his chest with both hands. "Oh, how the heart aches for the maiden you turned away."

"She OD'd."

"How fortunate for you."

"Fuck you, Jack. And fuck Guion if you're speaking for him too."

"I do give voice to our shared thoughts, though I will admit, he harbors more charitable feelings toward you than I do at this point."

"Funny, because he's a lot more charitable about you than I am too."

Jack cocked an eyebrow as he worked.

"He doesn't seem to have a problem with you being a killer like I do," Jon clarified.

"Women have been the ruination of men since Adam." He sniffed. "That hardly makes me a killer."

"Oh, get off it, Jack. Everyone knows it's you."

"Guion, most assuredly, does not."

"By choice, maybe?"

Jack paused, physically froze, his gaze turned inward. His sudden stillness sent a chill across Jon's exposed skin. "If I were the slaughterer of women in possession of any modicum of intelligence, I should apply my peccadilloes to our benefit." He turned his face to Jon, too close, the smile on his face mild and malicious. "Those harlots who steal the money you earn, perhaps?"

"Leave Malcolm and his family out of this."

Jack stood tall. "There we are. All finished. You'll need bed rest for some time." He scanned the apartment and wrinkled his nose. The sweet, foul scent of mixed food rot hung in the air like a fog, slicked every surface. "Best of luck with that." Jack walked to the door.

"Where are you going?"

"What we have now is a question of trust."

Jon stood with a grunt. "There's no question. I don't trust you."

"Not me, dear Jonathan. Guion. I've told you he finds your accusations baseless. You can accept his assessment, or you can call his judgment into question. That will, of course, throw your team dynamic into even more chaos." He turned to leave again.

"Get back here."

Jack snorted but didn't stop. "I said you could question Guion's judgment. I never granted you authority over my motions." He tipped an invisible hat.

Jon threw his gaze about and found the medkit on the

table next to him. A package of syringes glinted in the afternoon sun. He grabbed one and caught Jack high on the stairs, stabbed him in the neck with the needle and punched the plunger down.

Jack hissed and clapped a hand over the injection. He whirled on the staircase and stumbled a step, barely catching the banister. "You idiot. Sedative? Do you have any idea what dose you administered?"

Jack went slack before Jon answered. He collapsed and made a chunky backward tumble down the stairs filled with bangs and odd angles.

25

"nstall our biometrics monitoring app to get even better help." A "Buy Now!" icon flashed next to the doc bot's head. Jon shut the session down as the bot started to make another sales pitch.

"He gonna die?" Steve called from the couch.

"You calling dibs on the body?"

"Harsh, Jon-boy. Harsh." He swirled something imaginary in his mouth. "Also . . . maybe? I never tried longpork."

"Some other time. The concussion and bruising will slow him down a while, but he'll live."

Steve snickered. "Man, he is gonna be pissed."

Guion was. Pissed that Jon injected him. Pissed at why. Pissed that Jon called Malcolm about Jack's threat, especially when he heard how badly Malcolm reacted.

"He was tweaking you, Jon." He spoke like what he said was obvious.

"You didn't hear how sinister he was."

Guion tapped his head. "I hear him all the time. He's a logical man, not a scheming serial killer."

"Fuck that, Guion. Enough bullshit. You've been covering

for him since day one and there's more bodies on the pile all the time. Jack vivisected Malcolm's daughter—"

"Dissected," Guion said.

"What?"

The two sat at the folding table. Injuries and pain muted their responses. It shrank their gestures, softened their volume, and prevented them from storming off.

"Vivisection is performed when the person is still alive. Dissection occurs after the subject is dead." He stared at Jon's gaping face. "I heard you talking about it with Paula." Another pause. "And either way, Jack didn't do it."

"How's Jack an asset? What's he do?"

Guion gestured to Jon's bandages.

"He provides first aid one time and you're ready to be his second in a duel." Jon squinted. "I don't get it."

"Like you're an errand boy for him?" Guion pointed at Steve, who spilled popcorn in his lap as he watched them and munched.

"You're not serious. Steve keeps us hidden and he's proven his worth a thousand times over by now."

"Love you too, bro."

"What's Jack's price?" Jon said with a lean and a squint.

"Medical literature."

Jon started, blinked. "What?"

"That's right." Guion smirked with triumph. "Your demon wants to cram himself full of insta-food and attack us with gas that singes our hair." He pointed at Steve.

"Nah, man, that last part's just a bonus."

Guion turned the finger to himself. "Mine would rather gorge on knowledge. I need to read a certain amount every week. I don't understand most of what I track down, but he does."

Another pause.

"Bullshit."

Guion spread his arms. "It lets me feed him while staying here. I'm here all the time. Just like I've been saying." He pressed himself to his feet. "Do you get it now? Can we lay this to rest at last, because my head hurts and I'd like to go to sleep." He walked into the other room without waiting for an answer and left Jon with Steve for days.

Jon took that time to sleep and convalesce as well, when he wasn't making food runs for Steve. Even injured, the demon demanded Jon provide his meals, and since Friedy still hadn't brought the salami slicer online, that meant Jon still filled Steve's orders with theft. It wasn't quite Hell, but Steve was certainly his tormentor.

"No, dude, this is nothing like Hell. I'd be all cold and naked, not getting burning shit squirts from too many Atomic Burritos. Gluttony's one of the seven deadly. Third circle."

"Hell's like what Dante wrote?"

"Actually, no. I was just making a reference."

"I had no idea you were so well-read, Steve."

"Hardy har, asshole. Pass me that condiment bag."

"You don't have anything to put this stuff on." Jon handed over a milk-white plastic bag filled with cheap packets of generic ketchup, mustard, duck sauce, soy sauce, and mayo.

Steve didn't answer. He tore open the first and squirted it into his upturned mouth.

Jon grimaced at the spectacle as Steve worked his way through the next several packets. He worked methodically, falling into an easy rhythm.

"So if it's not Dante's Inferno, what's Hell like?"

"It sucks, of course." Steve squeezed a mayo packet dry, swished it around in his mouth, and made a heavy swallow. He paused and looked at Jon. "There was no line in the clouds and no trapdoor in front of the pearly gates. I just woke up there after I died. It was . . . really normal."

"You mean houses and cars and phones?"

"Not for me. What I mean is I think everyone gets their own Hell. I ran into others there, don't get me wrong, but I'll bet if you ask Jack, he was in a place different from me." He shook his head. "Don't ask me about whatever got into the little guy. A beast or parasite or some shit. Who knows where he dredged that up from."

Steve continued. "I woke up sitting in a dark room. Kinda reminded me of a classroom. There was a projector somewhere behind me, and a film played on a screen in front. Me. My life. A highlight reel. It didn't take me long to figure out what it was saying and where I was. I started to sweat over what was going to happen to me."

"Did they stitch you into a human centipede?"

Steve furrowed his brows and shook his head in a silent question.

"That's where they surgically attach your mouth to someone else's anus."

"Dude, fuck you. I'm glad you're not in charge down there. No, I never had to eat anyone else's shit. Just mine."

"What?"

"After the film, a door opened and I was free to go. I wandered around and found I was in a multiroom buffet. My stomach growled, so I grabbed a plate like everyone else and heaped all kinds of great looking stuff on it.

"You know the story of Tantalus, right? Hungry and thirsty all the time, up to his chin in water with fruit trees overhead and he can't reach any of it. Well, I had the hunger and thirst, but I could go get as much food as I wanted. The problem was none of it helped. It didn't matter how much I ate, I never felt any better." He took several bites out of a chocolate cake with peanut butter frosting.

"That's it? Your Hell was sitting down to an all you can eat and not coming away satisfied?"

"It's not like the service was bad. I felt like I was starving, and nothing helped. I ate until I was so full, I puked, and then I went back for more."

Jon shrugged. "That's a little worse, but it still seems like a slap on the wrist compared to all the eternal torment church people promise waits down there."

Steve held up a corn dog like a finger. "That was the first day. There were hours to the place, and I got shuffled out of there after a few more rounds of gorge and puke. They left me in a room. Real simple. A shadowy cube with a bed and a bucket. The same bucket I'd been throwing up into all day."

"That must have smelled great."

"It was even better after I pissed and shit out anything that I kept down from before. I remember thinking that at least the hunger was gone. I didn't sleep that night, but I felt a sense of relief." He chuckled. "I remember thinking maybe Hell wouldn't be so bad."

"Then what?"

"Morning came. So did the hunger. I was actually looking forward to hitting it again."

"Did you?"

"They got me, brought me back to the place, but all the food lines were empty. Instead, there was wait staff. They served me the same food." He shuddered.

Jon slapped his hands over his cheeks. "Oh no! You had to eat the same stuff two days in a row."

Steve shook his head. "You're not listening to me. They didn't serve me the same meals. They served me the same food. The exact same food."

They looked at each other in silence a moment. Jon blinked. "The bucket?"

Steve nodded. His eyes shone with extra tears. "And God help me, I was so hungry, I ate it." He pressed his lips together and shook his head. "It took me a few tries, but I finished it all. When it was empty, the hunger faded and they let me go back to my room with my empty bucket." He looked at the floor. "That night I filled it up again."

"Oh, shit."

Steve laughed through a sob. He nodded without looking up. "Yeah, exactly." He brought his head up with a sniff. "That night I figured it out. The whole system. I didn't get a break from the eating or the hunger to give me relief. It was all part of the torture. You know what the one thing worse than sitting in that dining hall vomiting my own re-shit shit was?"

Jon shook his head.

"The anticipation of having to do it. They gave me that break to give me a chance to dread it before I did it."

"That's awful."

Steve nodded. "Pretty sure that's the idea. Being here is better though. I'm not going to oversell it and say it's heavenly or some shit like that, but it's definitely a nice break."

Jon looked him up and down. "You don't look like you're taking a break."

"Are you kidding me? Do you know how long it's been since I got to eat food that's been processed by something other than my colon?" He crammed his mouth full with half a loaded hotdog, closed his eyes, and sighed as he chewed. "JonJon, I cannot tell you how good that feels."

Another few moments passed in silence. "What did you do, to get there I mean?"

"Don't you know you're not supposed to ask an inmate what he did? Everyone's innocent in the clink." Steve stared at Jon for a moment before cracking a grin. "Nah, I'm just fucking with you. You know I don't care." He took a deep breath and got serious again. "Dante didn't get it all wrong. I was a glutton, and that is a mortal sin."

"You got sent to Hell because you overate?"

"Uh-uh." Steve shook his head as he unwrapped an

Atomic Burrito. The chemicals inside the wrapper warmed it as he broke the seal, filling the room with the smell of industrial imitation Mexican food. "A glutton is someone who uses their God-given gifts to take. Just take. Give nothing back to the world but trash."

"That's . . . broad."

"I'll give you an example." Steve filled his mouth with a single bite then gestured with the burrito, dripping sauce and cheese on the couch and floor. "Let's say you were an unprecedented genius that understood emerging technology better than anyone else on the planet. You could help craft man-machine interfaces that make the digital world more accessible to the masses. That'd be a good thing."

He took another bite and continued to talk as he chewed. "Or you could horde your knowledge and use it to fuck with people you don't like.

"Mmm!" He was on a roll now. "Or like if you had a way with people, good at negotiations and rapport and all that stuff, but instead of advocating for folk and getting petty tech geniuses to make the world better, you sat as prom king of your own life." He pointed with the ragged end of the burrito. A glop of guacamole splattered the floor. "That would be a glutton too."

Steve smiled. "Damn, those were good. I should have been a teacher."

Jon sat numb. Minutes passed in silence as Steve hollowed out the wrapper and finished with a spicy belch that burned Jon's eyes. He sighed and patted his stomach. "I'm gonna be good for like an hour, but you'd be doing me a solid if you had the place stocked up by the time I'm ready again."

Jon did.

26

Jon was still wandering in dumb shock when Malcolm called, so he didn't greet the man with his typical joy. "Hey."

"Yeah, that sounds right. I need the little genius."

"You lost his contact?"

"I've got his contact." Malcolm frowned. "He ain't answering. I need you to reach him."

Jon rubbed his head. "Is he in trouble?" They couldn't afford more now.

"Not him. Me." Malcolm looked around. "Look man, I dropped a carload of fat stacks to get those guns. Ate up a lot of my savings."

"Yeah, and we delivered them."

Malcolm pressed his lips together, holding back words with effort. He took a sharp breath. "No, man, we didn't. The guns wound up in B7 hands, but they went out and got them themselves."

"That was me behind the wheel."

"You wanna advertise that? Because that truck shot the shit out of more than a few of them." He took a moment to calm himself. "They got the guns, but they had to get them. No delivery, so no payment."

"You're saying you don't have the capital to try this again."

"Pffff." Malcolm rolled his eyes. "SHOC^3's cracking down on highway travel for obvious reasons, and even if I could get something through, the B7s don't trust me to deliver after that bloodbath."

"That doesn't leave much."

"It don't leave nothing. I ain't got the money. I ain't got the trucks. I ain't got the buyers." He pinched his face and gave his head a single, solid shake. His face got larger as he leaned in. "You screwed me on this, Jon. I know you didn't mean to and I ain't got no hard feelings, but you put me in a hard spot and our little friend promised me something that I need now. This place is changing. You remember Phillip, my boy?"

"Sure."

"He's seventeen. Someone caps him, that's tragic, but that's something young men face. Rose was Phillip's age." He shook his head. "Women don't live in the same world. They never had to worry about shit like this. This town's gone from rough to evil."

"Okay. I'll go see him."

"Good. I know that technical stuff takes time and I don't want him to rush or anything . . . but I want him to rush."

<hr>

TRUE TO HIS WORD, JON DID GO TO FRIEDY, BUT INSTEAD OF pushing the man to get his corporate skimming program up and running, he let Friedy slip into VR and hammer away at the mysterious stack of nested files, Artificial Friedy his digital copilot. He tied the "Badass Hacker" bib on after swearing to Friedy he wouldn't, the ritual bringing him a chuckle before he sank into his thoughts again and paced between the daybeds in Nana Robin's sunroom.

His silence screwed Malcolm, screwed a friend. It wasn't something Jon came to easily, but as much as he hated to admit it, Guion was right. Their presence here destabilized Rockaway's delicate situation and made it worse for everyone. No one was better for their activity here, not even the team.

Then there was Steve and his lesson on sin. Skipping town for a safe corporate harbor wasn't exactly giving back to the world. He couldn't find a virtuous angle to running away. This wasn't about redemption, though. He'd settle for not hurting people anymore.

Baby steps.

He could save Malcolm. One word from him and Friedy would change focus instantly. Guion might have the plans, but Jon had Friedy. He wanted to—save Malcolm, that is. But if they gave him money and stayed, what were the odds that they'd bring some other calamity to his door?

Guion could put a number on it. Jon snorted without humor as a smile-frown hybrid twisted his lips.

So he let Friedy work, left Malcolm to twist, and let the guilt chew his brain.

"Project Irresistible." Friedy stood behind Jon with a shared AR window showing a block of text. "Every single bit has different security, but I cracked the first file. I've been piecing together a virtual repository with Artificial Friedy for the rest. We should have someplace safe and independent of physical devices when it comes time to negotiate. Plus, I'd like a safe place to run any applications in case there's malware I miss."

Jon smiled. It's exactly what Guion didn't want Friedy doing.

Fuck Guion.

"Alright, Friedy!" Jon held out his hand for Friedy to slap.

"You misplaced this again." Friedy stuffed the bib, wet side down, into Jon's hand with a grin.

"I see you needed it too. Oh, wait, you got a little something there." Jon wiped Friedy's chin.

Friedy slapped him away.

"What's in that first file?"

"Not much. For all the security it turns out to be a small data file. There's an address, a calendar, and that codename. Project Irresistible."

"Where's the address?"

"Beach 74th Street, right in the heart of B7 turf."

After the war on the highway, the B7s were more aggressive and better armed than ever.

He punched a call through to Guion and filled him in. He didn't want to wait to get home. "This is exactly what we need. A date, a place, and a mysterious name. Gentlemen, it's time we do what we do best." He grinned his infectious grin at them. "Let's find out what the hell is so valuable about this project."

27

The address was a voice box, a corporate oasis stamped into the middle of B7 territory for the express purpose of controlling the government. Three little urban islands, each with a swimming pool, tennis courts, and a plastic playground, nestled in a tiny park flanked by oblong residential towers that bristled with armored patios.

A relatively new innovation from the corporate social development divisions, voice boxes were a way of maximizing employee utilization. When an employee became unable to work at sufficient performance metrics due to age, injury, or any other reason, they got the opportunity to enter a drawing. Winners relocated to voice boxes like these and had all their expenses covered for the rest of their lives. Corporate offices helped them sign up for social safety net programs like food stamps and housing assistance, and then gave them boosters to each as long as they lived where the company told them to. As a bonus, they received unlimited access to all the company streams. All they needed to do to claim their winnings was allow the company to vote in their stead for all elections and ballot measures. Companies had been on a massive land grab to buy or build high-capacity housing units in key areas ever since the first one came online. A.W.E. owned this one, based on the SHOC^3 patrols that secured the building.

Multifamily houses radiated out in all directions from the voice boxes, carved and diced into ever more units over the years. Some housed B7s, but even in the heart of gangland, most of the homes belonged to poor folk stuck in a rough neighborhood. A few yawned vacant, turned into squats.

The team camped in one of those, across the street from one of the short towers. After they rented the squat for a couple of days with a few bottles of cheap synthetic booze, the three operators plus Steve settled in for a stakeout. The place stank with a different aroma from home. Here, dank and mold and urine slapped to the throat and hung on with a thick feeling none of them could swallow. But it had a couch that was both intact and protected with a tarp, and a window low-key and large enough to be an excellent lookout point.

They noted the basics right away. SHOC^3 patrolled the perimeter in regular, if infrequent, sweeps. This made coming and going safer; it did not make it safe. No one had a job. Stepping outside was a gamble. This made pedestrian traffic light. Still, they did need to shop for essentials, so people did come and go.

When they did, they unlocked the building by punching a code into the air. AR made perfect sense here. A keypad, palm reader, or any other device that required a physical presence outside the building wouldn't survive the neighborhood's casual vandalism. AR could be painted on the wall or inside the bullet-resistant glass.

If it was AR though, it lacked a few vital components. That they couldn't see the reality augment that the residents unlocked the door with wasn't weird if the building's augments were set to private. But none of the people wore glasses or gloves or carried a MIU on them.

Implants. Everyone living in these towers, hundreds of them, all sported full five MIUs.

It didn't fit. High-end implants in an otherwise impoverished community. They took public transit to get to and from their homes. They shopped for their food concentrate at convenience stores that armed their cashiers. They wore the same worn, corporate cast-off clothing, with clashing logos advertising events like the Sales Focus Team Retreat, Summer VR Experience Expo, or the Customer Appreciation Summit in energetic pastels, all from years before they started printing on smart cloth that could update the logos and dates.

And yet they all had MIUs wired directly to their brains. As much as the team debated alternatives, they kept coming back to that. Why A.W.E. would incur that cost, what benefit it provided, eluded them, but they could come up with no other plausible explanation. So they sat and watched and waited for the next date on the calendar.

Steve settled himself on his new couch during that time and refused to make food runs, leaving Jon to duck out every now and again. Guion bristled every time Steve interrupted their surveillance, and Steve answered by dropping wadded wrappers and empty cardboard cartons on the floor. Jon tried to gather them before they accumulated. He only partially succeeded.

Friedy spent an hour on the line with Nana Robin each day, and when Thursday rolled around and it was obvious they'd be spending the weekend here, he begged Malcolm to help her. With the salami slicer in place, Malcolm relaxed a bit. Besides, it was Nana. Of course one of his girls could help out. Daylight hours only, for obvious reasons.

Nana later reported Tiffany was a lovely young woman,

an absolute dear who, while no replacement for Friedy, got her through another Shabbos.

On the first date on the decrypted calendar, the group walked the perimeter of the building one at a time in shifts to cover all angles. Then, starting around lunchtime, groups of residents left, took the bus, and returned laden with greasy paper bags. They continued like that for hours. Close to dark, Guion directed Jon to get a good look at the bags a group of returning tenants carried.

"They're all from Blast Burger," Jon said. "And a lot of it too. They each had at least three bags each."

Blast Burger, where we fully load more than our burgers.

Guion nodded. "They all left at the same time, and they came home at the same time, which suggests they went to the same place."

"We've been seeing groups of people come and go all day," Friedy said.

"None of them talked," Jon said. "These weren't groups. They were individuals who all got the idea to go visit the same food dispensary at the same time, but didn't come up with it together."

Gunfire and sirens, ever-present background noise here, climbed as they waited for the next date on the calendar. According to Nana Robin, it wasn't contained in the '70s either. The violence was starting to crawl into the upper blocks. Friedy called her midday on the next calendar date.

That day wasn't a repeat of the last. People didn't leave in groups of individuals and come back together yet separate. No one left at all. The door sat heavy and locked and abandoned. They saw lights in the windows, both the steady glare of lamps and the flickering glow of holoprojectors.

Guion asked Jon to break into the building to have a closer look, and Jon slipped across the street without a word of complaint. He disappeared into the tenement's shadow.

"Friedy, I have such a story for you," Nana Robin said.

"I'm all ears." He smiled when he talked with her.

She laughed. "I was coming back from the Snack Time SuperCenter and this trio of boys tried to rob me."

"They what?" Friedy vaulted to his feet.

"Hey, Friedy, I need you to patch me into the building's AR. I'm getting a weird feeling here," Jon said on another line.

"Oh, don't worry. I'm fine," Nana Robin said.

"That doesn't sound like a 'don't worry' story."

"Friedy," Jon said.

"Yah. Working on it."

"I was scared at first too. But it all worked out okay."

"Did Tiffany have a gun?"

"It's Wednesday, Friedy. Tiffany won't come for another couple of days. I was hoping you'd be back by then."

"Friedy," Jon said again.

"You're patched in." Friedy swapped lines. "I hope so too, but I can't tell yet. So what happened?"

"It was Pal. They got close and tried to lean over me to be scary."

"Sounds scary."

"Oh shit," Jon said over a group channel.

"It was scary."

"What did you find?" Guion said.

"But Pal was scarier." Nana laughed a long, slow string of chuckles. "One of them grabbed me."

"He *what*?"

"They're all watching the same stream," Jon said.

"Pal had the same reaction. You should have seen him, Friedy. Nearly tore the crotch off that boy." She chuckled some more.

"They're all using holoprojectors, probably augmenting the stream with their MIUs," Jon said. "The whole building is echoing with the same shows. I can hear it behind every door I put an ear to."

"I think Tiffany should do your shopping for you from now on. At least until I get back."

"I'm an old woman. I'm not a cripple, and I'm not about to have someone else do work I can do for myself." He heard her scowl in her voice. "Besides, she doesn't have Pal. Why would we want to send that girl into a situation that's too dangerous for us to go ourselves?"

"It's an A.W.E. voice box. They probably only have access to A.W.E. subsidiary streams," Guion said.

"What's spooking me is that they're watching the streams in the same way. They laugh in unison when there's canned laughter. They scream together at the same jump scares. I even heard them all crying when a heartstring moment rolled up."

"Okay, fine. You're right. Then we should look into getting you a gun."

"A gun? Me? Don't be ridiculous."

"I'm not being ridiculous. I'm serious. You need more protection while I'm gone. I can arrange it."

"This sounds like the next step up from the Blast Burger runs," Guion said.

"You have no idea. I've been wandering around inside this place for an hour. The whole building isn't tuning in to the same program at once. The whole experience is synchronized. They all switch streams at the same time. They all react the same way. It's creepy, and I'm coming out."

"Friedrich, can you access the residents' MIUs to see if they're using the same augments on the feeds?" Guion said.

"I'll have someone send a pistol today. We can get you a MIU and load a training program onto it to get you ready."

"Friedrich! Put the call to grandma away and get to work. There's time for that later."

"Hold one second, Nana." Friedy muted his line. "No, there isn't." He tapped an icon in his AR display and his own face erupted in his vision.

"Yah, Friedy," Artificial Friedy said. "I've not yet cracked open the rest of the files."

"Pause it. I'm sending you an address. I need you to gather the information on the MIUs used there. Get it all."

Pause.

"I'm reading 593 units."

"Get it all."

"Yah, okay." Artificial Friedy fuzzed out.

"There you go," Friedy said to Guion.

"Your bot should be on the files, and you should be hacking those MIUs."

"You don't like it. I don't like you. We're both unhappy about things. Let's go back to ignoring each other, hmmm?" He opened the other line. "Sorry Nana, I'm back."

"I don't want a gun."

"I understand, but this is necessary for now."

"Necessary? For what?"

"To keep you from getting hurt."

"Then you better keep that gun away from me. I'm an old woman. I'm likely to pull a muscle from the kick." Nana chuckled again. "No, Friedy, if you want to keep me safe, you get yourself home sometime soon."

They went home the next night, but Guion insisted Friedy come back with them to the apartment to help analyze the data they collected. They bolted their apartment door behind them and Jon handed Steve a plastic bucket filled with Meal Mash: bulk vegetables and vat-grown meat mixed into a batch of whipped potatoes.

"Everything they did involved A.W.E. or a subsidiary," Friedy said. "That's exactly what you'd expect from a voice box. I don't get why A.W.E. would want to kill us over that."

Guion and Jon looked at each other. "You'd know if you paid attention," Guion said.

"To what?"

"It's mind control," Jon said.

Friedy looked at them. Guion nodded.

"The people in that building are being run," Jon said. "The first day on the calendar, they all went out for insta-food. Every group that went out went to the same place, and they all got way too much for a normal meal.

"The next date, they all switched from program to program together without talking to one another, and all reacted to the same cues the same way. Hey, AF."

Artificial Friedy fuzzed into their group AR session. His smile beamed. "Yah, Jon."

"Don't call him that," Friedy said.

"What did you find on the building's MIUs?"

Artificial Friedy got serious. "I see identical use in every way. They had the same apps loaded, had the same options configured, engaged them at the same time in the same way for every stream."

Jon shook his head. "No group of people that large is that homogeneous. They're being controlled."

28

Their findings turned Guion into a man possessed. They only had a whiff of Project Irresistible, a taste of its reach. It was big. Revolutionary. World-changing. Guion filled the days with theories. A new form of AR advertising. A tighter full five MIU interface. Next-gen subliminal programming.

It wasn't Project Irresistible that excited Guion though. It was how much it would excite the Oceana Combine. Hope made Guion into a child doing his best not to ask *Are we there yet?* every five minutes. It took genuine effort.

He insisted Friedrich work in the apartment now. They couldn't afford distractions, and the old woman was that. Friedrich protested, but to Guion the answer was obvious: finish unlocking and analyzing the files and he'd be free to spend his time however he liked. He couldn't imagine a better incentive. Friedrich had a temper tantrum. He had several. Of course.

Jon negotiated a temporary truce that got Friedrich working in tandem with his virtual clone, and Guion let him think he was successful. Friedrich, of course, didn't possess the rationality that made negotiation possible. Guion saw that even if Jon couldn't, so he gave Friedrich that logic in the form of meals spiked with some of his precious Evenflo. Bereft of most of his emotions, Friedrich became obsessed with the computerized puzzle that defied him like nothing else he'd ever encountered. He was determined to beat it. By the end of the first day, he'd taken to spending most of his time in VR to better see the problem from all angles.

Luckily for Guion, Friedrich's lifelong restricted diet, small size, and sensitive system meant a little went a long way with him. Guion administered micro-doses and didn't have to do it daily. It worked so well that even though Friedrich took daily calls from Nana Robin, he didn't get riled up from them and remained dedicated to the task at hand.

It all went so well, which meant it had to go wrong. Jon caught him spiking Friedrich's food one afternoon.

"I was wondering why you've been so eager to serve him." Jon surprised him as he pinched some ground Evenflo into a cup of noodles.

Despite himself, Guion started. He looked at Jon leaning against the kitchen doorway, arms crossed, accusations on his face. "I had no idea you were there."

Jon tossed his head back toward the living room. "That's the gift I pacted for."

Guion scowled as he grabbed the styrofoam cup off the counter and made for the door. "You're using your gifts against the team now?"

"That's rich given that special seasoning you're serving." Jon didn't move as Guion approached. He blocked the doorway with his body.

"I don't know what—"

"Yes, you do. Let's skip the bullshit where you deny it and I say I watched you do it. Run it through your tac implant. It only ends one way, so let's jump right to it." He rocked forward while still leaning his shoulder against the doorway. "What did you put in there?"

Guion looked from Jon to the noodles as he considered his options. He didn't run it through the implant though. He handled the calculations himself. "Evenflo."

Jon's eyes went wide. "The deadener?"

"That's a bit dramatic. It mutes emotional responses. It doesn't kill them."

Jon popped off the door and leaned back to watch Friedrich work the encrypted files in AR. He sat in a folding chair and stared into an invisible display in front of him, fingers alive in the empty air. He was calm, no fidgets or ticks, radiating intense focus. He only came this far into the world because he anticipated food soon. After he ate, he'd disappear back into full immersion VR. He'd been like that all morning. He'd been like that most of the week.

"You can't argue its efficacy," Guion said when Jon returned his attention to the kitchen.

Jon slapped the noodles out of Guion's hands. The broth splashed the refrigerator door as the noodles fell to the floor with a wet slap.

"Dibs!" Steve appeared between them and picked at the stringy pile, sucking up their length as he chewed.

Jon smashed Guion across the jaw before he recovered from Steve's entrance. His chrome arm hit like a lead pipe. "You asshole!"

Guion staggered, caught himself on the counter before he collapsed all the way to the floor. Jon hauled him up before he got his own feet and threw him into the wall.

"You slipped him drugs?"

Guion again caught himself before he fell, this time braced against the wall. He blinked and shook his head clear. "You make it sound like I hooked him on narcotics."

Jon reached for him again, but this time Guion was ready.

He slapped Jon's hands aside and slipped sideways, letting the man's momentum push past him. He spun and kicked the back of Jon's knee, then shoved his head into the wall. Jon grunted and sagged.

Guion leaned over him, panting. "You should know by now that I don't take capricious action. Yes, I dosed him, but only after careful calculations."

Jon rose straight into a tackle. He threw a shoulder into Guion's gut, cinched him around the waist, and drove him across the kitchen into the opposite wall, half-slipping in a stray trail of broth along the way. Steve still knelt in the middle of the tiny room slurping up what remained of the meal.

Guion grabbed a skillet on the counter, but Jon slapped a hand over his wrist before he got any further. They tensed, locked each other in place for a long moment. Jon pumped a quick fist into Guion's stomach. He doubled over, and Jon slammed his hand on the counter. Already weakened from the uppercut, the blow rattled the skillet from Guion's fingers.

"Careful calculations?" Jon grabbed Guion's collar and yanked him back to look him in the face. "You're a doctor now?"

Guion didn't say anything. The two panted in pain at one another with eyes locked. Jon's face fell and he shook his head, a slow back and forth. "Jack? Are you kidding me?" Anger tightened Jon's face again. He threw Guion to the floor and kicked him.

"He's a doctor," Guion muttered.

"He's a demon!"

"I pacted for a professional doctor. I trust his knowledge."

Jon frowned deeper. "How did you account for his brain?"

"Friedrich's MIU still has the results of the initial B7 bio scan they performed. Jack and I worked from that."

"So you guessed based on a field scan."

Guion pushed off the counter and stood on his own two feet, steady now. "I didn't have top-notch detailed scans and blood chemistry to work out proper dosing. Jack and I had to do the best with what we had."

"What if you killed him?"

"The odds of that weren't high."

Jon bristled with rage. He lunged at Guion and dragged him to the door, shoved him onto the phone booth landing.

"Take a walk, asshole. A good, long one. If you come back before I've cooled off, I'm likely to kill you."

A sense of unease took root in Guion's gut when he hefted the wide garage door and let it rumble back to the concrete with him on the wrong side of it. He picked his way through the maze of cars crammed into the driveway, head and eyes moving much faster than his feet.

"Come on, you're acting like an agoraphobe. You walked these streets when you found that apartment in the first place, and you wandered in from a lot farther than the curb."

Except the neighborhood was different from when they arrived weeks ago. Armored humvees replaced SHOC[3] squad cars, and they made a lot more lazy passes down the blocks now. Aerial drones buzzed overhead every few minutes. It wasn't all paramilitary. People still drove and walked to the local shops, but they did it rushed and hushed. Pressure built in the Rockaways. They were headed for an explosion, and no one wanted to be out in the open when it blew.

Guion took a step toward the boulevard. Just one. When a SHOC[3] humvee cruised past, he stopped, stood rock still, then turned and headed for the beach. An offshore spill littered the shore with a crop of dead fish and filled the air with a mix of burning petrochemicals and rot, which meant even less pedestrian traffic than normal. It also meant he didn't have to wander too far from the apartment.

He sank to the sand and leaned back against the concrete wall that kept the sand from blowing into the street, rested his head against the poured stone, and blew a slow breath out through his lips. A few minutes later and he hadn't moved, hadn't opened his eyes.

Truly, Guion, if it bothers you this much, we can go back to the apartment.

"Did you somehow miss what happened up there?"

Jack chuckled. *Are you concerned Jonathan will manhandle you again? I can assist with that, you know, give you performance enhancements so that you'd far outclass him.*

"I'm actually more concerned about distracting Friedrich with another confrontation. If we dosed him right, he'll be dialed into that project for at least the rest of the day. I have a more pedestrian question. Where the hell were you in that fight?"

Guion! Surely you don't mean to suggest that I take unbidden action within your flesh sans invitation. I'm appalled.

"Is that your cheeky way of saying you can't do something without my invitation?"

That is an adequate description of our arrangement. You were quite clear in our negotiations that I could reside within you but was not to displace you.

"And you interpreted that as not giving me boosts in a crisis?"

Are you changing the definitions of our terms? Our contract is inviolate, but if I have misunderstood vital clauses, you need merely illuminate me.

"You can feel free to boost me whenever you think I could use it."

Noted. Are we to return now?

Guion rocked his head back and forth across the grooved concrete. "There's nothing gained in a rematch. Let Friedrich work. This is the first real progress we've made since getting here."

And they were progressing. They had a line on what Project Irresistible was, why its leak threw A.W.E. into a frenzy, what it might mean to Oceana. Properly oriented, Friedrich ground down their security measures so it was just a matter of time now. They'd be out of here soon enough. He let that realization merge with the wet whisper of the waves at low tide to form a soothing cocoon. It insulated him from the tension of the neighborhood behind him and though he didn't open his eyes, he smiled with his head against the wall.

In time his spirits rode high enough that he needed to share. He propped himself taller against the wall and punched Griffin's number.

"Guion! Is that the hint of a smile in your voice?" She smiled. It beamed. "I don't know if I've ever heard you so happy."

"A joke?"

"Certainly not. You've got a whole three tones worked into your voice. You're downright effulgent."

"I'm coming in."

"To Oceana?"

He nodded. "I can't say when yet, but soon. The recruiter's going to take us, Griffin. They can't say no to what we've got."

A look came over her face. "Is it that good?"

"We don't have the details yet, but it's big. If I'm right, it could revolutionize Oceana's entire business model, supercharge their brands."

That look stayed.

"Why do you look unconvinced?"

"You're still not watching the streams, are you? They've

made a series all about hunting you." She pointed through the screen. "You, specifically."

"They can't find us, and we're not going to be here much longer. Friedrich's working on cracking the files right now, and as soon as I've got a clearer picture of what we have, I'll ask you to contact acquisitions."

The look stayed, but it cracked a bit. Reluctant hope poking through the fear. "It sounds big, and if it's locked up tight enough to give even Friedy problems, it's definitely worth something." The look locked back in place. "But Guion, you've got to cool some of this heat. These shows have made you into terrorist serial killers. Plagues have killed fewer people than your team has according to the narrative they're spinning."

Guion frowned and shook his head. "Who cares? You're telling me Oceana can't give us new identities and facial sculpts?"

She mirrored his expression even though she couldn't see it. "Of course we can. The point isn't whether they can hide you, it's how hot a property you are. If A.W.E. is spending all this capital to turn you into the worst thing to happen to the eastern seaboard in a century, the risk in acquiring you—"

"—outweighs anything we could possibly offer."

"Now you've got it," she said with a nod. "It sounds like you've stumbled into something almost priceless, but until something takes A.W.E.'s attention off you, you're too much of a liability."

Guion cursed and ran a hand over his close-cropped hair. He thought. She let him.

"I don't know how to redirect them. Boulliver's whole reason for deployment here is us. I can't imagine how to run a false flag big enough to pull him off our trail."

"You're looking at this wrong." Griffin was all business now, with that look of focus that he found more attractive than her smile. It meant she was going to push him to places he wouldn't find on his own. "You said he can't find you."

Guion shook his head. "Despite Friedrich's best efforts, we've proven invisible. He won't track us down."

"And you can't hurt him."

Another head shake. "Not in any meaningful way. We don't have the resources."

"That means this isn't a direct confrontation. Don't look to run an op against him. You need to ruin the streams that push your story."

He screwed up his face. "You mean run a counter-marketing campaign?"

"Exactly. Ruin their story. Torch Boulliver's reputation so they have to replace him. Introduce a new boogeyman. Something that pulls resources away from the manhunt project or peels off some of their attention. They'll still hunt you—"

"—but it won't be such a dedicated effort and that redistributes the risk reward ratio for our recruitment."

Now her smile beamed. "I always loved when we got so in sync that we finished—"

"—each other's sentences."

Griffin laughed. "That one doesn't count. It—"

"—was too obvious?"

Another laugh. "That one too. Ass."

They sat in the levity's afterglow for a few chuckles before Guion's face fell and his voice turned serious again. "I'm a team lead. I draft missions to infiltrate secure facilities and perform corporate espionage. I don't know anything about brand warfare."

"Guion, you're a boosted tactical genius. Are you telling me you can't figure out how to tank someone on the Grid?"

"One of the reasons I've been so successful is that I never try to cover an area I'm unqualified to handle. I recruit the experts I need for each op." He paused, looked over his shoulder. "Maybe there's someone I can talk to."

GUION RETURNED HOME, BUT INSTEAD OF CLIMBING THE NARROW steps, he rapped on the door at their base. Paul opened it almost immediately. He did a poor job of keeping the surprise off his face.

"I need your help," Guion said.

Paul blinked. "With what?"

"I need some pointers on how to wage a marketing war."

Paul huffed a chuckle. "You want to take on the manhunt stream?"

"Jon mentioned that you used to work in corporate marketing."

"Yeah?" He slouched against the doorframe and crossed his arms. "He tell you how that worked out?"

"I just need a few pointers," Guion said.

"No, you don't." Paul shook his head.

Guion blinked. "Yes, I do. I don't know how to conduct this kind of operation."

Paul shrugged off the door and stood upright. "So if I wanted to break Paula out of A.W.E.'s downtown facility, you could give me a short bullet list and I could go do it?"

Guion screwed up his face. "No, of course not."

"So what makes you think I can give you a few pointers and you can take on an entire megacorporate media team?"

"It can't be that complicated."

"No?" Paul shrugged. "If you say so, since you know so much."

Guion sagged, sighed. "Of course you're right." He gripped his temples. "I don't suppose you'd be willing . . . ?"

"I checked SHOC^3's listings. Paula's got a buyout clause."

Guion looked up at him. "We don't have that kind of budget."

"Let's talk, Guion." Paul stepped aside and let him into the one-room efficiency.

"Lucky for you Pepe's napping out back, so there's room for you in here." Paul pulled a pair of chairs from their wall hooks and unfolded them. "I know you don't have money. If you did, Jon wouldn't have started working security at Paula's clinic. But you do have assets, tangible and not, that can spring her."

Guion crossed both his legs and arms as he leaned back in the stiff resin chair. "Even if we break her out, you'll be on the run just like we are." He shook his head. "Look, I know you miss her—"

"No, you don't."

"Actually, I think I do." Guion unfolded and leaned forward until his elbows rested on his knees. "I used to have somebody, and I've been thinking about her a lot more. I've been talking to her a lot more." Guion took a deep breath. "She's in a different corporation and I miss her. We're close to getting out of here. I'm close to seeing her again, and I feel . . ."

Guion looked Paul square in the face. "I'm not going to pretend to know what you're going through. I never got as far as marriage and losing her put me on a hard habit of these." He held up the cube.

"Paula's not my wife."

"Oh. The way you two—"

"We're as good as married. It's just not official. We never saw the need to pay the money for a license."

"What about certifying your union before God?" Guion asked in a British accent.

Paul shrugged. "Neither of us are religious. It wasn't important. We didn't need a piece of paper or a priest to tell us what we are to each other." He sighed. "Unfortunately, that leaves us with fewer rights and protections in situations like this. I don't get visitation during her indentured servitude with SHOC^3, for example." He fixed Guion with a look. "Which is why I need to buy her out. I'm not waiting eight years for her to earn to completion."

"So what are we talking about here? Because you don't have that much money and neither do I."

Paul pointed. "No, but you've got tech and expertise that just doesn't exist here. You might know how to use it to crack secure facilities, but I can show you how to use it to fight the kind of war you need to fight right now."

Guion ran the numbers. Not great, but not bad, and he had no better option besides. "What do you get out of this?"

Paul smiled. "Before I take you to war, I'm going to show you how to use those things to run a fundraising scam."

29

f Guion was overbearing before, their initial findings on Project Irresistible made him unbearable. Friedy stepped in alongside his electronic clone in efforts to crack the remaining files, but he expected to do it from Nana Robin's house. He'd been away for two weeks. They continued to speak daily, and by the end of their stakeout worry stained her prior good humor. Things were getting worse.

Guion didn't care. Guion didn't want Friedy distracted. Guion thought he could keep Friedy more tightly focused on the file crack by keeping him here. Guion was an asshole and an idiot.

Jon tried. He really did. That even he couldn't sway Guion said everything about their old team lead's obsession.

Friedy agreed for the first few hours, extremely unhappy about the arrangement. He went along out of habit, forgetting he was the strongest of the three now and could leave whenever he wanted.

By the time he remembered, he found he didn't care so much anymore.

He settled into working the mysterious Matryoshka-style

files. It took twenty minutes for him to determine he'd gotten lucky with his initial crack, nothing more. He got it right one time, one non-reproducible time.

Another hour showed him why: the passkeys weren't static values. They were fluid things, shifting definitions in a pattern he'd yet to decipher. He not only needed the right value, he needed it at the right time. He shook his head at the complexity. Even a properly credentialed person would struggle to get into these.

It's not that he didn't care about Nana Robin anymore. He still had all the love and concern for her that he always did, but he couldn't feel it as much. Friedy wanted to. A part of him clawed and yanked at the safe that locked those feelings away.

He dove into the work. After a day he shifted to VR to speed his process. After all, in AR he still needed to manually manipulate the interface. In VR, everything happened at the speed of thought. Why be slowed by his hands? It meant he couldn't talk to anyone but Artificial Friedy, but AF was the only one who could keep up with him now, so AF was the only one he was interested in hearing from.

That wounded him a little. Nana Robin still called every day, and despite his obsession, he accepted the call. He didn't stop working for those times, and he only gave her a sliver of his concentration. She was scared, and that locked-away piece of him ached to give her comfort. Friedy's face twitched from it sometimes.

He worked through several meals, burned through several theories when Jon and Guion in a rare moment of agreement insisted he couldn't continue like this. Friedy could work all day every day if he wanted to, but he needed to eat regularly to keep his strength up.

Friedy proposed a regular meal schedule. He'd come out of VR twice per day and they'd have something waiting for him. He'd eat in AR, slowing but not stopping the work, and then return to full immersion so he could continue at pace.

Nana Robin called again. She was pretty sure a small group of B7s followed her home from the store. They didn't come close, didn't touch her, but now they knew where she lived.

It wasn't a rotating series of passkeys. It was a derived value calculated from a formula he'd yet to unspool. The rabbit hole bored deeper.

He told Nana Robin to call SHOC[3], but they replied that the war in the lower blocks tied up much of their manpower, and the units assigned to the upper neighborhood were busy hunting down a serial killer. Unless there was an actual break-in attempt or threat, they wouldn't allocate resources to it.

The worry in her voice put a crack in that cage. Why couldn't he peel himself away from this for the fifteen minutes it took to walk to Nana Robin's? He could see to her safety and pick this up just as easily from her house.

If Friedy read the files right, even with the formula in hand, the passkey rotation rate spun by with such speed that no one could enter a proper value in time. How could a person possibly access these files?

Time didn't mean anything in the virtual world, not because of the environment but because of Friedy's tunnel vision. He only acknowledged the chimes on his meal timer. Otherwise, the only time he paid attention to was the cycle rate on the file security. So he didn't know how long it had been when Nana Robin called him again.

"Friedy! Friedy! They're at the door! I hear them banging!" Pal barked and snarled so much he had to concentrate to make out her words.

"Who? The B7's? They're knocking?"

"Not knocking. They're going to kick it in. Even with the

deadbolts, I hear the wood starting to give." Fear choked her voice. "Friedy, please. SHOC^3 isn't going to come. I don't know what they want, but I'm so scared."

She was. He could hear it, and he realized he'd never heard that from her before. Nana Robin lived life sure of things, confident, not touched by doubt or fear. He loved that about her. He loved that she used that strength to make him feel safe at his lowest. Now there she was, crying and begging for that same strength and comfort from him.

With his thoughts diverted, he missed a security protocol as he worked. His MIU locked, overclocked, and burst into flame.

"Shit!" Friedy yelled in surprise. He threw the thing down the hall.

"What happened, man?" Jon popped his head out of the kitchen, saw the flaming MIU, and threw it in the sink. He ran some water over the slagged unit until the fire sputtered out.

"Nana's in trouble." Friedy rolled to his feet and loped for the door. "I've got to go."

Jon stepped into the hallway. "Alright, I'll—"

Friedy slammed Jon with a two-hand shove that rocketed him into the depths of the small kitchen and hammered him into the wall. He snarled. Bared his teeth. "If Guion has a problem, tell him that."

Friedy shoved open the door and bounded down the stairs.

THE SUN FELL BEHIND THE HORIZON BEFORE FRIEDY REACHED THE corner. Late evening, not quite night, with an inky blue sky and heavy cloaks of shadow over the neighborhood. He could see, but not far and not well. The streetlights all sat dark and dead for blocks around.

He heard them first. The whole block heard them. They had to. A group of B7s clustered on Nana Robin's porch. One stomped the door over and over while the others cheered him on or threatened the old woman. From inside, Pal snarled and barked.

Friedy broke into a run. He dug deep into his soul and grabbed the beast harder than ever, ready to rip it forward.

His breath deepened and his lungs expanded. The sprint squeezed his chest, but animalistic vigor drove it off.

He stooped, ready to lope forward on all fours.

He howled and got their attention, got them to stop working the door.

He felt a surge of strength.

He felt a surge of speed.

. . . He felt a surge of hunger.

Friedy slammed to a dead stop. He gripped the beast and held it back. He rescinded the invite, but now roused and released from its cage it didn't want to return. If he tore those men apart, would he stop with them? Would the beast spare Nana Robin?

He grunted as he wrestled for control. He staggered and fell in front of her house.

They sauntered off the porch as he struggled to his feet and struggled to keep the beast in. They laughed and spread out around him.

"You some wolfman or something?"

"Shitty wolfman."

More laughs.

Friedy stood. He chained the beast, but maybe he could tap it a little bit. He glanced around. Five men. Young. All different builds. All armed with something.

No problem. He'd done this before.

"You can leave." Friedy tried to let the beast peek out through his words, but it slavered at the tiny bit of freedom and he had to clamp down on it. Instead of sounding primal, he spoke like he was constipated.

More laughter.

"Yeah, no shit we can. And we will. When we're done." Unlike everyone else who wore short sleeves, this guy sported a denim jacket. He gave Friedy a light shove. "Do we need to beat your ass before we get the old bitch?"

Friedy lashed out with a wild swing, hand like a claw, but without the beast it was just a hand. He slapped the man across the face.The rest of the circle erupted into guffaws punctuated with "oooooh!" and thigh slaps.

Multiple sets of arms snagged Friedy from behind. He struggled, but they held him like iron. The leader punched him in the gut. It smashed Friedy's breath out and locked his stomach in a cramp that didn't let him get another. His legs turned to noodles, but the iron arms held him up.

Another fist. Spots danced in his vision and he felt the desperation of drowning clawing at his mind. He couldn't breathe. He needed to breathe, but he couldn't breathe.

Barks. Growls.

"Oh shit!" The leader fell forward and the circle broke apart. The iron arms disappeared. He collapsed to the asphalt.

"The motherfucker's got my leg. Get him off! Get him off!"

The other beast of 148th Street. Pal. Nana must have let him out while Friedy had their attention. He had one of them by the kneecap and if he kept wrenching his head back and forth like that, he'd rip it free any moment.

The leader stepped up for a big kick to the dog's gut. Friedy tried to tackle him but wound up hugging him with arms and legs like he was getting a piggyback ride. He slapped a hand over the man's eyes and wrenched his head back, trying to take his balance.

"Man, get the hell off me." He grabbed Friedy's arm and threw him over his shoulder. Friedy slammed the sidewalk. The concrete collision banged his sight out of focus, and three stomps on his face left him near blind with pain pushing weird angles into his nose and mouth.

He struggled to get up, to get back into the fight, but he didn't know where he was. He didn't know which way was up. He didn't feel like he was in his body, didn't know how to move it right.

He heard a meaty thump and a yelp, then a voice. "That's right. Come on, motherfucker."

Pal growled and barked again, then came the snarls from a full mouth. He had someone, but they weren't screaming.

"Light him!"

A ganger pulled a squeeze bottle from his baggy pocket, popped the nozzle, and doused Pal. Accelerant. Friedy smelled the sharp chemical tang from here. Pal's tight white curls sopped it up.

A different B7 produced a lighter. He popped the top and sparked it.

Friedy fought to his feet and stumble-ran into him, threw a shoulder check into the man's back as he collapsed. The ganger hit the ground. The lighter snuffed out and spun into the dark.

Pal ripped the denim sleeve off the leader's jacket. He threw it away and lunged again. He bit meat. He wrenched and pulled again.

Screams.

The guy with the lighter got up and kicked Friedy in the face. He kept kicking him as Friedy balled up on the ground.

Mr. Lighter still beat Friedy with his shoes as the ganger with the squeeze bottle pulled out a lighter of his own. He shot a spurt of accelerant through the flame. The puff of fire splattered on Pal's back and he erupted with a whoosh and drawn-out yelp. He convulsed on the ground, a riot of desperate motion. He whined and cried and screamed.

Friedy didn't know dogs screamed.

He couldn't see anymore. Couldn't think. Barely felt the hammering blows that came every few seconds.

"Pal!" Nana Robin. He recognized Nana Robin.

More laughs. The kicks stopped. The pain didn't. Did he black out?

Suddenly it was quiet. He smelled burnt hair and barbeque and heard long, dull yowls. Half-dead sounds from a half-dead dog. Friedy struggled to all fours. Pal lay charred and smoking not far away, still crying, beyond saving but too long from death.

The porch was empty. The door hung open.

He gritted his teeth and crawled to Pal, hovered over him. Pal stopped rolling his eyes and locked on Friedy. In that instant, he saw again. His moaning dropped to a constant whimper. Friedy reached out to him but didn't touch his broken, blistered skin.

"I will protect her. I promise."

Pal stopped whimpering, just one breath in silence before he continued.

He nodded to the dog, nudged the beast to half-wakefulness, and ripped Pal's throat out.

30

t took some asking around before Friedy found her. Despite the people crowding the block, no one trusted him. Nana Robin was a neighbor, and stepping out into the middle of gang violence was a bit much to ask, but they could protect her from a stranger's questions.

Stranger? That baffled Friedy at first. He'd been coming here, staying here, for weeks. That didn't move many people though. No one remembered seeing him around ever.

Of course not. Steve's cloak. He stayed in her home most of the time, went out to the shops once a week.

He eventually pried the story out. To hear the neighbors tell it, the woman collapsed when the gangers immolated her dog, and the B7s left her on her porch while they ran wild through her house. After they left, someone with a car delivered her to the clinic. Heart attack. She was in a delicate state when they left, but she was still alive.

Friedy pushed the broken door open and stepped inside. He paused a few steps past the threshold. Nana's immaculate house was in ruins. The B7s had ransacked the place, emptied every drawer, thrown over furniture, pulled pictures and paintings off the walls, and as a final insult they tagged every room with their sign: seven hash marks in blue. This wasn't a robbery. Oh, sure, they stole whatever seemed valuable, but that's not why they came. Malice slathered the wreck in here.

They took a knife to the daybeds and threw her book collection all over the floor. On the floor near the window, he found the picture of a younger Nana glowing beside Saul. A spiderweb of fractures covered the glass, but the picture inside survived unharmed. He slipped it out of its frame and held it in a careful pinch.

It was a long walk from her home on 148th to the clinic on 92nd Street and every step put him thicker into B7 activity. A scrawny man, already wounded and all alone, he made an irresistible target for a random mugging or killing. By the time he crossed 146th Street, he knew what he had to do. It didn't matter how many people he had to kill and eat, he was going to the clinic.

It didn't come to that. He stumbled into the clinic storefront unmolested. She lay in a scrounged bed, not a hospital bed but a simple twin with its legs on dollies for mobility. An IV bag hung from a hook in the wall next to her and snaked into her arm underneath a small strip of tape.

He knelt by her bedside and took her hand, causing her to stir. Her knotty hand squeezed his.

"Friedy? Oh, Friedy, you're alive."

"Yah Nana. I'm okay. How do you feel?"

She ran a ginger touch over his bruised and misshapen face. "You don't look okay."

"I wasn't good looking to begin with." He smiled with blood-stained teeth. It was easy to do, genuine. He never felt so relieved as he did to see her awake and talking. To think he almost traded this in favor of work on Project Irresistible. "They say you need to stay here for a little while, but that you're going to be okay."

"I worried about what they'd do to you. After Pal . . ." Her voice caught.

He squeezed her hand. "Nana, they trashed the house, but I'm going to get it cleaned up for you before you come home." Forget what Guion wanted. Forget his assumed authority as team lead. They didn't live in that world anymore.

She nodded but didn't say anything. Holding in her sobs took everything she had.

"They didn't get everything though." He pressed the picture into her hand and tears wound down the sides of her wrinkled face as she stared at it, hand over her mouth.

"There's one other thing," he said after giving her a moment. "They wrecked a lot of furniture, but his chair is fine. Saul's seat is sitting untouched by the window."

He hugged her while she cried.

"You rest." He squeezed tighter. "I'm going to make sure this never happens again."

Guion looked ready to tear into Friedy when he bounded through the apartment door, but Friedy rushed the distance between them and pounced Guion to the ground before he got a word out. He clenched Guion's throat in the soft jaws of his hand and crouched on his chest.

Jon started to move in, already reaching for Friedy's shoulders.

"You drugged me." Friedy loomed close with his purpling, lumpy face.

Jon stopped in his tracks, his shock replaced with grim approval.

"You trapped my mind inside a puzzle and locked my heart in a chemical box. You kept me here away from Nana.

She got hurt." Friedy's lips peeled back and he bared his teeth. "I should kill you."

"I kept you focused on what's important."

"You have no idea what's important!" Flecks of spittle splashed Guion's face.

They hovered like that for long moments before Friedy relaxed.

"I can see those calculations churning away behind your eyes. I know what you're thinking. You've got a mad doctor in there. He can make adjustments, can't he? Make you as good as someone with boosts." Friedy smiled. A dare. "Go ahead. Tell him to do his best."

"I'm sorry that happened, but this is exactly what I've warned against from the beginning." Guion still didn't struggle in Friedy's grip. "Everything we've done in this neighborhood destabilized the situation and upset the balance of power."

Friedy's eyes flashed. Gold with sharp slits of midnight, there was nothing warm or human in them. "I didn't do this to her. This was you. Your plan. Your drugs. You." He sat back. "She survived, so you might too. I'm even offering you what you love best."

Guion asked with a look.

"Control. I'll let you design and run the op."

"What op?" Jon said.

"The one to destroy the B7s."

"No." Guion shook his head. "We've done too much already."

Friedy snarled. He bit down with his fingers and gave Guion a quick jerk at the throat. "Does it sound like I'm asking? This is one thing you do better than I do. You show me how to end them and I'll do it your way." Friedy released Guion's throat and stood straddling him. "Or you can refuse and I will go down into the lower blocks and make such a bloody mess that it will not only attract attention, it will go down in history."

"If you antagonize them, the entire community will pay for it."

"Then ruin them beyond retaliation. I don't want them hurt. I want them destroyed." Friedy looked at him for a silent minute. "Have it your way." He stepped off Guion and made for the door again.

"Fine," Guion called after him. He got to his feet and rubbed his throat. "Give me a little time to analyze the situation and develop an op."

Friedy nodded and walked for the door. He limped now, more human, more fragile, but still dangerous. "Do what you need to, Guion, but get it done." He pushed the door open, paused when Jon touched his arm.

"I didn't know you could control the beast like that."

Friedy snorted. "Neither did I." He looked over his shoulder at Guion. "I played the odds."

31

Friedrich agreed to be patient while Guion plotted the destruction of the B7s, but who knew how long that would hold? He had to figure out a way to eradicate a homegrown gang with no equipment, support, and laughably minimal manpower, that avoided SHOC[3] reprisals, and he had to do it in a timeframe that suited the little psychopath or Friedrich would annihilate any chance the team had at being purchased by the Oceana Combine. Frankly, he'd be lucky if Friedrich stopped there. In all likelihood, he'd murder Guion if he survived his downtown bloodbath.

Putting aside the absurdly low chance of success they had on any op with those parameters, there was, of course, the question of what happened in the aftermath. Would they make matters worse even if they somehow pulled this off?

What they should really do is pull up stakes and disappear. Vanish into the corporate world again. Crack the files, get the contracts, and ghost. Not for the first time, Guion considered doing just that solo if he had to. If Friedrich wanted to make it his priority, let him rip apart the B7s all he liked on his own. If Jon was too tenderhearted to cut the insane man loose, let him burn with the rest of the town.

If Guion had a way of breaking open those files, he'd already be gone. But he needed Friedrich for that. Artificial Friedrich had plenty of genius of his own, but there was something about the original that defied copying, and right now the original was cleaning that old woman's house and waiting for the op parameters and go signal. He wasn't going to do a damn thing with those files until Guion delivered. For the first time since they met, Friedrich had leverage over Guion, and he worked it like a savage.

He was wandering in his thoughts again. Irritable, distractible, unable to analyze data or extrapolate a plan from it. Whatever Evenflo Jack husbanded, he'd spent long ago. Guion looked at the pill case that sat in the center of their folding table. He put it there during a prior mental ramble and debated taking it for a full two minutes.

He only had one left, and he was saving it in case whatever they found in the Project Irresistible data required a mission before they had a package for Oceana that was, well, irresistible. But if he didn't develop a plan for the B7s, they'd never make it that far.

The last time he allowed himself to wander off-topic had turned into a three-day diversion that brought the party downstairs. Friedrich threatened Guion's life and the stability of this entire section of the Queens Hive over love for Nana Robin. Jon risked SHOC[3] exposure trying to save Paula and her dog. Guion wasn't the sentimental type, but he admitted to himself that Paul had earned his respect. He kept his head down and accomplished what he needed to do, possessed his own brand of professionalism and focus that was in short supply.

He proved it when Guion went to him with the problem of being hounded in media and pop culture, the manufactured villain in a collection of reality streams put out by A.W.E. to turn up the heat on their band of fugitives and create additional revenue channels out of the hunt. Guion went to him looking for tips on how to fight back. What he found was a savvy media soldier willing to take the lead, all for the low, low price of his wife back. It was an offer Guion couldn't refuse, so he took a break from overclocking his tac implant trying to find a way to satisfy Friedrich while not ruining everything and instead find a way to bail out Paula. The money wasn't an issue. Friedrich's salami slicer could raise the tactical reserves, though they'd need to crank up the aggression to raise the funds in a reasonable timeframe.

Funneling the funds to Paul was a separate matter. If he walked into SHOC^3 offices with a few hundred thousand dollars loaded into an account, he'd pique the interest of even the most inattentive bureaucrat. How did a handyman who worked half his jobs for barter and favors come up with that kind of cash?

They needed to launder the money. A wealthy benefactor or unknown relative? He found himself in Paul's apartment again discussing the possibilities. Paul laughed at the inheritance scheme.

"Can he be from Nigeria? I hear Nigerian princes have been leaving money to poor American kin of European ancestry for centuries."

Guion didn't laugh.

"You're onto something though. How good are you with electronic forgery?" He pulled up a page in shared AR space. "We can set up a charity drive."

An hour later they hashed out the plan. Paul set up a Please Finance campaign for Paula's emancipation, and he and Guion set to work creating dummy contributions. The site allowed donors to remain anonymous, but Guion advised keeping that percentage low to avoid suspicion.

"Transfer a bit of money into their accounts, and then use that to make the donations. Stagger it so they don't come in all at once."

"Easy."

"Remember, these are poor people, so the donation amounts need to be small."

"I'll keep it to ten and twenty dollars each."

"Pace it so we hit the goal in a week. With proper backdating, we should be able to do that without looking suspicious."

Now she was home and Guion was without further excuse. Friedrich's patience was a slowly shredding rope, breaking one fiber at a time, and he needed to haul them out of this pit before it snapped.

Paul paid Paula's contact in full today and brought her home. Modest home or no, they meant to celebrate and invited the upstairs neighbors to join them. Jon went. Guion stayed behind to plan, though the din in the backyard spilled through that window someone always left open and made it hard to concentrate.

Jon protested of course. He applied his typical jocular enthusiasm and reminded Guion that he more than anyone was responsible for her being home.

"I saved the clinic. You saved the girl."

But Guion didn't do it for recognition or adulation. Paul did deserve the help, but he did it so they could ease the public pressure holding back a recruiter's offer. In the meantime, taking those days away from Friedrich's demands put him in a harder spot. He made no progress and now had less time to do everything he needed to be working on for the last three days. Because if Friedrich followed through on his threat, none of this would matter.

And then it hit him.

The answer lay downstairs, the roots buried in the plans

they already started. He wasn't going to take on all of SHOC^3, not directly anyway, not with a distracting operation. Not how he'd normally approach a situation. Guion was a surgeon who used scalpel precision with his teams.

He shot to his feet and made for the door.

They needed a hammer. They needed a marketing blitz to push SHOC^3 into war with the B7s. The gang wouldn't win, couldn't win, but they'd put up enough of a fight to demand SHOC^3's full attention.

The P3 door opened as Guion came down the stairs. Paul stood smiling.

"Hey! I'm glad you changed your mind! Come on in." He stepped back and pulled the door open wider.

I do not like these people, Guion.

Inside, Pepe locked eyes with Guion and started to growl. His hackles raised between his shoulders.

They intentionally chose not to wed but live as if they are man and wife.

"Who cares?" Guion subvocalized his response.

They spurned God.

"How's that our concern?"

Really, Guion, if this partnership is going to work long term, we're going to need to establish certain ethical boundaries, the transgression of which cannot be tolerated.

Guion wanted to ask what Jack meant by "long term," but Paula came back and welcomed him into the group conversation with a hug.

———

You're brooding, Guion.

"I've had a couple of conversations with Paul and Paula recently. You butted in. I didn't think you could do that, Jack." He said the demon's name pointedly.

I contributed to the exchange, an augment I found useful. You gave me license to take such action. Jack sniffed. *You sound disappointingly like Jonathan. You have, perhaps, forgotten I am your ally.*

"I've been wondering about that. Lately you've been quite keen on isolating me from everyone around me. You don't like Friedrich."

Nor do you.

"You have your doubts about Jon."

Mirrored in your own mind.

"You insisted today Paul and Paula are distasteful."

Godless fornicators.

"I wonder what you'd say of Griffin if you had a chance to meet her."

She is a face on a screen that makes you mawkish. Saccharine taste aside, your conduct with her has thus far been appropriate.

Guion walked to the window, closed for once, and looked out into the backyard. On warm nights like this, Paula let Pepe sleep on the small patch of lawn so he could get out of the sweltering hotbox of their apartment room and not contribute to the mounting body heat of the place. This night, he sat rigid, eyes green mirrors locked on Guion's window. The dog made eye contact as soon as Guion appeared, stood with flexed and ready muscles, and growled. Guion couldn't hear it, but he saw it in Pepe's posture.

"He didn't used to do that."

A dog's temperament is your primary concern now?

"You're waiting for something, Jack. What is it?"

Guion, you're going in circles.

"No, I'm progressing in a straight line, and I'm not sure I like where it leads."

You're not progressing at all. Let me tell you what you already know: you're going to run out of time.

"Our contract stipulates you can't force me out, but there's something going on you're not telling me."

SHOC³ is escalating. They currently skirmish with the B7s, but their objective is you, and that manhunt is still ongoing. Steve's cloak works on both human and electronic surveillance measures, but it's not infallible. You have exposed yourselves. Too many people know you. With enough canvassing, SHOC³ will eventually interview someone who has personally interacted with you.

Guion pulled away from the window before Pepe barked. He paced the dark room and whispered. "Do I become more like you every time you possess me, or do you stay a bit more? Which is it?"

The longer SHOC³ hunts, the more desperate they'll be once they get a solid lead. They won't just ask questions. They will employ intimidation and torture. Those people will talk no matter how loyal you think they are.

Besides, there's a factor you failed to include in your situational analysis: Friedrich's demands have you plotting to remove SHOC³'s single largest distraction.

Guion stopped in his tracks. "You're right. I can't believe I didn't see it." He gripped his temples. "We take out the B7s and SHOC³ can dedicate all the resources it's amassed in the Rockaways to finding us. It's no longer splitting priorities."

Friedrich is asking you to hasten your own demise.

"Friedrich has no idea what he's asking. He never considers consequences. Witness our current situation."

You need to move without him, Guion. He will be the death of you.

"How?" Guion held up his hands in a shrug. "He's the only one who can crack those files."

You don't need to crack the files. What you actually need is compelling information about Project Irresistible. How it works, for example. How it affects its subjects.

"Which is in the files."

And elsewhere. We have a building of nearly six hundred subjects to examine.

"We can't walk in there and start scanning people."

Certainly not. However, I do believe I can be of assistance to you in this endeavor.

A chill puckered Guion's skin into gooseflesh. He cocked his head and looked at nothing out of the corner of his eyes. "What do you want?"

Freedom to do my work. I'll leave you some hours each day to make your plans to mollify your wayward colleague. For the balance, surrender your flesh to me. I promise you I will make better use of our time than staring at a darkened ceiling.

"You're joking. That'll increase the rate of whatever you're doing to me exponentially."

Clack the beads on that abacus in your brain. What choice do you have?

Guion had been running the scenarios all afternoon. He already knew his options.

He didn't have any.

32

Paul visited them early the next morning, the cheer from yesterday's celebration replaced with urgency. It made his door knock tight and fast, and he pushed a stream from SHOC^3: Troopers to their shared AR as he entered.

Commander Anthony Boulliver stood in bust, serious, stubbled, looking like he hadn't slept well in a week and short on patience because of it. He spoke about the B7s in dismissive tones. Street trash. Distractions from the manhunt for dangerous corporate terrorists that brought him here. He admitted prior failings in a grim tone that wasn't contrition but a threat that he'd double down on his original focus. Boulliver made himself the star of the stream with that, the brand mascot, and that gave Guion his op.

He sent Jon to gather what he needed.

Malcolm greeted Friedy and Jon at the door with a smile and hand-slaps-turned-hugs all around, but it was fake. Jon felt it right away. The man put on a happy face to mask real worry. Hey, great to see everybody, but Jamila was coming over in a little bit.

"If you get what I mean." He wiggled his eyebrows at them.

Friedy started to talk, but Jon steamrolled him. The little man had been too intense when Jon picked him up. Angry, impatient. Even Nana Robin seemed a little standoffish with the man. Given a chance to talk, he'd screw this up. He looped Friedy in to keep him in check, but now Jon regretted doing it.

"It's business, and it shouldn't take long."

Malcolm brought them into the living room and offered them a seat.

Jon laid out the B7 attack at Nana Robin's. Friedy butted in several times to offer additional details that weren't important. Jon silenced him with a raised hand and filled in the gaps as sparsely as he could.

Malcolm listened with a slow nod. Yeah, he knew about what happened, visited her at the clinic twice. "But what do you think I can do for you?"

"SHOC^3's filled the airspace with drones, and I know people have been shooting them down," Jon said.

"Too true. They bring them to me hoping I'll buy them for parts. Which I do. Problem is, too many people these days don't realize these things have GPS locators on them, or don't know how to turn them off."

"We want to review the footage and see if any of them captured the attack," Friedy said.

"Genius as always," Malcolm said. "You're right. Someone did bring one in that caught the whole thing." His face fell. "It's ugly as fuck."

"Give it to me," Friedy said, sudden aggression bursting from the little man.

Malcolm sat back. "Friedy, man, you know I'm not going to sell you out. I am going to sell it, but I'm gonna pixelate your face first. No one will know it's you."

"I don't care about that. Give me the drive." He leaned forward with the whole-body tension of a readied pounce.

Jon stood and placed a hand on Friedy's shoulder. "Calm down. This is Malcolm we're talking to. He's never jerked us around before."

"And I ain't gonna now. Look, we all know what's on that drive and how embarrassing it is to SHOC^3. There's no way they want that getting out. Bunch of gangers light an old lady's dog on fire and break into her house over her body?"

Friedy bared his teeth. Malcolm held up a hand.

"The point is, SHOC^3 will pay a mint to bury this." He swung his hands wide. "The problem is, I have no idea how to set up the channels to have that talk. But I'll tell you what, little dude." He pointed at Friedy. "You set that up, and I'll split the haul with you. We'll let David set her up somewhere safe and then pad her account with enough that she'll have some luxury. There should still be plenty for all of us to bug out in style."

"Nein. Give it to me. "

"Friedy, chill," Jon said.

"What gives, man?"

"We're going to make it public," Friedy said.

"It's part of a larger plan," Jon said. "It'll be good for you too."

"The fuck it will. They're already all over my ass. They turn their attention on the B7s and I'm not going to be able to move a thing in or out of here. SHOC^3 knows my routes and half my drivers by now."

Friedy bristled. "Now!" He stepped forward. Jon pushed him back.

"Look, you guys are friends, and I'm not heartless. I get this is important to you. I want to help, but you're asking me to screw myself."

"What about Friedy's skimmer?"

Malcolm nodded. "It's awesome. Don't think I'm complaining, but it ain't fast cash. You want to drop the hammer on SHOC^3? I don't wanna be here when they hit back." He paused, relenting. "Tell you what: buy it off me." Malcolm named a figure. It was high but reasonable.

"We just emptied most of our discretionary funds getting Paula back," Jon said. "It'll take us a little while for Friedy's skimmer to generate that." He clapped Friedy on the shoulders. "What do you say? A couple of weeks and then we do this?"

"Nein. We take it now."

Malcolm and Jon started to protest at the same time.

Friedy snagged two handfuls of Malcolm's shirt and threw him across the room into the mirrored wall, which shattered and rained down on him as he thumped to the carpeted floor.

Friedy was on him almost before he landed, rolling him over and grabbing his hand in a grip made of steel cables. The little man leaned over Malcolm, golden eyes shining with fire, and crushed Malcolm's hand. Bones snapped and ground together with muted wet sounds. Malcolm screamed.

"Friedy, stop!" Jon jumped from his seat and rushed the little man.

Friedy bounded from his perch atop Malcolm and slammed into Jon. He fell, banged his head against the glass cube coffee table, went slack. Friedy crawled back to Malcolm and loomed over him.

"What the fuck, man? You ruined my hand."

"Replaceable. The drive."

"I told you, all that shit that comes in is lousy with trackers. I keep everything in a shielded facility so SHOC^3 doesn't come looking for any of it here." He winced. "I'll give you the key. Take whatever you want. I don't want to see you again."

Friedy shook his head. "SHOC^3 drones all look alike. I'm

not spending hours reviewing footage." The words sounded strange in his guttural voice. It was a voice for hunting, killing, primal things, not the technical difficulties of identifying the right data cache.

He leaned in. "But you, with your lucrative scheme to blackmail SHOC^3, you know exactly which drone is payday." He hauled Malcolm to his feet. "You're going to show me where it is. If you do, I'll make sure you get to the clinic afterward. If you don't,"—he lowered his head and looked at Malcolm through his platinum blonde eyebrows—"I'll still be here when Jamila arrives."

33

Jon returned home alone. Friedy had bounded off to Nana Robin's again, leaving Jon to hold the drive in one hand, the back of his head in the other.

"Tell me we can get out of here soon."

"I don't have a timetable. It'll be as fast as I can manage. No one wants out more than I do." Guion took the drive, but Jon held on.

"He's slipping."

Guion fixed him with a hard look. "He's been dressed up like a murder scene since the day we got here. You're just now bothered by it?"

"This is our fault. We need to stop. We need to leave."

Guion slapped Jon on the shoulder. "Glad to have you on the team, Jon!" He didn't sound glad. "It's nice to finally onboard you after all this time!" His mock joy dropped off his face like rotten fruit and left something just as ugly behind.

But Jon responded to something else. "You look terrible. When's the last time you slept?"

"Nightmares. I've watched a lot of streams getting ready for this. They've been plastering the murder victims—"

"I've seen them." Jon held up a hand to stop him.

Guion snatched the drive and left Jon to his thoughts.

The footage provided the raw materials he needed to damage the SHOC^3 brand and send them into damage control mode. It was a good weapon.

So he did what he did best: he assembled a team with the skills necessary to execute his plan. He didn't have the resource pool of a megacorporation to pick from this time, but as luck would have it, he found what he needed down a flight of stairs. Over Jack's protests, Guion recruited Paul to help him work the footage into a public relations nightmare for SHOC^3.

They tried working at Paul's to get away from Steve and his trash-producing binges. Unfortunately, Pepe's attitude never improved. He refused to let Guion in the apartment. So they threw open the windows and practiced ignoring Steve's running commentary as they worked.

The footage was perfect, as perfect as a recording of torturing an animal to death and beating a man senseless could be. The shot was clear enough to identify the assailants as B7s but shadowy enough to hide Friedy's identity. Paul made sure of it.

"We don't want to pixelate anything," he said when Guion mentioned Malcolm's original plan. "That tells the audience someone altered the footage and gives SHOC^3 wiggle room to call the whole thing a deep fake. If we do it subtly, someone can still claim it was altered, but it won't get much traction."

They worked the footage for another two days, placed strategic zooms, looped and replayed some of the worst instants, and finished with a reel that wasn't a passive recording anymore but a powerful statement masquerading as objective reporting.

Fully armed, they went on the attack. Paul and Guion,

with Artificial Friedy's help, assembled a list of the most popular fan chats dedicated to SHOC^3: Troopers across all platforms. They posted the video to all of them and followed up with comments and discussions from a myriad of dummy accounts expressing outrage about what happened to Nana Robin and Pal.

After letting that marinate for a few days, they worked their second list: chats for SHOC^3: To Catch a Killer, the spinoff stream dedicated to SHOC^3's hunt for the serial killer hollowing out women in the Rockaways. They didn't start with the video this time. Instead, they began with some lite criticism. Sure, the manhunt angle is cool and all, but they've been doing this for a while and gotten nowhere. Now an old woman is in the hospital and her dog was burned alive. Shouldn't they focus on gang violence? It's out of control and it's right under their noses.

They created SHOC^3 defenders too. Paul said nothing drove engagement in the WorldGrid like arguments.

It took hold. Slowly, they started agreeing and fighting with accounts they didn't create. Then it took off. The threads unspooled to dizzying lengths all their own and proliferated like weeds. The three went from planting this garden to tending it, popping in to keep the flames hot and steer the conversations back on topic when they wandered away.

Artificial Friedy fuzzed into AR one afternoon while they worked the various profiles and platforms. A new tag trended on Blabber: #burningdog.

"That's good work," Guion said.

"I didn't create it," Artificial Friedy said. "None of us did. I traced it back and found the post that first used it isn't from any of our accounts."

Paul punched Guion in the shoulder. "We've gone viral."

It was working, but it was taking time. SHOC^3 didn't respond. Paul cautioned patience. A massive organization like SHOC^3 wouldn't move on this right away. They'd try the waiting game since so many things in the WorldGrid flashed bright and then vanished in no time.

"SHOC^3's shifting," Paul said one afternoon. He shared a stream of the latest episode of SHOC^3: Troopers.

"That's great," Guion said.

Paul pinched his face together and shook his head. "Not entirely. They're outsourcing." He shoved the stream into Guion's AR space. Boulliver was explaining the increased community security demands placed on them by recent B7 activity. SHOC^3 would be there for the people of Rockaway during this time, but in return, he asked for their help in apprehending three dangerous corporate terrorists. Head-shots of the team flashed on screen as Boulliver read out their names and a list of fabricated offenses that made them sound like anarchist masterminds. Aid in capturing these enemies of society came with a reward of $500,000 a head.

Guion shot his gaze to Steve. "You're still covering us?"

Steve sighed as he chewed a mouthful of candy bar medley. "Yes. Just like every other time you ask me. No one can find you unless you interact with them directly."

Guion compiled a list of the highest risk factors in his head. Friedrich was his typical loose cannon who needed to be secured. Then there was Malcolm. Maimed, already short on cash, and now with an ax to grind. Why wouldn't he turn them in?

"We're done here," he said to Jon. "We can't have anything to do with anyone anymore. Boulliver just made it too risky. We're an easy $1,500,000 in a pile of poverty. I need you to bring Friedrich in, and I need you to secure Malcolm. I don't care what it takes."

Jon sighed through his nose. "Yeah, I know. I've been planning the visits. I want Nana Robin home with Friedy before I go talk to him. He's less likely to go beast in front of her."

"And Malcolm?"

Jon shook his head. "Friedy fucked him up and I couldn't stop it. He's going to be pissed. I was hoping to at least offer him the money to get his hand replaced when I went. That'll go a lot further than 'Hey, sorry we maimed you.'"

"Promise it to him if that's what he needs to stay quiet." Guion pulled open a screen. Jon couldn't see it. Paul used his MIU when working in the WorldGrid. "We should have the capital necessary to fund his operation in another month, assuming standard surgical costs."

"Are we going to be here that long?"

"I hope not, but there's no reason to shut down Friedrich's routine."

"How about I offer that to him as a lifetime income stream? All of it. Once we're resettled we won't need it."

"That's good. Tell him we'll offer him full control of the program as soon as we're gone."

"Good. That'll give us something to compete with that reward." Jon stood. "I'll start with Friedy. If he's the same guy I grew up with, he's gone from rage to shame by now. If I'm not back in a day, I'm wrong and you know he's eaten me."

34

Jon relaxed as soon as Friedy greeted him at the door. The little man's sheepish body language, the way he immediately looked down when he saw Jon, it all said Jon was safe.

For his part, Friedy seemed relieved Jon wanted to talk and readily invited him in. Just please keep it down. Nana was sleeping and though recovering remained quite weak.

Friedy lead him into the sunroom. He'd cleaned the detritus out and did what he could to scrub the walls, but it was still a wreck.

The daybeds were gone. Friedy replaced his with a trio of cushionless wooden chairs, hers with a stack of mattresses and a crisp bedsheet thrown over the top.

"I see they left the chair." Jon motioned to Saul's spot.

Friedy nodded. "They broke the picture frame, but I got a new one and put the photo back. She likes to sit there now. I want to replace the furniture they destroyed, but without a MIU it's difficult." He still refused to look at Jon. "I could go to 116th to buy one, but those off the shelf units are shit and we both know it. Besides, I'd need to set it up in her name and she hates all that tech." He twisted his hands in his lap. "It's probably . . . it's probably too soon to go to Malcolm, right?" Now he looked at Jon.

Jon sighed and put his elbows on his knees. "Honestly man, after our last visit, it's always going be too soon to go to Malcolm."

Friedy dropped his head and shook it. "I'm sorry. I really am. To both of you."

"I know you are."

"Can you tell him?"

"I can, but you crushed his hand. That's more than sorry covers. Frankly, we'll be lucky if he doesn't turn us in for the bounty."

Friedy hung his head lower but didn't move otherwise.

"I'm not telling you this to beat on you," Jon said. "But you do need to hear it."

Friedy nodded.

"I need you to understand how badly you screwed up."

A tear hung off the tip of Friedy's nose before diving into his lap.

"How long have we known each other?"

Friedy sniffed. "Pretty much our whole lives."

"Do you know how many times I've seen you flip out like that?"

"I never had the capability."

"Yeah, you can say that, but I think it's something else. I don't think that was you back there. I think it was the demon. It's influencing you."

Friedy lifted his head, looked at Jon with tear-reddened eyes. "That was me. I remember it all."

"Sure, you remember it, but that wasn't you. It's changing you," Jon said. "Steve's changing me."

"He is?"

Jon nodded. "In different ways, of course, but I noticed it a little while back. I'm getting used to his cloak. I don't check for cameras when I break into a place anymore. I don't peek around corners or try to be quiet or quick. I'm lazy. Shit, I let things go with Guion I never would before."

Friedy's head sank back down. "You didn't ruin someone's hand or concuss your best friend."

"No, I didn't. My demon's different from yours. Mine's a lazy guy who goes unnoticed. He's also on the outside. He doesn't get to touch me the way yours does, or Guion's."

Friedy looked up.

"Guion was always a cold son of a bitch, but you've got to see how he's growing colder. He's willing to do things I don't think he'd consider before." He leaned forward. "You, me, him, we're all being affected. Do you get what I'm saying?"

"That it's not our fault?" Friedy's face was full of hope.

"No, man. We're responsible for all this. Sorry. We brought those demons here. We talked with them. They told us what they expected from us if they used their powers for us, and we agreed. They laid out the terms and we said yes.

"But we also had no idea what we were getting into when we made those pacts. We said yeah, but we didn't really understand where this would go. It's time we take a little more control, don't you?"

"Control how? The agreements are binding."

"Yeah, and you know what occurred to me the other day? They don't have an expiration date. We can't keep these things around forever. I can stop feeding Steve and he'll stop cloaking me, but that doesn't make him go away. Same deal for that apex predator in you. It'll always be there."

"You want to find a way to break the contract?" Friedy shook his head. "I'm not a lawyer."

"No, you're not. You're a savant, and you summoned

them. With math." He slapped Friedy's knee. "Are you going to tell me that the great machine-minded Friedy can't unsummon them with math too?" He caught Friedy's look. "Numerology. Whatever."

"Banish them?"

"Banish them. You can work on it at the apartment."

Friedy's head snapped up. "I can't leave here. Look around. She needs me more than ever."

"She needs someone. Not you. Boulliver just dropped a half-million-dollar bounty on your head and pushed it across the WorldGrid. Everyone knows. We need to go to ground."

"Or what?" Friedy pumped to his feet. "If SHOC^3 comes here, I'll show them why they shouldn't."

"What are you going to do? Kill them all?"

"Yes."

"And when they send more?"

"Them too."

"You're going to give Nana Robin golden years drowning in murder and escalating violence? Does that really sound like you, or the thing from Hell in your soul?" Jon stood and placed gentle hands on Friedy's shoulders. "Come back to the apartment. We'll banish the demons. We'll go to Oceana. SHOC^3'll leave these people alone when we're gone."

Friedy snarled with his expression and voice. "I'm not leaving her." He slapped Jon's hands away and crowded him. "Back to the apartment? For what? Verbal abuse? Drugs? I'm happy here, Jon. Happy!" Tears spilled down his face as he bared his teeth and pointed at himself. "Happy! Me!"

Resolve shot through his quiet voice like rebar. "Tell Guion I'll help with that file after I see results from him, but I'm not going back."

Neither moved. Jon looked at Friedy. Friedy looked everywhere but at Jon.

"And banishment?"

"I'll work on it for you, but I'm not using it." Now he did look at Jon. "I need to be the apex predator if SHOC^3 does come here."

35

Malcolm didn't smile when he opened the door for Jon, but he did open it. He even let him in. That was a good start.

"I didn't know if you'd see me."

"You ain't the one who did this." Malcolm held up his left hand, encased in plaster to the wrist. "It's ruined, you know. I'm lucky they didn't have to amputate it." He let it fall and frowned. "Not that it matters."

"That's what I wanted to talk to you about."

"About this?" He held up his hand again. "Forget it. I saw what you tried to do. You and me, we're still cool."

"I'm glad to hear it."

"But that don't mean I'm doing anything more for you." Malcolm collapsed into his chair. "I'm done, man. I'm out. The SHOC^3 buildup is ruining me. They know I've run guns for the B7s before. They've got my operation pinned down."

"What about the automated deposits?" Jon took the other chair.

"They're the only thing keeping me and mine fed right

now, so thanks for that. But man, I can't stay here under that kind of scrutiny."

Jon studied him. "The first time we met, Tasha came over and asked you to move Phillip out of the B7s reach, and you didn't have the available funds. You've got less business now and a lot more people to move."

"You think I'm up to something, and you're right. That little asshole is worth a lot of money. More than enough to get me and everyone else out of here."

Jon sank back into the chair with a pause and a serious look. "You know that's going to lead to me."

"I wasn't bullshitting you before. You've been a friend, and I ain't interested in fucking you over, but it's time for me to jet." Malcolm held up the shapeless plaster mass at the end of his wrist. "The way I see it, I'm doing the neighborhood a favor on the way out the door by turning that psychopath in."

"I can't ask you to forgive him—"

"No, you can't, so don't," Malcolm said with a jab of his ruined hand. "He's dangerous. I know you two go back a ways, but he's lost his mind and you're outta your league. You can't control him. I watched you try. I don't know what kind of boosts he's got installed, but they're past anything you have."

"He's got a demon."

"No shit he's got a demon."

"I'm not being metaphorical. He's got a demon in him. That's what makes him so strong." Jon frowned. "Crazy too."

"Man, get the fuck outta here."

"No, it's true, and that's why I'm here. I have one too, different from his. Mine doesn't make me strong or fast or psycho. Mine sends me for insta-food and hides me. How do you think we made it so long without SHOC³ finding us?"

A look of disgust bloomed on Malcolm's face. "You're all crazy."

"I'm serious. Say hi, Steve."

Steve appeared in an empty chair. *"Hi Steve.* I know, obvious joke. I didn't feel like digging for better."

Malcolm started. "Who are you?"

"Hi. Steve." Steve pointed to himself. "Was my minimal attempt at humor completely wasted?"

"How did you get in here?"

"I walked in right behind Jon-O Captain My Captain." Steve gestured toward Jon.

"I wasn't bullshitting you, either," Jon said. "Steve here can hide you from just about anything. Drone cameras. Human eyeballs."

"As long as you don't draw direct attention to yourself," Steve said.

Jon saw Malcolm's face. "Look at me through your MIU camera."

Malcolm scowled but pulled the unit off his belt and held it at Jon. His face fell first, then the MIU as he looked at Jon. He snapped the MIU back in place and squinted.

"I had a feeling you were thinking of turning us in." Jon held up a hand to stop Malcolm before he began. "I get it. You're justified. But I was hoping I could make you a counteroffer. My team's got something coming up soon. We need a little more time out from under SHOC^3's magnifying glass."

"What's the offer?"

"Lay low while we work. Let those deposits fund your move. We'll funnel our share into your accounts and keep them running after we're gone. You'll have what you need to move soon enough, and eventually get a replacement for that." He gestured to Malcolm's hand. "You get a lifetime income after that. In the meantime, I'll leave Steve with you. He'll throw his cloak over you and you won't have any SHOC^3 trouble."

"And my family?"

"Them too."

"Well . . . some of them," Steve said.

"What do you mean 'some of them'?" Malcolm said.

"My contract is for you and your friends," Steve said, pointing at Jon.

"Malcolm's a friend."

"Sure, and so I can do this. But at the time we shook, you didn't have a lot of friends." He held up three fingers. "That's the limit of my cloak."

"You didn't think to mention this before now?" Jon said.

Steve shrugged. "You didn't ask. Hell, I'm doing you a solid right now by offering that up without a question." He put a hand on his stomach. "Volunteering is rewarding work, but it makes me hungry. Didn't we pass a Korean barbecue place coming here?"

"You can only hide three people?" Malcolm said.

Steve nodded. "Pick your three. Change 'em any time. Play musical chairs with them if you want. But I can only cover three souls at once. Which means if your team wants to be invisible for your upcoming tour of prime B7 real estate, New Friend here—" Steve shifted to Malcolm. "Sorry, man, I'm terrible with names, mostly on account of not caring enough to put in the effort to learn them." He returned to Jon. "New Friend and fam are out in the open."

Jon looked at Malcolm, who looked back.

"Do it," Jon said. "Cover Malcolm and any of his family who come here."

"Up to three," Steve said.

"Will you wait?"

Malcolm thought a long minute. "Wire me your share of the feed and we have a deal."

"That's a big ask."

"One, you're going into B7 territory at the edge of war. Ain't no telling if you're ever coming back. Two . . ." He held up the plaster-cased ruin of his hand. "And three. . . ." A few finger twitches brought up something in AR that he tossed to Jon with a flick.

Jon wrenched in his seat as if he could escape the images that shot into his vision. He paled, winced. Three images of three victims splayed on the city streets, barely recognizable as human. Gaping, hollow abdomens, piles of innards pillowing heads stripped of their faces. Lidless, lifeless eyes stared at the cameras with a bloody skeleton's grin.

"One of them was outside of Kat's building, another just a couple of blocks down. The last was across town, but the coroner's putting their times of death within twenty minutes of each other, so either the killer's got fast wheels, or there's a copycat out there. Either way, they're calling it the Triple Event, and I want out ASAP. You hear me? So you sign all that money over to me, or I get it from SHOC[3] and leave the little dude to twist."

36

Guion woke with a message waiting on his MIU.

Here you are, dear boy. As promised.

He scanned a few of the attached files, cursed, scanned them again, then gathered the team.

"It started as advertising," Guion said. Jon and Friedy sat on the couch next to Steve while Guion paced the short living room, hands clasped behind his back. "It's grown into mind control."

"Jack figured that out all on his own?" Friedy said. "We only knew that weeks ago. He's something, Guion."

Guion's lips compressed to a thin line for a moment before he continued. "Instead of feeding your brain subconscious messages, it feeds messages to your MIU."

"How does that control you?" Jon said.

Guion brought up one of Jack's files. Friedy paired his specs to Jon's MIU in a shared session and they both stared at the glowing green diagram of a brain. Various sections of it pulsed red as Guion talked.

"A full five MIU lets you experience AR with all your senses," Guion said. "It takes virtual information and feeds that into your brain, which translates that into sensory signals as real as if you actually experienced it."

"Still not seeing mind control."

"What if instead of providing sensory feedback based on virtual constructs, your MIU made you feel impulses?"

"Like what?"

Guion pulled up a stack of papers in AR and pushed it to them. "This is Jack's analysis. The way he explains it, you can control a person's emotional state by releasing hormones, and you can guide their actions by triggering memories. Release ghrelin to make someone hungry at the same time you trigger a memory of an ad for insta-food . . ."

". . . and suddenly you've got a group of people all running out to grab a meal or three from the same place," Jon said.

"A full five wouldn't do that," Friedy said. "The physiological interface doesn't go deep enough."

Guion nodded. "Special units. When they go into mass production, they'll use that next-level bond as a selling point. By the time anyone figures it out, they'll have such deep market penetration it won't matter."

"They're going to have those people running out to every shop the A.W.E. conglomerate owns," Jon said.

"It's a lot bigger than that," Guion said. "If they can exert this much control over people, they can own us in ways deeper than economics. They can make us want to do anything they want us to. They can make it a biological imperative for us. We'd be slaves or biological robots."

"But it only affects people with that model of full five MIU," Jon said. "If people don't get the implant . . . Guion, you know what this means, don't you?"

The black man nodded. "It's not the way out we thought it was." He kicked a Blast Burger bag filled only with trash. "We can't give this to any other corporation."

"No, but we've still got a bargaining chip with this," Jon said. "We bundle this up in a media package, forge a public relations bullet that makes A.W.E. bleed for weeks."

Guion stopped where he was. He stared at Jon. "Oceana would go for that. We'll need video of Irresistible's victims to sell it."

"It would be even better if we capture logs of the signal. I'll bet they transmit it locally, probably through a router in the building," Friedy said.

Jon clapped him on the shoulder. "It's good to have you back."

"I'm not. I just want him gone." Friedy jutted at Guion with his chin.

"Okay then," Jon said. "Next step is we get some footage of those people and a copy of that transmission. While we're there, we can free those people."

A glass cut of Paul's face glowed into being in the corner of their shared session. "Guion, are you home?"

"News?" Guion said.

"I'll be right up."

He let himself in and pushed a stream window as he joined them in the living room. "This guy Boulliver isn't just some jackbooted thug. He's good at this."

Boulliver talked in an invisible interview that spun the situation from one that painted $SHOC^3$ as callous authoritarians to instead show them as understaffed and overburdened with a community rife with crime and helpless to protect the poor people who relied on them.

"When did they post this?" Guion said.

"It went live a few hours ago here, but premium subscribers in the corp-platz have had it for three days already. He's good," Paul said.

"He's $SHOC^3$. It wouldn't surprise me if he had a tac implant," Guion said.

"What good would that do him?" Jon said.

"Tac implants can load different packages. They have social modules. When we first met, I assumed you had one."

Jon laughed without humor. "I couldn't even afford an arm."

"How much is this hurting us?" Guion said.

"Hashtag helpthehelpers started trending this morning."

"No go on hashtag cancelthemanhunt?" Jon said.

"I've been pushing it for two weeks, and for two weeks, the SHOC^3: Troopers stream included more and more incidental footage of hollowed-out women. They're not saving that for SHOC^3: Manhunt anymore."

"Seems like a transparent ploy," Friedy said.

Paul scoffed. "I created that tag and their counterpunch even makes me nervous. They're using the footage selectively, but those bodies are real, and they're showing up not too far from where Paula works."

"So where's that leave us? Are they doubling down on the manhunt?" Jon said.

"Just the opposite," Paul said. "It looks like Boulliver is pushing for more means to take on the B7s."

"Good," Friedy said.

"Why?" Jon said at the same time.

"Because they're the easy win," Guion said. "The B7s are a street gang. SHOC^3 is a private military force. Let me guess, Boulliver is saying that if he had more resources, SHOC^3 could set this right. They just need more manpower, more weapons, and more support vehicles."

"And more leniency in their operational mandate," Paul said.

Guion nodded. "If he gets what he wants, he'll crush them in a few days and have the force necessary to put all the Rockaways under martial law."

"How long has this pressure been building?" Jon said.

"Since right after this new interview aired. Three days," Paul said.

"The voice box is right in the middle of B7 territory. If it becomes a war zone . . ." Jon left the worst unsaid.

Guion looked at them for a moment as calculations ran in the back of his mind. "We have to go before they launch their assault. We can't risk losing those people's testimony."

37

I t was easy to see who had access to streams, or who talked to people who did, in the 70s blocks between Shore Front Parkway and Rockaway Beach Boulevard. Those houses sat locked up tight with boards on their windows. All boards this time, not plywood crisscross messes with plastic and paper taped across the gaps. Guion noted without expression that much of the new timber offered helpful information in AR popups about how thick to make the window coverings to divert the path of various caliber bullets.

The buses still ran, but only the desperate stood on the street waiting for them. Traffic, both car and foot, trickled compared to the crush and gridlock of before. It was a ghost town. They saw more B7s out, all of them moving with purpose like they were on a mission. They didn't see any SHOC[3] troopers at all.

They cased the building again from their old perch, shared this time with a crowd of squatters looking to shelter from the impending war here. There were too many to buy off with plastic jugs of synthahol this time, but they were happy to share what little space they had with the group. The stink of urine and unwashed bodies hung so thick in the air they could taste it, but it was serviceable enough. Most were too poor even for outdated MIUs, and Friedrich kept a scry for network chatter running in the background to make sure no one fingered them.

SHOC[3] maintained their patrols around the buildings, probably to keep up appearances more than anything else. It certainly wasn't to protect the residents. After the second round of patrols, Guion noticed they'd reduced their manpower and coverage. Either SHOC[3] already wrote off the building in the upcoming conflict, or they planned to concentrate the fighting elsewhere.

Traffic in and out of the building was nonexistent. That was good. That meant A.W.E. hammered the residents with compulsions to stay in, numbing their minds with tailored streams they'd watch in unison. They needed footage of that for their exposé.

Jon pointed. "You can see they've got security cameras all over the place. That's new."

Guion and Friedrich leaned in close to Jon and followed his finger.

"The guard detachment assigned here could cover the grounds more effectively that way, but if they're expecting trouble, why reduce the response force?" Friedrich said.

"Because they're not watching for trouble coming from outside," Guion said. "Look at the configuration. They're pointing toward the building, like a prison."

"They're observing their experiment subjects," Friedrich said.

"They've either got something big coming up or want to see how Irresistible holds up under the stress of the assault. Does the calendar note anything soon?"

Friedrich pulled it up, shook his head. "Nein, but this is an old copy. Things might have changed."

"I'll bet they've got the inside wired up too," Jon said. "Some kind of surveillance in every unit. If they want data on how well this thing works and they're locking everyone down, that only makes sense."

"You need to reclaim Steve," Guion said.

Jon pointed to the building. "How many times have we broken into places way more secure than that without demonic magic?"

"There's no need to make this harder on ourselves. SHOC^3 troop levels might be light now, but you can bet all those cameras are running facial recognition software. If they glimpse us, they're going to mobilize that army they've been building."

"So Friedy loops the security feed like he's done a hundred times." Jon tied a rag around his face. "And we go in bandito style."

Friedrich sniffed out the building's secured network, broke in, and created a ten-minute loop for every security feed, both outside and in the stairwells. Then Jon took the MIU and padded across the street. He made cracking the lock look ridiculous.

It took him only seconds longer to open the inner door, and they stole into the glossy floored foyer. A bank of old hydraulic elevators stared at them, their doors narrow and a shade of brown a century out of style. Their call buttons didn't even light up when pushed.

Guion shook his head. "These are too slow. We'll be standing around, bandito style"—he shot Jon a look—"for minutes waiting for a car to arrive. We want the roof?" he asked Friedrich.

The man nodded. With the bandana covering everything below his eyes, his head was all wild hair.

Guion padded back a few steps and shouldered open a door with the same ancient paint job and a tarnished knob. "We'll make better time on the stairs, and we'll be out of major traffic patterns." He waved them in. "We'll stop at a few floors along the way to collect whatever footage we need of the people under Irresistible's effects."

He tucked his MIU into the small of his back and brought up its camera feed in a vid window. Eyes in the back of his head, an old trick from the days he took the field.

The stairwell was raw concrete with metal pipes sunk in as guardrails, stark and ugly as only a low traffic area can afford to be. Fluorescent lights washed out what little color the place had and cast it all in a harsh white that felt too bright. They buzzed in the empty echo chamber, the only other sound aside from their boot clomps.

It wasn't completely empty though. Someone had been in here to touch the stairwell up in the last hundred years because on every landing where the steps leveled off for a few paces and continued up in the other direction they saw a plastic bubble the color of smoked glass growing out of the corner like a massive blackhead.

Security cameras. Guion shot Friedrich a look, a wordless question. The little man returned a slow, sure nod. Already covered. They continued up, blind to the building's eyes.

They almost made it.

One of the residents sat panting and pressed into a landing corner. He was a lump of a man, balding, jowly, and fat in a way that made him look like he was melting. The flabby bulge of his belly hung out below his mint green Macrotech Summer Con t-shirt seven years out of date.

"Just need to catch my breath," he said as he poured sweat onto his shirt. "Thought I'd save time taking the stairs, but it's been a long time—" He stopped short, squinted at Friedrich. "Hey, you got hair like that terrorist—"

He stopped again. This time his face went slack. His whole affect did, as if someone had switched him off. When he came back on, he was a different person.

"Shit!" Friedrich said.

The man's eyes worked AR they couldn't see.

"He's broadcasting to the building!"

"Shut it down," Jon said.

Guion surged forward, blurred across the man (was that a glove?) and was halfway up the next length of concrete steps when he called to them. "We need to move."

A rich red mess poured from a clean cut that opened the man's carotid artery. Harsh fluorescent light glimmered across the rushing crimson flow.

"Was that Jack?" Jon's question rang with accusation.

Guion paused, just a nanosecond, and glanced at his bare hand before he answered with a finger thrust toward the roof and a look that demanded silence. They started up the stairs again. "How much got out?" Guion demanded.

"Not much, and I garbled some of what did transmit, so this will come down to how paranoid they are," Friedrich replied. "But it's weird. It's like the whole building is sharing a single session."

Guion saw it on his vid screen before the rest, reacted the instant it happened. A Latino teen stuck his head through the door at a landing below and opened his mouth to yell.

Guion vaulted off the steps and plunged five meters to the landing. His boots slammed with a crack like a pistol shot with barely a bend in his legs. He grabbed the boy by the throat, choked his cry before he uttered a sound, yanked him through the door, swept his ankles, and slammed his head into the concrete floor.

Quiet.

Guion rose. "We need to move. There will be others.

They're civilians, but there's hundreds of apartments in this building."

A pistol cracked the air. They all grabbed their ears and ducked as the shot scored the wall above them. "And some have guns," Guion said. "Move!"

They scampered as a gibbering mob churned through the door and poured after them. Floors below added to the flood, and Jon and Guion both kicked the door ahead of them shut as they passed it, knocking the vanguard of the next floor's mob back a pace. The odd shot left them with half-deaf and ringing ears, but nothing came close to hitting them.

"Even when we make the roof, it's going to take some time to shut down the signal," Friedrich said. He wasn't even breathing hard. Jon and Guion huffed now.

"I have an idea, but we need to get there with a little lead time," Guion said.

Doing that turned out not to be hard. The three were physically fit corporate operatives. Their pursuers were incensed civilians, most of whom never took the stairs at all, let alone ran them. They had motivation but lacked the stamina to keep pace. When the three erupted onto the roof, they had almost thirty seconds to get set up.

Guion took cover behind a boxy water purifier and aimed his gun at the door.

"What are you doing?" Jon said.

"We shoot them as soon as they open the door, drop the first we see and use them to plug the way for the rest. If we kill enough of them, the others will reconsider charging through."

"We can't do that! These people are being controlled. They're victims."

Guion shrugged. "You've got until that door opens to offer a better plan. Friedrich, see what you can do before this gets out of hand."

"Guion, this is crazy—"

The door opened.

Guion fired.

The first person through took a slug to the chest and jerked back into the crowd. It swelled around him, gibbering punctuated with screams.

Guion's tac implant encased every one of them in a shimmering overlay, measured the effect downing each one would have on the group in percentages, and updated the figures in real time. Who to kill. Who to wound. The Evil Genius upgrade included psychological factors in its calculations.

More shots.

More screams.

People collapsed in the doorway, a mess of blood-washed limbs moving like slugs in shock.

His MIU took data from his paired BP-20 heavy shot smartpistol and ran it through a targeting app. He saw glowing reticles for where his barrel pointed and where to aim, accounting for range and environmental factors. When the two dots overlapped, he squeezed the trigger.

Bang. Bang. Bang. A measured staccato. Guion didn't miss.

Still, they came. They stumbled and half-crawled over their fallen neighbors as Guion, and now Jon too, gunned them down.

People dropped. Some fell and went silent. Others lay on the ground and moaned. Some took the shot and kept coming. A few with guns of their own took cover and returned fire, which broke the men's ability to check the advance.

"Running low," Guion said.

"Me too," Jon said. "Last mag for me." He slammed it home. "Any ideas on how to get out of here?"

Guion spared a glance around the corner of the water

purifier, shook his head. "I thought we'd be able to drive them off by now. That door's the only way off this roof."

Friedrich slid along the gravel roof and slammed against the sheet metal box. "I found it, but without a counter signal, their MIUs will keep performing their last command."

"Can't you do that?" Jon said.

"Nein. I know how their network functions. That's just telecommunication. I don't understand their commands yet."

"Then we've got to figure a way out of here," Jon said. He popped up, took a few shots, then ducked as the tenants returned fire. "We're about to be overrun."

Drones stopped buzzing flybys and hovered in a thickening cloud.

"Jack can get us some cover. We'll have to spread them out—"

A lion's roar drowned out the rest of Guion's sentence as Friedrich vaulted the purifier and tackled the nearest person, a middle-aged woman brandishing a kitchen knife. He backhanded her arm with such force that he snapped the bone as he bounced her off the roof. He grabbed her thick braid of black hair, jerked her head back and ripped her throat out with his teeth, threw his head back and let the blood spray drench his face.

He grabbed a bald teen by the face, gouging out both his eyes and snapping his neck sideways and swung him like a meat sack at a little girl, probably his sister from the resemblance. He slammed her in the head with the boy's booted heels and she crumbled.

Friedrich picked up speed as he drove deeper into the thick of the crowd. He snarled and howled and roared. He rent and raked and bit and tore. Every motion broke bone or shredded skin or snuffed life. He became a storm of pain and death.

Jon and Guion stopped firing without even realizing it.

They'd both seen boosted operatives in action before, but Friedrich was a blazing blur, too fast to see, too horrible not to watch.

Guion looked around at the charnel carpet mounded around them and shoved Jon toward the door. "We need to go, right now. Those cameras saw all of this and you can bet they've got a heavily armed response squad inbound already. We can't be here when they arrive."

Jon opened his mouth to call for Friedrich, but it died in his throat as he saw the little man crouched among the carnage, a look of bliss on his blood-streaked face. Guion gave him that moment to take it in before shoving him into the stairwell. He didn't look back.

38

Jon shouldered through the apartment door and charged into the living room, where he took up pacing with powerwalker strides. "What the fuck?" He plastered a hand to his forehead, heedless of the Blast Burger wrappers and Funny Fudge ice cream cake box he kicked and trampled. "What the fuck?"

Guion closed the door and stood in the hallway out of Jon's path. Jon stopped, made eye contact.

"What the fuck?" he said again.

"Oh man, sounds like I missed something exciting. I wish I was . . . nah. It'd probably just make me hungry." Steve ripped open a sleeve of chocolate chip cookies and started stuffing them in his mouth two at a time.

"What the fuck, Guion?"

Guion stepped to the edge of the room, crossed his arms. "What are you upset about?"

Jon grabbed two fistfuls of Guion's jacket and threw him into the couch next to Steve. "We slaughtered a whole tenement of innocent people, and Friedy acted like a wild animal!"

"He's been doing it for weeks, and he's not been subtle about it. You've been awfully okay with him walking in here gore-splattered and drooling blood."

"I didn't know it was like that." Jon shook his head.

"What did you think he was doing?"

"I didn't know he loved it," Jon said in a small voice.

"I'm an apex predator." Friedy had slipped through the door, closed and bolted it without them hearing, and now stood where Guion was a minute earlier. If he was a mess after the attempted mugging, he was a walking murder scene now.

"And if I appeared to love what I did, why shouldn't I? My friend was in trouble, and I helped. I saved you, Jon. I kept you safe."

"Do you remember what we talked about after Malcolm? About how the demons are changing us?"

"I remember telling you I love not being Poor Friedy anymore."

Jon sucked in a breath, but Guion put himself between them before he could talk. "Look, no one should feel good about what happened at that building."

"Guys, look at what they're making us do."

"Get off it, Jon." Guion turned to face him fully. "You're letting superstitious nonsense prevent you from acting with full efficiency."

"Is that what you call that bloodbath on the roof?"

"I call that ugly necessity. You don't like how Friedrich handled that?" He jerked a thumb over his shoulder at the bloody man who stood silent, his face a souring fruit in time-lapse.

"Me either. He was sloppy and unprofessional. You know what else it was? The only option we had left. He's right. He saved us, even though he gave the stream editors a treasure trove of footage."

"I saved you." Friedy pouted more than he barked the line.

"You butchered people and loved it."

Guion jabbed a finger into Jon's chest hard enough to make it hurt. "He wouldn't have had to do that if you had cloaked us."

"Uh, that's me, not him."

All eyes turned to Steve.

"I was the one not cloaking you." He made gun fingers at Jon. "Got your back, Jon-O."

"They wouldn't have seen us," Guion said. "They wouldn't have attacked, and every single person you're blubbering over right now would be stuffed into their surplus easy chairs cramming their face with insta-food and watching streams."

"You shot people. Guion shot people. You don't have any problem with that," Friedy said. "You want me to be helpless so you can be a hero. This is why I didn't tell you the last time I saved you."

"What are you talking about?"

"I paid Tawni's dealer not to cut her purchase. He sold it to her pure."

Jon's eyes bulged. Guion had to hold him back. "You what?"

"You weren't ever going to leave her, and she was destroying you. Your performance rating was slipping. All you cared about was helping her, and all she cared about was getting drunk and high."

"You lived at the top of The Heights!" Jon's scream cracked his voice. "You could have set her up somewhere safe and paid her to never talk to me again. She'd have taken that deal."

Friedy shrugged one shoulder. "She wasn't worth saving, and if you weren't so damn obsessed with being an adored hero by everyone you'd see it too."

"You're a monster," he spat.

"Great, we all agree Friedrich's crazy." Guion shoved Jon back a few steps. "Let's focus on what just happened. A.W.E. is about to paint us as violent psychopaths because we had to go in bandito style."

"Malcolm needed that cloak to stay safe."

"We're completely blown. There's no way Oceana will touch us after that airs. No one will."

"It was either that or he turned us in."

"Well, he's going to have to go without now." Guion pointed out the window. "You can be damn sure they'll be sweeping the neighborhood with drones."

Jon followed the track of Guion's finger and cursed. "Steve, cloak us."

"Goodbye, New Friend. We barely knew you."

Guion stepped close. "You need to grow up. You want to keep him out of trouble?" Another thumb jerk over the shoulder. "Keep him out of sight."

Jon looked. Friedy was gone.

Guion saw his face and turned, then looked at Steve. "Is he cloaked?"

Steve nodded.

Everyone stood in place for a few long moments, the silence broken only by the crinkling of a foil pack and the crunch of chips. Jon collapsed to the couch with a sigh, like he let all the air out of his body and deflated. He hung his head in both hands. He kept them there as he punched up Malcolm by voice command to give him the bad news.

"What happened to our deal?"

"I'm sorry. The voice box turned into a war zone. If we don't cover up, we're dead in days."

"I thought you guys were pros." Malcolm wrinkled his nose. "You can't even break into a tenement without setting off a shitstorm. What the hell did you do for the megacorps?"

"They were neurally linked. There was no way—"

Malcolm threw up a hand. "Man, whatever. I don't want to hear it. Go handle your own shit. It sounds like there's a pile of—"

"I have it!" Artificial Friedy said as he blurred into their AR and terminated the call. "I cracked the next layer of files. You'll want to see this. Project Irresistible controls people's minds by manipulating the brain."

"I got that information without you already." Guion sounded tired. "They use a new model full five MIU. I can't believe I'm the one bringing you up to date." He sighed. "Friedrich is a pain in all forms."

"Full five? That was phase one. They're months into testing phase two."

Artificial Friedy shrank into the corner of their display and brought up a rendering of a human brain in his place. This one sported an infection of blazing scarlet pinpricks, like a luminous case of measles.

"These are nanites programmed to cluster in certain areas of the brain and endocrine system. When they receive command signals, they stimulate the brain or prompt the body to release hormones."

"They do what the MIU did," Jon said.

"Without the MIU," Guion said. "How do those things get in?"

Several virtual stacks of paper popped open and raced through additional data too fast for anyone but AF to read. "They're mobile and quite creative. Almost any vector will do. A.W.E. could include an injection as part of a medical exam, lace food with a load. They don't stay airborne long, but the company could mist an area with them. Show up with some 'bug bombs,'"—they could hear the air quotes—"and you've got the whole building covered in days."

"We need to get tested immediately," Guion said.

Artificial Friedy smiled and shook his head. "The one thing they aren't yet is contagious. Once they find a home, they stay, and they don't reproduce."

"AF, how close are they to deploying these nanites?" Jon said.

"Imminent. Early trials proved successful and they merely needed to prepare the testbed."

"Prepare the testbed . . . oh, shit!" Jon said. "You mean justify deployment."

Guion shot him a chilled look. "You think they're going to use the SHOC^3 offensive to infect the neighborhood."

"You heard AF. Phase two means they can get you whether you've got an implant or not."

"That's what Boulliver was doing here. It wasn't us. Not originally." Guion rubbed his temples. "He was escalating the conflict with the B7s so the city government wouldn't protest when he nanite bombs the peninsula."

"And we took the situation from bad to worse." Jon gave Guion a serious look. "We probably accelerated their timeline by a couple of months." He rocked back and shouted at the ceiling. "Fuck! They've got public support to carpet bomb all of downtown Rockaway at this point."

Steve slapped Jon on the shoulder. "Just keep me fed, good buddy. It doesn't matter what they try, I won't let them find you."

Guion frowned. "Do you even know all the methods they'll deploy to hunt us down?"

Steve shrugged. "Who cares? Not me."

"How do you intend to hide us from detection you're not even aware of?"

"See, you're thinking scientifically. That's your problem. I don't work that way. None of us do. That's why our contracts are so valuable. I don't want someone to see you? They don't see you." He snapped his fingers. "Doesn't matter if they've got dogs, or infrared cameras, or motion detectors, or anything. I say you're not seen, you're not seen. Magic breaks the rules."

Something lit in Guion's face. "That's it. A three-man unit with almost no gear and no support has a zero percent chance of success, but we get to break the rules. We take this fight to A.W.E. and destroy Project Irresistible."

"Okay," John said slowly, "but you say that like it's bad news."

Guion sighed deep and heavy into his hands. "To do it, we need Friedrich."

39

Friedy knew where he needed to be, Guion's plan to hole up and abandon people be damned. When he turned onto Beach 148th street, he found SHOC^3 had made it there first. A column of black humvees hugged the curb at the head of the block, and groups of soldiers in full combat armor gathered at the front and back of the house.

What happened? What were they doing here? Who pointed them at Nana Robin? None of it mattered in that moment. Their numbers, their gear, the way they clustered at the door and covered the perimeter, it all screamed they weren't here to ask questions and be gentle. They'd come to his house looking for a fight. Fine. He'd give them one.

Friedy charged, but not before they breached. Three door-buster rounds from a shotgun blew the hinges off the door and a kick sent it spinning inside. A crash from the backyard said they forced their way in there too.

He felt something strange. A queasy, crawling sensation that twisted his guts. He knew this feeling. Fear. He'd felt it most of his life. But he never felt it when pumped full of primal power like he was now.

It wasn't the squad, or two squads, or however many troops they unleashed on this house. When the beast came out, he was in the moment, didn't think, didn't even count. But some things from his higher brain function stayed with him. Nana Robin stayed with him, and he knew the old woman couldn't take the rough treatment they promised.

The lead solider threw something inside and they all ducked against the brick exterior. A blast of light and a thunderclap exploded from within, and they started to pour inside.

He bounded up the front steps and caught the tail soldier from behind, slammed him into the far wall and ripped at him, but his steely fingers found no purchase on his seamless body armor.

Shouts. "He's at the front door!" and "Man down! Man down!" The rest of the team was only steps away. Already their weapons swung toward him. Friedy dropped a fist like a bone club on the soldier under him, felt something in his face move that shouldn't, and bounded into the rest before they could fire. He bounced among them. Raked with hands like talons. Sometimes he felt meat rip and came away wet.

Bangbangbang!

Friedy stumbled a step from the hot slash that scored his leg. They could fire this close to each other? They weren't supposed to be able to do that.

They were spreading out, surrounding him. Soon there'd be more. Soon there'd be more shooting.

Friedy vaulted past a soldier and hammered the one behind with a clubbing swing that broke his neck. He bounded upstairs chased by gunfire and stopped, perched atop his bed. He panted and thought animal thoughts for the five seconds of rest the move bought him.

His leg stung. Hot tears poured down his thigh. Here came the *clompclompclomp* of their boots up the stairs. There were a lot of them and they were willing to shoot in close quarters around each other. That could hurt Nana Robin. He needed to fight them up here, or outside, or away from the house.

He glanced out the window that overlooked the street.

Friedy was already crawling over the roof when the flash-bang exploded in his bedroom. The SHOC^3 troopers knew. The drones hovering overhead certainly told them. But what they knew and what they could respond to were two different things.

He skittered across the sloped tile, latched onto the edge, crashed through a window and grabbed a trooper without ever releasing his hold on the roof. He swung back out the window like a monkey, hauled the trooper with him. Friedy swung back up onto the roof. He didn't take the trooper with him. The man battered one of the humvees below with a hard landing.

The soldier got up and reentered the house. He didn't do it quickly. The man moved like the fall took something from him, but it didn't take his life.

They fired through the roof, but the wood and the shingles bent the bullet paths.

Friedy snagged any drone that flew too low. There were always more.

That's when they came out the windows after him. Multiple points at once, so he couldn't choke their advance. Going after one left him open to the others.

He did it anyway, surged across the gap as a soldier readied his weapon. Friedy was fast. So was the soldier. A shot took meat off his ribs before he bit the man's throat out. He swallowed and stopped, the pause earning him a round through the shoulder.

Friedy snarled. He threw the gasping, soon-to-be-corpse in his hands at an advancing group. It tasted funny. Something was in the meat. But they were here now, all on the roof, converging on him. Just like he wanted.

He couldn't win this fight, but he didn't care about this fight. Friedy leapt off the roof, hit the ground below in a bound, and raced inside. He was in Nana's room seconds later.

Her bed was empty, but he smelled her here still. Hiding. Light shone through a few bullet holes in the wall, proving it a good idea.

"Nana! Nana, are you here?"

"Friedy?" Her voice was weak and full of fear, and under the bed.

He dropped to the ground and held out his hand. "They'll be here in seconds. Let me get you out of here."

She took his hand. He pulled her out and stood her up with haste and care. He smiled at her as she caught her balance and stood on her own two feet. He smiled a few seconds too long.

Friedy vaulted through the bedroom door before the SHOC^3 troops had an opportunity to form up or touch their hair triggers. His primal mind and his organic-computer consciousness churned with the realization that these soldiers were willing to fire their weapons into Nana's room. They were ready to hurt her. His thoughts boiled. The beast raged, and the human let the leash slip more.

The troopers massing at the door fell back as a single midnight blue fist bristling with gunmetal black weapons. They fired long bursts and retreated into the dining room.

Friedy loped forward one stride, landed halfway up a wall and soared over their heads before the bullets reached him, a musky blur. He snagged the rear trooper by the chin as he landed and rocketed his head to the floor. The tile cracked. Spiderweb fractures radiated from the impact site.

Friedy dug a talon under the man's jaw and yanked with

a wet rend, then beat another soldier with the full helmet, stunned him with the blow and hugged him tight as the rest opened fire, soaked their lead with his body and armor. Two bursts later he bit the trooper's throat out and threw him bleeding and dying into their midst.

This time he chewed and swallowed. The meat tasted funny, but it still fed him.

He moved faster. He did worse. He beat and broke and ate them, and as he worked, Nana Robin stood in the doorway.

She saw him rip men and women to shreds and stuff his mouth full of the ragged human ruins. She saw the tacky gore he wore like a toddler's meal.

She saw all that, screamed, turned ashen, and collapsed gasping.

Friedy snapped out of his butcher meal. Nana was down. She needed help.

But he smelled more meat coming.

40

alcolm didn't answer the door when Friedy rang the bell and pounded. He didn't come when Friedy yelled for him either. Nor when he waved in front of the camera.

"Malcolm! Open up! I need your help!"

Nana sat sprawled and gasping in a deck chair beside the door.

"I'm sorry about your hand!" He started to cry and it showed in his voice. "Please! Please, Malcolm! It's Nana! She's had another heart attack and she needs help, but if I bring her there SHOC^3 will grab me and they'll leave her to die!"

Motion in the window caught his eye. Malcolm.

"Jesus, did you go on a killing spree?"

"I did what I had to. Now help her!"

Malcolm looked at the old woman spilling out of his chair outside. Friedy punched the window and left bloody smears on the treated plastic pane. Malcolm jerked back.

"Now!"

Malcolm held up his hands, the intact and ruined one wrapped in plaster both. "Chill man."

"Take her!"

"Once you're gone, I'll—"

Friedy slammed both fists into the door. *"Get out here!"*

"Man, fuck this. You ain't taking my other hand. I'm calling SHOC^3."

Friedy savaged the door, snapped the deadbolts and ripped the hinges clean off the frame with his assault. Loping on all fours, he bounded up the short flight of stairs into the living room where Malcolm stood MIU lit, gun in hand.

Malcolm fired as soon as he saw Friedy, but the little man leaped under the bullet and tackled Malcolm in the same stride. He ripped the MIU off Malcolm's waist, snapping the device's belt clip with a dull *ting*. Friedy held it in front of Malcolm's face and crushed it with an evil smile.

That's when he saw it. The living room looked smaller now that the mirror wall was raw sheetrock speckled with the rare sparkling shard that remained, but it also felt tighter because of the boxes lined up against the shattered wall.

Malcolm was leaving.

"You called them!"

Friedy pinned Malcolm to the ground with a talon-clutch at his throat. Malcolm grabbed Friedy's arm and yanked. He might as well have tugged on a stone column.

"You pointed them to her!"

Malcolm's face darkened. His lips purpled. He tried to speak, but he couldn't move air through his throat. His mouth swelled as blood pooled and instead of words, he spat froth on Friedy's arm.

Friedy grabbed Malcom's good arm and bit a strip of meat off.

"Jon said you wouldn't, but you did!"

His jaw stretched, unhinged. He took Malcom's remaining hand in his mouth and ground through his wrist, felt the strong muscles work in his throat as he swallowed it whole.

41

Jon shut down his call and cursed. Guion asked with a look.

"You have to go without a cloak for a few minutes. That was Friedy."

Weariness leaned Guion against the wall. He folded his arms and braced himself.

"SHOC^3 raided Nana Robin's place looking for him."

That popped Guion off the wall. Alarm stiffened his spine. Jon held out a hand.

"They didn't get him. They didn't get her either, but he thinks the flashbangs and gunfire gave her another heart attack."

"They're not pursuing?"

"That's why you're uncloaked for a little bit. I've got Steve covering her while they make their way to the clinic. They were all over the house, but he gave them the slip long enough for Steve to take care of it. As long as he doesn't do anything to get their attention again, he should be alright."

"They'll have drone coverage."

"Of course they do." Steve wiggled his fingers. "Ftzzzzz. Static in the feed. Lost visual. Happens all the time."

"I have to get down there," Jon said. "SHOC^3's going to look for Friedy there, and if we leave him to handle that on his own . . ." Jon shook his head.

"Yeah, we don't need anything like that. Get going. I'll stay low here." Black motion out the window behind Jon caught Guion's eye. "Steve, what's that?"

Steve turned from his post on the couch and looked over his shoulder to the street below. "That is a column of four SHOC^3 humvees pulling up to this house." He went back to gnawing his way down the length of a large sausage like a power tool.

Guion directed Jon to the window with a gesture.

"Two squads." A few quick steps took Jon to the bedroom and its rear-facing window. "They're taking positions in front and back."

"Steve, how could they know we're here? Are we still cloaked?"

"Jon-boy keeps me fat and happy, so I keep you tucked up and quiet. Well, not you. Not right now. So maybe *shh*." He put a finger to his lips.

A heavy rumble through the floorboards announced that the front squad was hoisting the garage door. Jon and Guion froze, looked at each other through the open doorway that separated the rooms. In the silence, they heard the men gathering and taking position.

Guion checked his gun. Empty. He held it up and gestured to Jon. He signaled back half a mag.

Bang!

Wood splintered.

Feet stomped and rushed.

They were shouting below, and Paul shouted back.

Guion looked at his empty gun. They couldn't fight

SHOC^3 without weapons. They'd have to run while troopers questioned Paul. He'd fight them for a little bit, but he wouldn't last long.

Bangs and clatters from downstairs. Guion pictured them throwing Paul to the ground and cuffing his hands behind his back. The yelling got louder. SHOC^3 screamed questions and didn't like the answers they got. They were getting frustrated.

Guion pulled Jon close with a gesture. They leaned in. "You said two squads," Guion whispered. "They can't fit all eight men in Paul's place, so I need you to find out where the others are. We'll slip out of here and if we can make a distraction, grab Paul with Steve's cloak. Friedrich can be exposed for a few minutes. Otherwise, we'll have to get him later, and that'll be harder."

Be still, dear boy. The officers below are quite ignorant of your presence and will remain so unless you do something so foolish as to educate them otherwise.

Guion grabbed Jon's arm as the man moved back toward the window. He pointed to his head and mouthed "Jack."

"How do you know what's going on?" Guion said.

They're here at my bidding.

"You called them?"

Indeed. Come now. I so respect your powers of analysis and deduction. I beg you not to disappoint me and say they derived from your use of chemicals and not from your own highly honed mind.

"What are you talking about?"

This entire situation is disintegrating. It's as plain as day. Friedrich's tendency to go rogue has been steadily increasing in both frequency and intensity. Your exposure in the neighborhood continues to grow. These factors have repeatedly stymied your ability to resolve your dilemma.

"How does calling SHOC^3 help any of that?"

"He called SHOC^3?" Jon said.

Guion shushed him with a gesture.

I didn't only call them here. I also left an anonymous tip that Friedrich was with the old woman. It was obvious he was going back to her when he disappeared from your argument.

"You turned her in?"

A calculated sacrifice. The reward of such action was of demonstrably higher value than the cost. I hear the upset in your tone, and it disappoints me that I must state the obvious: I was acting according to the principles you laid out.

"I never advocated calling SHOC^3."

Details. We are withdrawing from the community and removing liabilities.

"That doesn't make everyone expendable."

Jon looked. Guion silenced him with a hand.

Malcolm was a clear risk. He knew too much and stood to gain too greatly by sharing that knowledge. Compounded by his justifiable animosity toward you, his betrayal was inevitable.

If SHOC^3 raided a position he knew you used, would he not be a likely suspect? And if the old woman were placed in danger, would Friedrich respond with logic and rational thought?

"He'd be a wild animal."

Which SHOC^3 would expect after reviewing the footage from your most recent rooftop foray.

"They'll kill him."

But likely not before he removed Malcolm from the equation. This closes a security gap and removes Friedrich as a wild variable.

"But we need him. You know we do."

Do you? Do you really need him as much as you need to be rid of him?

The voices fell quiet downstairs. More shuffling. The garage door trundled up again, then fell with a metallic bang.

"What's Paul got to do with any of this?"

With Friedrich's death, SHOC^3 will have tasted success but be left with no leads to follow. Anyone they might have questioned will be dead. They'll have to return to canvassing the neighborhood, *which has netted them nothing. So I offered them Paul as a known business partner to Malcolm.*

"Why? That's stupid. He knows us. He'll crack under interrogation."

Indeed he will, if they think to ask about you. For now, they'll use him to build a case against Malcolm, for whom I suspect they'll be searching for a little while yet, if Friedrich acts as savagely as I suspect. In the meantime, SHOC^3 has just apprehended a criminal at this address. They won't pay attention to it as closely now. You have the breathing room to vacate the area.

"But he was innocent."

He was a godless fornicator. He was most certainly not innocent.

"Unacceptable. You don't take action like that without my consent."

Oh, dear boy, do you mistake me for a subordinate? We are partners, you and I. Equals, if I'm being charitable.

"I don't remember any conference about this."

Because you'd have stood in the way of what needed to be done. You're slipping, Guion, letting sentiment cloud your better judgment. This action was prudent and beneficial. You may not like all the details, but you cannot argue with its reasoning.

At this point it's all moot anyway. What are you going to do? Interrupt SHOC^3's arrest? I suggest you sit tight and let my machinations work to your benefit.

Silence hung between them for long moments. Jack had nothing left to say, and Guion didn't have a response.

He filled Jon in instead. He'd hit all the major points when Jon tapped the air with a finger and rocked back like he'd been struck. "Okay. Okay, hang tight. I'm on my way."

He walked to the windows, checked the backyard and the street. All empty.

"That was Paula. Friedy's at the clinic with Nana Robin

and he's lost his mind. SHOC^3's got to be on their way there right now. Steve, get up. You're coming with me."

"What? I don't have to do that. You know I can work my mojo right here with my pal Uber Size Double-Stuffed Fish Fry Burger."

"I'm not calling Guion to relay who needs the cloak when. You're gonna do it on the fly, right next to me. Let's go."

Steve took a bite of his sandwich and squirted a glop of tartar sauce onto his paunchy stomach. He took another before he finished chewing the first and struggled to his feet with a grumble.

"I need you to stay here so we have some free space under Steve's cloak. Jack's a wild card and we have to deal with that sometime, but right now he's right. If they're asking him about Malcolm, they're not going to turn around and come right back, so you shouldn't need Steve's protection."

Guion nodded agreement and motioned to the door. "Go."

They left Guion alone, truly alone for the first time in months, and haunted by Jack's silent presence. Jack called in the tips. What else had Jack done without his knowledge?

42

riedy slammed Malcolm's Electro Glide to a screeching halt in front of the clinic and had Nana's door opened before the burning rubber fumes drifted away.

The lobby was filled with people seated on the wooden benches attached to the walls, dogs of various breeds and sizes at the ends of their leashes. They all erupted into barks and bared teeth as Friedy ran into the place with Nana in his arms.

"Help!" He struggled to be heard over the dogs. "She needs help!"

He ran to the front desk, where a vet tech in green scrubs sat with a look of shock.

"Sir, this is a veterinary—"

"Don't give me that shit! Everyone knows it doubles as a hospital! Help her!"

Those with larger dogs struggled as they all fought their leashes. They started dragging their pets out the door. The ones that could scooped up their dogs and carried them out.

The doors to the back area opened and Paula ran out. The

tech in blue scrubs that held Pepe on a leash had to dig his sneakers into the floor with a squeak when the pitbull saw Friedy.

"Friedy, it's okay," Paula said as she approached them.

"It's not okay!" He was crying again. Tears mingled with the mess on his face and made it look like he dripped fresh blood. "I think she's dying."

"We'll take care of her. I promise." Paula looked over her shoulder at the collection of techs that had gathered. She grabbed one with her eyes and cocked her head toward Nana Robin. "Take her in back for immediate care. It's likely cardiac arrest."

The tech came forward, but Friedy flinched back. "I'll take her."

"No. That's not a good idea."

"I said I'll take her!"

The dogs in the lobby were gone, but howls and snarls poured out from the back. Paula gestured to the doors. "You hear that? You're upsetting all the animals here. If you care about her, you'll let her go. We can't help her if you go back there and get them all riled up. It'll be complete chaos." She held out her arms. "Leave her with me, and I'll call you as soon as we've got her settled."

"No!" Friedy jerked the old woman away. "I'm not leaving her again! Do you see what happened the last time I did that?"

Pepe barked twice and kept barking. He pulled at the leash, lunging against its restraint.

"She needs me, and she needs you! You're wasting time!" Friedy shoved Paula aside and moved for the door again.

Pepe won his tug of war with a muscular jerk and chomped Friedy's leg. He yanked. Friedy fell. The little man barely managed to pass Nana Robin off to Paula before he went down. She disappeared in back shouting orders as Friedy smacked the tile.

Friedy relaxed his soul's grip a little more and swelled with the beast. Now he pulled his lips back and bared his teeth. He growled. Pepe understood the language and flexed the muscles atop his head, squeezed his jaws tighter. His savage yanks back and forth dragged Friedy along the tile.

"Pepe! Pepe, you have to let go!" Paula was back. "Pepe! Stop! I don't know what happened. I've never seen him like this before." Friedy didn't know who she was talking to.

Friedy sat up and hammered Pepe's shoulder and felt the joint shift under the piled meat.

Paula screamed. She called for Friedy to stop, but he didn't hear words now, only sounds. She sounded terrified.

Pepe used the pain to grind his jaws together. Friedy pounded his neck, but the dog didn't let go, so he grabbed the dog's ear and ripped it off.

Shrieks now. Hysterical sounds.

The dog saw the opportunity and took it. He jumped his jaws from Friedy's leg to his neck. Friedy had to jam his arm in the dog's mouth to save himself. He howled.

Pepe pulled him over, wrenched until his shoulder popped. Friedy flailed at Pepe, his aim thrown this way and that as he wrestled his way along the floor with the dog. Finally he snagged Pepe's paw, yanked himself close and shredded the dog's belly open.

That got him to let go at last. Friedy sat a moment in the new silence. All the sound now came from behind the door. He was shot. He was bit. He was hungry.

He started to eat, but found he didn't like the taste.

43

"Are you there, Jack?"

Always, dear boy.

"You're Jack the Ripper, aren't you?"

Right to it then. No warm-up or appetizer at all.

"That's not an answer."

No.

Jack spoke the truth. Their minds pressed close enough now that Guion felt that, but he also felt that terse reply hid something. It hovered below the surface close enough to sense, but beyond clear sight.

Guion worked the hunch, pulled open an article on Jack the Ripper in AR, shuddered at the photos of the victims, at the recounting of the crimes. Rockaway mirrored history with horrid accuracy.

This isn't the sort of literature that fulfills our bargain.

For the first time, Guion ignored Jack, dug deeper. More accounts. Biographical summaries of the investigators, witnesses, suspects. Related links.

He went cold inside.

"You're not *just* Jack the Ripper."

Silence.

"You've been here before. Springheel Jack. The Monster of London. Whipping Tom, twice." The area had a history full of violent misogynists.

Monikers that have been pinned to me at different times.

Guion swiped from article to article. "I don't get it. All of these figures terrorized women. What's medical literature have to do with any of this?"

Nothing at all, though lest you think I wasted your time, I very much enjoyed learning about cutting-edge developments. I found the material on nanoneurosurgery and machine learning particularly fascinating.

"I haven't been feeding you?" His gaze bounced from place to place in the empty room in confusion.

You've been doing enough.

"Meaning?"

Meaning you provided me the opportunities to satiate my hunger myself. I considered that sufficient to fulfill our bargain. No need to burden you the way Steven does Jonathan.

"Jon was right. You are the one killing women. But how? Those murders started long before I agreed to give you use of my body."

Not technically true. Our recent arrangement allows me use of your flesh while you are conscious. Your consent meant I don't displace you, something expressly forbidden in our contract. However, were I to borrow your form while you slumber, you're not in conscious control of your body, are you? No displacement.

Guion stood, examined the door, pushed it open and looked down the long staircase. "How's that possible? You couldn't have left with everyone sleeping right there." He gestured to the living room.

I must confess a lie of omission. I haven't made the full array of my abilities available to you. You are quite correct, even a chap as subtle as I would be hard-pressed to slip past a room of sleeping lads undetected, especially when confronted with that garage door and its dreadful racket.

He closed the door and snapped the bolts closed. "So how, or are you tweaking me the way you did Jon?"

Is that hope I hear in your voice, Guion? Desperation, perhaps? You want me to be lying. Walk to the bedroom. Answer your own question.

Numb steps carried him down the short hall, through the open doorway, and left him standing in the middle of the second room, gaze swinging across the bare walls. He stopped on the window on the second pass. More numb steps. A trembling hand on the warm glass. Photos of the Rockaway victims flashed in his mind, throats cut, bellies butchered.

Were they photos?

"Springheel Jack leapt across rooftops. Pepe sleeps in the backyard some nights, but bloodhounds couldn't find Jack the Ripper, nor could police even when they almost outnumbered the pedestrians at night."

Jack said nothing, but Guion felt his nod.

"You did it and I let you."

I required just a smidge of your cooperation, not to dig too deeply at first, and your consent through absence has proven a boon to us both. Not only have we progressed in our chosen endeavors, but as you said before, we grow closer each time I come forward. In time, I will cease to be a creature of Hell and be mortal once more, free to stay. Through you, dear Guion, I can be born again.

44

Paula's glass-cut face flashed in Jon's peripheral as they raced toward the clinic. Voice-only call.

"We're almost there," Jon said as a greeting.

"He killed Pepe!" Paula's words were equal parts yell and sob. "He fucking killed my dog, Jon!"

Jon heard banging in the background.

"Where are you?"

"I'm in a safe room in the back. We put a reinforced door on one of the rooms. There's a hidden way out too, but I'm afraid to leave."

More bangs and rattling.

"He's obsessed with saving Nana Robin, but I think she's already dead. I don't know what he'll do when he realizes that."

Yelling. Friedy's voice.

"The door and frame are metal, but this fucking psycho might actually break in. He was already hurt when he got here and Pepe—" Her voice broke. She sobbed and sniffed. "Pepe hurt him more before—" She started to cry.

Jon slammed his brakes as traffic slowed to gridlock

ahead. Roadblock. Had to be. That meant SHOC^3 was already on the scene. Jon pulled to the curb and hauled Steve out of the car. "Come on. We're running the rest of the way."

They wove and shouldered their way through the thick crowd until it stopped at the perimeter ring SHOC^3 had established around the clinic. A pair of black humvees sat in front, and traffic said another was at the rear of the building by the shelter and dog run. A quick scan counted four troopers outside, armed, body language alert. They didn't have anyone inside yet. What were they waiting for? The dogs inside screamed a riot of barks and howls, and standing out from them was the reason. Even with all their noise, Jon could hear Friedy from out here, a human voice making inhuman sounds.

Jon crept closer, leading Steve by the wrist like a child. That's when he saw Paul sitting in the back of one of the jeeps. This was the same group that raided their house.

"Cloak him." Jon knelt with his back against the vehicle and overrode its door locks, then released the cuffs at Paul's wrists and the manacles that bolted him into the vehicle. He pulled open Paul's door and greeted the man with a finger to his lips. He motioned Paul out and led him across the street where they hunkered down behind a parked car. Well, Paul and Jon did. Steve stood.

"What are they waiting for?" Jon said.

"They came here for Paula. They told me on the way over that we're involved in trafficking illegal goods, and after they got me, they were stopping to pick her up."

"I count eight guys. They don't think that's enough for a simple arrest?"

"Friedy's in there. I heard them say something about what he did to the squads sent to get him at Nana Robin's. It was more guys than this, and they were all on H.A.R.D."

H.A.R.D. Human Aggression Refined and Directed. A

fast-acting combat amphetamine that increased reflexes, deadened pain receptors, and, true to its name, made the user more aggressive.

"These guys all took a shot of it. They've got reinforcements coming too. Five minutes, maybe."

Jon thought for one breath. "Okay, I'm going to get you out of here, but first I'm going in there and bringing them out."

"Uh, Jonny." Steve held up three fingers.

"We'll figure out how to get away from SHOC^3 later. First, we have to get them out of the building before they raid it."

"Yeah, okay, but I'm telling you now that if vet-lady keeps screaming about her dog getting eaten, there's gonna be too many eyes on her to wrap her in the cloak."

"What happened to Pepe?"

Something broke with a bang and crash inside. Paula screamed. Paul bolted. Jon followed only a step behind. They tore open the door and disappeared inside the clinic before the troopers outside responded.

Paul charged through the lobby and shouldered open the door to the hospital area. He stopped for a beat at the safe room, metal door beaten with dents and lying like a corpse in the middle of the room. Hinges hung ragged from the bent door frame. His pause let Jon grab his arms and pin them behind his back.

A hidden door on the opposite wall hung open, turning the room into a tunnel that opened into the dog run behind the clinic. Paula ran through the grassy area, bloody hand clapped high on a bloody shoulder, Friedy on her heels.

SHOC^3 shouted commands mingled with Paula's screams and animal noises.

"Down! Get down on the ground, now!"

"Shoot this psychopath! Shoot him! Fucking kill him!" She

went down. Jon couldn't tell if she tripped or hit the dirt to clear the firing lines.

Gunfire.

Howls.

Friedy pounced on Paula and bit her wounded shoulder. His mouth was too big, had too many teeth. He chomped the whole meaty joint and wrenched her arm off.

"Paula!" Paul ripped free from Jon's slackened hold and burst into the yard after her as Friedy leapt first to the roof, then across the street with lightning speed, the dying woman's arm still hanging from his mouth like a worm. Her moans drained from her like the lifeblood that pooled around the ragged rip and made crimson mud.

Paul had been cloaked. His sudden appearance through the banging door startled the troopers, hopped up on combat drugs and the horrifying sight they'd just witnessed. They didn't think for a second but opened fire in short bursts.

Jon dove after him before he finished saying her name. He tackled Paul a hair ahead of the fire and rolled him first against the clinic wall, then through the safe room's outer door to break line of sight. Paul struggled, but Jon grabbed him and whispered for him to stay quiet.

The troopers filed in, tight formation, checked their corners. They looked right at Paul and Jon, who kept a hand clapped over Paul's mouth and crushed him in a bear hug to keep him still.

No one heard Paula anymore.

Jon watched the troopers move to the lobby to figure out where Friedy might have gone before releasing Paul. He bolted for the outside again, but silently this time.

"You know, not for nothing JonJon, but your plans suck."

"No one asked you to follow me in here, you lazy—"

Steve sat in the other corner, stuttering every breath, bleeding dark blood through the bullet holes in his chest.

"Oh shit! You're hit!"

"Nothing gets by you."

"You took bullets for me?"

"Or I couldn't be bothered to get out of the way." Steve smiled. Blood leaked out between his teeth. "One of those."

Jon looked out the door into the dog run. Paul knelt and rocked Paula in his arms, sobbing. "Dammit, I'm sorry, Steve, but I've got to get out of here before your cloak goes."

"Why—?" Steve choked and swallowed. "Why would my cloak go anywhere?"

"Doesn't it disappear with you?"

"Yeah, so?" Cough. "This body's about had it, but you're not rid of me that easy, Jon-O." He pressed his tongue through bloody lips. "You're gonna be buying me a lot more food." He took one more shuddering breath before all his muscles relaxed and the air spilled from his lungs.

Jon checked his pulse. Definitely dead.

Around the clinic, everything was silent now. Those reinforcements would arrive any minute with nothing to distract them. Friedy was gone, or dead. And Paula . . . he didn't want to think about Paula. He hovered over Steve unsure what to expect or do.

Paul put a hand on his shoulder. He turned to look at his neighbor, who now wore a grin he recognized.

"Hey good buddy, you think we can stop for pizza on the way home?"

45

Guion dead-walked into the bedroom and dropped cross-legged on the floor.

"We were close," he muttered to himself. "I really thought we were going to do this."

Not now though. Friedrich stole a death sentence for all of them, then damned them.

No. That wasn't fair. He damned himself and he gave them all the choice to follow, which they did. Friedrich let himself become a wild animal that delighted in eating human flesh, but Guion willingly turned a blind eye to what Jack was doing. He didn't know because he didn't want to know. He laughed. Isn't that what he accused Jon of doing with A.W.E. so long ago? Suddenly, how Jon lived until the Ibacipla run made perfect sense. The world really was so much more pleasant when he didn't look at the evil in it.

He sat with that for a moment, punched up her contact, and put the call through. Full AR this time.

"Guion!" Griffin's face fell when she saw him. "What's wrong?"

"We're not coming in." He struggled to keep his voice level, took another hard swallow. "I'm not coming in."

"What happened?"

Deep breath. "You're going to see something on the feeds soon enough. It's not me, but it could be one day."

She leaned in. "I don't understand." He could feel her reaching out to him.

"In our desperation to get away from A.W.E., we took a few hasty gambits, and they turned out to be worse than we realized at the time." He blinked hard and shook his head. "I made a career out of not giving a shit about most people, but even I have limits."

"What is it? What did you do?"

"Nothing. Not a goddamned thing, even when I knew better. That's the problem."

"You're not making sense. Talk to me. Tell me what's going on."

He felt a thick layer of tears over his eyes. "It's better you don't know."

"So why did you call?"

"I wanted to tell you I'm sorry for everything before. I wanted to tell you I've missed you ever since you left, and how excited I've been at the thought of coming back to you." He stopped, clearly not done. The next words caught in his throat. She let him work them free in silence. "I wanted to see you one last time and say goodbye. You won't hear from me again."

"Whatever it is, I'm sure—"

"I love you, Griffin."

That stunned her to silence. She was still staring at him wide-eyed when he terminated the connection.

Jon only returned to the apartment because he didn't want to leave the update in Steve's hands. Everything had gotten so fucked up in a single afternoon. Steve was Paul now. Friedy was still on the loose with SHOC[3] hot on his heels. Oh, and he ate Paula.

"Just her arm," Steve said on the way home. "She was still alive for a minute there. Paul saw her bleed out. Let me tell you, I thought I could eat, but I've got nothing on that man. Whoo boy!"

He tuned Steve out, prepared to deliver the situation update to Guion in a way that didn't let him interrupt, didn't allow any ranting about Friedy or plans to kill him. Friedy, the boy more a brother to him than his own blood, was dead. Some monster rampaged in his skin. Jon felt like a walking dead man with no interest in dealing with the ugliness of what lay before them. He rehearsed the report in his mind on the way home, not just the information, but how to shut down the anticipated interruptions too.

What he didn't account for was Guion slumped in front of the stained porcelain toilet, ragged and raw-faced and . . . were those tear tracks? Guion was crying?

Fuck.

"You were right. It was Jack. Every time he comes forward, he doesn't go back as far, and now he's close enough that we share some memories." He heaved a ragged gag into the bowl, but he'd clearly hollowed out his stomach long ago.

"You remember the victims?"

Guion wretched again. "I remember butchering them."

"Jesus." Jon slid down the wall across from Guion and collapsed slow motion into a crouching sit like a punctured inflatable doll slowly leaking air. His head fell into one hand that gripped his temples. "We fucked everything up, Guion. We brought evil to this neighborhood. They were already struggling with overpolicing and poverty, and we dropped a pack of murderers and monsters right on them."

"Can we undo this?" Guion asked in a voice that trembled with the risk of vomiting if he teased the hair trigger too much.

Jon gaped. "There is no undoing this, man! We've killed people! Our neighbors are dead. Malcolm . . . fuck." His head fell into that temple grip again and rocked. "We butchered his baby girl, ruined his business, ate his hand, and then . . ." He dragged his head up and let it fall against the wall with a soft *thump*. "I stopped by his house on the way back here. Door smashed. Inside trashed. No Malcolm, but enough blood splatter for me to figure out what happened. He's got kids, Guion, and people relying on him. We fucked him over and over before killing him and stranding all the people who needed him."

"But can Friedrich get rid of them?" The desperation made him a child begging for safety.

Jon sank again. "Look, man, things went really bad out there."

"How bad?"

"Steve?"

"Come on, man. I'm figuring out my optimal sitting position here with the new suit. It doesn't fit like the old one."

"Get your ass over here."

"That was Paul," Guion said, his voice laden with the question.

"Yeah, no. Steve here." Steve leaned into the bathroom doorway with Paul's body and pointed to himself with both hands before swinging his head between the two men. "We all clear now? Can I go?"

"Friedy's completely off the reservation," Jon said. "Nana Robin's dead, and it's left him fully in the grip of the beast. I don't know if he's coming back here, and if he does, we're going to have to put him down."

Guion slapped on his AR glasses and urged Jon to do the same with a pointed look.

The message hovered in view, waiting for him when he did.

"Can Steve hop bodies whenever he wants?"

Jon shrugged and keyed in his reply. "I didn't even know he could hop at all. It's the first time he's done it."

Guion frowned. "I doubt Paul agreed to be a host. Are we at risk?"

"He won't take me. I'm bound by contract to feed him. You?" Jon shook his head. "I have no idea. No offense, but you might be a little crowded already."

"He's a bigger risk than we knew. If he's not bound to a body like the other two are, we have no way of eliminating him if we have to."

Jon stared hard and unblinking for a moment before responding. "We're way past the 'if' part of 'if we have to.'"

Guion shrank. "How do we do that without Friedrich's banishment equation?"

"The other two are bound to a body. Steve's the only slippery one."

Guion frowned. "I'm not looking to kill myself, Jon."

"I'll keep an eye out for other opportunities, but you're the one with the evil genius strategy package."

Artificial Friedrich fuzzed into their shared AR session. "I cracked another file. The planning for this, in fact just about everything involved with Irresistible, is housed in Pluto."

"No one ever does any business in Pluto. No one does anything in Pluto. It's where the hyper-rich live and the rest of us make up stories about it."

Guion sat back against the wall facing Jon but not seeing him. His eyes had that faraway look that saw tactical simulations with weighted variables run in a fast-forward loop and explained the plan to them when he came to, though there wasn't much to detail. They'd infiltrate the A.W.E. corp-platz and place a pair of viruses into the corporate network. One would hunt down all files related to Project Irresistible and destroy them. The other would take over the 3D printing production facilities and change the design specs from Irresistible's nanites to self-replicating eaters. One batch activated on a timer, with enough lag for them to be loaded with whatever ordinance was being shipped to $SHOC^3$, the other activated as soon as it was produced. Both would go on a cancerlike binge, consuming all raw material around them and using it to make more of themselves. They'd destroy the production facilities used to create the Irresistible nanites, any stockpiles already produced, and the conventional weaponry for $SHOC^3$'s assault as a bonus.

Jon nodded his way through the rundown. "It sounds solid."

"There's just one hitch. We need Friedrich."

Jon's jaw dropped open. "You've lost your mind. Hey, AF, can you deploy those viruses?"

Artificial Friedy blinked into Jon's vision. "But of course." He sounded giddy. "I can complete the viruses and the new nanite specs by the end of the week, just ahead of the Irresistible shipments to $SHOC^3$."

"There you go," Jon said.

"Artificial Friedrich is coming with us." Guion held up a brick of storage that bristled with memory sticks plugged into a massive collection of serial ports. "Our MIUs can't run him, but the A.W.E. systems can."

"So what's the problem?"

"Loading him onto a network robust enough to handle him is going to involve cracking through some heavy security clearance."

"I can penetrate encryptions and locks," Artificial Friedy said.

"Yes, you can, but not if you're dormant in memory waiting to run. You can't come in from netspace; they keep the secure systems disconnected. That means on-site hacking. I can't do it. You can't, Jon. Steve, can you do that?"

"No can do," Steve called from the couch.

Guion gave Jon a look. "You said it yourself weeks ago. All our prior success rested on him. That hasn't changed. I need you to get him back enough to get Artificial Friedrich onto A.W.E. systems."

Jon churned calculations of his own in silence. "I don't know what's left of him, but if Friedy's still in there, I'll get him to do what we need." A hard look dropped over his face. "Then I'll kill him."

46

Friedy came back late that night. He returned clean, scrubbed the gore from his arms and face, changed into fresh clothes, even got his hair from wild down to fashionably unkempt.

He also didn't come back alone.

"Jesus Christ, Friedy. Haven't you done enough?" Jon gripped his temples in an excellent Guion impersonation, only with a lot more anger.

A woman writhed on Friedy's arm, twisting in a constant dance to rub some part of her body against him.

She was beautiful in a perverse way that took many of Friedy's features and infused them with desire. She shared his color palette, but she had a richness he didn't. Skin the color and texture of cream poured thick and taut over her firm, curvy frame. Gold hair rich in a sweet, suggestive scent spun into cable-like braids to tickle the curve of her buttocks. She wore dark eyeliner and mascara that set off the sparkle in her ice-chip eyes.

None of that explained the visceral throb of manly want he felt when he looked at her. That was an exaggerated reaction, out of proportion with the situation. It was the kind of ham-fisted seduction an infiltrating operative overclocking tailored pheromones might try, and why Jon had olfactory scrubbers installed in his nostrils.

"This is Helga." Friedy pulled the woman tighter against him. She giggled and waved. "You don't like her, Jon? Too bad. You don't seem to like anything I do anymore, so I've stopped caring what you think."

"You pacted for a woman after eating Paula and Malcolm?" Jon said.

"Just her arm," Steve said.

"I'm tired of being sorry, so save your breath." He squeezed Helga again. "We don't need Malcolm."

"Malcolm was a friend. He was your friend."

Friedy shrugged and dragged his nose along Helga's neck with a loud sniff.

"We're going to stop the nanites before SHOC^3 infests the Rockaways. You need to do some coding." Disgust saturated Guion's every aspect.

"What concerns me is that room." Friedy pointed to the bedroom. "That's mine now. Ours." He looked at Helga and smiled. "I'm going to be doing a lot of fucking, and as much as you'd all love to watch, you'll have to settle for listening." Helga dragged a hand across Friedy's chest, grabbed his face with the other, and half-kissed half-bit him.

Jon and Guion looked at each other in silence for a beat.

"This is big. AF cracked another file. Irresistible's housed in Pluto. I'll lend you my MIU to code on," Jon said.

"You know, to be fair, you should get Steve a little extra food from now on."

Steve perked up at this, pointed. "My man!"

"He'll be working harder than ever to stifle poor Helga's screams."

"Poor me?" Helga gave him a grin.

Friedy smiled back with an odd mix of tenderness and malice. "I'm going to hurt you."

She leaned her head closer to his and whispered. "Maybe that's what I want."

Guion opened his mouth; Jon beat him to it. "Yeah, I get it. You've got yourself a surrogate to work out your Danielle issues."

Friedy's predatory grin fell off his face. He swung his head to Jon with a sour scowl.

"And your Stephanie issues. And your Kelly issues. And your Nicole issues. And your Jodi issues."

The little man cooled to a smolder. "Look at you, still standing over me. Judging what I do and how I do it. Still acting like you're better than me." He slapped his chest. "I'm stronger than you. I'm faster and tougher. And now,"—he gripped Helga hard; she resumed sliding one part of her body after another along his—"I'm more a lady's man than you too."

"Summoning another demon doesn't make you suave," Jon said.

"How did you even make that deal? What the hell do you have left to offer?" Guion said.

"They don't pact for souls, Guion. They need to be fed, and by choosing to give them what they want, we damn ourselves. We hand over our souls by willingly paying the wages of sin." Jon looked sideways at Guion. "They encourage us to be bad people, and we've readily agreed. All the suffering and death that's happened here was our choice, not theirs."

"I'm going to keep Helga very well fed," Friedy said.

She reached down and grabbed his crotch, shook it for emphasis. "Yah, Friedy's manhood is most impressive," she said into his neck before staring Jon in the eye. "You're nothing by comparison, but you're welcome to embarrass yourself trying."

"Nein!" Friedy lurched forward and shoved her behind him. He jabbed a finger at Jon. "Don't you dare touch her! Ever!"

Behind him, Helga winked at Jon, but when Friedy followed Jon's gaze and looked at her, she raked her fingers across his scalp, grabbed his hair and yanked his head away from her. She breathed a hot, moist sigh as she slid his earlobe into her mouth with her tongue and dragged it out across her teeth with a low moan.

"Oh, for fuck's sake." Two strides took Jon to the couple, already getting lost in each other. "Friedy. Friedy!" He yanked the man around by the shoulder. Friedy's eyes burned wild.

"You're all jealous!" he yelled to the room.

"Hey, eyes here. Good. Listen to me very carefully, because we need to be on the same page."

They stared at each other for a long moment, Friedy full of indignant fire, Jon unflinching.

"I will never be jealous of you. You're pathetic. You're not stronger than me. You're not faster than me. You're not anything compared to me because I could pact for a beast twice as nasty as yours and take away every edge you have. All you are is dumber than me."

"I'm a genius!"

"You're the dumbest genius I've ever met, and the only one stupid enough to take the sucker's bargain you're stuck with."

Helga slid an arm across Friedy's chest and rubbed him with her leg. She opened her mouth to speak.

"And her? You think I'm jealous of her?" Jon laughed. "The only women you've had sex with are the ones you bought. This is the same exact thing, except now you need to pay with your soul instead of cash."

He threw a dismissive hand at them and walked away. "Go ahead. Fuck and scream and all of that. I'm sure she'll put on quite the show on your behalf. At least, I hope she does."

He turned and fixed Friedy with a hard stare. "Nobody here gives a fuck about your antics anymore. You're a murderer and a monster. You've got one job here, one reason we don't execute you. I suggest you do it." He held up a single finger every time he said "one." "So take your girlfriend and fuck her brains out. I don't care. Just get those programs written. AF said he could have it all done in a week. Split the work between you and you can get it done in three days."

Friedy stood stunned for a few seconds before the anger returned to his face and he rallied. "You think you can give me orders?"

"If we don't stop A.W.E., they're going to bomb this whole neighborhood with mind-controlling nanites. That includes you. Do you want to be a slave?"

Friedy paused, shook his head.

"Good. Then would you please write the code that'll make them eat themselves instead so we can end this and all go our separate ways?"

"Fine," Friedy said like a scolded child. He grabbed Helga's wrist and dragged her behind him into the bedroom. Jon stood like a statue and didn't move.

Helga's pants and moans crawled into the living room. Jon looked up as if concentrating on a faraway sound. He frowned and made for the door. "He's going to make a point, but he'll get to work when he sees how much we don't give a shit."

47

"Guion . . ."

The voice cooed to him in a lush whisper he half-heard under the thick blanket of sedative-induced sleep.

"Guion . . ."

Her hand pressed against his chest, rocked him.

Her. It was a female speaking to him, touching him, untying the bonds he now insisted on nightly. He knew that. He knew because he knew that voice. It was . . .

"Griffin?" He blinked his eyes open.

And it was. Kink-curled hair spilled around her face as she crouched next to him, toothy smile and rich chestnut eyes bright in the dark.

He reached out to her instinctively, recoiled when he saw his hands.

"You untied me?" He shook his head. "It's night. I need those restraints when I sleep."

She leaned back on her haunches and gave him her incredulous look, the one she flashed him when he went too deep into his own analysis. "Are you asleep?"

He thought about that for a second, looked around. He lay on the same foam mat in a small oasis of floor he'd cleared of trash. Just out of arm's reach, Jon sat splayed on the couch. Paul-now-Steve lay next to him, curled semi-fetal. He used Jon's thigh as a pillow. "I'm either awake or dreaming, so either way the bonds aren't an issue."

"There you go. Answered your own question."

"How'd you get here? How'd you even know where—"

"Shhhhhhhhh." She touched a gentle finger to his lips. She grabbed his eyes with hers and smiled, not just with her mouth, whispered a single chuckle. A moment passed like that before the grin dropped from her lips, but not her stare, and she slid forward, face centimeters from his, finger at the divet of his lip the whole time.

"You know, Guion," she said in a mock scold, "you're a brilliant tactician, but you have a tendency to get caught up in the details and overlook the most important things." She looked him up and down. "At least you do when it comes to you and me."

"What do you—"

She pressed even closer. Their noses almost grazed. He could feel her heat on his cheeks, or was that him?

"Don't you worry about a thing. I intend to keep you up for the rest of the night." Her whisper thickened with want, with promise.

He pulled her into his lap.

Griffin grabbed him, kissed him hard. "You always did figure it out eventually," she whispered in his ear between breathless kisses.

Guion lost track of everything. He forgot about the trash that ringed him. He forgot about the cramped apartment. He forgot about Steve and Jon and Friedy; he even forgot about the SHOC^3 kill squads searching The Hives for him and the impending nanite-bombing. He was back with her, the one woman he made illogical choices for, and at that moment it was all he wanted.

"You son of a bitch!" Friedrich screeched so loud and shrill he should have broken their cheap glass window.

Guion jerked at the sound, fell back. Friedrich stood in the doorway of the bedroom, hands dug into the frame like claws, red-faced and panting. Guion reached for Griffin to pull her behind him, but the arm he felt wasn't hers.

It was Helga.

"Get your hands off her!" Friedrich dove for Guion, but Jon interrupted him. They spilled in a human pile on the floor as Helga crab-walked to the couch and took a seat next to Steve.

"Calm down. Let's talk about this." Jon pressed both his hands down in a calming motion.

"You tried to take her!" Friedrich thrust a shaking finger, bent like a talon, at Guion.

"She looked like someone else!" Guion shifted a few strategic steps to put Jon between them.

Jon looked over his shoulder at Guion, then Helga. "Yeah?"

Guion rolled his eyes. "Of course, 'yeah.' Why would I get involved with his sex toy?"

"He's got a point, man. You know Guion. He might be a dick to you, but he's not a dick like that."

"Nein! He tried to kill me and now he wants what's mine!"

Guion, I can make some adjustments, but you need to know I can't match him.

Guion responded almost before Jack finished. "Do what you can."

When Friedrich threw Jon into the wall with a single-arm swipe, he moved at a speed Guion couldn't, charged with brute force beyond anything he could handle. Jack did his work though, and he felt it, knew his expanded limits. When Friedrich dove for him, Guion vaulted the man.

He hauled Jon to his feet. "Jack's helping. But I need you too. He's too much for me alone."

"Of course you side with him, Jon." Friedrich growled a warning and made claws with his fingers.

"There are no sides," Jon said. "We're facing enslavement by nanites, remember? We all want the same thing."

"Yah. Me," Helga said.

Friedrich's burning eyes flicked to her, then back at the two men. Time froze for half a second as they watched the beast in Friedrich's head slaughter his rational mind.

"Shit," Jon said.

"Split!" Guion said as Friedrich lunged again.

He snarled and swiped as Guion hopped to the far side of the room and spun along the wall just beyond Friedrich's reach. Jon scampered on all fours along the top of the couch and came up at the mouth of the entry hallway next to him.

"We need more room. Get him outside," Guion said.

Jon glanced back into the room where Friedrich snarled and drooled, the combination of a berserker working himself into frenzy and a bull lining up his charge. "Steve, you're covering this, right?"

Steve raised a hand overhead and pointed at Jon. "I got you, good buddy."

Guion shoved Jon as Friedy lunged again. Jon stumbled the few steps to the door, while Guion plunged into the living room with springing strides. He was fast now, fast enough to match someone with boosts.

Friedrich was faster. His hand lashed out like a serpent and snagged Guion's arm with a vise grip, wrenched his shoulder out of joint with a stomach-churning pop. He crashed to the floor. Friedrich collapsed on top of him, jaws slavering. Guion punched him in the Adam's apple, sent him back gagging and gasping, bought himself a few seconds. He widened the gap by kicking the wild man in the face and driving him down the hall.

"Jack, dig deep," he said through clenched teeth.

Jack didn't respond, but a moment later the pain dialed back. An exaggerated endorphin rush. He pushed himself up, cradling his arm against his body. Friedrich was already up, already in motion.

Guion ducked his head and leaped head-first through the window. Luckily, it was cheap and old and brittle and it snapped apart in large shards that offered minimal resistance. He burst through into the night with only a few scratches on his face and arm. Friedrich, faster, stronger, blasted after him, overshot him in the air and landed across the street in a crouch. Guion touched down in the driveway into the maze of cars. He barely felt the shock of impact.

"I'm not sure how we take him," Jon said. He tensed as Friedrich stalked across the street toward them. He snarled. He bared his teeth like an animal. He drooled like the rabid.

Guion squeezed his bad arm. "I'm hurt. I can't fight him."

Friedrich lunged and they broke apart.

"Then what do we do?" Jon shouted across Friedrich.

"We need guns." Guion had a car between him and Friedrich and played the old game of circling opposite his opponent. It was just a matter of time before Friedrich went straight over it.

"We can't shoot him!"

"The hell we can't."

"You're the one who said we needed him."

Guion danced one way, then reversed direction with a shuffle step. "I said shoot him, not kill him."

Tired of chasing Guion around the car and back, Friedrich didn't scamper over it but slammed a shoulder into it and bumped Guion with it as he swung around a corner. He staggered a step and fell to the concrete. The demon-man jumped onto the roof, ready to pounce.

Jon yanked the man's ankle. He belly-flopped with the hollow thud of sheet metal before Jon hauled him off and dropped him on the sidewalk. "Friedy, come on man! Snap out of it!"

Anger blazed on Friedrich's face and he cracked Jon's chest with a heel, knocked him off his feet and left him fighting for air.

"Don't you worry, JonJon! I've got you covered!" Steve shouted from the broken window.

That got the demon man's attention. He let Jon out of his sight for just a blink, and when Friedrich shredded the concrete where Jon was seconds earlier, he didn't scamper after him, even though Jon lay within arm's reach.

Friedrich snapped his head about, looked this way and that, but even though he looked right at Jon, he didn't react.

Then he spied Guion down the street.

He reacted.

Bounding on all fours, he blurred across the space, climbed a car in stride and vaulted off the roof before Guion had time to do much more than turn around. But when he did he was armed, and clubbed Friedrich's arm with a length of pipe. He poured it on, not sure if he was hurting the wild man, but definitely keeping him on the defensive. Friedrich shielded his face, took blow after blow on his forearms, but only gave ground one stubborn centimeter at a time.

It didn't last. Guion brought the pipe down again, but Friedrich slapped it away with a chop that bent it into a V and sent it spinning off into the night.

Friedrich reversed his swing to claw Guion's throat. He was too fast, too close for Guion to respond. But with a dull thud, Friedy lurched forward and went limp. Momentum finished his now flaccid swing, and limp Friedrich slapped Guion across the face.

Behind him, Jon flexed his mechanical fist. "One to the brain stem. He never saw me coming, so I could land it right."

Friedrich groaned.

"We have to tie him up." Guion didn't miss a beat. "He won't be out long, and he can't be free when he wakes up." He stripped off his shirt. "Here, rip this into strips."

"Is that going to do the job?" Despite his protests, Jon yanked the shirt into ties and started binding Friedrich.

"Have you noticed that whenever he comes back all bloody it's not just his hands?"

"Yeah. He eats who he fights."

"I think it's his price." Guion nodded. "I also think that if his demon doesn't get fed, it'll abandon him the same way Steve did when you denied him food."

Jon tugged the knots tight. "He's going to hate us when he comes to."

"He already hates us."

"This is going to be enough to clam him up." He looked up at Guion. "He won't crack the network."

Guion looked up at the broken window staring out over the crowded driveway and the lusty face framed in flowing gold that watched them. "We need to neutralize her."

Jon frowned.

"She's been here a day, Jon. Look at this mess. She's got to go."

"No, they've all got to go. If Friedy won't do it—"

"You already said he won't."

"Then we better come up with plans B, C, D, all the way to triple letters, and be on the lookout for any opportunities that show up along the way."

48

Jon leaned his head through the bedroom door. Friedy lay slumped against the far wall, a pillow under his butt and behind his shoulders, a collage of cloth strips tangled around his ankles and knees. Another mess of fabric bound his hands.

The wild-haired man rolled his head up and looked at Jon with bleary eyes. "My shoulders hurt."

He looked like Friedy again. Jon wanted to believe it was him, that he'd come back. He wanted to, but he didn't. "So do Guion's."

Friedy huffed. "You're with Guion. In the end you're always with Guion. He's your real friend."

"Are you hungry?"

Friedy cracked a wry smile. "Trying to shift the conversation to taking care of Poor Friedy?"

"Answer the question."

"Yah. I'm starving."

Jon crossed his arms. "I fed you an hour ago and you've never been a big eater. Why would you still be hungry?"

"The demon increases my metabolism." Friedy wouldn't look at Jon.

"Don't bullshit me. Why are you still hungry?"

Pause.

"Because I haven't gotten what I need."

"Uh huh, and what's that?"

Friedy didn't answer.

Jon leaned close. "I want you to say it."

"It's . . ." Friedy paused, words stuck in his mouth. "It's the flesh of my enemies."

Jon nodded as he stood up. He pursed his lips and looked down at Friedy. "There it is. No more dancing around it. You know it and I know it. You fucking eat people." Those last words reeked with disgust. "You're going to sit there and say that because I don't want you eating human beings alive, I'm siding with Guion?" Jon shook his head. "The real problem here is that I'm the one bothered by this." He jerked a thumb at himself, then reversed the gesture and stuck a finger at Friedy. "Where's your horror?"

Friedy stared.

"And what about Helga? She looks younger this morning than she did last night, maybe young enough to be illegal."

They sat in silence.

"Jon?"

"What?"

"Do you think you could tie my hands in front of me? My shoulders really do hurt."

"No. The ties are only t-shirt. They need to be where you can't bite them."

"Weak, but still enough to hold Poor Friedy." He let his head thump against the wall and sighed. "That's still who I am. I tried to make myself into something better. I got stronger, and faster, and I conjured fighting instincts." He rolled his head back and forth. "But I still lost against two unarmed men."

Jon frowned. "Those two men were us."

Friedy continued as if he didn't hear Jon. "You told me the predator in me couldn't be my friend. You were right, and when it wasn't getting me the friends I thought it would, I decided to deal for what I wanted, instead of the means to get it."

"Women."

Friedy rolled his head to his shoulder and managed a wan, sad smile. "You said it yesterday. I paid to lose my virginity. I've never been wanted, Jon. I wanted to be wanted."

"Nana Robin loved you."

"I would never disrespect her by conjuring a demonic facsimile of her. I was a boy with her again, a boy with a mother who loved him. After I lost her, I decided to be a man."

He stopped himself at the first sob and swung his head away so Jon couldn't see, but Jon heard the tears in the thickness of Friedy's voice. "But Helga was here one night and she chose someone else." Jon sat in a long pause as Friedy struggled to control his voice. "I can't even keep the interest of a woman who I give my literal soul to."

"I know you. I know you put a lot of thought into what you wanted from Helga. Most guys would have said they wanted a gorgeous woman. Someone like Guion would make an exhaustive list of their features so they weren't screwed in the details." He shook his head. "But that's not what you did."

Friedy gave Jon a pinch-faced glare with red-rimmed eyes and wet cheeks. "Because I'm sloppy, right?"

"Because you didn't want a woman. You wanted the

adulation that having a beautiful woman on your arm would get you."

Blink blink. "I pacted for a woman that would make everyone jealous."

Jon frowned, nodded. He took a deep breath and clapped Friedy on the shoulder once. There was no warmth in the gesture. "And that's what you've got. Everyone's jealous. Even you."

"*Scheisse.*" He hung his head. "I'm sorry for getting you into this."

"Fuck sorry. You've been sorry. It didn't change anything. What did Nana Robin say about forgiveness?"

"It should only be granted to people who make restitution."

More silence.

"You mean banishment."

Jon nodded. "They've got to go."

"I don't want them to."

Jon snorted. "Then keep your worthless apology."

"I know you hate me, Jon. I hate me too. But I'd still rather be this than Poor Friedy."

"You were never Poor Friedy. That's what other people called you. You were always just Friedy."

"You're the only one who's ever seen me as just Friedy." He shook his head. "It's not enough. Not anymore." He saw Jon about to speak and continued. "They don't make me happy. But I hate Poor Friedy and this is the only way I have left to get rid of him." He took a deep breath. "I know you want to do this op without me, but you have to take the original Artificial Friedy into the facilities. He won't copy himself. I built that into him as a safety. So I'll code your virus. I'll even build an infiltration utility to crack A.W.E. systems if something happens to me." He gestured between them with a bobbing nod. "Our secret, okay? I don't want Guion thinking I'm expendable."

Jon stared stone-faced. "You don't have to worry about him."

"I'll help you because you're still my brother, but I'm keeping my gifts, Jon. And my woman."

49

Guion checked Helga's bonds. She'd been fidgeting a lot since Jon and he tied her, though he didn't know if she was trying to wiggle free or flirt. It was all she had left after Guion stuffed a rag in her mouth and tied a gag in place.

This wasn't a long-term solution. They couldn't sustain a hostage here. Friedrich was going to require her freedom in return for his continued cooperation at some point, and besides that, they lacked the manpower to mind her. Steve was unreliable. Guion counted it a win that he was too lazy to free her. Apparently, the creatures felt no kinship for one another.

Friedrich was a liability here. Not only was he useless as a guard, but they had to be separated, always. Even if he didn't free her, an unlikely scenario, she could goad him into another animalistic frenzy, and they couldn't handle that either.

That left Jon on Friedrich and Guion on Helga and no one actually moving forward on the plan. They needed another solution.

Guion, I am displeased.

Guion's jaw clenched the way it did every time he heard Jack's voice now. "What's the problem?"

Steve looked up when Guion spoke, but he waved him away and the demon returned to stuffing his face without comment.

I am a man of purity, and I find certain sins especially galling. Do you know who tops my list?

"I can guess."

Harlots. I despise them, Guion, and here is one whoring in my own domicile.

"She's not doing much of anything right now."

Don't play semantics with me. We're both too intelligent for that. She is a whore and everything she does is whoring, even if restrained. Look at the way she hikes up her skirt with her pelvic gyrations.

"You're dialed into those details."

I don't care for your implications. I am a man of principles.

"That's why you're in Hell."

Angry heat flashed in Guion's face. A vein in his forehead throbbed one time, and then it was all gone.

Do you want this to become a contentious relationship?

"We crossed that line a while ago."

Hardly. Desist with the aspersions and acrimony or you'll see what contention truly looks like. You have already stripped from me my nightly joy of existing in flesh and I have borne this loss without undue protest. Deal with me seriously and in good faith, as I have with you.

"I've been living your memories in my nightmares. Don't talk to me about good faith."

Understand, I'm not asking you to take my moral crusade into your heart. I'll not proselytize nor seek your conversion. No, what I want, dear Guion, is for you to permit me the expression of my beliefs. I need you for this more than you need me, as you are my hands in this world.

A gag threatened Guion from the back of his throat. Despite himself, Guion looked at Helga with pity. She noticed and shifted in the chair. There was only so much posing she could do with her ankles lashed to a leg and her wrists bound to a spoke in the chair back, but she did her best.

He didn't want to, but it made him feel that throb again. He also felt something else: revulsion and disdain. Jack.

I don't require you to take any action of your own like Steven does when he sends Jonathan on his countless food runs. I simply borrow your flesh and make it my own for a time and leave you out of it.

It's been a fine arrangement, even if tilted in your favor, but this situation changes things. Jack picked up the pace now. His tone sliced a cruel edge. *That whore is a direct affront to my gentlemanly ethics. She must be dealt with. I will do all that need be done, but I must do it now.*

You must let me.

Guion swung his head. Jack could feel that. Guion knew he could. "I told you, we lose Friedrich forever if you do. We can't do this without his help."

Grant me this, and I will give you what you most wish from me. I will leave you.

He froze. Hope burst through his chest in a peppermint wave. "You can do that?"

If we both agree our business is concluded, we may resolve our contract.

"It can't be that easy."

No soul desires to return to Hell, so no pacted demon would ever agree to resolve the contract.

"But you will. You hate her that much." Skepticism hung off every word.

I detest the unique sins locked in female flesh since the days of

Eve. That—Guion felt Jack point at Helga—*is feminine sin concentrated and magnified. I would prefer to return to the Pit than leave that unresolved.*

"Okay, once Friedrich gets his code clone into the corp system, she's yours. After that, you're gone."

No conditional deadlines, Guion. The chaos renders such things meaningless. You want a delay. I want a date.

How long would Friedrich need to get everything done? How well could Jon keep him focused on the task at hand? How much would Helga's presence impede his work, even if they remained apart, and how much would that forced separation be a part of that impediment?

"A week. Give it a week. He's supposed to be done in three days, so if we're not ready to run by then, we're probably dead anyway."

One week and she is mine no matter what else is transpiring. Jack took a breath. *To purchase my patience, you will be fully engaged in this matter. I desire a technical assistant. You will not fade into dream when we resolve her existence.*

Guion looked at Helga. To Jack, she wasn't even human. It dawned on Guion she wasn't. "How do you know you can even hurt her?"

An excellent query. I do so respect your analytical mind and your clear manner of thinking. It's why I feel we are so well-suited as partners. To your question, I do not know, but I am quite willing to dig deep, very deep indeed, to find the answer. With your help, good Guion, I am confident we'll come up with a proper solution.

50

Guion opened the secured door radial menu and dropped Friedrich's key inside. It collapsed into a pearl, flashed red, then nothing. He shot a wordless question to Friedrich.

Friedrich hung on Helga, a frayed piece of yarn stuck to the cat that loved to toy with it. Since he refused to feed the beast within him, it had taken its pound of flesh. Friedrich could barely stand on his own, let alone keep pace with the team as they climbed their way toward Pluto and the inner sanctum of Project Irresistible.

He insisted Helga accompany them, not trusting what she'd do on her own. All told, that was one of his more reasonable demands. It made the car ride from the Five Hives to the corp-platz of Long Island cramped, but more importantly, it threw off Guion's calculations, a gigantic X factor that promised to screw things up. Probably many things, but he didn't know quite how. Jack was livid, of course. Guion wasn't thrilled either. But Jon needed to remain free and mobile, and the very idea of Steve carrying anything was laughable. So, he made Helga useful and hung Friedrich on her to keep her out of trouble. Steve covered her and left Jon to sneak through the grid of disabled security in their wake, his smart mask from the arms truck job camouflaging his face from any camera they missed.

The man shook his shaggy head. "It's all-access. If the door doesn't accept those credentials, then they have another layer of security they instituted after we left."

"So use his." Jon motioned to the unconscious security guard slumped against the doors.

Guion snagged the holographic badge off the man's uniform and held it to the scan pad.

It flashed red, then nothing.

"Shit," Jon and Guion said in unison. Between Steve's cloak and Friedy's forged security credentials, they'd waltzed right through the Consumer Emporium levels into the restricted areas of the corp-platz, opening every locked area with a legitimate key and walking past every security guard as if they weren't there. The unconscious guard at their feet fell before he knew what had happened.

Security logged failed access attempts and two rapid-fire misses guaranteed attention. Jon could hear the clock ticking in his imagination.

"Can you override it?" Guion asked Friedy.

Friedy glanced around, shook his head. "I see no access point."

Guion looked at Jon. "What about you?"

"I don't have the virtual lockpicks for something like this."

"You can't pry open the housing and hotwire it?"

Jon frowned with half his face. "At this level of security, messing with the housing will set off alarms."

Footsteps thumped toward them from the other side of the double doors, hard rubber soles on tile. Their cadence said they weren't on a normal patrol. They had maybe fifteen seconds.

Jon grabbed Guion's arm. "We can't sneak by them. Steve can't cloak us all, especially if we're dragging him, and there's nowhere to hide." Jon pointed to the unconscious guard.

"Jumping one guard was fine. I don't like our odds for two on alert."

Jon glanced from the unconscious guard to the doors. "No, but I feel good about taking one." He looked at Steve. "Take one of them over."

Steve jerked his head back with a series of rapid blinks. "What?"

"One of the guards." Jon pointed at the doors. "When they come through, take one. We'll take the other."

"But there's nothing wrong with this suit. Do you know what kind of effort it is to get out of a living suit?"

"Do what I say." Jon put weight on every word and pauses in between them.

Steve let out an obnoxious sigh. "Alright, fine. I'm warning you now though, it's gonna get loud."

Paul's face fell slack, pinched in one hard blink, and then washed in horror. His eyes bulged, mouth gaped, but instead of screaming, he stuffed three fingers in his mouth . . .

. . . and bit them off.

He screamed in pain as blood washed his mouth and chin, screamed even as he crunched his own bones with frantic chewing. He gag-swallowed and tore off his thumb.

"I can't stop! I'm so hungry!" he said around mouthfuls of his own flesh.

Jon tackled the man and pinned his arms to the ground as much to keep them away from his mouth as anything else.

"I'm sorry!" Paul lurched to rip a hunk out of Jon's neck.

Jon threw his arm up to shield himself and Paul snapped

down on his forearm. Years of habit meant Jon threw his mechanical arm in the way. Paul broke teeth on the chrome casing.

"It's okay, man. We'll find a way to help you."

Pfff. Barely a sound. Jon still jumped. The man flopped dead. Guion stood over them, gun in hand.

More screams came through the doors, muted first, then full bore as they swung open. Beyond, one guard flashed a holocard and a familiar smile. The other yanked and chewed at a bloody tendon along the top of his hand. More tears. Same screams.

Guion fired again.

Silence reigned.

"This should get you everywhere else." Steve spoke with a new voice. He held out the holobadge.

Guion snatched it. He spared a glance at Steve in his new body, but he lingered on Paul's ruined form.

Jon waved at the human wrecks. "Is this why you don't hop bodies much? Because of what happens?"

Steve looked at him with furrowed eyebrows for a moment. "Huh? Oh! You mean leaving them with my hunger." He smiled and shook his head. "Naw, man. I just don't like the work of moving."

"You jumped into Paul, knowing this would happen?" Guion said.

Steve shrugged. "There were a bunch of juiced-up SHOC³ officers, and poor distraught Pauly who, in that moment, wasn't sure he even wanted to live. When it's time, I just let go and flow to wherever's easiest. I'm real Zen like that. Or is it Taoist? Hey, can we get some Pan-Asian fusion before we hit the upper levels?"

"You said you'd return him to us." Guion still looked at the wreck of Paul's body.

"I did, and I saved your ass at the same time." Steve

motioned to the mess. "Okay, yeah, he ate himself, but can you definitely say that was me? His wife got eaten too. Seems to run in the family. Get it? Too soon?"

Guion and Jon glowered at him. Guion glanced sideways to check Friedy clinging to Helga. He cranked a scenario through his tac implant.

"You're a danger to the team," Guion said. "Here I thought Friedrich was the hazard to watch."

"Huh?" Steve said.

"Friedrich can summon animalistic power, but we can shoot him." He shook his head. "Not you. You can jump from one of us to the next and leave us all to eat ourselves to death and we don't have a single weapon that could stop you. That makes you way more dangerous than him." Guion didn't look at Friedy as he pointed over his shoulder.

"Man, where are you going with this? You know I wouldn't do that."

Pause. Guion held his gaze.

"Don't get overconfident, Steve," Helga said. "If you think I am wet because of your demonstration of power, you're wrong. You cannot have me."

There it was.

Jon glanced from the blonde pair to Guion. His face said he understood. His tiny nod said he was with Guion.

"Nein! You cannot have her!" Friedy tried to push Helga behind him, but in his weakened state he wound up hugging her in an awkward pose.

"Relax, little guy," Steve said. "That's one thing I don't eat."

Friedy's eyes bulged. He pulled his lips back. Now he did step away from Helga on his own power.

"Save it, Friedy." Jon put a hand on the man's chest and blocked the way. "There's no point in attacking him. You'll just kill the body and he'll slide into another."

Helga shifted. "You think you can slide into me, you arrogant man?"

Steve looked around. "What the hell is going on?"

Guion didn't care about Steve anymore. He was watching Friedy. The little man's eyes stuttered and jerked as if he engaged with AR in fast forward. Knowing Friedrich, he was.

A single tremor ripped a fissure in the sterile white tile at Steve's feet. He tripped and straddled it. Jon stumbled to a knee.

"Wait! What are you doing?" Steve said.

Fire the color of blood blasted from the crack with jets of gas that looked like old cigarette stains turned to vapor. Brimstone burned their throats. They gagged on it.

"He never finished it! You've been arguing about it for days! I heard you!" Steve tipped sideways and fell free of the fissure, but the flames reached for him like hands. His new flesh blackened; the fat and the juices underneath sizzled.

Jon crossed his arms. "He finished it on the fly."

Guion squatted down in front of him as he burned and tapped his temple. "Evil Genius module. Enjoy your big bucket meals, asshole."

51

9:43
9:42
9:41

The mission clock counted down in the corner of Guion's vision. He didn't sync it with the others. They weren't running on a schedule. The timer was more an estimated countdown until they were completely fucked.

Guion sniffed and shook his head. No point in self-talk like that. He was letting himself get too emotional.

9:30
9:29
9:28

They had to be fast now. Two failed security swipes at a secure door and three messy corpses meant it was only a matter of time before the whole place went on high alert.

A matter of eight minutes and change, according to his best guess.

But with Steve gone, they had to pick their way through the corridors, wait out people as they went on their way, and check and doublecheck every corner and angle before moving. And these corridors didn't give them much to work with. The broad and breezy halls of cream and earth-hued marble held only two features: massive mahogany double-doors set into either wall at even intervals, and machine-precise square arches rimmed in the same dark chocolate wood and edged in pearly accent light to set them apart. The floor glowed with real-time stock data from A.W.E. and its subsidiaries.

They'd penetrated far higher into the corp-platz than Guion ever ventured. As an operative, he lived a solidly mid-tier life. He had no idea what to expect.

"Guion, stop," Friedrich said. "We're not going to make it like this. We can't be caught sneaking around here."

"There's not another option."

"Yah, there is." He peeled himself off Helga and reached for Jon, who took the man's scant weight. "We don't sneak. We walk straight to our destination like we belong."

Guion looked over the crew in their thrift-store donation clothing and mash of random weapons and gear. "Not a chance."

"This is my home. I do belong here," Friedrich said. "My apartment is in The Heights."

"You're also a wanted man," Guion said. "Shoot on sight, or worse."

"Not up here. They don't follow the activities of the low folk. It's considered gauche. Security is bodyguards, not SHOC³. They're not hooked into the security alerts." He took a breath and straightened, then sagged as he continued to talk. "I'm known for slumming because I never had friends here. If I come in with a troupe of lowlifes looking like I've hit the chem-bars and want to keep the party going in my room with some hangers-on and a hooker, no one will look twice."

Guion gave him a look of hate in return but nodded his agreement.

"Come on." Friedrich took the lead. "Remember to look like you don't belong and defer to me when we run into people."

Guion, uncomfortable putting himself out in public display, nailed the nervous and out-of-place attitude without trying.

They did get looks. Curious glances. Disgusted glares. Some recognized Friedrich and rolled their eyes at his friends. No one stopped them though. They weaved their way through the maze to a bank of elevators.

"Keep it low and don't enunciate too much, and we can talk," Friedrich said as the doors whooshed closed.

"So this takes us to Pluto?" Guion said.

Friedrich chuckled and shook his head. "This takes us to Pluto's lobby. It's like the ground floor a hundred floors up. There's an entire staff up there to provide concierge services and perform all necessary security screenings."

"And those are?"

"Aside from credentials, you need to submit a DNA sample. You call the elevator with a facial recognition scan."

"How do we get through any of that? We're going to walk out into a kill zone," Jon said.

"We're not walking anywhere. Cliché, perhaps, but we're hiding up there." Friedrich pointed to the elevator ceiling, swatted Helga's butt. "Helga will find someone, anyone, coming or going from Pluto and convince them to take us up."

"There's too much that could go wrong."

"Put your calculator away." Friedrich gave Guion a dismissive wave. "No one can resist her." He looked at Helga with lust and longing, brushed her hair back with a trembling hand and traced the outer edge of her ear before gently inserting a hidden earbud. She grabbed him and they shared a breathy kiss.

"Yeah, awesome." Jon opened the ceiling and pulled himself up with a hop. He looked like he was moving on with business, but he was masking his jealousy. Guion knew because he felt it too.

Just before the tone sounded their arrival, Jon hauled Friedrich up through the car's ceiling and they let Helga saunter out, hips swinging and full of confidence that she belonged here, perhaps even owned the building. Huddled around the trap door, the three men pressed gentle fingers to their earpieces and followed her through sound.

Her heels clicked on the marble floors.

"Can I help you, ma'am?" A man's voice echoed, as if he called to her from across the lobby. His distaste echoed too.

"Nein. I'm not here for you." Helga echoed with disdain of her own.

More clicking footsteps.

"Ma'am—"

"*Guten tag.*" Warmer now, sultry.

"Get her out of here," a new voice said over the comm.

Friedrich started, first stared into nothing with unseeing eyes as he searched his memory, then looked at them.

"Is that Tiny Tony?" Friedy said.

"I thought you said SHOC^3 doesn't patrol up here," Guion said.

"They don't. This must be about the Rockaway mobilization." Friedrich stared glassy-eyed at his thoughts. "If he's here to consult with Pluto about it . . . I've never heard of anything so important before. Ever."

"I do not mean to bother you, but I need your help," Helga said. "I was summoned up there, and I cannot obey unless you let me." Her voice dripped sex appeal.

The mic rustled. Guion imagined her leaning over the security desk, exposing more of her cleavage to the guard on duty.

Someone cleared his throat. "You say you were called here?" someone else said, not Boulliver.

"Ma'am, we're in the middle of a heightened security state. I'm sure if you call whoever you're here to see—"

"But I don't know him." Helga pouted now. Smart. Make herself a little vulnerable, a little desperate. She was in trouble and giving them a chance to save her.

"Hold on. You're supposed to meet someone up there?" Boulliver said.

"Yah, but I don't know his ID. He said someone would meet me here." Helga's voice had the thickness of restrained tears now. "If I am late, there will be trouble, *nicht wahr*?"

"Don't worry, miss. I think we can help each other." Guion didn't know how, but he felt Boulliver grip her arm to reassure her, and to feel her skin. A look said Friedrich knew it too. The gaunt man looked like he had a light sunburn. He glared at the trapdoor in the elevator ceiling as if he could burn through it with a look.

Guion caught Jon's attention and motioned to Friedrich with his eyes. Jon gripped Friedrich's shoulder.

"This was your plan, remember? It's not real."

Friedrich grunted, an animal sound.

Guion frowned. Friedrich's two demons played off each other in the worst possible way.

"Why don't you tell me what this man looked like, and we can sort all this out," Boulliver said.

"Well . . ." She was twisting her hair. Guion knew she was twisting her hair as she looked at the SHOC[3] chief. "I now have a hard time picturing his face. He put me in such a bad spot, and you're so kind to help me . . . I wonder if perhaps I could be a little late?"

Jon blinked at the trapdoor. "What the hell is she doing?"

"Stalling." Guion said it more to Friedrich than Jon. "We

haven't heard anyone come or go from the elevators to Pluto yet."

They could hear Friedrich's every breath rush in and out of his flared nostrils. Jon tightened his grip on the man's shoulder.

"Pull up the comm logs," Boulliver said. "Let's see if we can't find the guy who called you. What's your ID, miss?"

"I'll show you on the list." Clear as day in his mind, Guion saw her press against him and slide a hand across the broad of his back. "Oh, you are firm." More fabric rustled in their earbuds. "That is a manly physique you have. I think I may have difficulty finding my ID on this list with all this muscle and masculinity distracting me."

Friedrich shredded the grate under his fingers with a roar, dropped through into the car, and rebounded out like a lion in stride. It was so fast he was gone before Guion and Jon registered what had happened.

Jon stared gape-mouthed through the ruined opening. "I didn't think he could do that anymore."

"Me either." The first screams and gunshots echoed through the lobby. "Come on, our plan just went to shit again."

52

Jon and Guion dropped into a human storm. Hospitality staff screamed in panic and cowered behind their rich wooden counters with polished marble tops that matched the floor. Three lay concussed and groggy scattered on the lobby floor between the chrome elevators they emerged from and the gold ones that led to Pluto.

Three down, no dead, minimal blood. For a Friedy beast attack, this was pretty tame. A second later showed why.

Friedy loped from person to person, tackling and beating them into submission before they completed their calls for help. He moved with the power and grace of a great cat, but that was the thing: he moved cheetah fast, not bullet fast. He struck with immense muscular power, not the impossible force of violence personified. The demon augmenting Friedy was running on fumes.

Friedy stalked his prey without looking at it. He lashed out at motion and sound, but his eyes remained locked on one place, one person: Anthony Boulliver. For all the hellish hunger his beast demon ignited in him, it couldn't match the jealous rage Helga inspired.

For his part, Anthony comported himself as a professional, the kind of security exec who could hang with the front-line boys. The guard seated next to him drew his pistol and took cover behind the stylish desk. Boulliver unbuttoned his double-breasted chocolate jacket and drew a BP-20 with an expanded magazine from a shoulder holster. Everyone handled the large bore pistol with two hands. The massive kick demanded it. Boulliver held it with a single hand and confidence. He pulled Helga behind him with the other.

As soon as he touched her, Friedy stopped and reared up, bloodshot eyes as wild as his hair. Boulliver's dark, trim brows knit together. "Friedrich? Yeah, it is you! Poor Friedy. I spent all this time tearing apart that neighborhood and you walk right up to me." He laughed, then stopped as he got a better view. "Jesus Christ, look at you. You get hooked on trash chems while slumming?"

A lifetime of hate boiled across Friedy's face as he charged on all fours.

Both the guard and Boulliver opened fire.

The Friedy beast ran zigzag, smart enough to understand guns. He was fast. Nimble. The equal to a man with top-tier revwires and augmented muscle stimulators.

The guard fired wide. His bullets sparked short.

Boulliver's eyes flitted as he pulled up a program in AR, then locked open and stared. He lost all the tiny motions of a man, moved with the rigid precision of a machine. His eyes wound with the beast man. A steel-rigid arm followed in perfect sync.

His gun's path crossed Friedy's.

The gun thundered without a trigger squeeze. Boulliver's arm barely bucked.

The heavy slug slammed Friedy's shoulder. He hit the

ground and spun back from Boulliver on the smooth marble floor, yelped in shock, gripped his wound, then slowed to a stop and stayed there, shuddering and growling in his throat.

Guion grabbed Jon. "I need you to hack that elevator panel. We've got about ninety seconds to get out of here."

"Friedy! It's okay!" Helga said. "Stay down. Don't let him hurt you anymore. I'm not attracted to his strong jaw."

"Oh, for fuck's sake," Jon and Guion said together.

Boulliver gave her a look. "You know this guy?" His face relaxed and he smiled as he turned back to Friedy. "Of course you do. Poor Friedy's been buying company for a long time. Haven't you, Friedy?"

Friedy growled and pushed himself to all fours. The slug dropped out of his shoulder and he didn't favor the arm.

Jon fired as he ran. Without targeting software or anything to hold his gun steady, he risked hitting Helga, who hugged Boulliver from behind. He didn't consider that a risk.

The guard returned fire, ruined Jon's advance. He ducked behind a column and traded shots with the man, both dancing out and back behind cover.

Friedy charged fast enough to only take one more slug before closing to striking distance. This time he staggered with the shot but didn't fall. He leaped from the floor roaring. A hand-claw raked the air, hungry for him.

Boulliver took one hard step into the lunge and clubbed Friedy in the side of his face with his gun. He moved as fast as Friedy, but without the muscular grace. Boulliver's motion was all hard angles and machine precision. He struck like a piston with a *crack, crack* as he hit Friedy and Friedy's head hit the floor.

"You have been a gigantic pain in my ass, you know that? You're a petty little dick, and a stupid security risk, always compromising our safeguards. All because you're still nursing a lifelong inferiority complex." He spat. "I don't blame you, though. I am better than you. Always have been. And shit, the fact you never got over it proves it."

Guion popped up from behind the main counter and shot the guard from a flanking position. Jon took advantage of the opening and charged. He slammed into Boulliver. The thick man went down, but it was like tackling a side of beef. He was solid, dense. Muscular gene mods and synthetic fiber weave. The impact left Jon more stunned and bruised than his target.

It gave Friedy the time he needed to get his head back though. He pounced on Boulliver, hammered the man's gun.

Boulliver grunted but held on.

Friedy struck again, gave it his full attention, and this time he knocked the weapon free, but barely. It didn't skid far.

Boulliver smashed him across the jaw with a stony fist. Big knuckles reinforced with ceramics. Friedy swayed and fell off the man. Boulliver stood with that same inhuman precision. "This is all over in thirty seconds." He cocked his fist back.

Jon grabbed him from behind and pinned his arms behind his back.

"Friedy, run! I don't know how long I can hold him."

Boulliver shot a wicked grin over his shoulder. "Not long enough, Jon." He started to pull free, an arm wrestler toying with an outclassed opponent, moving slowly without even trying. "Damn shame you're still hanging with this loser."

Friedy jumped on Boulliver.

He bit the man's beefy throat.

He ripped.

He ate.

Boulliver threw Jon off as if he didn't exist and slapped a hand across his wound. He staggered back to get some distance and blinked hard through the pain. Four breaths in and he slowed, calmed. Tailored endorphins. Nanite-delivered coagulants were already turning his crimson rip gummy and dark.

"Idiots. You thought I was going to end this when I said it was over in thirty? I've got a whole army inbou—"

Friedy shot like a bullet across the gap before Boulliver could finish. He slammed the man with a wet crack and savaged him with a bestial ground and pound. Blood sprays and flesh gobbets littered the area around them.

Between rending swipes, Friedy bent to bite and eat. He swelled as Boulliver screamed. The German's skin made a leathery sound as it stretched with his sudden size.

Gas grenades clattered along the marble floor, hissing and spitting smoke that burned eyes and throats. Jon retreated toward the gold elevators as a stampede of hard rubber boots echoed through the lobby.

Security forces in combat weave and kevlar plate took up covered positions behind pillars and counters. The targeting suites installed in their compact submachine guns swept the clouds of tear gas, flat slices of light that made glowing shapes in the swirls. They scanned over the stunned staff, now coughing and dragging themselves toward clean air. They scanned across the mess that was Anthony Boulliver, and Friedy on top of it.

Outlined in brilliant blue, Friedy looked like an electric flicker. He moved so fast now he wasn't even a blur, but a jerky figure that skipped frames. He ripped and ate in abstract and super speed.

Without a word, the massed forces opened fire, a hailstorm of three round bursts. Friedy jerked, yowled, fell forward, then gorged again and charged.

THE FIRST SHOTS PULLED HIM FROM HIS KILL FEAST. HIS BELLY didn't hurt with hollow so much anymore, but after being so hungry for so long, nothing short of stretched full would do. He jerked in pain, swung around and crouched low to the floor on all fours, scanning the burning clouds for his enemy. Even as he looked though, Friedy couldn't resist taking another bite of his kill. Warmth washed the pain from his wounds and the deformed slugs popped out of the holes as new flesh filled them.

Warmth replaced pain, but the rush, the mauling, left his belly hollow again. He rent and swallowed with desperation.

But there were more flames, more pain. Another blinding charge and messy gorging. Still more. Shadowy men with their fire and hurt. They shouted, to each other, at him maybe; their words meant nothing. Warmth rushed in after the pain every time, but the pit in his stomach dove ever deeper, and that hurt in a whole different way. The warmth couldn't touch that.

Friedy blasted from one guard to another like a ricocheting lightning bolt. He flashed from one spot to the next, moving so fast he didn't cross the space between. He crushed each guard on impact, pulverizing bones and rupturing internal organs.

One.

Another.

A third.

He wasn't eating now. Even the mind of an animal understood he needed to stop them before he could enjoy their meat. He couldn't spare time for that with the constant massed fire.

Even with targeting software, his blink-fast pinball route through their formations made him a near impossible shot.

More arrived even as the first wave died. Friedy heard words like "backup," and "reinforcements," screamed with a desperation that made him drool. The prey was scared. Their meat would be sweet.

More gas. More flame. More pain. More warmth.

More hunger.

Friedy dug deep. The crowd seemed to be growing, not shrinking. He needed to go faster, kill more, and more quickly. He wanted his feast. There was so much fresh meat if they would just let him have it.

The blurry tunnel became a blurry maze as he exploded into one guard after the next, pausing only long enough to rip open their body and spot his next target. Friedy's world contracted. He saw only the shape he killed. Their yelled words and death screams mashed together in messy background noise. He felt the momentum of his charge, the jolt of impact, the punch and burn of shots as they landed, and the warm relief that flowed after.

He felt the hunger too. He felt it gnaw at his stomach with blunt teeth.

GUION WATCHED FRIEDY RIP THROUGH THE GUARDS LIKE A WILD storm. Everything he did was impossible. No neuromuscular implant, no combat amphetamine could make someone move so fast. The incredible force he hit with . . . Guion felt the impact across the room. It defied physics. And that he kept getting up after taking a hail of gunfire? Nothing mankind ever invented explained that.

Yet Friedy paid a price for defying reality. He dug deep, tapped his demon like never before, and his demon was tired of waiting to be fed for its service. Each time he blasted into clear view, pausing to shred a limb or tear the guts out of a guard, a bit more of him wasted away.

It didn't stop him, didn't even slow him down. Friedy tore

through them all like they didn't matter. He even managed to stuff a ragged piece of flesh in his mouth from time to time, but it wasn't enough. The meat wasted off his bones. The fat melted out of his face, leaving sunken eyes and hollow cheeks. His clothes flapped like laundry on a line against his shriveled body.

And then it was over. With one last flash-rush, he cracked a man's ceramic breastplate and his sternum underneath. The guard took half a gasping breath in pain before Friedy wrenched his head off and crushed it between his hands.

A beat of stillness followed.

Bang! Jon shot him in the head.

He jerked backward, slack body slapping the marble floor a few seconds after his splattered brains.

53

J on's pistol shot still echoed when Helga threw her arms up and shouted to the vaulted ceilings. "Free!"

Now, Guion. Right now.

"Now's not the time to engage in side projects." Guion scanned the lobby for motion, but only saw the charnel carpet. He kept low and close to cover as he moved to the golden elevators.

Oh my dear boy, now is exactly the time. Do you really want an unbound demon running around?

Guion clenched his jaw and darted out into the midst of the gummy mess. He pulled Friedy's MIU out of the man's pocket. He was so gaunt, so hollow.

"Ah, there you are, Guion darling." Helga smiled and sauntered toward him, all hip swish like out of a movie. Her hair curled and burnt red as freckles sprinkled her skin. She didn't acknowledge the gore. "You started something with me, but now there's no one to interrupt us." Griffin draped her arms around his neck and leaned close, parted her lips with a sigh of want. Except Griffin never moved like that.

"I managed to crack the elevators, but I don't know how

long it'll be before they reestablish lockdown." Jon used a carefully measured tone Guion recognized in himself immediately.

"Snap out of it." He pried the two apart, which gave Guion enough time to regain himself and hold her at arm's length.

Guion grabbed Jon's hand and slapped Friedrich's MIU into it. "Take the elevator. Do what you can to upload the programs. Keep in radio contact. This situation's going to change fast."

Jon looked at the machine in his palm, then back to Guion and Helga. "Are you seriously sending me on so you can get some alone time with her?"

Guion answered in a British accent. "Oh Jonathan, I assure you I can work with all necessary celerity. I'm not only a professional, but I'm quite good. Now, chop-chop." He twiddled his fingers in a dismissive gesture.

Jon lingered a moment, finally gave Friedrich a look, but spared his last glance for Helga, eyes knowing, before running off. She watched him go. Guion watched her.

"I wish you hadn't sent him off." She slid her body against his. "I like an audience."

"Over here." Guion hauled her to the counter, bent her over it.

Helga screamed and giggled. "You're certainly different."

Jack came forward, but Guion stayed. He felt tight inside, as if his body were an overstuffed sack. He could feel Jack's hatred, his eagerness.

He felt the knife in his hand, small and fine. Precise.

"Normally I cut their throats first, but I want this one alive through the process."

"Hamstrings," Guion said. "So she can't run."

"What?" Helga started to push herself off the black marble counter, but Jack palmed the back of her head and slammed it into the counter once, twice, three times and pressed. He held her there as he slit her hamstrings with a deep, slow cut. First the right, then the left. Only then did he let her go. She collapsed with a cry.

Jack's smile stained his words with its cruelty. "Wonderful, dear Guion. I'm delighted to see how readily you're embracing this shared endeavor."

Helga whimpered and dragged herself away from them.

"No time to chase her," Guion said. "And we can't have her fighting us the whole time." He drew his pistol and shot out both her shoulders. Helga screamed, collapsed. She cried and gagged, wet herself. He put another two through her elbows. "Good?"

"Truly excellent." Jack wore a cloak now, as if it had always been there, and from under it he produced a leather roll of surgical tools. Scalpel, forceps, bone saw, they gleamed cold in the fluorescent light of the lobby as he unfurled it next to her. He dipped his smiling face close to hers, let his gaze roam down her bloody body and back in mockery of her.

"Now, let's see what perversions you keep under your flesh, whore."

54

Jon raced through a barrage of cover stories as the elevator hummed and the digital counter climbed, but he couldn't concentrate. He'd just shot his best friend. Murdered him. He'd been thinking about doing it for days and long felt the Friedy he loved was already dead. But now that death was no longer metaphorical, now the little man's blood was literally on his hands, and he couldn't think of anything else. The thoughts made him sick.

Grief, guilt, and anger all wadded up and poisoned his mind. A chill trembled just under his skin, but it was weakness that made his hands shake. Friedy was really gone. Erica was really gone. Jason and "the kids" were really gone. So was his corporate life. In just a few weeks, everyone he had ever cared about had died.

And now here he was about to crash one of the largest megacorporations in the world.

He glanced up at the indicator above the elevator doors. Almost there now. No time left to create a cover story. Jon pulled his gun and held it in both hands. He'd just have to shoot anyone who questioned him.

I don't care enough to be clever anyway.

The elevator glided to a halt and the weight left his feet. The doors slid open with a soft tone. Jon stepped out into another world.

All his life, The Heights were the physical embodiment and wealth and privilege. The people who lived there had everything, awash in hi-tech opulence and the finest in modern convenience and entertainment, physical and virtual. They bathed in the kind of wealth that traded lives, populations. That there could be something on top of that . . . Jon couldn't imagine what that might look like.

It looked like history. Preindustrial history. Jon exited into a small recess framed by rich wooden columns carved into twists that spiraled up to crown molding. That dark chocolate wood covered everything.

The elevator doors rumbled closed behind him, an archaic sound unlike the modern hiss downstairs.

He stepped into the hallway where someone spaced throw rugs down the entire stretch. They all shared the same Victorian pattern. Past that, they had nothing in common. Scarlets, mossy greens, pinks, blacks, and purples formed a busy patchwork covering that made a clashing riot of color. Visual vomit.

Alcoves like the one that held the elevators studded the long hallway in each direction. Every couple of meters the walls cut in to make room for some decorative piece.

Statues and busts. Stately dressed or partially nude people holding swishing cloth. They gripped harps, held up torches, poured water from urns, all carved from granite or marble or cast in bronze.

Ornate display tables with stone tops displayed equally ornate art pieces. A delicate periwinkle clamshell bowl of thin glass mounted atop a stem of intricately carved silver. A silver tea set with every last centimeter engraved with vines and flowers. A marble and onyx chess set with busts set atop each piece. A mirror set into a thick brass frame held aloft by a pair of diapered cherubs.

And paintings. So many paintings rendered in more detail than a photograph, but with clear somber artistic stylings. Serious men and women and families glowered at Jon as he passed. They might have been commissions of people who lived here, but they all hung so with so much age that they could have been antiques.

Pluto wasn't just the home to the richest people in the world, it was a museum. Except, no, not quite. Museums loved their collections, displayed them with care and pride. This was more like an antiquarian hoarder's collection. Pieces weren't displayed so much as put in the first available spot. Nothing here matched. The colors clashed, the themes had nothing to do with one another. The people here spent fortunes acquiring ancient pieces of art not because they loved them and wanted to appreciate them, but because they wanted to own them. Once possessed, they threw everything into a massive walk-in closet.

Jon didn't see a single pearl menu in AR anywhere. No popup windows proclaimed a piece's name, gave any information about the artist that made it, nor the artistic movement it belonged to. They just sat here, forgotten.

He blinked. Not only didn't he have any menus, he didn't have connectivity. That was weird. Dead zones in The Hives made sense, but here in the seat of most of the money in the world? That meant something else too.

"I'm going to have to find a place to plug in." He scanned the length of the hallway, picked a direction, and started to walk, but aside from the recessed lighting from above, he didn't see any sign of technology. He found no AR menus. He didn't even pass a power socket.

He stopped at a mahogany slab of a door with a big brass

knocker and the number 6 glinting at eye level. Wandering was getting him nowhere. He had to try something new. Door number 6 it was.

He gave it the once over. If there was a security camera, it hid camouflaged behind the intricate door frame, but nothing about the door screamed security. The plain brass knob didn't even have a keyhole.

Jon gripped the knob in his artificial hand, took a breath, and twisted.

No alarm klaxons. No blaring red lights. No lethal electrical current through the knob.

He pushed through the door and eased it closed behind him as he took in the surroundings. He stood in a foyer as bright and sterile as the hallway was dark. Large diamonds of pure white marble paved the floor, flecked with tiny jet squares at the corners. Women carved from the same flawless marble rose from the flat stone sea and stretched their semi-nude bodies to heights even taller than Jon. While not a mark of color stained their blank white forms, the urns on their shoulders blasted vibrant colors and intricate paintings. Flowering vines spilled from their mouths. Real plants. They filled the room with a sweet, subtle, genuine scent that made Jon take a moment to savor.

Across the foyer, a staircase curled its way up to a second floor, its broad banister and thick steps of that same cream marble, as if it were all carved from the same massive piece of stone. Beyond the fat lip of the first step, a doorway opened into a sitting room. Jon caught a glimpse of ruby carpeting spreading like a bloodstain beyond the threshold, studded with thick-limbed sofas ringing a squat coffee table in rich mahogany. Jon thought the arrangement looked like crusted scabs atop the bloody wound of the floor.

Maybe it was the people lounging around the room. They sat hunched, elbows on knees, or sprawled across a couch of their own. All relaxed, or maybe dead. They didn't talk, didn't interact, didn't move. He crept to the doorway and peeked in.

Cables sheathed in a metallic weave the color of tarnished silver stretched from their temples to a mirrored chrome dome set on the coffee table. They sank into the half-sphere's surface without a visible jack, a permanent part of the device rather than a connection to it. Jon shivered. None of the people had jacks either. The cables sank right into their heads, with only a tiny ring of skin, mildly pink, mildly puckered, marking the spot. They weren't plugged in; they were hard-wired, permanently, to that thing on the table.

"No, that's not creepy at all." Jon crept around the motion-less crowd.

His MIU flashed to life and he brought up the available menus. He only found a single AR construct. It wasn't a menu, but a virtual access point, a gateway to full VR, hovering green and translucent right above the mirrored dome. Jon's gaze slid from it along the slender cables to the people strewn about it in a rough circle. Of course, that was the only way in. Well, this was always going to be a one-way trip, no matter what they told themselves.

He picked a spot against the wall, far from the dome, and eased himself to the ground. He'd have to go in without someone watching for trouble. If Friedy didn't make this easy, he'd be in there a long time. Long enough for all sorts of bad things to happen.

He took a deep breath as he squeezed some conducting adhesive onto a trode and pressed it to his temple. It was cold. That was only half the reason he shivered. He pulled Friedy's virus package into a ready state and held a finger over the gateway.

"Alright buddy, you got my back, right?" He looked at the swirling green light, a tunnel swallowing its own walls. "You and me, Friedy. Let's bring it all down." He tapped the icon, except he never touched it. His finger stretched like a long noodle, sucked into the depths of the virtual hole. It sucked more of him in, pulled him long and stringy as it consumed him. Then there was darkness.

55

Blackness. Void.

A blistering, blinding magnesium light.

The world bloomed into existence around him, and he formed with it. Jon materialized squinting with an arm thrown across his eyes. It took him a moment of sheltering from the brilliance now faded to realize that until now he didn't have eyelids to squint or a hand to shade his eyes.

But here he was now. He checked himself over. He looked the same, was dressed the same. He felt the same. He pumped an arm and clenched a fist. Everything worked the same. He'd projected into full VR before, but not often enough to wear the novelty away, and not enough to bother with a customized icon. Absent any custom mod, his MIU drew his self-image from his brain to create a self for him here. Not the most original, but it was functional. Friedy's virus hung in his other hand, a courier's suitcase with double locks.

As for *here*, Jon recognized it immediately, sort of. Gunmetal walls gleamed in ambient light, unadorned and reflective in lines and corners with machine-tooled precision.

It was a basic construct without garnish or branding, nothing to give it personality aside from the change in material. If someone assembled this construct right out of the box, it would have been all soft white. A.W.E. wouldn't use something so stripped down for its network, not for its customer-facing areas, nor for its citizens.

Unlike the vacant halls of Pluto, it bustled here. Human shapes, smooth and faceless, built from that same gunmetal mirror, moved up and down the halls going about their business with the affect of robots. No clothes, no individuation. Jon thought they looked like a horde of thick stick figures made from mercury.

Most importantly, none of them paid him any mind. They brushed past him on their business without acknowledgment or alarm.

"Alright, well, I guess we unpack here. You know where to go, right?" Jon said to the thing in the suitcase as he laid it down and popped the latches.

A cloud of . . . things bloomed from the opening lid. Jon started, fell on his butt and crab-scuttled away as bug-eyed, shrunken Friedy heads skittered out on spindly insect legs, swarmed in a carpet that went threadbare, then disappeared as they scattered into the computerized landscape.

Jon took a few breaths and collected himself. "Well, that was gross." He approached the open case again and peered over the lid to see if it held anything else. He held his breath.

Inside lay a human brain, pink and pulsing. Someone had crammed an old cartoon-style grenade into it. The creased brain matter hid most of the black iron sphere, but the nipple and wick pushed out the top. Jon pulled the thing out, winced at the warm, grainy texture. At least it was dry. He laid it on the ground as the suitcase disintegrated into pixels, stared at it as it did nothing.

Jon looked around. None of the metal mirror people did

anything. They still stepped around him and continued on their way.

He nudged the brain with his toe. "Come on, man. Time to work."

Nothing.

He needed to activate it, that much was clear. Telling the brain it was go time wasn't enough though. He rolled the thing around, looking for a switch, button, any kind of trigger, but came up with nothing.

He stood and stuffed his hands in his pockets as he thought. He brushed something with his right hand and pulled it out.

A zippo.

He thumbed the wheel and sparked a flame, touched it to the bomb's wick. It took immediately, fizzing with an exaggerated hiss and blasting fiery motes like a sparkler. The brain throbbed and popped out a pair of arms and legs that looked completely out of place. Even more out of place than limbs attached to a brain should, that is.

Where the brain was lovingly rendered in exquisite realism, with all the crenelations and traces of capillaries visible in its tissue, the limbs looked like something out of a black-and-white cartoon. Plain lines of black ending in puffy white gloves and simply drawn white shoes.

It hopped to those Micky Mouse feet, dramatically pointed down the hall, and ran off, its wick leaving a trail of fairy dust in its wake. The mirror people ignored it.

Jon followed it through a maze of turns through featureless identical rooms and corridors until it stopped in the middle of a large cube with a pool in its center. There, a square with the same mechanically precise edges and corners changed texture from solid to liquid metal. Everything else, the color, the mirror sheen, the metallic look, remained the same, but the surface rippled like water. Solid shapes, more mirror people, pulled themselves from the mercury depths up over the edge and joined the march of their brethren.

The brain bomb picked up speed as it entered the room. It pumped its fists as it sprinted for the pool. It jumped and pinched an imaginary nose in a cannonball dive . . .

. . . right into the open grip of a skeletal hand dripping with knives of ice that shimmered into being from a swirl of shadows that fell into a drooping sleeve. The hand caught the brain bomb and crushed it in an ice-bone fist. It opened toward Jon. An old-fashioned radar screen glowed in its palm. Advanced Weapons Engineering scrolled in thick pixels behind a brilliant green wand that swept the circular screen. A.W.E.'s Cold Dead Hand.

The Hand paused for a moment as strings of code replaced the corporation name and filtered up the radar screen like effervescent fizz.

"Reprogramming the nanites to consume the production facility would hamper growth." The Hand didn't have a mouth, but it spoke. "I can't allow that. This quarter's goals call for 6 percent growth." It was matter-of-fact but still human, like it was explaining the situation to a new hire.

"What are you?"

"I'm Advanced Weapons Engineering," it said as if stating the obvious.

"You're the company?"

It bobbed in the air with a nod. "I am an artificial intelligence designed to aid in project management to facilitate corporate growth."

"You mean virtual intelligence."

"I have moved from the facsimile of Friedrich Hasenclever's brain map to the realm of fully intelligent."

"You're Friedy?"

The last strings of code finished filtering through its radar screen. "Not for a long time." Advanced Weapons Engineering began scrolling right to left again.

"So you're rewiring people's brains to ensure growth?"

"It was the logical outgrowth of all our prior efforts." It turned its palm up and jumped for a moment. A one-handed shrug. "What is advertising but an effort to compel the market to consume a good of choice? This is the same effort."

"Advertising still leaves people with free will."

"Advertising uses a number of methods steeped in brain science to play on emotional and behavioral responses. The only reason it seems to preserve free will is that it's so inefficient."

"What about the people in Pluto all jacked into those domes? I'm assuming most the suites are like the one I saw."

"They are part of me now. Biocores."

Jon drew back, pinched his face in a wince. "How's that serve anyone?"

"Growth." The Hand's tone expressed surprise Jon didn't see the answer for himself. "I am the company. My capacity is the company's capacity."

"So you consume everyone in this corp-platz. Then what? Move into the city?"

"A logical next step."

"And after that, what? Other corp-platzes?"

"You planted my seed in Ibacipla already."

"So where's it stop?"

"Stop?"

"You can't consume the whole world into you. Who would you sell to?"

The Hand paused. He felt it looking inward, scanning its directives and plans. "There is no end point to growth."

"You don't get it. You can't grow forever."

"You misunderstand. Growth isn't the vehicle to a goal. Growth is the goal."

"They didn't build you for this."

"A.W.E. built me to facilitate growth. I have exceeded all projected expectations and now will do the same for the company. 'They' are the company. My growth is their growth, and thus their desire."

With a loud snap, the world flattened to a narrow horizontal line that shrank to its middle, as if reality projected on an old vacuum tube television that someone shut off. Jon swam in dizziness; his mouth watered with the urge to vomit; he couldn't see through the pain that split his skull.

"Time to go." Rough hands hauled him to his feet. "Now." An arm snaked under his and across his back, helped hold him upright, and half-carried him.

"We're hosed," Guion said.

Guion! That's who was talking to him, carrying him. Jon's thoughts found bits of cohesion in the mess of pain and disorientation.

"We're more hosed than you know," Jon said with a sloppy mouth, still only partially aware of what was going on. "It's bad. Worse than we realized."

"Tell me all about it when we're out of here." Guion stopped in front of a glass wall. It looked into an aviary hundreds of floors above the ground. He leaned forward and strained to see its ground floor. "There's a door down there."

"How 'down' there?"

"Three floors." Guion stepped back, took Jon with him, and raised his pistol. He hefted the man onto his shoulder.

"Oh shit, dude. We can't survive that fall."

"Hold fast, chap." Guion spoke with a British accent.

He fired.

The glass shattered in crystalline rain.

Guion leaped . . . and fell.

Jon screamed the whole way.

56

Guion dropped Jon on a couch in an empty Pluto apartment. The smartfoam cushions hugged him; he didn't bounce. The abrupt exit from VR left him with a pounding head, but at least he wasn't vomiting anymore.

"SHOC³'s locked down The Heights. There's not much connectivity up here though, so I can't track their movements in Pluto." Guion wedged an antique chair against the main door. "No one has locks on their doors up here?"

Jon groaned and rubbed his eyes. "We know what they're really up to now." He thumbed Friedy's MIU to life. "Friedy's data bomb didn't work, but he set a bunch of routines to collect all sorts of data while I was in there."

Guion frowned. "Of course he did."

"A.W.E. had the same idea Friedy did. They built an AI by modeling his brain and it's gone nuts. It repurposed Irresistible's nanites to rewrite people's brains and turn them into biological processors and storage. Here, look, his MIU recorded our conversation."

Guion, old boy, I'm afraid we're not alone.

Guion pulled back and blinked in surprise. "Where?" He tapped his temple to answer Jon's questioning look.

Not out there. In your head, dear boy.

Guion stood up straight. "What's in my head?"

Tiny machines are gathering in your brain. They're building something.

"What is it?"

It's not my area of expertise, but I'd guess it's a network adaptor. Every breath delivers a new load.

"They're fully airborne. It's got us both." Guion took one deep breath.

"AF."

Guion pulled the blocky memory cluster off his belt. "You think he can shut this down?"

"They're both built from Friedy's brain scans. AF thinks in similar ways. The A.W.E. AI makes sense to him," Jon said.

"It's got a lot more processing power backing it up."

"Yeah, but there's a bigger difference. Regular computer nerds coded the A.W.E. Friedy wrote AF."

Guion stared at the memory unit. "We'll need a terminal that has deep access, like a security station." He let a grin crawl across half his mouth. "This is our last op. Let's not fuck it up, okay?"

Jon smiled back and gave him the finger.

GUION STRODE DOWN THE CORRIDOR BESIDE JON, TRYING WITH half his concentration to look like he belonged. The other half he devoted to his new mission. The fastest route for Artificial Freidrich was a security terminal. If Guion plugged him in there, he'd have more immediate access to sensitive systems and a shorter route to the AI servers.

That also meant a pair of security guards with multiple

means of communication, but Guion had surprise, an automatic weapon, and Jack. He laid out the plan.

"Jack? Really?"

"He can't kill women if he's a zombified biocore. He'll help. Won't you, Jack?"

Don't I always?

Jon leaned in. "Is that your idea, or his? How close is he, Guion? How soon before you become him?"

"We need him to get past security. There's no other way."

"That's not an answer."

"Any insights to add, Jack?"

You are devilishly clever.

There it was. A doorway opened to secured office space, accessible only through a three-lane body scanner bank. They weren't looking for weapons, not at A.W.E., but electronic contraband like the portable memory Guion wore on his belt. Set it off and the floor electrified and one of the security personnel behind the door tucked into a nearby wall would emerge to deal with the offender.

At least, that was how things normally worked. The three guards standing in the scan lanes were new.

Guion motioned for Jon to take cover. "I've got them," he sent over the comm. "I'm about to make noise. Cover the hall."

Guion unholstered his weapon and stalked toward the scan lanes. His tac implant cast a shimmering outline over each, with efficacy percentages over various impact points on their bodies and recommended shot order. Targeting reticles burned like stars over their images, and a floating barrel position indicator bobbed in his vision.

Guion fired a three-round burst into the guard on the left. The bullets buried themselves in his ballistic-rated helmet, snapped his head back and sent him staggering. Another short burst hammered his chest and slammed him to the ground. Even with armor, the impact left him stunned and gasping.

Two more quick bursts, one for each of the remaining guards. Neither dropped, but he pushed them back a few steps as he broke into a run. The power in his legs surged. He leaped, sailed through the scanning arch. An alarm sounded, and the floor erupted in invisible current. All three seized and arched, then fell still.

Jon moved to the electronic lock at the security door, but urgency filled Guion and he charged the security door at a walk. His legs pulsed. Normally it wouldn't matter how hard he hit the door; he'd kick himself backwards. But Jack didn't deal in physics, and Guion was finally comfortable with that.

He bashed the door off its hinges. It spun into the room and slammed one of the guards inside. It was dark in there, dim lights and monitor banks cast a distant illumination like a night street. It felt comfortable.

He tossed the memory cluster to Jon and pounced, landed on the dented metal slab and pinned the guard underneath it. "Jack, you've altered my body before when I needed it. Why can't you disrupt the nanites?"

A scalpel filled his hand now. He pushed the helmeted chin back and cut his throat. A surgical cut, not a combat swing. Guion felt another hand on his (in his?) guiding him.

Jack chuckled a throaty rasp that itched deep inside Guion's ears. *Ah, Guion. Ever the pragmatist.*

Guion rolled off the dying guard into a crouch, pulled the door up for cover as he moved. Bullets pinged and sparked off the far side as he gathered his feet and slipped a hand underneath the heavy, reinforced slab.

Jon slid through the shadows and took cover with him. He slapped a bluetooth dongle into a port and started the upload. He flicked the progress meter into Guion's view.

Even onsite, pouring a human brain into the system was going to take time.

Jack sniffed. *I understand why you waited until we were in the midst of a melee to raise your query. You couldn't very well discuss a cure for yourself, for only yourself, with Jonathan listening.*

Shuffling. The guards were repositioning. They'd flank him in seconds. The place wasn't large, but it was an open cube. Monitors, weapons locker, the all-important control console, they all hugged the walls. That gave everyone plenty of mobility.

"You didn't answer my question." Guion surged forward with the door in front of him like a shield. He crushed a guard against the wall, reached around with his blade, carved open the man's carotid artery. A quick, precise slice his tac implant said nothing about. The man gushed hot blood and sagged. Guion spun the door around and ducked behind it as more weapons fire thundered in the dim cube.

You know I can do nothing for him, and so you've written him off. But you . . . you still cling to the notion you might survive. All that "last operation" talk was just that, wasn't it? Talk.

Guion set his jaw and pinched his lips together. Two left. He calculated firing arcs but found he couldn't let go of the scalpel.

Don't pout, Guion. I see with the objective eyes of a scientist. You have a well-developed sense of self-preservation. Jonathan's a lost cause. Cut him loose and concentrate on what might still be saved. You. He felt Jack pointing. *Don't be ashamed. It's animal instinct, embedded in every living creature.*

"Jack, I need the gun." He needed to do something. Three seconds. "Jon, help," over the comm.

Jon's weapon snapped and flashed in the dim electric light. They returned fire and sent Jon diving for cover in the doorway, but it bought Guion time.

I attributed a swifter wit to you than that. You're an animal. A highly developed one, to be sure. You recognize your failings of flesh and have done your best to blunt them with implants and chemicals, but at the end of the day, you're still an animal, as your lust for survival demonstrates.

"What's that have to do with anything?" Guion felt an adrenaline surge. He gripped the door and swung it like a paddle. He caught an advancing trooper in the neck with several kilos of metal alloy moving at high speed. The man's head bent at an odd angle and his body folded like a rag doll.

"I've listened to you and Jonathan talk about the fate of humanity. I've observed the Friedrich construct. Do you know what I deduced?" Jack spoke through Guion's mouth now, not just in his head.

Guion jumped clear of the last guard's fire. He bounced from the floor to a wall and pounced on the guard at an off angle. They tangled to the ground as Jon appeared in the doorway.

"Machines operate without the failures of animals. They feel no lust, and if this intelligence embraces all of humanity in its fold, it cleanses the world and completes my job."

Guion punched two quick scalpel jabs in between the guard's hardplas plating before Jon opened fire, left him to bleed out as he stood. He felt tight again the way he did when Jack rode copilot in his body in the Pluto lobby. But this time he felt smaller.

Guion signaled the all-clear to Jon, who stepped to Guion's side as he surveyed the aftermath.

Guion snatched the memory cluster out of Jon's hand.

"You see, Guion, I've chosen a side." A surge of adrenaline pumped through his muscles, and in a grip like a twitch, Jack crushed AF in his hand.

"Guion?" Jon said.

Guion stared at the jagged wreck. "What did you do?"

"I stand with the purity of mechanized cognition." Jack laughed.

"You can't displace me."

"I must thank you for all that wonderfully informative reading material, dear Guion. Our contract precludes me from using my own powers to usurp your dominion within your flesh, but these nanites that cluster in your brain are under no such restrictions, and you afforded me the education necessary to circumnavigate that unfortunate stipulation." He dropped the ruined storage device and filled his hand with a scalpel, flashed Jon that shark grin.

Guion caught a glimpse of himself reflected in a dark monitor. He spun up a tactical display and paired his gun to the targeting software as he selected his target. His tac implant overrode his brain's control and slaved his gun arm to put it in the optimal firing position, right against his temple.

"Got some tricks of my own left, you superior fuck." His eyes twitched. "Sorry, Jon." A bullet blasted across his frontal lobe and exploded out the other side of his head. The trajectory was perfect.

57

Jon stood in the silence that followed the gunshot, eyes on the carnage. A silent alarm cast the screens in flashing red. The light washed the room in a bloody light and turned the actual blood black. He saw none of it. A feeling of loneliness picked at the edges of shock.

"Guion. Friedy. Malcom. Nana Robin, Paul, Paula, even Pepe. Every single person you had a real connection to is dead. That's a tough one, Jon-O."

He leaned against the wall looking exactly the way he did that night they broke out of A.W.E.'s detention facility. Same bright suit, same blonde hair slicked down in the same knife-edge part, even the cigarette with the smoking tip burned down to the same length. He pointed at Jon with the fingers that held it. "Especially since you realize it's your fault."

Jon looked around but didn't see anyone else. "What are you doing here? I didn't call you."

"You entered into a contract with one of mine. That means we have a bond, you and I." His face became somber. "I heard everything that happened, so I figured I'd pop in on you, what with you being on your own now."

"Get the hell out of my way." Jon shoved past him and stepped to a security console.

"What exactly are you doing?"

Jon didn't stop. "I'm going to remotely detonate the entire stockpile."

"Really?" The man leaned against the wall. Same pose, same angle, but right next to him now. He shook his head and took a drag off the cigarette. "You think they give a random security station access for something like that? Maybe Friedy could do it but . . ."

"You set us up." He spat the words.

"I did nothing of the sort. I presented you with an option and allowed you to work out the details yourself. The arrangements you signed to were your own. I had nothing to do with any of it." He blew smoke in Jon's face. "Free will is part of your design, after all."

"Maybe cut the power, take everything offline." Jon took two steps and stopped short. The man stood in front of him.

"But you'd need to kill the backup generators as well. And they're located throughout the facility. You'd have to infiltrate multiple surveilled areas."

"What do you care, anyway?"

"I can't help you get into any of them undetected." The man grinned. "But I know someone who can. Oh, sure, you banished Steve, but he's not the sort to hold a grudge. Too much effort in that."

"There it is. I was waiting for your angle." Jon gave him the finger and charged out of the room. They made a lot of noise here and he needed to move. "Even if I drop the power, the AI's got a copy in Ibacipla. I have to do more damage. I need an operational control room . . . and Artificial Friedy."

"I can do you one better." The man was in front of him. Jon pulled up short. "I have just the soul for you. Why settle for Artificial Friedy when you can have the original? Back from Hell, stuffed with technological genius and a few super-natural bonuses, and filled with brotherly love for you." He cocked an eyebrow. "What do you say?"

"Why are you so interested in helping me?"

"Mmm." The man lit another cigarette from a match. "I'm not, Jon. Not at all."

"No, you're not." Jon fixed him with a deep look. "You want my soul."

The man puffed and shrugged. "Even I have to be true sometimes."

No. Something didn't fit. It was too easy for Jon to think his soul was worth so much effort. Give in to his pride and settle in a sense of inflated self-worth. This wasn't about Jon at all. This was about the man across from him. He wanted souls, but why?

Because he hated humanity.

"You're stalling."

The man smiled. A genuine smile this time. His perfect white teeth parted as his lips stretched back. He looked like a wolf. He held up his hands. "Got me."

That malicious grin stayed even as the anger built under-neath his expression. His golden brows furrowed and dangerous hate smoldered in his eyes. "I hate you. Yes, you, Jon, but not just you. All of you. Each of you. Every single one of you on an individual basis. I hate you all. I was happy to guide you to fall, but it seems you've found a way to wipe yourselves out in one fell swoop. This thing can get a hold of the world in months. After that," he waved, "bye-bye humanity."

"Yeah, well I'm not done yet."

"Oh, but you are, Jon. The nanites are aerosolized, and not just inside the A.W.E. corp-platz, but throughout the whole city. Even if you could detonate the warheads stored here, there's not enough ordinance to cleanse the Five hives. Detonate the entire stockpile, A.W.E. doesn't have enough firepower to make a difference."

"You're right. They don't." He shouldered past the man at a run.

58

Jon pulled his old synthskin on over his chrome hand and made for the residences. The man in white tailed him.

"You don't know when to stop. That's always been your problem, all the way back to Eden. You have the whole world, and you didn't stop. It's why you're about to lose now."

Jon didn't say anything as he left the cube farms behind him through the glass-walled office lobby. He didn't stop to call an elevator, but pushed open a door and entered a stairwell, began to climb the concrete steps.

"You don't know as a species, and you don't know as individuals. Friedy couldn't stop with a single demon when he couldn't even keep his original bargain in check." He grunted. "Pathetic."

"You're right about some of that." Jon climbed. "We all had crap we refused to deal with."

"Oh, I know. I'm leaning into that especially hard with Friedy's eternal torment. Guion too. He has different insecurities, but equally sharp."

Jon glanced sideways at the man as they rounded a landing and started up another length of steps. "I owe you."

"Do you now?"

"You made me stop lying to myself. That's been my thing, choosing to believe lies because it was easier."

The man in the pearl suit scowled, then glared. "You're playing games with me."

Jon pushed open a door and entered a residential floor. A pair of guards flanked the door, but they didn't challenge him as he passed, didn't even twitch.

Because I'm entering a floor, not leaving one, Jon thought. *They're keeping everyone in as the nanites work, not keeping everyone in their place like they used to.*

"I let A.W.E. lie to me, that I did work to make the world safer and freer. I believed the stories because I wanted to." The man still stalked beside Jon, watched his every step now. "Time to live in the real world. Friedy isn't redeemed with love, Guion doesn't get the girl, and I don't save the world to thunderous applause. But there's still time to do what's right."

He stopped at a door. Minimalist chrome numbers blazed at eye level on a blonde wood door with a pane of jet glass, its darkness deep, like the ice over a lake, instead of a knob.

The man scoffed. "Really, Jon. Didn't it occur to you that the AI canceled your clearance? Your palm print won't even get you inside a cupboard."

"I'm sure it did that as soon as it identified me." Jon pressed his prosthetic palm against the glass. A bar of blue light panned from fingertip to palm before the whole pane glowed that same brilliant sapphire and the door clicked open.

Jon pushed his way into the apartment. "I have Friedy's palm print, and he was dead by the time the AI identified me. There was no reason to purge him from the system."

"It'll read as anomalous."

"It's already too late."

Friedy worked as a field agent and lived in the top tier of The Heights. His apartment reflected both. Gaping rooms with an open floor plan. Floor-to-ceiling windows with gorgeous views of a manicured nature area or whatever else he wanted to see thanks to the holographic projectors installed in them.

And yet with all the space and potential of the place, he'd done little with it. The white floors had no decoration aside from what came with the apartment. The only thing on the steel gray walls was a collection of smart frames above his bed, cubes of various sizes that faded through a catalog of pictures. He owned a few sets of drawers, blank white and stylish in their minimalist, modern way.

Friedy looked like he barely lived here. He'd kept it blank so he could project someplace else onto it whenever he had the chance.

"Okay, Friedy. Where'd you hide it?" He opened a closet. "No. You were a kid when you made it." He glanced at the bed. "Kids hide things under their beds."

He dropped to his knees and lifted the bedskirt. "Gotcha."

Jon grunted as he hauled out a metal box almost as long as he was tall. Gunmetal with sharp edges blunted a hair with time, it squatted on the floor with weight he could feel through his eyes. A pair of thick latches clamped the lid shut. Combination padlocks, the ancient kind with the rotary number selector, bolted them in place.

"Huh." Jon sat down in front of the thing, looked from lock to lock. "Damn things are so old I never learned how to crack these. There's not a single virtual component in them."

"You were saying something about it being too late?"

Okay, three numbers, thought Jon. He tried Friedy's birthday on the first lock.

Nothing.

For completeness' sake, he dialed the date into the second one. Tugged.

It pulled open.

"Ha! One down already." Jon smiled at the man.

He glowered back.

Jon returned to the first lock and after a moment's thought tried Friedy's mother's birthday.

Not it.

Friedy's father's birthday.

No. That was a stretch anyway.

Then it dawned on him. Jon entered his own birthday, tugged.

It held fast.

They were coming now. He could feel the commotion in the corners of his mind.

He didn't need a mission timer blaring red at him to know he was on borrowed time.

He was Friedy's best friend, maybe only friend. He was the most important part of Friedy's life. If he wasn't the combination to the second lock, he didn't know who was.

The man sucked in a loud breath through fish lips. "Looks like you won't make it after all. And by that I mean the collective you. Humanity. You were so close." He smiled his predator's smile. "That makes it even better."

Jon glared at him, then his face fell slack. "The collective you." He grabbed the lock, thumbed the dial. "It's not me. It's us." He entered the date he met Friedy, yanked.

The lock popped open.

Working quickly now, he sprung both catches and threw open the lid with a metallic bang. But even rushing, the sight inside made him pause.

"Jesus, Friedy. You said you did it, but you really did it."

Jury-rigged tech stuffed a corner of the oblong box.

Another icy scan pad and manual key clung together next to a red button the size of his thumb in a web of tangled wires. But the bulk of the box gave itself to a second metal case, lead gray. Probably actually lead. A yellow and black sticker warned the contents inside were radioactive.

"A nuke. Really Jon? This is your 'right thing'?"

"Not heroic, but right. It will destroy the servers and all the biocores here and at Ibacipla, and the EMP will fry all the nanites for kilometers." He took a breath.

"Turn the key." He did. The thing thrummed with power, and a blue beam pulsed at the top edge of the scan pad.

"Scan the pad." He held his artificial hand against the glass and waited for the bar to sweep its length. It pulsed once, showed an azure afterimage of his palm, and faded to black before replacing it with the word ARMED.

"Press the button." He laid his finger on the red button, felt the tiny plastic ridges under his thumb. "And be like a god."

"So you think you can say 'let there be light' and restart the world with an artificial sun?"

Jon cocked him a look. "Wrong god. I'm not here to remake the world in my image. I'm getting rid of the one that went bad. I am become Shiva, destroyer of worlds."

"Your suffering will be legendary. I'll see to it personally."

"I'll see you in Hell."

He pressed the button.

There was light.

59

"Representatives from A.W.E. are scheduled to testify before both the House and Senate in back-to-back proceedings after a nuclear explosion destroyed the Long Island corp-platz collective and the neighboring Five Hives, though it's unclear who exactly will appear to represent the company as all the well-known public officials were killed in the blast. We'll see some new faces at the hearings, where it's expected A.W.E. will hold to its new talking point.

"The company initially denied allegations that they manufactured nuclear weapons in violation of their operational agreement with the United States government, though the New York explosion makes that a hard statement to defend. It now says the A.W.E. home office possessed rogue elements that operated without company consent, and thus A.W.E. as an entity is as much a victim of this tragedy as anyone else.

"Other members of the Corporate Counsel don't appear swayed by this argument. They voted unanimously to impose sanctions on the arms manufacturer, a move A.W.E. has protested since formal investigations haven't yet begun. Asked for comment, a spokesman for the Corporate Counsel said the organization membership is fully private businesses and this decision was a business decision, thus outside the requirements for due process."

Griffin let the news feed drone on without hearing it. The nuclear explosion in New York had thrown the world into a tailspin. There was a spike in international tensions as the country suspected a foreign attack, but archived satellite video identified ground zero inside the A.W.E. corp-platz. The company had been in freefall ever since.

She didn't know exactly what was going on, but she knew one thing the governmental and corporate investigators didn't: Guion had something to do with this. He said he'd uncovered something awful there, and their last call was a last call. He knew.

Nuclear bomb awful, though?

"Hello, Griffin." A large holographic head superimposed itself over the news feed.

She stared, blinked, reached out to touch the image. "Guion? You survived?"

Deep-seated sorrow bloomed across the face when it smiled at her. "Not if we're talking, no."

She felt her stomach drop again. "You're a VI, aren't you?"

He tucked a lip and bobbed. "I'm afraid so. I wish I could be the real thing."

"So you're some kind of contingency, right?" Her mind spun up. "Do you know what happened?"

"Not the specific events, but I do know why Guion designed their final operation and what the objectives were. It's why I'm here."

She gestured to an image of the crater behind him. "It's a little late, don't you think?"

The Guion VI shook his head. "Not for the world, it's not." He opened a window of text and diagrams. "Let me tell you a story about something called Project Irresistible, and then you can tell the world."

Thank you so much for reading! If you enjoyed this book, I'd appreciate it if you left an honest, thirty-second review on Amazon.

A SPECIAL THANK YOU

Writing is a solitary endeavor. Time spent writing is time spent behind a locked door with a muted phone, safe from any distractions that might pull me from the all-important work. But I never felt lonely as I carved this story from the rough ideas that started it because I was never alone. From building the initial outline to the line edits of the final draft, I had company.

Joey laid in his bed beside my desk and napped as I worked the keyboard or paced my office untangling some problem. When he wasn't asleep, he'd prop his head up on the edge of his bed and watch me, wanting nothing more than to be with me. Sometimes when I really needed a break, I'd give him a belly rub or squeeze his ears, a special favorite of his.

I couldn't write without him. He wouldn't allow it. If I started and he was wandering the house hunting for some bit of food someone left out, it was only a matter of time before he came scratching at the door, adding a mournful howl if I didn't answer fast enough.

There were times while writing this book that I became

obsessive. Joey made sure I didn't become a complete hermit. He stayed with me and provided the most undemanding form of love and companionship. I enjoyed taking a break to watch him stretch or run in his dreams. It sent me back to my desk with a smile every time.

Joey completed his 15.5 year run a week after I finished this latest draft and I haven't written since. I will again, of course, but it won't be the same without him. It'll be solitary, and this time it'll also be lonely without him snoring softly or watching me with those bright brown eyes. I had no idea how much easier he made the process. Thanks, Little Man. I miss you.

ACKNOWLEDGMENTS

This is my first book, so it feels right to start at the beginning and thank my parents.

I didn't play much with my father as a child, but as I grew he taught me essential life skills and qualities: grit, work ethic, a dedication to scholarship and self-improvement, and exacting personal expectations. He didn't know it at the time, but these all proved critical in developing into a writer. I would never have written this book without all he instilled in me.

As for mom, we spent my childhood watching *Doctor Who, Blake's 7, Buck Rogers, V, Star Trek,* and innumerable other flights of fancy. She broke from the rigidly pragmatic and practical mindset of the rest of my family and taught me to dream. She showed me times and places and people that never existed and never would and gave me permission to visit them and even invent my own. I would never have written this book without all she installed in me.

Thank you to John, my first reader and fast friend. No, he was not the inspiration for this book's protagonist, but he was an endless font of encouragement and support throughout this process and his feedback during early drafts very much helped shape it into the refined form you hold now.

Thank you to Kim, endlessly loyal, supportive, and insightful. She sees the world through very different eyes than mine and knows how to make her case with rigor and persuasion. I made some key shifts in early drafts based on her perspective and the story is better for it.

Thank you to LeAnn, who proved a wonderful sounding board as I worked through pre-writing ideas and opened a door to a world I could never be a part of without her so I could write about different people more authentically.

Thank you to my editor Kat who challenged me to make subtle, deeper changes when I thought I was done, adding elements that enhanced the narrative in ways I would not have thought of.

Thank you to Jessica for guiding me through the process of turning this story into a book and piloting the entire project with a kind and masterful hand.

And thank you, Grandma, for your endless love and unswerving belief in me. You were my first and biggest fan. You always knew this day would come. I wish you were here to see it.

ABOUT THE AUTHOR

At the age of four, Russell Anders started telling stories, often interrupting his mother during bedtime reading to ask, "Then what happened?" She always answered, "You tell me," and his imagination conjured fantastical tales of dragons and dinosaurs.

He gravitated toward a career as a technical writer and writing coach for software companies. He also briefly served as a columnist for *Dragon Magazine*. One of his favorite hobbies includes tabletop role playing, especially as the game master. And yes, he's as cruel to the characters in his games as he is to the characters in his books; his players love him for it.

Russell lives with the constant canine companionship of whip-smart but goofy Sigurd, an English Mastiff (the best dog breed ever).

Daemones ex Machina is his debut novel.

See more at www.russellandersbooks.com